The Brim Reaper

"A page-turning journey through the Civil Rights and Women's movements, where Lester marched and protested and explored the meaning of race and being female in American society. Those battles gave her the strength to claim her rightful position as an acclaimed essayist, biographer, and novelist. You will be cheering for the heroine all the way through the book."

—FRANCES DINKELSPIEL, *New York Times* best-selling author of *Tangled Vines*

"This book is laced with passion and anger—both personal and political—that buffets and thwarts Lester but forces her to hold tight to her dreams. Her triumphant path to publication is an ending we can all savor. Over the years, her mentors are often books that come to her at just the right time, and seeing them through her eyes is a glorious reminder of their power. Perhaps with this memoir, Lester will slip into the canon alongside her mentors."

—ELIZABETH PARTRIDGE, author of National Book Award finalist *Marching for Freedom*

"From her unique vantage point, Lester delivers a beautiful memoir about being a white woman married to a black man when it was illegal in more than two dozen states—from being a single mother to being an avowed radical. This memoir, written with a skilled, wholly human hand, is as intensely personal as it is universal."

—KATIE HAFNER, author of *Mother Daughter Me*

To the beautiful world that we so fortunate to inhabit! ♡

Loving
before Loving

A Marriage in
Black and White

Love! ♡

Joan Steinau Lester

Joan Steinau Lester

THE UNIVERSITY OF WISCONSIN PRESS

The University of Wisconsin Press
728 State Street, Suite 443
Madison, Wisconsin 53706
uwpress.wisc.edu

Gray's Inn House, 127 Clerkenwell Road
London EC1R 5DB, United Kingdom
eurospanbookstore.com

Printed in the United States of America
This book may be available in a digital edition.

Library of Congress Cataloging-in-Publication Data

Names: Lester, Joan Steinau, 1940- author.
Title: Loving before Loving : a marriage in black and white /
Joan Steinau Lester.
Description: Madison, Wisconsin : The University of Wisconsin Press, [2021]
Identifiers: LCCN 2020035445 | ISBN 9780299331009 (cloth)
Subjects: LCSH: Lester, Joan Steinau, 1940– | Women authors, American—
20th century—Biography. | Interracial marriage—United States.
Classification: LCC PS3612.E8195 Z46 2021 | DDC 323.092 [B]—dc23
LC record available at https://lccn.loc.gov/2020035445

I have changed several names. Otherwise all is as I remember it—
surely not "objective" truth, but accurate to the best of my recall.

For
Carole

What if the mightiest word is love?

—ELIZABETH ALEXANDER, *Praise Song for the Day*

Contents

Illustrations

Loving
before Loving

Metamorphosis

1962

It was the sound of his guitar that initially caught my attention that summer of '62. But instantly I registered the remarkable fact that the man was the lone Negro at this Catskills camp full of white people. Strolling on the lawn beside the dining hall, he softly sang words I couldn't catch.

Stirred by the music and the sight of this surprising person, I sauntered over. "Are you a counselor?"

"Yeah, the music counselor," he said laconically. "Wouldn't you know it?"

His faded red-plaid flannel shirt hung off a bony body. Medium height, long face with a large nose, he wasn't physically impressive. The high forehead, droopy mustache, heavy eyebrows, and small pointy beard lent him a mournful look. Yet he radiated a magnetism.

"Can you play the blues?" I asked, cocking my head to one side and placing one sandal on top of the other.

His brown eyes, amused, searched my face. He nodded, slid his fingers up and down the frets, cocked his head to one side, and began to sing in a deep bass voice, "Wade in the water, wade in the water children, wade in the water, God's gonna trouble the water." His long fingers lingered on the strings, giving the notes a melancholy shimmer. I shivered, awed at the power and beauty in his voice. Later I would understand that this spiritual wasn't the blues, but at the time I didn't know the difference.

"Name's Julie," he said, still strumming. "Julius Lester. From Nashville. Where you from?"

"Connecticut. Well, my parents are, out in the sticks. I've been working in New Haven, at Yale Medical School. And all over. Different jobs through my college," I explained.

He looked puzzled.

"I went to Antioch College. Every six months we went off to work for a couple months. Real-life experience through jobs the college set up. Co-op jobs."

"Antioch? Where's that?"

"Yellow Springs, Ohio. But I'm moving to California after the summer to go back to school. Finish my degree." I felt a breeze ruffle my long hair.

"Hmm. I just got mine. From Fisk. I'm on my way to New York in August."

Fisk? Now it was my turn to be puzzled.

As if reading my mind, he explained, "Fisk University. In Nashville." He waited. "Tennessee. The Jubilee Singers?"

I shook my head.

"They're famous. It's a well-known college." He squinted, looking surprised and maybe a little offended that I hadn't heard of it. "Now I'm off to New York City to make my fortune as a writer. I already have a room lined up." His generous mouth twisted into that same wry grin: half mocking, half satisfied.

A writer? Electricity shot through me. There could have been no greater aphrodisiac. That, a twelve-string guitar, and the fact that this stranger came from a land I knew little about: Negroland.

"My parents went to Black Mountain," I stammered, nonsensically free-associating that tiny, experimental North Carolina college with his alma mater. They were both in the South. Hey, Tennessee, North Carolina, one giant blob of fake white gentility and Negro lynchings on my map.

This conversation wasn't going well. But how many times had I talked to a Negro man? When I had worked in New Haven, my friend Eleanor Holmes, three years my senior, had often taken me to her Yale Law School dining hall. There I had stared at dark waiters in white gloves who stood silently in front of red velvet drapes covering the windows. It looks like the Old South, I had thought, though I dined with a Negro woman.

"How can you stand seeing them all lined up on the side of the room?" I once asked Eleanor.

"Look, they have jobs!" she barked. The clatter of silverware rose behind us so loudly, Eleanor turned to stare the diner down.

"But it's a segregated job," I argued. "And wearing those red jackets and white gloves. It's humiliating. This is 1961!"

"It's just like a white liberal to want to take away their jobs," she muttered.

"Okay," I said with a sigh. "I'm glad they have jobs. But these are so embarrassing. How must they feel?"

"Grateful!" she spat out. "They can feed their families, pay their rent. Get practical, girl. This is a good job."

"If they can swallow their self-respect." I bit into my chicken, which tasted of the bile rising into my mouth.

"Self-respect doesn't put food on the table," she snapped. "A paycheck does. I give them respect every time I see them. And they acknowledge me." Here she waved to one of the waiters, who hurried to our table. "Sir," she began, showing me how it was done.

I had chatted with a few Negro men on a New Haven picket line when we were protesting Woolworth's segregated southern lunch counters. But I had never flirted the way I was with this guitar-playing man. Actually batting my eyelashes.

Evidently I was equally beguiling on this first day at Camp Gulliver. After twenty minutes of chatter, Julie smiled broadly, no half-grin now, and asked, "Want to walk into town after lights out?" He kept lightly plucking the guitar, pinging each string like a silvery chorus to his question.

"Sure." I nodded, pleased. And then, wanting to continue the conversation, I blurted, "Boy, it's hot."

"Don't call me boy!" Julie whipped around, dropping his guitar on the grass so fast dust rose. His large eyes glared through his glasses.

I stepped back, confused. "I wasn't calling you boy. It's only an expression. Just a word," I faltered. "It's so hot." I wiped perspiration from my face to demonstrate.

"Not to me, it's not just a word. Grown Negro men have been called boy for generations." His deep voice turned sharp as he spit out the words. "They're not called by their name, or mister anybody, by white people. They're called *boy*. Don't you ever say that to me!"

"I won't. I didn't know about it. I'm sorry." I shook my head, mortified, and blotted the word *boy* forever from my speech.

Still his generous mouth turned down, and his jaw muscles clenched.

"I'm sorry," I said, again. "I wasn't calling *you* that." Who could know about all this history, about a simple word that could make a grown man jump?

I held my breath.

His jaw muscles rippled.

As he stood draped in his fierce pride, I liked him even more. What could I do to make up for my blunder? "Do you still want to go into town tonight?" I asked quietly.

He remained silent.

I waited. His thin, tense face looked as if he might explode again.

When I began to walk away, I heard a soft, "Yeah," and the sound of an exhale.

I turned back and said, "I'm sorry," once more for good measure.

That night, once my co-counselor Claire and I got our group of ten-year-olds to bed, Julie and I strolled through the dark to the nearby town. I happily inhaled the moist evening air and the sharp smell of pines that reminded me of woods I had loved as a child. Crickets chattered.

He seemed to have forgotten my mistake and his outburst. Instead we both stammered, seeking a mutual topic, finally landing on books. Our words spilled over each other.

"I majored in English lit," I said.

"Me too! I already have one novel completed and I'm working on another." He sounded confident, as if he had always known his destiny. As if he were sure of publication. I admired that he dared name himself Writer, while I never had the nerve to call myself one despite my poetry and the stories I tried to write. Despite the essay I had published at fourteen.

We scuffed at the dirt, laughing and talking until we reached town.

"Who's your favorite author?" he asked, perched on a stool next to me, before turning to the bartender. "We'll have two Heinekens."

"How do you know that's what I want?"

"Oh, I assumed," he said, looking surprised.

"I do, actually. But next time ask me." I smiled to soften the request.

"Sorry." And he looked it.

"It's okay." I glanced at the wizened white bartender hunching over a sink and wondered what he thought of us. Would he call the cops? I didn't want to get Julie in trouble. But the bartender hardly looked our way, acted like seeing a Negro man with a white woman was an everyday occurrence. I had only seen one such couple in my whole life and thought them odd, if vaguely admirable.

"I like Thomas Mann," I said, watching the tip of my cigarette, an eerie glow brightening red when I inhaled. Tapping its gray ash into a dish on the counter, I blew a perfect smoke ring into the room.

"Mann's one of my favorites, too. *Magic Mountain.* You know he said, 'To be an artist, one has to die to everyday life.'" Julie's eyes shone.

"What does that mean?"

"He has to devote himself completely to his art."

"Who does the dishes? And his laundry?"

"The dishes?" Julie acted like I had asked the most irrelevant question in the world. "I'm talking about Art."

Why did I keep upsetting him? "It's not important," I said.

"And *Steppenwolf,*" Julie continued, oblivious to my lack of enthusiasm about Thomas Mann's manifesto. "A classic." He nodded approvingly.

I agreed with that. We had devoured the same novels every young seeker was reading, from *The Brothers Karamazov* to *Siddhartha.* These authors were our mentors, passing on their anguished observations about the world. Hesse, Balzac, Dickens, Stendhal, Hardy, Kafka. I had absorbed them the way I soaked up sunlight on my skin. These men were the solar system of my world. It was thrilling to find a fellow devotee.

"Kafka," I said, wrinkling my nose. "So much suffering in *Metamorphosis.* His sister . . . I mean the bug's sister . . ."

"She was cruel," Julie agreed. "The story is about the suffering of the artist."

"I thought it was about the suffering of the office worker. Believe me, I know. I just did it for two years."

He looked thoughtful. "*Metamorphosis* is one of my favorite novellas."

"Lawrence Durrell wrote a great book," I added, beaming at the memory. "*Alexandria Quartet.*" I lit another cigarette. "It's about these expats in Alexandria before the war. It's four novels, each told by a different character. They talk about the same events, but everyone tells a completely different story. And each one seems real." Durrell's assertion of relative truth continued to unnerve and fascinate me. "Maybe the authors we've studied, with their absolutist proclamations, aren't the last word. Durrell's writing reminds me of koans, like in Alan Watts's *Way of Zen,* where nothing's like it appears."

He looked interested, so I continued. "Hasn't Einstein showed that even our concept of time is relative? *The Alexandria Quartet* makes me wonder about everything. How do other people see what I see?"

"But there is some deeper truth," Julie said. "Some absolute truth."

"Is there? How do we know? Did you see *Rashomon?*"

Julie shook his head, sipping his beer and twirling on the bar seat. His brown eyes sparkled with interest.

"It's a Japanese movie. You see the same scene over and over again from four people's views. It's like *The Alexandria Quartet*. You never know what *really* happened."

He grew still and said quietly, "It's like the elephant and the blind men."

"What's that?"

"An old Indian story about six blind men who meet an elephant for the first time."

"I never heard it," I admitted.

"Each man feels a piece, trying to figure out what it is. One says, 'It's like a rope.' 'No, it's long and sharp, like a knife with a point,' another one says. 'It's the side of a wall.' 'No, a pillar.'" Julie laughed. "The one who feels the ear says it's like a fan.'" He gave me a piercing look. "Maybe you have to take the sum of everybody's perspectives to get to 'truth.'"

The tale enchanted me, and so did the man. Most men didn't want to talk philosophy with me, or literature. He was taking me seriously. All of me.

Each evening after that, Julie and I talked our way through the night, strolling into town. We sang, too, belting out folk-singer Josh White's "One Meatball." Soon we began holding hands on our walks. When darkness fell and our work for the camp was done, we slid into a magical realm where he and I existed only for each other.

"Stealing," I said one night, my hand tingling from the warmth of his, "is all right from large corporations. They steal from us. Why shouldn't we steal back what is ours?"

"It's never right to steal," this son of a Methodist minister answered, dropping my hand. "No matter who it's from, it's still theft. It's not your property!"

"Property *is* theft. Why should we pay them again?"

"It corrodes your soul." He frowned.

"Soul? This is about our rights. How they pay shit to workers and then charge exorbitant rents!"

"It doesn't matter," he said. "Stealing is not ethical. Period."

Though I disagreed and thought Julie politically naive, his talk of "soul" intrigued me. His insistence that soul mattered, that we harbored a dimension I hadn't considered, made him even more alluring. Not only was he a writer who loved books, but he held keys to whole spheres of consciousness I had never thought of. Spheres my atheist family considered verboten.

One night we paused in our walk, lingering on the deserted road under the sweet-smelling pines. I inhaled the woodsy scent, amazed simply to hold hands with this remarkable man who thought so deeply about life. He bent to kiss me. I slid my arms around his neck, stood on tiptoe, and felt I could sink forever into his ample lips, soft as pillows. At twenty-two I had kissed many men, but this was the first time I had merged so fully. How could something the world insisted was so wrong—black man, white woman—feel so right, so natural?

Maybe my intoxication came from hearing Julie name himself Writer. Maybe it was his soulful guitar, or the low, deep drawl of his seductive voice. Maybe it was my attraction to the unusual, to an exciting adventure. Or maybe we really were the intellectual soul mates we believed we were, and some sixth sense let me know it.

Was I as forbidden to him, my access to a white world equally beguiling? He gravitated to me as much as I to him, as if we were two magnets being pulled toward each other.

Every night we dallied on the walk back from town. We kicked pebbles back and forth, seeing how long we could keep them going, laughing when one went awry. The dark enveloped us until we felt wrapped in its velvety cloak. I began to enjoy a bliss I was sure no one before had ever experienced to this degree. Being loved by such a man, one I admired more each day, was as intoxicating as any drug.

Now I wonder: What did people in cars speeding past on the lonely road think when their headlights showed us holding hands: Julie, with his tight dark curls and deep brown skin; me with wavy blonde hair and pale skin. President Dwight Eisenhower, recently retired, represented white America when he told Chief Justice Earl Warren, after the 1954 *Brown v. Board of Education* decision, how revolted he was at the prospect of opposite-sex Negro and white children in school together. "Who knows what kind of race-mixing might develop?" he asked.

Eisenhower's predecessor, Harry Truman, expressed similar sentiments when he told a reporter who asked if school integration might lead to intermarriage, "I hope not. I don't believe in it. The Lord created it that way. You read your Bible and you'll find out." The reporter for the *Chicago Daily Defender*, a Negro paper, followed up by asking President Truman if he would want his daughter to marry a black man "if she loved him." The president shot back, "She won't love anybody that's not her color."

Every poll showed virtually unanimous white opposition to interracial romance. Thousands displayed their resistance by assaulting Negro children trying to attend school. The common white argument was, "If people fraternize, anything could happen. Would you want your daughter to marry one?" They assumed the answer was evident. If it wasn't, they brought out their clincher, which was used successfully even in court: "God made the races different colors so they'd stay apart."

Surely some white people with those sentiments passed by Julie and me on those balmy nights. Had any consumed a few drinks and thought of swerving to scare us? Or run us down? The road was deserted. Did anyone who came upon us carry a gun, out here in the country where hunting was popular?

I wonder now and shiver, but back then I felt no fear, never considered danger. That summer I was so ignorant, with little understanding about the long white reign of terror. Julie was surely not so oblivious, but in the ecstasy of the moment, we were too wrapped up in each other to worry about hostile reactions. That would come later.

Instead I focused on one question: How had the universe thrown such a brilliant man across my path and led him to choose me? All summer I existed in a daze, unable to believe my good fortune. We paired off every evening until August, when on a full-moon night he said, "Come to New York after the summer."

I looked at that dear face, already familiar, and the shy look in his eyes where hope fought with fear. His lean, angular body pressed closer. "Live with me," he said, squeezing my small hand with his large one.

I breathed the heady pine that puffed around us, warmed by the rush I always felt in the woods. When he wrapped his arms around me, my entire body responded.

"Come," he whispered, pulling me close, until my desire merged with his. Exhilarated by the thought of living with this marvelous man in New York City, I wanted to agree.

But all spring I had worked on my application for Mills College in Oakland, California. I had spent weeks arguing with their admissions office, begging them to honor every Antioch College credit on my transcript. Finally all were awarded. I would enter the women's college as a junior with a full scholarship and was headed for the center of Beatdom, San Francisco Bay.

Ready to spread my wings and go west alone, I was poised for a grand adventure, far from the crowded streets of old New England, with its stuffy clam chowders, its tidy greens in the center of town, and its ancient, cramped, shingled houses like the one I had grown up in. If I followed

Julie to New York, I would lose everything I had worked to set up and would share his single room with no plans at all. How would I finish my education?

"I don't know." I stepped back and gazed at my boyfriend. Here was the intimacy I ached for: union with a soul mate, a man who respected me and my ideas. Who found my laced-to-the-knee leather thong sandals sophisticated, imagining me the bohemian intellectual I longed to be. A man who was a writer.

He also opened a door that segregation had nailed shut, entry to a world I knew little about. Only my Antioch friend Eleanor had escorted me inside briefly, when she took me home to DC over a college break and I marveled at her Negro family, who appeared to me upper class with their polished antique furniture, ornate rugs, and framed pictures with real glass, so unlike the one poster thumbtacked to my parents' living room wall. Then in New Haven I hung out occasionally with her two Negro girl-friends vigorously debating everything: boys, the Movement, and the rad-ical Warren Court decisions reshaping American law. Yet it was clear that I wasn't one of them. I didn't know the music they played, popping their fingers as they listened—the Jackson Five, the Four Tops, Stevie Wonder—and had never heard their lingo, like starting every sentence with "Girl," or saying, shrieking with laughter, "He better kiss my black ass." Eleanor, with her fierce style, lightning-quick brain, and generous friendship, had introduced me to another cultural world. But with Julie, I would move inside.

And if independence in California was one dream, life with an intellec-tual, a writer, a man I loved, was another dream. It might be worth it. I could find another college, a job.

Leaning on his arm in the moonlight, I felt California slip away as if it had been a mirage. Maybe someday we would venture there together, stand hand in hand on the continent's western edge, soak up a land bursting with creativity.

Meanwhile the intense energy of New York and life with Julie the writer could fling me to the center of a radical literary life. This new lover might be inviting me into another universe I had sought to enter, the world of publishing.

The previous year, feeling bold, I had stepped into a Sheridan Square phone booth, tapped out a cigarette from its blue Gauloises packet, slid my dime into the slot, and dialed a New York publisher.

The phone rang on and on.

"Simon and Schuster," a bored voice finally answered.

"I'd like to speak to an editor."

"Which one?"

"I don't know."

"You have to give me a name."

"Any editor."

"What do you want?"

I stayed silent, unable to voice it. What did I want?

"Do you have a manuscript? I can give you the address for unsolicited submissions."

"No."

"What is it?" Annoyance.

I steeled myself to say it. But what came out was a hoarse, "Could I please speak with someone. An editor."

Weariness. "I'll connect you to Somebody Gobbledygook." The name was garbled over the wires running between us, or perhaps my terrified brain couldn't hear it.

I waited. Had to put another dime, then a nickel in the slot. When Mr. Somebody got on, he said brusquely, "What do you want?"

My armpits grew wetter while trucks and cars clattered across pavement, rattling my bones.

"I'd like to get a job in publishing," I whispered. "Writing or something."

"What have you done?" he asked, not in a friendly way. Not "How can I help you?" But at least not "Come into my bed," as an Antioch professor I admired had begged me in a long handwritten letter, pages of tiny ink script pleading on onionskin paper. The man was as old as my father. Older maybe.

"I majored in English literature," I said, not mentioning that I had dropped out of college. Instead I said in my brightest voice, "I love to read."

"What have you done?" he insisted, his voice turning harder.

I'll do anything, I wanted to say. For six months I had proofread the *Current Digest of the Soviet Press* in English, and I spent evenings nodding to a jazz beat, hanging out with poets at the West End Bar on Broadway, near my shabby apartment. We had eaten cheap beef from the steam table bisecting the room and stayed late, smoking, talking of Sartre and Camus, who'd recently died in a car crash. *What was the meaning of existence? My existence?*

I knew the Dewey Decimal System.

What could I tell him? That I had applied for a job at a venerable West Fourth Street bookstore, full of old-book smells, where you stepped down from the street into a narrow shop crammed with books. Heaven. The pimply white man at the counter had said, "We only have one toilet; we can't hire girls."

When I argued, "I can use the same one," he sneered, "That's not possible." In 1960 that was legal.

"It's not fair!" I had said, but he only shrugged.

What else had I done? I had made my way alone to my first Broadway play, *Raisin in the Sun* at the Ethel Barrymore Theatre, paid a dollar for standing room, and gawked at the dilemmas playing out onstage. Sidney Poitier and Ruby Dee hollered, Diana Sands pranced, Claudia McNeil watered her shriveled plant and her dream, and my education that day equaled at least a year of college.

Into my silence, Mr. Somebody said abruptly, "We don't have any jobs. Thank you for calling. Good-bye."

I dropped the receiver. Embarrassed. Humiliated. Shame flamed through my body. How had I imagined they would be interested in me?

But now here was this exciting man, a writer, begging me to live with him in New York, the capital of publishing. He could introduce me to a literary world I had only dreamed of.

Primed to throw myself into the winds of the '60s, I flung my arms around my love and said yes. At twenty-two I was ready for love, ready for adventure. And like young lovers everywhere, I believed our passion was stronger than some musty old history.

The Mandarins

1962

Julie's small Manhattan room held only a single bed, a hot plate, and a bureau. Writing papers for the New School, where I enrolled, was hard to manage in the cramped space, so I created drafts in the library and balanced his typewriter on my lap to finish them. Compared to Julie's glorious writing—with sentences infused by the cadence of his Tennessee father's preaching—I found my own, which had drawn praise at Antioch, rather pedestrian. His stories, read aloud, awed me with their beauty.

"I don't write for readers," Julie told me one evening, lying back on the narrow bed, barely more than a cot. "I could live in a cave and write. Or a monastery." He gazed steadily at me. "Publishing contaminates art."

The purity of his artistic dedication dazzled me. Here was a genius mysteriously dropped into my life, reading his brilliant stories to me. Finally I wasn't waiting for my life, I was living it. This was it, here in the flesh, with a writer who enjoyed the added attraction of being close to Nashville sit-in leaders like Diane Nash, his Fisk classmate. Everything I cared about was wrapped up in this one poetic package: a man who, mysteriously, was ferociously in love with me. He brought home handfuls of daisies he plucked in the park, beamed when I walked in the door, and let me know every time he touched me how equally astonished he felt by my presence. Our first weeks in that cramped single room were everything I had ever imagined.

"I'll meet you after class," he reminded me each day as I left. And sure enough, that night when I raced out of the New School building on Twelfth Street, there he was, standing directly across the street scanning faces. Once he saw me, he opened his arms and I ran over, folding myself into his embrace. We would hop on the subway, chatting eagerly all the way home. "I started a new story," he would say, squeezing my hand. Eager to hear each other's thoughts, we talked rapid-fire.

He listened carefully when I explained, with great excitement, details of my day's learning. "The economic history of capitalism is shocking. The capitalists take surplus profits from workers. Labor hardly ever gets its fair share!" When I related a funny anecdote about a fellow student's over-bearing father, mimicking the student impersonating a bossy old man, we laughed so hard on the subway that other passengers chuckled. Attentive and supportive, Julie was everything I had ever imagined a lover could be.

One evening on the subway, he said, "I finished that new book by Nabo-kov. *Pale Fire*. He's a genius. The structure is amazing, it's so complicated." His eyes widened with awe.

"I hated *Lolita*," I said, pulling my hand away.

"What? It's a masterpiece."

"Masterpiece?" I looked at him in horror. "It's disgusting."

"It was hilarious! A beautiful love story." He seemed truly confused by my response.

"How can you call it funny? A love story? A book about a twelve-year-old's kidnapping and her rapist's obsession with her, that's a love story?"

"That's the surface story," he explained patiently. "There was so much humor in it, and sadness. But above all, love. A brilliant cautionary tale about lust. Remember, he goes to prison."

We had reached our stop, 110th Street. "It was repulsive," I said, and for once I strode two steps ahead, almost running on our way to West End Avenue.

"It was a farce," he said when he caught up. "It's full of puns, it's a mas-ter class in style. You're not seeing what a genius he is."

"No, I'm not. He's a sick man with no moral compass," I exploded. "Why was the book told from the old man's sick point of view? What about Lolita's?"

"Because that's the choice the author made! It's a commentary on the greed of American life."

I looked away. Our first real fight. And over a book. While we continued, not speaking, up to Julie's room, I remembered the English professor, an ancient man to my teenage eyes, who had recommended *Lolita*. He was the same man who had written me a letter begging me to come to his bed— the pleading letter I never answered. It was an unfortunate introduction to the writing of Vladimir Nabokov, whom I've never been able to read since, despite his reputation.

Yet once Julie and I lay down, twining our bodies until heat melted us, anger fled and throbbing bodies reminded us of our unbreakable bond. Who cared about Nabokov in the face of this gigantic love?

Yet strangely a call for something else began bubbling up inside. For days it pressed: a lust for the independence I had dreamed of finding in California. I didn't want to lose myself, even in this magnificent love. For I had been building a self after all, though I was only dimly aware of it: a self dedicated to civil rights and to literature.

What if I got my own apartment, I wondered, and was surprised to feel my heart lift. Each morning when I first woke, the thought, light as a breeze, tempted me. But I didn't dare mention it to Julie. Would he be angry? And wasn't the idea insane when I had found True Love, exactly what I had yearned for? After all, wasn't this exactly what every woman wanted? How could I risk losing that for a bit of independence?

I tried to ignore the odd hunger. Yet it refused to die. When I rode the subway, I began to scan apartment listings and imagine cooking alone, sleeping alone, reading alone in the 1 BR, Cozy LRs described in ads. Queen of my own quiet domain. I had lived alone only briefly before, for a month or two here and there.

After my daydreams I would crumple the ads, pitch them in a garbage can, and scold myself. What was wrong with Julie's simple room and the reassuring sound of him pounding on the typewriter at night, sitting three feet away at the card table we had found on the street? We loved each other. Lovers lived together. What was this heretical urge?

Nevertheless I couldn't shut it out.

Finally, when I couldn't hold back the insistent longing anymore, I named it. Out loud. "I want to get an apartment, my own." Julie and I lay facing on his single bed, my hands stroking his forehead. "You're my soul mate," I quickly added.

"It's fine for you to stay here," he said, pulling me tight, caressing my naked breasts until my nipples hardened.

"This room is too small for both of us." I wrapped a curl of his hair round my finger. Tightly wound in its natural state, it looked short, and I was always surprised when I pulled a hair out straight and observed its length.

"Everything's so steep." He caressed my back. "We can make this work."

"I know, but I'll find something cheap. I need to be closer to my job." My Camp Gulliver bunkmate, Claire, had referred me to a settlement house, Church of All Nations, where she worked, and they had hired me. I ran an after-school program for Puerto Rican girls from the neighborhood around Houston Street and already loved them all. But it took nearly an hour to ride the IRT, with two changes from Julie's Upper West Side room all the way down to the Lower East Side.

"We could find something . . ."

"I need my own place. Just for a while," I murmured. I hardly know what I envisioned, but the idea wouldn't let go: living in New York at twenty-two, alone. A freedom I only sensed, like an animal finding its way in the dark, knowing what it needed for survival. "And it's hard for me to write here. You know, my papers," I hastily added.

"I want to be together."

"We will be, but I need my own place," I dared to insist.

He looked so wilted that I reassured him again and again, "I love you. More than anyone I've ever loved."

"We're soul mates forever," he swore. And then we made love, our merging bodies cementing the deal. Later I looked down at us. How normal this color contrast was beginning to look.

⸻

Giving up on *Village Voice* ads as too expensive, I scoured NYU listings that were open to the public.

"Yes!" I shouted aloud one day in NYU's housing office. "Basement, three rooms, 329 West 21st Street. $35." That would be perfect. I could walk to classes at the New School, saving a subway token. Be closer to my job. And on the West Side, an easy subway ride up to Julie's.

"Come on over," a husky male voice said on the phone. "It's available. Starting immediately."

Striding across Twenty-Third Street from the Seventh Avenue subway, I dodged traffic and angled my way over to Twenty-First. My eyes tried to take it all in, this neighborhood that might be mine. The block was barren, without trees. An antiquated brick school loomed over one side. On the other a young woman crouched on a stoop, rocking a carriage. Three small girls played around her legs. She looked radiant. "Hola, buenos días."

I smiled back. "Hola." Maybe we would be friends. She lived three doors from my new maybe apartment.

"Hey sugar, give me some sugar," a friendly man squatting on the stoop next to 329 called out, with an easy smile that matched the sun warming my back.

A pudgy woman with freckles sprinkled across her face appeared. "Joe's drunk," she said, laughing. "Like every day."

"That's OK." I stared, curious. "I'm going to look at the apartment next door. The basement."

"Oh, it's real nice around here." She stepped forward to shake my hand. "We look out for each other. Joe here sits out all day long. Nobody will mess with you as long as Joe's on the job." She chuckled. "Theresa, who owns 329, she's another story." I followed her eyes up to the second floor. "An Italian lady. She screams all day." She looked away. "Nasty things. Theresa's rotting up there in that wheelchair, hasn't been out in ten years. No legs. She leans out the window, throwing her whiskey bottles onto the street." The woman sucked her teeth. "Child, she pisses all over herself."

Oh my.

"I'm Serena. We're always here." She grinned. "Hope you like the place."

I stepped gingerly into 329, feeling my way down two steps into a dim hall. It's the only door, he had said. On the right.

I knocked.

A tall Negro man, gaunt, who appeared old to me though he was probably all of forty, said quietly, "Come in."

My eyes adjusted slowly to faint light filtering in through windows at street level. We stood in his living room, where a giant fish tank spanned half a wall, providing the only color. Ten goldfish swam, gleaming gold. The floor: black-and-white checkered linoleum. He had painted the woodwork black, reminding me of *Invisible Man*, where the narrator lived in a dark subterranean den.

"Look around." He motioned toward a short hallway bordered on one side by a row of built-in drawers and cabinets. Painted Pepto-Bismol pink.

The back room was a makeshift kitchen, with the stove tucked under a black cement overhang, clearly showing the actual basement this had once been. He had created a middle room with Sheetrock, cutting the dark apartment in two.

"Two hundred dollars key money," he said curtly. "Up front."

I looked around. Thirty-five dollars a month was a rent I could handle. But the $200 was steep. I had saved $160 over the summer and figured I could borrow the rest of the key money, which, while illegal, was common.

"I'll take it," I said, my heart flying.

I couldn't keep the smile off my face

Now I would have to tell Julie.

———

I walked slowly back to the Twenty-Third Street station, planning how to break the news. Now that I had found a place and committed, it felt equal parts thrilling and frightening. I didn't want to lose Julie. By the time I arrived at his room—it had never felt like ours—I still hadn't decided what to say.

When I opened the door, the room was empty. Close as we were, did he know what I had done?

I paced. Looked out the window onto the fire escape next door. Lay on the bed and tried to read an economics textbook, but couldn't concentrate. Where was he?

Cars honked outside. In the hallway a door slammed. Footsteps. Was it Julie?

No, the sound faded away.

I got up to use the hallway bathroom but the door was locked, so I jiggled the handle to let the person inside know I was waiting. After a minute I knocked. A man's voice shouted, "Go away!" I stood in the hall until, hearing nothing, I knocked again. Squeezed my legs together, my bladder about to burst.

Suddenly there was Julie, putting his arms around me from behind. I felt his bony body against me and leaned back into his embrace. "How long have you been waiting?" he asked, wrapping his hands in my long hair.

I turned to face him. "Forever."

Julie rapped on the door, hard. "We have to use the toilet. Hurry up, please."

No answer. But the door flew open and a short, brawny white man I had never seen bolted out. He hissed, "Goddam nigger" and fled down the hall to the stairwell, where he disappeared.

The ugly word bit into me like a corkscrew.

"Motherfucker!" Julie shouted and started after him.

"Don't," I called before dashing into the bathroom. "Please." What if the man attacked him, beat him up? Julie was a writer, not a fighter. That terrible slur, uttered with such hatred, lodged itself in my ears and wouldn't let go.

When I hurried back to the room three minutes later, I found Julie, head in hands, sitting on the edge of the bed. "I'm sorry," I said, sliding my arms around his thin shoulders.

He looked up with blank eyes. "Yeah."

How could I reach him? How many times had he heard that word? I sat next to him, holding his shoulder, silent, until my stomach growled. Still I didn't say anything, waiting for him to break the silence.

"Lord, Lord, Lord," he finally said, shaking his head. It sounded like a dirge. A lament from deep inside.

"Wade in the water," I began to hum. A song I had heard him sing many times. After a few bars, I quietly crooned, "God's gonna trouble the water."

He joined me and we sat, rocking, singing, cleansing our souls with the song his people had created for times like this. "Who's that young girl dressed in red? Wade in the water. Must be the children that Moses led." How wise his ancestors had been. I never knew music could purify like this, lift us up. "Who's that young girl dressed in blue? Must be the children that's coming through. God's gonna trouble the water."

After the music had soothed us, we sat quietly at the card table eating canned spaghetti I heated on his hotplate. All the time we chatted I remembered: I'm supposed to get the key tomorrow morning, so Julie will have to know. But after that word the man hurled, how could I break the news?

As I opened my mouth to speak, he leaned from his seat on the bed (I had the only chair) and said, "God's going to trouble the water. God makes the crooked way straight and the narrow path wide."

Never having been to church, I had no idea what this son of a preacher meant. But since he looked calm and satisfied, I assumed it was a good thing.

Fiddling with my spoon, I said nervously, "Julie, I rented an apartment."

He stabbed a forkful of the slippery noodles. "You know I don't have the money."

"No," I said quietly. "Just for me."

His face collapsed. He put his fork down. "Why? What did I do?"

"Nothing!" I rushed to his side and crouched down. "Nothing. I want my own place. I can't explain it. I'm so in love with you but I have to live alone for a while. I want to see you a lot, you're my soul mate, you know you are." The words rushed out, trying to erase his dazed, lost look. "Let's lie down. Please."

We lay back on the bed and I held him guiltily, wanting to promise anything. Except to give up the apartment.

Eventually we made love, as we usually did after dinner, and all that stroking and coming seemed to heal up the hurt. As we fell asleep in each other's arms, my last thought was, Am I a selfish person?

The Twenty-First Street tenant handed me his key "and goldfish food," he said, extending a small cardboard cylinder. "Sprinkle in a few flakes every day, and scrub the aquarium once a month." The filtration system looked complicated, but the fish came with the deal, which I had negotiated down by twenty-five dollars.

In a moment the apartment was mine. As soon as the previous tenant left, lugging a couple of suitcases, I skipped through the rooms. Again I couldn't keep a smile from my lips, though I had to fight a guilty conscience to keep it there.

For my first hour alone, I curled on the saggy bed that came with the place, reading Simone de Beauvoir's novel *The Mandarins*, which Julie had gotten from the library, introducing me to the author. De Beauvoir and her lover Jean-Paul Sartre were suddenly the couple I most admired. Scandalously unmarried. Speaking French! They lived apart but wrote side by side in the Café de Flore. Radicals who supported the Algerian revolution, they were photographed with Che Guevara in Cuba.

The Mandarins was about a group of Parisian intellectuals. I plunged in, identifying with Anne, the de Beauvoir character, as she navigated postwar Paris, delivering philosophical bons mots during sex with her lover Lewis, who was based on the Chicago writer Nelson Algren. What does it mean to be an intellectual, de Beauvoir asked. Why are we alive, and what is the meaning of it all? What use are intellectuals in a world of strife? How can they influence politics? This was the kind of writing that moved me, the kind I hoped to create some day.

But de Beauvoir had Paris, romantically destroyed by the war, and a group of high-powered literary friends to write about. What did I have? An after-school job with ten-year-olds, evening classes at the New School, and a boyfriend who, when he wasn't feeling inspired to be a monk, aspired to be a published writer.

My neck cramping after an hour of reading in poor light, I rose to sprinkle Ajax on the linoleum, then scoured it until it gleamed. Deep into the night, I washed the shiny black paint covering the woodwork and swept rat turds from the makeshift bathroom inserted at the rear of the apartment. I did have the luxury of a private bathroom, I had to remind myself after I saw how decrepit the old toilet was, with its rusty pull chain. It's all mine, I remembered, when paint flaked off the shower wall as I scrubbed it. When I realized the bathroom had no sink. But it was mine. My charmed apartment.

Once everything was in place, a sensation of spaciousness swept over me. This was the feeling that had tugged me along. I wasn't leaving Julie but I needed something more—the leisure to come and go without negotiation, read as long as I wanted, scrub the floor all night if I wished. No surveillance, no trying to please anyone else. Feel the air swirling around my shoulders, swish from room to room. Run, prance, tiptoe, slide. Shout. Or never talk at all.

Why couldn't Julie and I have the kind of intellectual lover/comrade relationship Sartre and de Beauvoir enjoyed, each with a separate apartment? We could make our own Paris.

Like most women in 1962, I had rarely lived alone, having gone from my parents' home to dorms to a boyfriend's apartment. Now I would have a chance to find out what life on my own could be like. Explore an inner life. What was inside?

A Room of One's Own

1962

Settling in for a quiet evening in my new apartment, I nestled into the faded armchair left by the previous tenant. Cozy in a gray sweatshirt and underpants, silence falling sweetly around me. The orange fish gleamed in their liquid home covering the front wall between the two barred windows. Light from the tank glowed softly. October twilight was falling quickly. My weak floor lamp barely penetrated the gloom, but my satisfaction was so great it lit the roach-filled apartment.

I opened a battered little book I had found in the same Village shop that once refused to hire me, saying they didn't have a toilet for girls. But they did have lovely, dusty piles of books. The title, *A Room of One's Own*, so expressed my passion of the moment that I had picked it up. The blue leather cover was worn, scuffed, torn at one corner. The author, a woman named Virginia Woolf, wrote that she had "an opinion upon one minor point—a woman must have money and a room of her own if she is to write fiction." Well, didn't I have a room now, three in fact, and two part-time jobs? What could I write, with my rooms and my salary backing me up?

Lazily, I fell asleep with the question circling round and round like a fly buzzing, until dreams overtook me. When I woke, I picked up the curious little book again. Now the author described going to Oxford College's great library, eager to research an original manuscript of Milton's "Lycidas." What words did he change in writing it, she wondered. But at the door she found a kindly gentleman who regretted, as he waved her back, that "ladies" were admitted to the library only if they were accompanied by a fellow of the college or carried a letter of introduction.

I understood her outrage. I had chosen Antioch in 1957 because it was the only college I could find without curfews for girls, whereas every other had them *only* for girls. Even at sixteen, I knew that was unfair. How interesting that this author was writing about the discrimination. Having the time to immerse myself in books like this was exactly why I loved living alone.

Julie and I saw each other every few days. "De Beauvoir's and Sarte's relationship is perfect, don't you think?" I had said just the day before, and to my surprise he had answered, "Yes, it's ideal." Now we were trying it ourselves. After three weeks, the arrangement seemed to be working.

In the morning, waking into that same delicious feeling of spaciousness, I wanted to read more of Virginia Woolf's book before I even washed my face. And here, alone, I could do it. Do whatever I wanted. I felt almost drunk with pleasure.

But before I could get back to *A Room of One's Own*, I had an assignment: Karl Marx's *Eighteenth Brumaire of Louis Napoleon*. My favorite New School professor, Dr. Karl Niebyl, a German refugee, had invited me in his thick accent, "Come to my private Marxist study group." Arriving at the back door of a Village apartment, I had found myself the only girl with two white men who worked in factories to "organize the masses."

Dr. Niebyl opened with a talk: Capitalism, given anti-colonial independence movements, was reaching the end of its ability to plunder resources from poor countries. Deprived of that prey, he predicted, the capitalist system would turn to looting wealth from its own population, "eating its own," pauperizing the US middle and working classes. They had been paid with imperialism's superprofits. Now they would be the targets.

It made sense theoretically, although in 1962 it sounded unbelievable. Our factories were humming, and most of the working class, the white part anyway, made decent wages, enough to afford a house, picket fence, and car. Plus sometimes a boat. Hopefully we would be able to stop the capitalists before they could fulfill their greedy ambitions.

Determined to finish at least one chapter, I curled up in my chair and skimmed the opening paragraph. "The tradition of all dead generations weighs like a nightmare on the brains of the living." What a sentence. How do we start fresh, the way my generation was, trying to wipe away centuries of white supremacy? Trying to escape the mistakes of the Old Left. I copied the sentence onto a yellow pad, wondering how we could ever extricate ourselves from the weight of segregation and the history of human enslavement.

Marx was analyzing the European revolutions of 1848–50 to understand these first organized European working-class actions. How did their battles end up, he asked, with an Emperor, Louis Bonaparte? What went wrong? I copied another sentence: "Just when [people] seem engaged in revolutionizing themselves and things, in creating something that has never yet existed, precisely in such periods of revolutionary crisis they anxiously conjure up the spirits of the past to their service and borrow from them names, battle cries and costumes in order to present the new scene of world history in this time-honored disguise and this borrowed language."

How could we apply that to the civil rights movement? It was employing tactics, like sit-ins, adapted from the Indian anti-colonial struggle. But Negroes were singing their own songs fitted with new words, not leftist anthems lifted from earlier revolutions. Perhaps because it wasn't a revolution yet, I thought, the movement hadn't fallen into the trap Marx described.

A knock at the door startled me. "Who is it?"

"Julie," he said in his deep voice.

Why was he here? He had walked me home from class two nights ago and slept over. We planned to meet again tonight.

I tugged at the metal pole anchored in the floor, lifted it aside, and unclicked the double locks. Opening the door, I saw my love, head hanging, a brown cardboard suitcase and olive duffel bag at his feet.

"What happened?"

"I've been evicted," he said, his eyes avoiding mine. "Everything was in the lobby," penalty for "nonpayment of rent," he mumbled.

In shock, I didn't speak.

For three weeks I had been free. Alive. Confident. Buoyant. I had found my footing at the New School, where I had gotten a ticket-taker job in exchange for tuition. All I had to do was arrive before class to collect entry tickets, which gave me a chance to meet other students. Even with two jobs, I had plenty of time to study.

My brain still entangled with Marx, I stood in a stupor, stammering, "Come in."

"I didn't know where else to go," Julie said, dropping to the makeshift couch, which I had constructed from scavenged pillows and covered with a red madras spread.

My forehead pulsed. Pain shaded Julie's narrow face. He clearly suffered, not only as a Negro but as all the great writers did, with their ponderous moods, heightened sensitivity, and profound silences. Writers needed tending to. I had read about it in every biography.

"Can I stay here?"

"I'm sorry you got evicted." I gulped, flashing to the Italian movie *Nights of Cabiria*, which I had seen several times in Yellow Springs, at an art theater where I worked. I had merged with the lonely streetwalker on screen who gave up her freedom every time a boyfriend called. Giulietta Masina's pixie haircut, just like mine, and her bounce made it easy to identify.

But now something inside rose up, rebelled. Simone de Beauvoir lived an independent life. Why couldn't I? And that woman Virginia Woolf who had written the book. She understood.

My female training, however, was powerful. Even in my offbeat family, I had watched my mother defer to my father. While my need for autonomy was strong, my capacity to say no was undeveloped. My friend Eleanor was one of my models for female independence, yet even she found a male mate necessary. "Finding a man" was the unquestioned necessity for every woman I knew. And now I had one. A good one.

I looked at Julie. White guilt merged with female conditioning, and I was gasping for air. Where could he go? He had just started work as a welfare investigator and didn't have money yet to put down on an apartment.

He was my boyfriend, after all. He had sheltered me; shouldn't I do the same?

He didn't speak, just stared.

I couldn't speak, either. Stalling for time, I said, "That was so mean, putting your stuff out in the hall!"

Still he was silent.

"You can move in here," I blurted. Then, devastated, I turned to prepare a late spaghetti dinner, biting my cheek to keep from screaming.

"He was so beautiful. I was angry, but I acquiesced," I typed that night on a piece of paper I tucked into a shoebox high in the hall cupboard, not daring to think of these typewritten scraps as a journal. "I didn't know there were men like him in the world . . . gentle, caring so much, thinking all that I'm thinking and all that I'm not thinking."

I stuffed my fury deep inside, hammering it down with a mallet until it splintered into my guts. Still, I knew I had let an opportunity slip away.

How different would my life have been if I had offered only a few nights, a week or two, until he found a place?

Instead I gave in and understood that I had let myself down. He was the Writer. The Negro Writer. And I turned out to be the Girlfriend, the white Girlfriend who gave him whatever he needed.

My collapse—or should I call it my love, my compassion?—set the pattern for our entire relationship. I could stand up for myself out in the world, but with him, whom I cared for so deeply, my boundaries blurred and I didn't know how to hold on to my own needs. That lack of ability had proven toxic before. This time all I lost was a piece of myself. But I stayed alive. One time I nearly hadn't.

Miss Lonelyhearts

1958

At the end of our first year at Antioch College, my roommate Jessie and I had co-op jobs lined up in Chicago, where we would live in Hyde Park. But just weeks before we left, the lab school where I planned to work rescinded its job offer when I refused to sign a loyalty oath.

"I am not now a Communist, and never have been," the school wanted me to swear, in print. Of course I hadn't been a Communist, had no idea how to be one, but such was the policy during the McCarthy era. Even a seventeen-year-old intern had to sign the oath.

"I really want to come," I told the school's director. "But I can't sign that anti-Communist thing. On principle."

"It's the rule," the director said. "I'm sorry."

"Can't you waive it? It's so silly."

But she wouldn't budge, and since I was adamant—I wouldn't dignify the witch hunt by participating—I couldn't join Jessie on what would have been our first great adventure. And now I didn't have a job for the six-month period when everyone in my class was supposed to be off working. In the Antioch job office, I scanned the few listings left, until I spotted one at the Evanston Children's Home near Chicago.

"I think I want that," I told my co-op counselor. "I like to work with children."

"Oh no." He shook his head, pushed back his chair, and stared at me with concern. "Sorry. The stipulation is that you be twenty. We've always held firm to that." He checked his file. "And you're still seventeen." He looked incredulous.

"I'll be eighteen in two weeks."

"These girls are quite disturbed," he said. "They've been raped and abused. You'd be living right on the floor with them, with only one day off a week." He sounded worried. "I don't think it's a good idea."

"I know I could do it," I said brightly, embroidering my past. "I've had a lot of experience with kids." Babysitting, where I suffered brats for the sake of leftover food in the fridge and a fistful of change. Tormenting my little brother before we finally became friends. Taking my baby sister ice-skating.

"You'd have to write up pages of notes on the girls every evening. It's a big job."

"I love to write. That wouldn't be any problem."

He looked dubious.

"Please," I pleaded. "I'm very mature." Which, if you judged by appearances, I was: poised, looking steady and strong. Academically I *was* strong. "I really want this job."

In truth I didn't. I simply wanted to be near Jessie in Chicago. But in the end, because I knew how to be persuasive and Antioch was committed to filling the job, the counselor let me go.

I rode the train alone from New Haven, staring out the window for two days, wondering about life in the Home while I munched on Muenster cheese sandwiches my mother had made. I couldn't wait to arrive. When the train finally pulled into Chicago, I scanned waiting faces on the platform, eager to find one looking for me. Slowly, I watched travelers greet people picking them up. But after all the other passengers faded away, I sat alone next to my trunk, still waiting. The loneliest I had ever felt.

Eventually I dragged my trunk into the empty station, found a pay phone, and inserted my nickel. A woman answered, sounding bored. "We didn't know you were coming today."

"Please," I said. "That's what I said. I'm here."

She sent an old Negro handyman, who arrived, complaining, an hour later. "We thought you were coming tomorrow," he grumbled. "Your room isn't ready and dinner is over."

Once I saw my room, I wanted to go home. A tiny cell, it rose three steps from the girls' quarters. Dirty sheets lay on the floor. The wastebasket overflowed with paper and crumpled Kleenex. The one small window, up near the ceiling, had bars. "Your room isn't clean," Jadwiga, the other staff member, mumbled, while making no move to help. I had to rummage in a basement closet for sheets and find smelly garbage bins out back to dump the wastebasket. A fog of sorrow seeped like a mist into every corner of the Home, and my room, inches from the girls' living quarters, had absorbed it all.

The five girls' bedrooms fanned out from a dreary living room stuffed with faded furniture. Four girls were white. Suzie, the oldest at sixteen, cackled in a high-pitched voice. Tina, a spunky, giggling fourteen-year-old, "like most of the others, was raped by her father," the director told me. Cynthia, the single Negro child, was twelve: chubby, with greasy, straightened hair. Mostly she cried alone in her room.

In my small room, the hard, narrow bed didn't offer the comfort I was used to finding in beds. Everyone appeared melancholy, counselors as well as clients, or inmates, as they seemed to me. My room, so close to the girls, was no refuge. Even books didn't give relief.

Each monotonous day was like the last except Saturdays, when the Home took all the girls out for a treat: lunch and a movie. All but Cynthia, who had to stay at the Home. With me.

"That's not fair!" I complained to the director, a well-dressed, aloof woman in her forties, when she and I stood in her office downstairs. It was my first Saturday, and the other girls, full of excitement, were upstairs preparing for the trip. "Why can't Cynthia go? That's horrible, how do you think that makes her feel?"

"Listen," the director snapped back, slamming a folder onto her desk. "We're extremely forward-looking to have her live here at all. No one else does this. If we were to take her out and there were a scene, if a restaurant didn't want to serve her, her presence might become public and the neighbors could easily complain. She's lucky she's here!"

"Maybe not," I muttered. Aloud I insisted, "She should go with the others."

"Listen, young lady. You don't know what you're talking about. Be careful what you say."

"This is 1958! It isn't right!"

She bowed her head to her papers and waved me off.

But the next Saturday morning, I spoke to the director again. "Everybody should stay back if Cynthia can't go. The girls talk about that lunch all week. And the movie. They act it out, they giggle about it. No wonder Cynthia's so miserable. Maybe everybody could go for a ride instead?"

"Somebody might see her."

"God, we have to hide her?"

"You are jeopardizing the safety of this Home," the director warned. "You don't have all the information. These girls have nowhere else to go. This is not your business, you're only here for six months, and you don't understand anything about the situation. It's very delicate. If you don't stop complaining, I'll be forced to write you an unsatisfactory report." Thereby denying me the twenty-six Antioch credits I would earn from this job, one for each week. Credits I would need to graduate.

I wish now that when I spent those Saturdays alone with Cynthia, I had had the wisdom to place her face in my hands and say, "You're beautiful. You're wonderful and special. It's stupid that you can't go with the other girls, but you and I will have an extra good time and do things nobody else gets to do." But at eighteen, all I could see in front of me was a fat blubbering girl leaking snot, so instead of lifting her misery I joined it, hating every minute I had to stay back from the fun.

The mind-numbing days dragged on, watching the unhappy girls play hopscotch on the roof, where sweltering sun melted the tar. Supervising them in dim light while they quarreled at Chinese checkers until red and green marbles flew through the air. Chewing carrot and celery sticks lodged in oval glass dishes, to start more-of-the-same lunches and dinners. Listening to Jadwiga, a Polish refugee with a pale moon face and dead eyes, throw up in the bathroom after every meal. When she confided her habit of sticking her finger down her throat, which I had never heard of, I wondered what hell I had come to.

Hours of writing reports ended each day, detailing each girl's behavior in multiple pages, with carbon copies that inevitably smeared: whom she fought with, whom she cursed, punishments imposed. Though I enjoyed the act of writing, the content was so miserable I couldn't imagine staying six months.

Yet I had made a commitment. I was trapped.

And I chose reading that matched the environment, dutifully plowing through psychologist Bruno Bettelheim's text on emotionally disturbed children, *Love Is Not Enough*. For relief I tried two famous Depression-era novels, Horace McCoy's *They Shoot Horses, Don't They?* and Nathanael West's *Miss Lonelyhearts*. The latter includes a scene where the protagonist, an advice columnist, sits with his drinking buddies as they complain about female writers, gleefully imagining violent rapes "to put these women in their place."

Only gorging on pints of cherry vanilla ice cream, which I stuffed down with a spoon stolen from the kitchen, gave temporary relief from the soggy gloom around me. But each time, after finishing the pint, I felt like a bloated glutton and hated myself. I imagined my slender body swelling like a balloon.

Four months into my stint at the claustrophobic Home, I rode the el as usual on my day off to Jessie's Hyde Park apartment. All week I looked forward to the break. While Jessie and her roommates were still at work, I would explore the city alone, dressed in my red paisley cotton shift tied at the waist. I haunted the university's broad lawns, sat in on classes, drank at an off-campus bar with new friends, and enjoyed every minute of freedom until my friends arrived home. I would sleep over, then plod back to the Home in the morning.

But this time my plans changed. In the apartment's low early-winter light, I sat slumped on the couch gulping Gordon's gin. Unable to face the thought of returning the following day to the Home, I watched the liquid flow through its clear glass bottle while I read *They Shoot Horses, Don't They?*, about a grueling marathon dance that goes on for days. One of the contestants, Gloria, keeps saying, "I wish I were dead" until the end, when she pulls out a pistol and asks her dance partner to kill her. Which he does, thinking, "They shoot horses, don't they?"

Exactly.

I kept sipping, my mind growing vacant. I watched a shadow slowly cross the floor, and listened to cars honking below on the street. Finally satisfied that the gin had mellowed my bones, I lurched into the kitchen and opened the oven door. Thick flakes of black grease covered the entire inside and smeared the door. It smelled like old fish.

I stumbled to a bedroom, grabbed a pillow, and placed it on the filthy oven door. Dark smudges would streak the white pillowcase. But I couldn't go back to the Home and I didn't know how to quit. Silently asking my friends to forgive the greasy mess, I knelt by the stove and lay my head on the soft pillow.

I reached up to turn on the gas.

How easy it was.

The world was silent back in the kitchen.

A large wall clock showed 1:22. Patience has never been a virtue of mine, but I remained crouched while the clock moved slowly, its noisy tick marking off the last minutes of my life. I cradled the gin bottle. The fishy smell in the oven made me gag. I sipped more gin.

1:35.

1:41.

I gulped gin and choked, sputtering. But I remained in place, my head on the pillow.

1:50.

I thought this would be faster.

At 2:05, surprised, I found I was still alive.

Shaking, I rose, suddenly horrified by what I had done. I turned off the gas, staggered to the telephone, and opened the thick Chicago phone book to the Yellow Pages. Psychiatrists.

I dialed one and listened to the phone ring on and on, its sound grating, echoing in my splitting head.

I chose another. This time a man's voice said, "Hello?"

"I tried to kill myself. I'm drinking gin, I had my head in the oven," I gasped, unable to believe it myself.

"Where do you live?"

"My parents are in Connecticut. I'm here on a job."

"How old are you?"

"Eighteen."

"Come to my house right away, to the back door," he instructed.

I splashed cold water on my face and walked unsteadily to the address he gave, ten blocks away. Seated in his brown leather armchair, I listened to the sympathetic man advise, "Go home to your parents. You're too young to be here on your own in that kind of situation. You must return home right away."

I nodded, relieved. I would have to quit the job. He had ordered it.

The next day, November 21, 1958, I bought a train ticket despite the director screaming, "You're leaving us in the lurch, a terrible staffing problem. I'll flunk you." Which she did, giving me zero credits for the four tortuous months I had worked.

My father met me before dawn in the echoing New Haven railroad station and folded me into his arms, the first safety I had felt since I left home. On the drive, when I told him what I'd done, tears wet his cheeks. "Why?"

I couldn't answer. All I felt was a vast emptiness, the tears of the troubled girls soaked into my soul. The Antioch counselor had been right. I was far too young. Possibly the wrong person for the job at any age, given my penchant for empathy and for blurring boundaries between myself and others, whose voices would linger in my head for days.

Ashamed, I had no idea how my porous skin might have indicated a writer's sensitivity, an activist's heart. Any strong character, fictional or real, could work herself into my consciousness until I felt even my walk or the way I spoke was the other person moving through me. Instead of seeing how this might be a strength, I faulted myself for weakness. After all, Sartre described the authentic person as one who has found a solid essence. Why was I so fragile? Was it part of being female, this inability to hold my own shape in the face of others' suffering, others' needs?

A terrible hopelessness settled into my heart. The depressing daily routine I had endured for four months—a lifetime for an eighteen-year-old—had crept into every cell, coloring the entire world gray. Maybe the professors at college, all men, applauded my English papers and gave me As, but how could I, a girl, ever become a writer like the men I read?

As for my political efforts, I hadn't even been able to convince the director at the Home to take Cynthia on any outings with the other girls. I had refused to sign the anti-Communist loyalty oath at the nursery school job, which had landed me in that terrible Home, but really, what did my refusal accomplish?

Fleeing the Home hardly restored my frayed identity. In the familiarity of my parents' house, I didn't know who I was either. Beguiled in Chicago by my first Indian film—Satyajit Ray's *Pather Panchali*, the story of a poor Bengali family—I edged my mattress off the bed and tugged it onto the floor. "I'm sleeping here in solidarity with the Third World," I announced.

During the night, I found that the thin mattress needed bedsprings to be comfortable, but I was determined. If people in India had to sleep on the ground, I would, too. I left my mattress on the floor, my bid for unity with the dark-skinned peoples of the world.

"Call me Krishna," I told my long-suffering parents, and insisted on eating with my fingers the way Indians did in the film. For my eight weeks at home, until spring quarter began, I would answer only to my Indian name. It was tough eating that way and sleeping on the floor. But I was committed.

Waiting at my parents' home, I often wondered, Why didn't all that gas kill me? Puzzled at the outcome though grateful for it, after the suicide attempt I was left with a belief for a long time that there was something wrong inside me, something shameful I needed to cover up.

I grew adept at cloaking my shame with intelligence and a naturally warm demeanor. But I felt like a fake. Except when I was composing words on a page. Then I was my genuine self, at ease and unaware of anyone else's opinion.

Back at Antioch, I threw myself into classes. And I deepened my friendship with Eleanor Holmes, three years older and my first Negro friend.

"Michael Harrington is coming to give a lecture tonight," she told me one afternoon, striding across campus on her long legs. I, four inches shorter, raced to keep up. "Do you want to come with me? He's a democratic socialist. Makes so much sense."

I didn't really understand his lecture, but I learned other things from Eleanor. After her white roommate got engaged and Eleanor told me, I murmured a conventional, "Congratulations."

But she erupted, "Only a white girl could come to college and get married! A Negro girl knows better. She has to take care of herself."

"Oh." I stared, chastened. And watched her with ever more interest. More and more, we spent time together talking politics.

Still, in November 1959, a year after my stint at the Home, I left college to "find myself." As if that were a solid something, lost temporarily—maybe back in that grimy Chicago oven. If I looked hard enough, I would find a Me inside, an essence, as the existentialists said. And I would know how to proceed with the rest of my life. So I moved to New Haven, thirty miles from my parents, to look for a job. But instead of the internal core I sought, what I found was an education about segregation, police ferocity, and the power of a people to change history.

The Souls of Black Folk

1960

On February 1, 1960, four Black college freshman in Greensboro, North Carolina, ordered "Coffee, please," at a whites-only Woolworth's counter. With liberation movements succeeding all over the world, the moment was ripe.

A server answered the students, "Negroes get food at the other end," and pointed to the other side of the counter, which held no seats. But the four young men—Joseph McNeil, Franklin McCain, Ezell Blair Jr., and David Richmond—remained, sitting at the whites-only counter until the store closed. In the morning they returned with twenty-seven other students and again requested, "A cup of coffee, please." Again the server refused.

On day three, the sit-in grew to sixty-three students and occupied all the whites-only seats. On day four, three hundred. On day six, over one thousand protesters jammed the store.

By the end of the week, the sit-in movement spread like wildfire across the South to scores of other lunch counters. The energy lit up the North, too, with Woolworth's boycotts springing up in every major city.

I had recently found a job at Yale Medical School. Somehow I had managed to sound competent enough that the doctor in charge said yes, hiring an inexperienced nineteen-year-old college dropout to administer a research project on women's health.

The last Saturday in February, I scooted over to the New Haven five and dime, where large gold letters over the entrance spelled WOOLWORTH against a red background. Stepping into a picket line, I joined a chant, "Can't eat, don't buy!" The boycott goal was for Woolworth's to stop segregating

CORE demonstrators outside Harlem Woolworth store, February 13, 1960.
(Bettman Collection via Getty Images)

their southern stores, which they defended by saying, "We don't interfere
with local culture."

Dressed in our respectable best—skirts and heels for the women, suits
for men—we walked in a circle chanting, "End lunch counter discrimination!" I called it out until my voice was hoarse, but my spirit grew stronger
the longer we stayed. "Every Saturday I'll be here," I vowed to a minister
behind me in the circle.

One Saturday in March was especially chilly, overcast and windy, but we
stayed, stamping our feet in the cold, because so many potential shoppers
turned away once they saw us. Then we clapped and shouted, raising our
voices in victory.

Most of the two dozen picketers that day were men. All but two of us
were African American. The other white person was a middle-aged man
in a wool suit, puffing along with an END DISCRIMINATION sign. All afternoon, drivers honked in support. Other drivers screamed ugly words: "Go
back to the zoo, monkeys!"

Near the end of picketing that day, I called out to my end of the line,
"I'm having a party at my place. Everyone's invited." My heart raced.

Despite the frigid air, I began to sweat. People were stamping their feet to keep warm, yet suddenly I wanted to unbutton my coat. Would anybody come?

"Is there food?" one good-looking young man behind me asked, laughing.

"Potato chips and onion dip. And salami!" I turned to smile back at him.

"Yes, ma'am," he said, tipping his hat. No one had ever called me ma'am before.

"Everyone's invited?" a scruffy older guy asked.

I looked at the disheveled, unshaven man. We were supposed to be wearing "business attire," trying to present the best possible look to shoppers we hoped to reach. Unnerved, I nodded. "Yeah."

"Okay, I'm down." He grinned, flashing large gaps between his teeth. "See you at your pad."

"Me, too," another man chimed in while we kept shouting, "North, South, East, West, we expect the best!" Everyone moved fast to keep warm. The wind was picking up, cutting into our faces, and dark clouds blew in front of what little sun there was.

"Dig it," I heard another man shout. "I'm in."

"Thanks," a woman behind me said in a beautiful low voice, adding, "What can I bring?"

Turning, I saw a plump, dark-skinned woman in her thirties, who was looking at me with a wide smile from under a large gray hat. It had a huge brim and black veil pulled up over the front, a kind of hat I had never seen. She looked as if she were going to church, I thought, although not being a churchgoer myself, I couldn't say for sure.

"Nothing, thanks." I had spent the morning fixing snacks and folding paper towels for napkins. "Glad you're coming."

By the time we finished picketing, I had at least fifteen or twenty guests—all Negro and all men except the dimpled woman with the hat—planning to come to my grimy basement apartment, where I had laboriously painted the cement floor fire-engine red the weekend before. I had only lived there a month but already loved the place. That morning I had scrubbed the windowsills and bathroom, swept the bumpy floor, and laid snacks on four chipped plates in the refrigerator. This was going to be a bash. A housewarming.

I led the group down Elm Street and Church, winding past the Green in the center of town, continuing on until we reached my imposing brick apartment building, set back from the street. We straggled along a walkway until we entered a side door and clambered down three steps, people chatting noisily. "Man, dig this place," I heard somebody shout to the end of the line. "Oh man, we home free!"

After everyone snaked around the furnace and ceiling pipes, my guests, making a racket with their clomping, filed into the apartment carved into a corner of the basement. They started pulling off winter jackets and coats, unwrapping scarves, and rubbing their hands for warmth. "You can put your coats on the bed," I called, waving to the bedroom before I headed for the record player and slid my one Sam Cooke album out of its sleeve. "Here, I've got that," the woman with the hat said, slipping the record onto the turntable and gently lowering the needle. "My name's Margaret." She stuck out her hand. "Got any Ike and Tina?"

I looked at her blankly.

"Turner." When I didn't react, she paused and looked at me, slant-eyed. "Ray Charles?"

"Ray Charles, yeah. 'Night time is the right time,'" I sang, trying to cover up my ignorance about who Tina was. "You can look in there." I pointed to a crate on the floor that held my small record collection: Billie Holiday, Chubby Checker, Charlie Parker (Bird), Fats Domino, and some old Beethoven 78s I had brought from home.

Running to the kitchen, I reached into the fridge for bowls of onion dip I had proudly made from a mix. "Let me help you," a young man offered. "Name's Edward." Despite his fedora, his sweet baby face made him look as if he were in high school. I had talked to him once on the line, speculating about when, if ever, Woolworth's would capitulate.

"Thanks. Maybe set these in there." I nodded toward the living room, where I had propped a wooden crate on a set of blue encyclopedias for a coffee table. Margaret cranked up the sound on the Sam Cooke record. "Everybody likes to cha cha cha," I heard and began to wiggle my shoulders and hips. "Little children like to cha cha cha." A few people began singing along, and the chatter of a party was starting while others were still stripping off jackets. "Took my baby to the hop last night."

I was handing Edward plates of salami and crackers when I heard the tramping of boots, angry shouts, and pounding at my door.

Edward froze. We stared in the direction of the noise. Suddenly a gang of white cops burst through the door holding clubs, swinging wildly and shouting, "Everyone out!"

Margaret leapt up. "What's happening?" she demanded. She frowned. I could see her hand shaking.

"Whose place is this? You're all trespassing!" a cop growled, raising his club to her head. His beefy face was red hot.

I pushed my way through the crowd, which had grown silent. Everyone was squeezed in the living room and kitchen, jammed now with a knot of burly white men shoving people toward the door. "It's my apartment. I invited them!" I thought that would end it. I *had* invited these guests. The cops would understand and leave.

The policeman leading the charge had a strong odor of sweat. His lips twisted in a snarl. His steely blue eyes glared. "Everybody out. Now!" He pushed two people toward the door. I saw Edward, who was slight, lose his balance. But someone else caught him and hung onto his arm. Edward looked as if he were about to cry.

"Stop it!" I screamed, confused by the mayhem. "This is my apartment. What's going on?"

"The floor won't hold so many. Regulations!" he bellowed, even though I was standing right there. "It's a violation." He swung his brown stick, tipped with metal, over my head. "Too many people per square foot."

"But this is the basement. The floor is cement. There's nothing underneath!"

Ignoring me, he kept pushing and shouting, "Regulations!" while people ran to the bedroom for coats. "Beat feet," I heard the scruffy older man mumble as he scurried past me. One guy hissed, "Fucking honkies" on his way out, while another man pulled him along, whispering, "Shut up, fool."

One man huffed, "You'll hear about this" as he stomped out, narrowly escaping a swinging club.

The cops, who looked huge, kept hustling stragglers toward the door while the record played "Twistin' the Night Away." People were running out when I heard Sam Cooke sing, "Here they have a lot of fun, puttin' trouble on the run."

The police were still yelling, "Get out!" while I stood helplessly by, repeating, "This doesn't make any sense. This is my apartment. I pay rent. The floor can hold us all!"

The police ignored me. One of the last to leave, Margaret, gave me a hug and whispered, "I'm sorry, baby."

In five minutes, everyone was gone. The guests, the cops. I stood in the doorway alone, trembling.

"Twistin', twistin'," Sam Cooke kept singing until, repulsed by the exuberance in his voice, I lifted the needle. Silence overwhelmed me. My building sat far back from the street, and the basement walls were so thick that no street sounds reached me. The place had felt cozy with noise for a few minutes, and now, other than the furnace clanking, I heard nothing, as if I were in a tomb.

I fell into my one easy chair in front of the makeshift coffee table. The brown corduroy chair, torn and musty, with stuffing leaking out the back, had been in the apartment when I moved in. Mindlessly, I began to eat potato chips.

As twilight fell, I remained in the dark, munching chips and scooping up onion dip, too dazed to turn on lights. How did the cops know a bunch of Negroes were here, I wondered, until I realized that tenants in the apartments above—all white—must have frantically called police when they saw a line of Negro men enter the building. So this was segregation, right here in my own apartment. I sat absorbing the reality, which of course my guests had understood immediately.

How could the neighbors be so mean? And the cops. They had no legal right to kick people out. I felt sickened by the cruelty, while the sour cream onion dip, beer, and potato chips churned in my stomach.

Should I have argued more, insisted I could have whoever I wanted in my private apartment? The segregationists loved to talk about private property and how they could control who was in it. But no matter how much I protested, nobody had listened to a teenage white girl.

I staggered into the bedroom. Someone had left a plaid woolen scarf tucked into a pair of black leather gloves with a hole in the index finger. Piling them carefully on top of my bureau, I fell into a deep sleep. Almost a coma.

The next day I tried to make sense of it all. When I called Eleanor, a law student now, she said, "Those fucking cops, you can't let them get away with it." But what could I do? Complain about cops to other cops?

On Monday at lunch, my best friend at work, Dee, a white X-ray technician with a lab across the hall, asked me, "Weren't you afraid the colored would steal things?"

"No!" I said, startled. "And don't call them that."

"Did you check after they left?"

"What? That's crazy."

In her late twenties, Dee was having an affair with a married doctor who had set her up in a remote apartment where he visited—sometimes—on weekends. This had shocked me as much as the cops bursting in, but her working-class bluntness felt familiar. She was smart and funny, and at lunch I loved sitting outside with her, swinging our legs on a low wall and eating corned beef sandwiches on rye, a sophisticated new food I had discovered. The day was chilly, but the noontime sun warmed my face.

"You're lucky they didn't rape you!"

"Dee, stop it," I said, inching away. "That's terrible."

She laughed.

"No, really," I said. "You can't talk about people like that."

"Okay," she said, but still with a wicked grin. I wondered, would she have called the cops if she had seen the protesters entering my building? I turned away and never again felt quite the same pleasure in her company.

Monday evening after work, as usual I opened up my gold mailbox in the apartment building's marble lobby. Reaching in, I saw a long, cream-colored envelope. Official looking. Puzzled, I ripped it open.

Running down to the basement, I called Eleanor again. "They're evicting me," I wailed. "Just for trying to have a party."

"Fight it!" she said. "Joan, you have to fight it."

"How?"

"You've got to get a lawyer. What they're trying to do isn't legal."

"I don't know how to go to court."

"That's why you need a lawyer. If you comply with the eviction, you're giving in to racism."

"Hmm." I would never admit to her how scared I had been of the cops, how big they were, how afraid I was of being dragged off to jail. Maybe beaten if the jailers knew who I had been fraternizing with, as they called it.

"You've got to fight it. You've got a case."

I hated to disappoint Eleanor, but when I called home in tears that night, my father advised, "It could be very unpleasant. Expensive." I didn't have the money and neither did he to pay for a lawyer. "You don't want to stay where you're not wanted. That would be awfully uncomfortable."

A few years later he would have offered different advice. He would have said, "We'll fight it. This isn't right. We'll find a way." His politics, like the country's, evolved until he and my mom grew deeply involved in civil rights. But in early 1960, he wasn't there yet.

"Eleanor," I called out the next evening when I saw her waiting for me by the law school. Late afternoon light burnished the building's stone a glorious, textured red. Yale's gothic architecture, with its many arches, ornate carvings, and stained glass windows, always awed me, as its designers no doubt intended. Each building was a medieval fortress, creating a granite skyline of turrets and towers.

A shaft of light caught Eleanor's cheek. She was pacing. "You're late."

"I know. Dr. Richards kept me after, correcting some damn form I gave him and I filled out one part wrong. He had to have it for a grant."

"Let's go, I'm starving."

Before we went up the steps, I blurted, "I can't do it. I can't fight the whole corporation that owns the building."

She spun around. "But you'd win! What they did was completely illegal."

"I found an attic apartment today. In a house near the medical school. It's nice. Same price." I looked at a leaded glass window over her head, avoiding her eyes.

"I could help you find an organization that might defend you."

"It could be a long case and they'd make my life hell there."

"I thought you cared about civil rights!"

"I do. But my father said it would be uncomfortable for—"

"Your father? What does he know about it?" She looked disgusted. "I'm in law school. I know the law!" This first-year student strode toward the heavy wooden front door, pulling it open.

I ran to catch up.

"White people," she fulminated, her long legs racing down the hall. "Just when you need them . . ."

"But I live there by myself. It could be scary," I said, trailing her.

"Yeah, well how do you think it is all the time being Negro?"

I didn't have an answer for that.

When we sat down, she glared, "We can't just pick up and leave. We're Negro all the time!"

"I'm going back to the picket line on Saturday," I said.

"Anybody can march on a picket line. That's easy. The hard stuff starts when they come after you!"

I gulped, and we sat in silence while the waiter poured water in our glasses.

"It was illegal," she repeated, poking her finger at me. "Illegal!"

"I know," I mumbled. "But they'd have all kinds of fancy lawyers, my father said."

"Your father. Is he a lawyer?"

"You know he isn't."

"Well?"

When the food arrived, Eleanor turned her attention to eating and seemed to soften. We had been friends for more than three years, confiding our dreams, crushes, and political hopes for the country. We had marched together and partied together. Perhaps she, a confident twenty-two, suddenly realized that at nineteen, living alone, I might not be capable of withstanding the pressure the landlord would surely exert. Though we had just joined CORE together, perhaps neither of us fully appreciated the support a civil rights organization might give. For whatever reason, my stern, chastising friend relaxed while she chewed her stewed chicken and changed the subject to a professor who had tickled her funny bone that day. When I heard her laugh, I knew she had forgiven me.

Three days later I moved, feeling like a coward. Enraged at the unfairness. All that red paint I had paid for and the weekend I spent slathering it on the floor. Having to pay a guy with a pickup to help move my stuff. The hassle of it all.

On Saturday I brought the left-behind gloves and scarf to the picket line but no one claimed them. A few people tried to console me. "You had to move? What a drag."

"Man, that's rotten."

"I'm sorry," two men said in unison, looking as if it were their fault.

"No, I'm sorry," I said over and over, the sorry carrying layers of meaning: sorry for segregation, sorry you've been treated unfairly all your life, sorry that after you gave so much on the freezing picket line you couldn't even enjoy a party. Sorry this probably wasn't the first time and wouldn't be the last.

So this is what happens when whites and Negroes try to socialize, I thought bitterly. Even here "Up South." What were white people so afraid of? Damn!

What I've only now realized is how little I understood about the lives of my guests, how totally segregation had kept us apart. How naive I was not to understand the jeopardy they put themselves in by entering my apartment. Though segregationists held a special antipathy for "race traitors" and "nigger lovers," it was my guests who risked the most. Whenever I've remembered this incident, I've thought about how it affected *me*. My eviction. My trauma. Not how it affected the others. Were any cops outside on the walkway waiting to get a lick in when the men and one woman were forced to walk a gauntlet? If so, I never heard about it. But I never thought to ask.

One afternoon I spotted a small paperback at the Yale Co-op. It was an old book and I had never heard of the author, W. E. B. Du Bois, but the title, *The Souls of Black Folk*, intrigued me.

Discovering fourteen elegant essays about Negro history, I gobbled them up. "The problem of the twentieth century is the problem of the color line," Du Bois had written in 1903. In 1960 it was still true: civil rights were splitting the country. *New York Times* headlines told me so. "Negro Sitdowns Stir Fear of Wider Unrest in South" told a typical story: North Carolina's attorney general Malcolm B. Seawell "asserted that the students were causing 'irreparable harm' to relations between whites and Negroes." Southern mayors and business leaders echoed his alarm, while Northern whites were divided.

Du Bois's chapter 9, "Of the Sons of Master and Man," explained exactly what had happened inside my apartment. "The police system of the South was originally designed to keep track of all Negroes, not simply criminals," he wrote. It was "arranged to deal with blacks alone, and tacitly assumed that every white man was *ipso facto* a member of that police." I had just experienced this modern-day police control, well outside the South. The immediate, violent response to a "Negro invasion" of my apartment building exactly mirrored the white response to the Greensboro sit-ins: You cannot come in here. Whites Only. Reading *The Souls of Black Folk* gave me another year of the liberal arts education I had missed.

On July 26, 1960, I sat at my office desk eating a jelly donut, a daily treat from an office pastry cart, when a *New York Times* photo of the iconic F. W. WOOLWORTH sign caught my eye. Six months after the Greensboro sit-in, Woolworth's had announced it would immediately desegregate all its lunch counters, North and South, exactly as we had demanded!

Suddenly giddy with power, I said to myself, "We won." The four students had started a movement. Thousands had been arrested, but we had toppled a historic barrier.

I broke into an ecstatic cheer, "Yes! Yes!" that brought my assistant, Lois, running from the next room. "Look," I shouted, "Woolworth's de-segregated! They opened their lunch counters in the South!" I pumped my arms in a victory salute. If we had broken nearly one hundred years of legal segregation, we could do anything.

Memoirs of a Dutiful Daughter

1962

After Julie moved into my apartment on Twenty-First Street, I turned to Simone de Beauvoir's *Memoirs of a Dutiful Daughter* as a manual on independence. How did this lonely girl, raised in a strict Catholic household, free herself from "the revolting fate that had lain ahead of us"? De Beauvoir had the audacity to create her own intellectual life, tailored to her desires. How did she do it?

Books, I discovered. De Beauvoir read books she found in a relative's home and others she borrowed from a friend. She asked questions relentlessly, everywhere, at school, at home. She ventured out into the world on her own, lying to her mother so she could visit clubs and cafés when she was supposed to be studying. She met Jean-Paul Sartre at university; he encouraged her thinking. Finally, she wrote the life she chose to lead. And her fiction became her truth.

As I studied *Memoirs of a Dutiful Daughter* (which she was not), Simone de Beauvoir became more than ever my mentor, providing a model of a woman's quest for autonomy. If she could do it, why couldn't I?

~

One fall evening, Julie and I wandered through Washington Square, where a band of young people sat on the edge of the central fountain playing banjos and guitars. The wind romantically blew yellow, orange, and red leaves around the plaza, so the musicians looked as if they were rising out of a multicolored whirlwind.

Julie, holding my hand, stopped by a sweet-faced older Negro man with a pompadour, a large guitar, and a cigarette dangling out of the corner of his mouth. "Hey, brother. Mind if we join you?"

"No, no. Not at all." He shifted his body on the bench to make room for us. "Sit a spell."

"Nice guitar," Julie said and sat back appreciatively, listening to the strings sing.

Once he started humming harmony, I joined in, lending my light soprano to the two growly basses. The three of us sat contentedly for half an hour making music, the musician occasionally handing over his twelve-string guitar to Julie. This is the life, I thought.

Afterward Julie and I ambled to Caffe Reggio, my idea of a Paris café: tiny round tables and wrought-iron chairs, the aroma of bitter coffee, and air gray with cigarette smoke. Several people in black turtlenecks sat alone reading in dim light. Others huddled in small groups.

Julie and I hugged a corner table, sipping coffee with bubbling milk made in an espresso machine. My eyes roved around the small room.

"I heard Pete Seeger's a Communist," an olive-skinned man at a nearby table said, shrugging one shoulder. With a scraggly beard, he looked like an intellectual.

"Daddy-O, then I'm one too," his companion answered in an accent I couldn't place, with a laugh.

On our way out, I overheard a pale woman in a black beret ask, "What's the meaning of life if there's no eternal essence?" Her companion, a tall woman in a pea jacket, said, "Camus shows the meaning of life is what we put into it."

What a perfect evening, I thought, snuggling into Julie's arm as we rambled back up to Twenty-First Street. I might not have a room of my own anymore, but I had him.

My contentment was broken by a shriek from the first-floor window of our building. "Nigger, get out!" Theresa screamed. The landlady, stuck upstairs in her wheelchair, kept howling, "Nigger, nigger. Goddam nigger! Get out! You don't belong here."

Ever since she had seen Julie, she had been shouting the same thing in her high, thin voice. The call of "Nigger, get out" followed him in the morning when he left for work, head hunched down, and escorted him when he returned at night.

"It's getting on my nerves," he said one evening. "Her voice echoes in my head all day."

"I know," I said, wretched that he had to put up with it.

"We've got to get her to stop." His thin face tightened and he paused. "She'll never listen to me. Would you go up and talk to her?"

"Maybe we should go together," I said, terrified of confronting her.

"She wouldn't even let me in the door," he scoffed. "She might listen to you."

Finally one afternoon I braced myself to go upstairs. Because I had paid key money to the previous tenant—and did he move because she yelled the same thing at him?—I had yet to meet my landlady.

Timidly, I walked upstairs and knocked on her door.

No answer.

I knocked again. "Theresa," I called out. "It's Joan, your downstairs tenant."

"Go away," she called out.

"I'd like to talk to you."

Silence.

"I have the rent check." I had decided to take December's rent up in person to sweeten the visit.

"Come in," I heard a scratchy voice say.

I opened the door to an overwhelming stench of urine and a messy room littered with whiskey bottles, clothing, old milk cartons, and banana peels. I could hardly breathe. Looking around, I saw a skinny old white woman sitting in a wheelchair by the window. Her legs were stumps, her gray hair hung in greasy strands, and her smell was unbearable.

Gagging, I took a step into the room and said, "I wanted to meet you."

She glared.

"We're good tenants. We keep our apartment clean. I sweep the hallway by our door. And the front steps. We pay the rent."

She grunted, burping loudly.

Nauseous from the stink of alcohol, stale urine, and rotting food, I said quietly, "Please stop screaming at my boyfriend. He's a good man."

"No niggers here," she said, slurring her words before she screamed, "Get out, nigger's whore, black bastard!" She continued ranting, repeating what seemed to be her favorite word, "Nigger, nigger," and started to wheel toward me.

I backed out of the room, relieved to close the door.

Her screams at Julie persisted.

One evening after he returned to an especially prolonged and profane barrage of her screams, he slumped at the kitchen table, a repurposed door with screwed-in metal legs. He looked as if he might cry. "All day I'm out dealing with poor people's traumas, and I come home to my own! 'Nigger, nigger,'" he spat out.

"I know," I said miserably.

He tilted his face up to me while I stood by his side, caressing his shoulder. "Should we move?" he asked.

"I don't know."

"Where would we find such a cheap place? I've already given two weeks' notice, and today I got another call for a guitar student, but it won't be as much money."

I sighed, knowing that with my own two jobs plus school I couldn't take on any more work. "I'd like to go up and push her out the window!"

He chuckled. "Yeah." And then, as he so often did, he leaned down, opened his case, lifted out his guitar, and began to strum. Here in the rear of the apartment, we were protected, safe from harassment. Theresa never went to the back of hers. Maybe she couldn't get there. We didn't know.

Later that evening Julie said, "Let's stay. I'm going to ignore her. Every time I hear her yell at me, I'm going to call it a blessing. She's blessing me!"

I laughed. What a creative and spiritual man, who could take shit and turn it into something good. Yes, I agreed, "We'll fill our heads with other thoughts—like our love—when she tries to clog our ears with that crap. Okay, I'm in."

Beginning the following month, Theresa stopped cashing our rent checks. Month after month went by. They remained undeposited. Finally, trembling, one evening I opened an envelope from the court. An eviction notice for nonpayment of rent. "What are we going to do?"

"We can't afford anything else," Julie said miserably. "I only have three guitar students."

"I'm not going to let myself get evicted a second time because of prejudice," I said. "Remember what happened to me in New Haven? Damn it, we're going to fight it. You know it's just because she hates Negroes." I wondered again if that was why the previous tenant had sold me his key. He probably didn't think he needed to warn me, a white woman. Or maybe Theresa hadn't harassed him. Maybe she only yelled at Julie because she couldn't stand seeing us, perfectly good tenants, together.

"What do you mean?"

"That time when I lived in New Haven and the cops kicked everybody out of my apartment after a Woolworth's demo, and I got evicted?"

"Oh yeah. But how would we fight it? She owns the building. We might have to move." He sighed.

"No!" Panicked, I was still determined not to back down. We had paid the rent, I had the check stubs. Wouldn't that be enough? Or would the fact that we had moved in illegally, with key money, make the eviction stand?

Researching tenant groups, I found the Metropolitan Council on Housing, a strong tenants rights organization. I called and talked to Frances Goldin, one of the leaders. "Don't worry," she said kindly. "You can contest it." She coached me on securing a show cause order against the landlady, which would delay the eviction.

We waited nervously. Finally a court date came in the mail. "Don't mention the key money," Frances cautioned. "You're on a month-to-month. Implied. And she did cash your first checks. You'll be okay. That established tenancy."

Since the eviction notice was addressed to me, Julie and I wondered who should go to court.

"If the judge sees us both, we'll lose the case right there!" he said, with a grim chuckle. "Or if he only sees me, he'd bang his gavel, say, 'Nigger guilty.'"

"And what would the judge think about us living in sin? Shacking up." I made a shocked face. "Plus, if we *were* married he'd probably think that was worse! Miscegenation!" We chortled, with complex emotions laced into our laughter: proud to be flouting these ridiculous old rules, nervous always about what violence might hit us, and a strong desire to simply be two young intellectuals in love, never having to worry about how our coupling might affect the way people treated us or what ugly words anyone might holler.

Julie and I practiced what I would say in court. I hardly slept, until, nerves jangling, I faced the morning of the court date. Julie, as nervous as I, kissed me extra hard for luck and said, "I love you," before I set out alone. Although I was a nonpraying woman, I did some form of it that morning on the subway, begging the universe to let us stay in our thirty-five-dollar basement.

Once I braved the intimidating fortress and located the room, I found a spot on a bench with a crowd of others. An air of desperation pervaded the room. I could almost smell it: nervous sweat, damp coats, unwashed people crowded together. An older woman, her face lined and scarred, with a colorful red scarf tied around her head, sidled up to me. "Court?" she asked with a heavy accent and tears in her eyes.

I knew how she felt. "Sí." I nodded, and motioned for her to sit by me.

She shoved a paper in my lap and pointed to the words. An eviction notice.

"Solo?" I asked.

"Sí."

I looked more closely. Nonpayment of rent. Same as mine.

"Money?" I asked as gently as I could.

"No dinero."

I felt helpless, wishing I understood more about tenant law, wishing I were a lawyer. But since I wasn't, I reached into my pocketbook and opened my wallet. Four dollars. I handed her two. Not enough to pay her rent, but a gesture of solidarity. She kissed my cheek and allowed her tears to fall.

Hearing my name called, I said, "Adiós," and rushed to the front of the room, expecting to confront Theresa's lawyer. But no one showed up to represent her. The judge waited five minutes past the appointed time, then declared, "Eviction notice vacated." Impassive, he said, "Next."

My legs rubbery with fatigue and relief, I looked around for the woman who had talked to me. She wasn't on the bench. I went out in the hall to search, but she'd disappeared. I wished I had hauled her up to the judge with me and asked him to help her, find a public defender, something. But I hadn't and she was gone.

Exhausted, I stumbled home. We could stay. That dim, depressing basement, despite Theresa's ugly taunts, had become home after all, sheltering my love and me.

Today when I reflect on Theresa cursing Julius and my court appearance, I remember how common the N-slur was in the early '60s. Even in the North. People flung it at us constantly. They yelled from cars passing us, slowing down to hurl the insult. Strangers on the street muttered it when they passed. That word was ubiquitous in our lives, conveying: "You may think you're Somebody. But you aren't." A constant reminder that Julius and I fought not only for civil rights—access to jobs, voting, and education— but for him to even be recognized as human.

I'm also aware now how often I was our front person. The landlady. Court. Renting a car. Applying for public housing. Shopping at the hardware store or for groceries. Buying a fifteen-dollar Plymouth at a police auction so we could spend a summer at a free New Hampshire cabin I had found in an ad.

Each time it seemed logical that I was the one to call, to go. He was busy writing or teaching guitar while I was the practical one, a woman who dealt with household affairs. But more importantly I was white, so more likely to get better treatment. And when I went alone, I passed as the white person I was, with no mention of a Negro partner needed. On the occasions we stopped in together at a bodega or another store, the clerk never recognized us as a couple, and acted as if we were two separate people waiting in line.

Once it became clear we were together, the clerk would speak only to me, even if Julie requested information.

"How much is this bread?" Julie would ask.

The clerk looked directly at me. "Twenty-two cents."

I learned to glance over at Julie, directing the clerk's gaze in the same direction.

In general, it was simpler to go alone. And as an oldest child used to responsibility, our arrangement felt normal, though I would have liked a partner in public dealings.

But what was it like for him that I was always out front? As a black and white couple in the '60s, this was one of the costs. I wonder how this added to other strains in our relationship, like our internal racial dynamics, for as a white woman I was surely imbued with bias despite my passion for equality. Did I place myself as the face of our public persona because I felt better qualified to navigate the world, more adept, as well as knowing I would be better received?

Our gender dynamics were difficult too, for I was a nascent feminist and he an unaware patriarch, much as he espoused equality of the sexes. He assumed that housework, and later childrearing, would naturally fall to me—assumptions I vehemently disputed.

Adding to our challenges were our dramatically different class backgrounds—class inflected by race. My parents, though coming from poverty, enjoyed the freedom of whites to flout convention, try different jobs, and be rule breakers scornful of manners, without fear of potentially lethal consequences. Atheists with no TV, we lived a marginal life outside standard American norms. Twenty years before the back-to-the-land movement, my parents were hippies, living on the fringe of society, both economically and socially.

Julie's parents were solidly middle class—Black middle class—devout Christians and proper Negroes whose strict home held doilies on living room furniture, a large color TV, and well-appointed rugs. They definitely didn't eat any food while walking down the street; "a credit to their race," they attended church every Sunday. His parents drove a Cadillac; mine were proud of a sputtering VW bug. His father dressed in a suit and tie, even at home, while his reserved mother kept an immaculate home with standards of cleanliness I did not share. My parents wore faded jeans; our living room, strewn with books and magazines, was otherwise spare, with several saggy, comfortable old chairs. Afternoon sun flooded the windows, creating a warm glow on the bare wood floor. Neither my mother nor my father felt any pressure to keep up appearances.

Julie, I only realized later, was essentially a conservative man whose artistic bent drew him, for a time, into bohemian environments that felt like home to me. And the fervor of the '60s thrust him into revolutionary politics, with views he would later recant. By comparison, I was a radical through and through, a true daughter of my people. The historical moment of the early '60s made it appear that we shared progressive values, but as the decade wore on, it became clear we did not.

He was also deeply spiritual, a devotee of Thomas Merton. Julie often dreamed, longingly, of being a monk. Such an idea was completely outside my ken. With no consciousness of a spiritual inner life, it would take me half a lifetime to develop one.

With such varied backgrounds, Julie and I had a lot to contend with in our early twenties, though I was naive about the impact of the differences. It's hard to overstate the limited amount of contact I'd had with Black culture and people in 1962, or how little I understood America's original sin. Other than *Raisin in the Sun*, I had seen no multicultural plays or movies except the film *Pinky*, about a tragic "mulatto." The only books I had read by people of color were Ralph Ellison's *Invisible Man* and James Baldwin's *Go Tell It on the Mountain*. I didn't have a clue about the vastness of African American culture and its myriad expressions, or the depth of white hatred and its lethal ferocity.

Julie, like most Negroes, was more experienced around white folks than I was around Black ones. Additionally, he had spent an uncomfortable college year as an exchange student in San Diego, which had given him an up-close experience of white culture.

Yet Julie and I were so passionate that none of that seemed to matter. In the bubble of youth, we bounced through our days, coming home at night to lovemaking in the privacy of our apartment. There, once we had suffered the gauntlet of Theresa's shrieks, no eyes could see our different colored skins, no one hollered at us, and we were free to explore each other's forbidden bodies and minds. Safe in our cozy New York basement, what could possibly derail our love?

Cinderella

1962

Julie proposed casually one evening in December, sitting on the living room couch with his arm draped over my shoulder while we checked *New York Times* listings for summer camp jobs. "We'll never get work together if we aren't married," he said. "We could make good money."

"Hmm," I said.

We had lived with each other for almost four months, except for that brief break after I moved alone to Twenty-First Street. I was proud of his gorgeous writing, happy at the New School and my settlement house job. I loved exploring New York with him, watching foreign films at the Thalia up on Ninety-Fifth Street, listening to folk music in the Village, or walking home from our branch library with armloads of books.

But marriage?

It seemed the practical thing to do. My mother had married at nineteen. I was already twenty-two. Yet a voice inside that still believed I could Be Somebody screamed, "No!"

"Maybe," I answered.

That night I began to decorate a Douglas fir we had dragged home from a stand on Twenty-Third. But I couldn't concentrate. What are you doing? I thought as I pitched tinsel to a top branch, inhaling the piney scent.

He's so sensitive. The strands shimmered through the air. He's amazing.

What about Simone de Beauvoir? Don't I want to be like her? Yes. I wrapped blue lights around the tree.

But she's fifty-four and I'm twenty-two. She's French, she looks grim, she's nothing like me! The abyss between us was so vast I could only admire her from a distance, never imagine myself into her life.

I hardly realized how much confidence I had lost in only four months, so slow had been the drip of erosion. Who was there to look to for guidance? My heroine Virginia Woolf had drowned herself, I'd discovered, weighting down her pockets with stones. If even she couldn't do it . . .

While I battled myself, a powerful undertow tugged. The Cinderella dream, as much as I consciously rejected it, had etched a groove in my brain. Here was Julie, my hero heretically recast from a white knight to a Negro intellectual, come to rescue me from my adolescent loneliness. From that awful suicide attempt.

Who cared about autonomy? I was happy with my academic career, where I was a star.

For two days the subconscious war raged. The practical matter of getting camp jobs kept surfacing; what was my resistance to this perfectly logical plan? Julie promised me, "We'll never be apart for a single night the rest of our lives." That sounded magical.

Should I or shouldn't I?

In bed one night I whispered, "Yes," stilling the voice that warned I would lose whatever shreds remained of a sovereign self. The same voice that had urged me to get my own apartment. But I drowned out its cry with the fantasy of happily ever after, cozily tucked in with my mate.

"Nothing will change between us, right?" I said, nuzzling into his shoulder.

"Of course not." He held me tight in his arms.

Since this son of a Methodist minister wanted a church wedding, I called the pastor at Metropolitan-Duane United Methodist Church on West Thirteenth Street in the Village.

"I can meet you both later today," he said, jovially. "Marriage. A happy occasion!"

Yet once he greeted us outside the sanctuary, I could smell his nervousness. Evidently he wasn't expecting Julie as my groom. But he collected himself and directed us toward the back of the church, where he motioned us into a windowless room. There he pointed to two chairs opposite his large wooden desk. "I'll be back in a moment," he said, scooting out the door.

I sat dazed, amazed that we were actually doing this. Julie was clearly excited, as well as annoyed by the white minister's obvious discomfort.

The minister returned and took a seat behind the desk. For a minute he simply stared. "Have you thought about your, uh, mixed-race status?"

He scrutinized us like lab specimens. "This could be very challenging. It's illegal—"

"I know," I interrupted. "In twenty-seven states. But not in New York. We never had anti-miscegenation laws here."

"We're not concerned," Julie added brusquely, squeezing my hand. I recognized the stony look: *You'll never know what I'm thinking, white man.*

"Have you considered, ah, the possibility of, uh, children?" The minister looked as if the words had been coerced by hot coals applied to his neck, which began to flame like his face.

"No," I said. "But if we do, they'll be fine." Bravado came naturally to me; I wasn't going to entertain any doubts.

Red-faced and oozing anxiety, the minister agreed to bless our vows after two sessions of counseling, which would commence immediately. I recall only a memory of how awkward they were. And, I believed, unnecessary. What could he know of the perfect merging of two compatible souls?

Both sets of parents, concurring with the minister's worry, refused to attend our wedding. "Stay away from white women," Julie's father had cautioned him all his life. "Don't even look at them." And now here he was, about to marry one, only seven years after Emmett Till had been murdered for whistling (maybe) at a white woman. As Julie said, "In the South, you keep one eye on the white girl you're walking down the street with and one eye on a lookout for the lynch rope." About the wedding, his parents told him, "Son, you're making a dangerous mistake." Still, after Julie wrote them about his determination, they called to give their blessing.

Mine worried about me until the last minute. My liberal mother came to New York to tell me, "We hate to stay it, but we think you're mentally unstable. This is a terrible mistake."

"Why?" I asked, chin out, while we stood in the kitchen.

"What about children?" she went on. "It would be very tough on them. They'd have big problems. Mental problems. Mulatto children have a terrible time." Her face was as set as mine.

"Don't say that word," was all I could utter. How could I defend my own mental health, never mind that of unborn children? I stared at my mother in disbelief. Was this the same woman who raised me on a gospel of racial integration?

"You already tried to commit suicide," she continued. "You had an illegal abortion and almost bled to death! And now this. We might have to have you committed. It would be for your own good."

"You wouldn't," I said, shaking. "*That's* insane. You can't keep me from Julie, the most wonderful man in the world."

Pulling out her ace, my mother warned, "Your father might have a heart attack. He's from Kentucky, you know. This could be fatal."

"He's not going to die," I affirmed, pulling every bit of swagger from my sinking heart. What if I killed my father?

Though I would never admit it to my parents, their disapproval fed my own sense of doom, which was still warring with my devotion to Julie. Staying loyal to him, two days before the wedding I called my parents to say, "We're getting married." Not waiting for their reply, I hung up, hardening my heart against them for six months.

Early on the morning of December 22, 1962, our wedding day, Julie knelt by our bed singing a love song he'd composed. His face was tender as he plucked the strings of his guitar, the same one he had played the day we met six months before. Proud of his gift, he offered it on bended knee.

"Thank you," I murmured as I lay stifling tears, guilty for my lack of cheer but unable to suppress a fear of vanishing along with my name. No more Joan Steinau. Now I would be Mrs. Lester. The archetype slid over me like a shroud. Never did it occur to me to keep my own name. Instead I blamed my ungrateful, selfish nature for my terror. Shouldn't Julie's love be enough to make me happy? What was the matter with me?

After our small church ceremony, Julie's friend Ann Mari Buitrago, a labor organizer he had once met at Highlander Folk School in Tennessee, came back to our basement with my brother, my aunt, and my Antioch friend Dee Dee, who showed up dressed admirably, I thought, in a long raggedy skirt and army boots. We all trooped to the back of the apartment.

There at the kitchen table we raised glasses of Gallo wine to this banned union, spitting in the face of ignorance. I laughed with the others, going through the motions while feeling oddly detached.

Ann Mari, short and squat with a square, weathered face, ten years older than I, brought her longtime partner, Mac, to the celebration. "I don't believe in marriage," she explained cheerfully to me, even as she celebrated mine. "Or having children. Bratellas," she chuckled.

Julius and Joan, à la Grant Wood's *American Gothic*, in their basement apartment, circa 1963. (author's archive)

I had never personally heard a woman say either of those things. Ann Mari's confident speech, sprinkled with Spanglish, inspired me. Her comfort with both decisions—her unmarried status and life without children—led me to immediately adopt her as a big sister and friend.

The night I married, I lay in bed worrying. Wife, writer, intellectual, activist; those words did not coexist in my brain. I felt suddenly thrust onto another planet. The planet of wives.

Who would I be in this unfamiliar place? And what would keep me alive?

The Fire Next Time

1963

Rage kept me alive. Like the flakes of soot coating our windowsills, rage was in the air. With every bombing of a black church, we inhaled it. When a killer gunned down Medgar Evers in his Mississippi driveway before the eyes of his wife and children, we screamed it. In every demonstration we chanted it. By the early sixties, for those of us who were politically engaged, rage was our default emotion.

My reading stoked the fury. I had evolved from the European writers of my college days, with their languor and private dilemmas, to books like Frantz Fanon's *Black Skin, White Masks*. Fanon, a West Indian psychiatrist, brought staggering news: most colonized people inhaled the toxic lies of their inferiority, which were rampant, thereby damning themselves forever until they excised the self-hatred.

"What can we do to help create the New Man if people are poisoned by the crap all around them?" I asked Julie one evening, evoking our phrase for the liberated man: one confident of his own intelligence, a man—of course a man—who had shed the internalized stereotypes.

Julie slowly shook his head and sighed. "The child beginning to know itself . . ." He stopped, and I thought his eyes briefly pooled. "'Even the stains of their tears have rusted.' That's from a poem I'm working on that I haven't read you yet. 'Boys growing up with the noose in sight, girls with white rapist bodies pressing.' I don't know, Joan. Lord, I don't know."

Stunned by this display of emotion, I could only stare and try to absorb his words. How could he shift a conversation so quickly, lifting it to an exalted sphere?

"Love," he finally said. "Loving each other, loving ourselves. 'Love is the beginning from which all else proceeds.' That's part of the poem."

"It's beautiful," I said quietly. And then I, who lived in the workaday world of practicality, answered my own question, "Education."

"Remember what Brecht said." He strode from the kitchen and returned with a book, which he opened and read aloud. "'Alas, we / Who wished to lay the foundations of kindness / Could not ourselves be kind' because of the dark time 'In which we are sinking.' It's going to take generations, Joan."

"Generations?"

"Yeah. This shit is deep. This is the year the Mason-Dixon line is disappearing. Niggers are niggers everywhere now," he said bitterly and trooped back to the front room, disappearing behind the burlap curtain he had strung—and I had embroidered—enclosing space for a private study.

What was I to make of his words?

When James Baldwin published a *New Yorker* essay, "Letter from a Region of My Mind" (later called *The Fire Next Time*), Julie and I read it aloud to each other, searching for answers. How could Negroes love themselves enough to effectively rebel? Baldwin wrote: "Negroes in this country—and Negroes do not, strictly or legally speaking, exist in any other—are taught really to despise themselves from the moment their eyes open on the world."

To counteract that self-hatred, he claimed a "Negro life force" that provided a strength people needed to survive a terrible past, which "yet contains, for all its horror, something very beautiful."

This beauty was the spirit I saw when Julie wrote, and when his friends laughed around our kitchen table. Or when they joined in harmony on a spiritual, updated with civil rights verses. These were civil rights workers up from the South for rest, or men from the New York SNCC (Student Nonviolent Coordinating Committee) office, where Julie started volunteering. I felt a comfort with these young men who seemed so at ease with themselves despite a history that told them they were dirt.

I was a white outsider, yet for the sake of Julie—and my cooking—they tolerated me. Late in the evening, after a few glasses of cheap wine, everyone smoking until the air was thick, someone would start the dozens. "Yo mama so stupid it take her an hour to cook minute rice."

Another man jumped into the duel. "Yo mama so fat she ain't got a waistline, she got a coastline."

"Yo mama so fat she deep fries her toothpaste."

They laughed uproariously. Not noticing the misogyny, all I saw was the deep camaraderie and shared history, the linguistically agile and humorous wordplay. As someone who loved words—and people—I wanted to be part of this warm, dazzling culture.

This "Negro life force" was a spirit I saw in Langston Hughes, whose "Simple" columns in the *New York Post* delighted me on subway rides up to City College, my graduate student home. Jesse B. Semple (known as Simple) was a lovable Everyman who acknowledged that "white folks is the cause of a lot of inconvenience in my life" but never abandoned hope. In every column Simple triumphed, outwitting the daily hassles of Negro life with dignity, even joy.

Studying economic history, I wrote papers trying to pull together these ideas from Fanon, Baldwin, and Hughes, filtered through a Marxist lens. Except Marx never included racism as a cover for the ruling-class divide-and-conquer strategy. And Marx never explained the resilience Negroes showed. Where was "soul," that faith-laden aspect of culture that kept people alive in hard times? And where in Marxist analysis were whites, who Baldwin said suffered "an inability to renew themselves at the fountain of their own lives." Had our racist lies drained us of humanity?

I sat at the kitchen table pounding on my Royal typewriter, searching for words to express the different strands of my life: de Beauvoir's female independence; Marx's analysis of a moribund, soul-eating capitalism; Baldwin's crystalline anger; Hughes's gentle yet biting humor. And the men sitting around our table singing the songs that had carried their ancestors through unimaginable horrors.

What was my place in this bifurcated life, where I sang with African Americans at home and mingled with white doctoral students at City College? Could I find a place at a graduate school where I was the only woman in economics? Where the Negro professor in economic history—the only Negro I had seen on campus—scorned my anti-colonial analyses? A thin, dour man, he walked with quick, nervous steps. I could hear his anxious shoes clicking on the floor whenever he approached the classroom.

Researching a paper on Egyptian history, I learned the British had seized huge plots of land (as in Kenya, India, and elsewhere), where they planted cotton, conscripting the newly landless locals for labor. With a ruined infrastructure, a new single-crop economy, and measly wages, poverty soared.

I labored over my statistics until I had a fifty-page paper demonstrating, with citations for every assertion, that the forced switch from diversified agriculture to one cash crop—cotton—had totally destroyed a functioning, complex economy. I was prouder of that paper than I had been of anything I had ever written. Finally my professor would acknowledge the wrongs England had committed, and my research capabilities.

I handed it in, expecting the same glowing response—"Beautifully argued"—I had received to my papers at Antioch and the New School.

But a week later the professor thrust the paper at me, hissing, "Propaganda!" Across page 1, he had written in red block print: "THE COLONIES BENEFITED FROM CONTACT. YOU HAVE IT BACKWARD."

How benign he made "contact" sound, I thought heatedly, as if guns, armies, and bayonets weren't involved. As if the native people weren't invariably impoverished. Not to mention raped. Murdered. Enslaved.

Devastated, I stumbled home right into Julie's arms. "How can he be so blind? Such an idiot?" I asked, sobbing.

"People can only see what they can see," Julie said sadly.

"I know, but he's not the king of England or something. He doesn't have an empire to protect!"

"He's an economist. An American economist promoting American business. He has a job to protect."

"But he's a Negro!" I wailed.

"Exactly what we were talking about. Self-hatred. He can't see what he can't see. And he's taking it out on you."

"Why?"

"You're challenging everything he's built up. He's made a career being a white nigger. An Oreo, an Uncle Tom. Supporting the status quo." Julie looked disgusted.

"What can I do?"

"Don't give up! He doesn't know who he is, so he's objectifying you. Making you the enemy because you're telling the truth about who he is, too."

Grateful to have someone who understood the situation, I sniffled, "It was a really good paper."

"Here," he said, pulling me onto his lap. "You're a great researcher. Keep going."

I nuzzled into his neck, safe at home. And I kept writing, believing that if I marshaled enough evidence, someday the professor would have to acknowledge the accuracy of my conclusions.

I persisted until the day a fellow student sidled up to me in the hallway and said, with an eager grin, "I'd like you to pose for my pin-up collection."

"What?"

"My pin-up collection. I've taken photographs of lots of beautiful women."

I looked at him, unable to believe my ears. "How could you ask that?" This young white man, though a businessman like the other economics students, had been my pal.

"I think you're cute," he added.

"I'm your study partner, not your pin-up girl!"

"Look." He opened his briefcase and whipped out a manila envelope. "See? I have a collection." He opened the envelope, showing black-and-white photos of scantily clad women in provocative poses. "You could wear a bathing suit. You wouldn't have to be nude. Although," and here a sly smile appeared on his pudgy cheeks, "You could be."

Horrified, I pushed the pictures away. "I thought you respected me." I began to walk away down the hall.

"I do," he implored, following me. "I thought you'd be honored. You're attractive."

"I thought you respected my mind," I snapped. "I thought we were friends, you know, equals."

"We are friends. I just wanted—" He looked bewildered.

"Friends don't treat each other this way!"

"Why are you so mad?"

"Because we're graduate students in economics! Peers. I thought you took me seriously."

"I do. I'm a good photographer," he pleaded.

I kept walking.

Once the semester ended, I changed my major to American history, where the faculty and students were more liberal, and there were even a few women students.

Fortunately for my self-esteem, the *National Guardian*, a prominent leftist weekly, invited me to review several economics books. The editor, a man I met through Julie, assigned serious political tomes, and I savored the chance to write for a radical audience. When I saw my reviews in print, with a byline, I was thrilled. But above all I wanted my writing to serve the revolution. When it came to literature, I understood that Julie, with his lyrical gift and suitably gloomy face, was the writer. I was only a bubbly girl who loved to write.

He was so clear about his purpose. Every night I heard his typewriter clickety-clacking while I read myself to sleep. How did men find their way so easily?

Yet in spite of my confusion and anger—against the men in economics, against racists and cops, against a system that branded me strange for wanting to study economics—daily life unspooled with its quotidian pleasures. Early each morning I bounced to the bakery for two twenty-five-cent cheese Danish, warm from the oven, which Julie and I ate while reading the *New York Times* aloud.

"Another so-called riot!" Julie would say, after carefully chewing his pastry. "Damn! It's white folks breaking heads."

Or, with a mouth full of food, I would stammer, "Listen to this! A huge demonstration. And they arrested everybody."

Evenings, Julie met me at the New School and we walked arm in arm, stopping at the library to browse. Once we were home, though, things were sometimes different. One evening he said, "The kitchen floor is dirty," casting reproachful eyes at bits of food, dust, and cockroach bodies. He looked pained.

Ashamed and resentful, I grabbed the broom and slouched across the floor, furiously brushing the mix from side to side before scooping it up. Then I hunched silently at the kitchen table, swigging beer from the can like my parents did, while I pored over textbooks. Julie slunk silently into the living room, and soon I heard the typewriter clacking, its bell ringing, interrupted occasionally by his crooning voice over the guitar. By midnight I crawled into bed and fell asleep to the sound of typewriter keys striking paper.

But in the morning we lay wrapped together after sleep had washed away all conflict. Well, not quite all. I felt as if I were living in one great raging cauldron of molten lava. Every day brought a cross burning, a police shooting, or a church burning. And my own seething resentment.

Wretched of the Earth

1964

I rushed in the front door brandishing a leaflet. "Look!" I dared to open the curtain blocking off Julie's corner. "CORE is planning a stall-in!" I pulled on the knot under my chin and flung my scarf to the floor.

"A what?"

"A stall-in."

"Mother of God, what is that?" His eyes looked bleary from typing in terrible light.

"Brooklyn CORE is organizing something amazing. They're going to shut down traffic to the World's Fair. On opening day! Nothing will move. They're going to completely stop traffic."

He rubbed his eyes. "Why?"

"The World's Fair is such a crock. Spending millions while people have crappy housing. No jobs. Segregated schools with no books. This tells all about it." I waved the flyer.

"Where did you get that?"

"Some guy was handing them out on Twenty-Third Street at the subway. I talked to him. They're serious." My coat followed my scarf to the floor. Since we had no closets, we folded our clothes on shelves in the hall, but I had no time for that now. "We've got to tell everybody about this."

"Hmm."

I shoved the leaflet into his face. "Look. Let's go!" I said.

"Of course. Maybe this will get some results. Those motherfuckers have to be shoved to the wall."

"Too bad we don't have a car."

CORE poster for stall-in, April 22, 1964. ("Poster for World's Fair Stall-In," corenyc.org, accessed May 4, 2020, www.corenyc.org/omeka/items/show/28)

"Yeah, but we can take the subway. That's gonna be tough too. Full of pigs."

I reached out to touch his shoulder, relieved this was one demo we would go to together. It would be scary. But necessary.

The 1964 World's Fair was set to open in three weeks. Mayor Wagner and Governor Rockefeller constantly talked up the benefits. Throngs of tourists would fill city and state coffers. Ever since the first shovelful of dirt had been dug in Queens five years before, the news had touted all the construction jobs. A five-year public works project, they crowed, and more jobs to demolish the buildings later.

"Using construction companies and unions that won't let Negroes and Puerto Ricans in!" I said. CORE and the NAACP had tried for years to integrate them. I knew. I had been on plenty of picket lines at construction sites, marching for hours. All in vain.

"Fantasy America on view," I scoffed. "No poor people. No dark people. The stall-in is brilliant. Get some attention for where the money really needs to go."

"I hope it works," Julie said, reaching up to pull me onto his lap for a kiss. "It'll be a mess."

"They're going to clog the highways. No tourist will want to be in that. Maybe the government will take these demands seriously. They can't go on forever—"

"Yeah, this could make a difference." He kissed me again before shooing me away. "I have to finish this chapter of my novel."

I trooped back to our bedroom in the middle of the apartment. Playing hopscotch and tag all afternoon with my girls at the settlement house had worn me out. When I joined their games, this sent them into giggles of delight. Seeing pure joy in the faces of these Puerto Rican children who lived such tough lives made me willing to do anything. I had visited tenements where an entire family lived in one dark room, cooking, sleeping, dressing. I had seen the girls' clothes hung on ropes slung across the room, coats piled in a corner, and beds where they slept three or four or five head-to-toe, like my friend Rosie Santiago's children. By comparison, our small apartment on a slum block felt like luxury housing.

Struggling to lift my heavy eyelids, I picked up a book Ann Mari had loaned me, marking a section to read. *The Wretched of the Earth*, another book by Frantz Fanon. What a heartbreaking title, I thought sleepily, turning to the essay she had flagged on page 206, called "On National Culture."

The opening sentence riveted me: "Each generation must out of relative obscurity discover its mission, fulfill it, or betray it."

Yes! My generation was finding its mission. While Fanon's generation of Africans was "breaking the back of colonialism," we would break the back of segregation. The stall-in would be one moment in our revolt, making visible to all America the terrible conditions of ghetto lives. Our lives. Like everyone else on our Puerto Rican block, Julie and I faced swarms of rats roaming our apartment despite poison and traps. Bed-Stuy and Harlem residents had even more. Since no one paid attention to our demonstrations, a stall-in might do it.

"Hey, Johnson is coming on opening day of the Fair to give a speech!" I told Julie one morning over breakfast, pointing to the article in the *Times*.

"That son of a bitch," Julie said.

"But it's good; that means TV will be there, for sure."

"Yeah, he would come to open a racist event," Julie spit out. "Goddam cracker."

Condemnation of the stall-in was front-page news every day. But the *Times* also published a statement by Brooklyn CORE's young leader, Isaiah Brunson. "While millions of dollars are being spent on the World's Fair, thousands of Black and Puerto Rican people are suffering," he explained. CORE had tried negotiating with city leaders about schools, slum housing, a civilian police review board, and reserving 25 percent of city construction jobs for Black people and Hispanics. But getting nowhere, they were resorting to this act of nonviolent civil disobedience. *Life* magazine quoted Herbert Callender of Bronx CORE saying, "The World's Fair portrays . . . the American dream. We want to show that there is also an American nightmare of the way Negroes have to live in this country."

Starting at 7 a.m., thousands of cars would stall on every artery leading to the Fair. People would sit-in too, and dump garbage to block traffic. Subway cars would stall with bodies jammed in doorways so trains couldn't move. Nobody would be able to ignore the gigantic mess on the biggest traffic day of the year.

Media outlets were hysterical. It's "a grab at the groin of a community of ten million New Yorkers," *Time* magazine wrote. The *Daily News* publisher proposed stallers have licenses, registration, and insurance permanently canceled.

"They've got a gun to the head of the city," Mayor Wagner screamed.

"Look at this!" Julie said one morning, reading aloud. "'A new city law makes it illegal to intentionally run out of gas.' Damn! 'Thirty days in jail and a $50 fine.' These people don't play. 'Police Commissioner Murphy promises thousands of police. Helicopters will fly over highways with tow-trucks ready.'"

"Look what they're willing to spend," I seethed. "Millions and millions of dollars. If they put half that into Harlem and Bed-Stuy, imagine what that could do!"

"That'll be the day!"

Debate about the stall-in split civil rights leaders. Malcolm X endorsed it on NBC news: "Nothing would spotlight the attention of the world upon the human rights violations of the 22 million African Americans more than tying up traffic that will make it impossible for the Fair to open up."

James Farmer, national CORE chair, called it a "hair-brained idea" and suspended Brooklyn CORE. The NAACP's Roger Wilkins scoffed. But Martin Luther King Jr. wrote Wilkins, "Which is worse, a 'Stall-in' at the World's Fair or a 'Stall-in' in the United States Senate? The former merely ties up the traffic of a single city. But the latter seeks to tie up the traffic of history, and endanger the psychological lives of twenty million people."

Southern senators had filibustered for a month—stalling—against a land-mark civil rights bill. Since the Senate had never gotten enough votes to end a filibuster on a civil rights bill, it looked like this one was dead.

Day after day the stall-in was front-page news. And we would be there. We were going to shut down New York City, the biggest, baddest city in the nation. At twenty-three, that was a heady sensation.

The night before the opening, Julie and I firmed up our plans.

"We should be on the subway by six," he said while I undressed for bed. "Cut the light on your way."

I nodded. "There are going to be cops on every car. As soon as they see us, they'll know."

"We need to stay with each other," he said. "If we're not doing any-thing illegal, well . . ."

We both knew what he meant when he let the sentence go. Not com-mitting a crime wouldn't necessarily stop the cops from arresting or beat-ing us. But for peace of mind we had to stick together. I couldn't ride alone to this one. And neither could he.

I had made a cardboard sign with large black letters: WE DON'T WANT A WORLD'S FAIR, WE WANT A FAIR WORLD. The cops on the trains would know where we were going anyway once they saw us, so we would have to take our chances with the sign.

I packed four bologna sandwiches, a thermos of peppermint tea, and apples. It was going to be a long day.

Julie carried the two bandanas I had bought to protect our faces from tear gas.

We were ready for battle.

At 5:30 in the morning, we prepared to set out into a cold and drizzly day. I pulled on my headscarf and warm coat, while Julie hunkered down in a hooded sweatshirt and raincoat. Since we tried to look respectable at demonstrations, I wore stockings and a skirt. We held hands, walking as fast as we could up to Twenty-Third Street. My heart beat fast with excitement and fear. "They're going to be picketing at the Unisphere," I said, breathing hard from our sprint. "I hope our signs don't turn to mush."

"There'll be a ton of us. Even in the rain."

When we descended into the station, we saw a train waiting. Julie dashed ahead to hold the doors open for me. Two cops on the platform raced toward him, evidently thinking he was going to stall the train.

They reached out toward Julie.

"Wait, I'm coming!" I yelled as I sprinted toward the doors, arriving just as the cops did. Julie and I lurched toward seats, with two glaring cops on our car waiting for us to block doors at the next stations.

At every stop, we saw pigs yanking protesters out of the doorways. We watched ten cops yank two women roughly onto the platform, while I screamed, "Stop!"

"Let's not stall the train," I whispered to Julie. The cops weren't gentle and they might "accidently" kill Julie.

He nodded.

I clutched the pin I had stabbed onto my collar, blaring: CORE Wants a FAIR World.

When we arrived at the fair, we saw how many other protesters had been on our train. We all faced a gauntlet of police in full riot gear. They held sticks horizontally, gloved hands holding each end, and blocked us from moving off the platform.

It was a face-off until, one by one, we slipped around behind them.

I had never seen so many police. Their presence at previous demonstrations looked like kindergarten compared to this. I was terrified. Julie and I held hands, which I knew was provocative to the police, but I needed to feel the warmth, the solidity of his body. He gripped me tightly too.

As we walked into the fairgrounds, I saw people surrounding the symbol of the fair, the Unisphere. "Jobs!" they chanted. "Decent schools!"

Cops ringed the marching protesters but we joined their chanting circle, peaceful at first.

"A civilian review board," we yelled. "Jobs!"

Suddenly, out of the corner of my eye, I saw a white man throw something.

"What's that?"

"Duck," Julie said as a small object flew by.

Eggs, it turned out, which hit a few targets but mostly splattered on the ground, creating a slippery, treacherous mess. A couple of other men joined the throwing spree, until some protesters were covered in slime. But we kept chanting, "We want a fair world!" while journalists snapped pictures of our signs—especially A WORLD'S FAIR IS A LUXURY BUT A FAIR WORLD IS A NECESSITY.

All morning Julie and I stayed despite the egg muck and screams from bystanders. "Commie bastards," I heard, and a few shouts of "Niggers, go home!" which puzzled me. Where were they supposed to go? Back to their slums?

We could take that—the eggs and the jeers—but a truly terrifying moment came when a large group of pigs in full body armor converged. "Don't say anything," Julie warned me, grabbing my hand. The cops surrounded a few of us, forming a barrier, shielding us from view.

"What are they going to do?"

"I don't know."

The cops started to move in, forcing us to back into the Unisphere, until one brave man with a huge voice called out to reporters, "Look what they're doing! The cops are squeezing us. We have a right to be here! They're about to beat us."

We'd heard that the cops beat up quite a few people at the subway stop where we had seen the phalanx in riot gear, so our fears that they would do the same to us were warranted. But suddenly journalists snapped pictures and in minutes the cops melted away, leaving me trembling.

Determined to hold our ground by the Unisphere, where lots of fairgoers would see us, we didn't leave our spot even when we heard that protesters were drowning out President Johnson, shouting, "Jim Crow must go!"

Back in our marching circle, I asked friendly journalists, "How bad was the traffic jam?" They shook their heads, as in the dark as we were. Finally news trickled in: the severe penalties had frightened stallers away. Although hundreds marched with CORE banners on highways to the fair, and some people dumped garbage, the roads were clear. No traffic at all.

Yet the stall-in had done its work. It created a giant transmitter, broadcasting photos of rats running through schools, tenements with falling ceilings. It called national attention to "the real world of discrimination and brutality experienced by Negroes, North and South, as compared to the fantasy world of progress and abundance shown in the official pavilions," one flier said.

When Julie and I finally staggered out at twilight, relief coursed through my body. We hadn't been injured or arrested. My legs weak as Jell-O, I said, "It was like Langston Hughes's poem 'Let America Be America Again.'"

"It never was America to me," he quoted the refrain and grabbed my hand.

"And now everybody can see that."

We trooped wearily back from our Twenty-Third Street subway stop, exhausted and eager to peel off our soggy clothes, climb into a hot bath in our jerry-rigged bathroom. But as we approached our building, Theresa's high whine, "Nigger, nigger, get out!" greeted us. The Greek chorus of our lives, I thought miserably.

"Shut up," I screamed up at her window. "Shut up!"

Soon we learned how successful the stall-in was. Only sixty-three thousand people paid the entrance fee for the opening, instead of the expected quarter million. Even Police Commissioner Michael Murphy, while criticizing the "shocking and disturbing" protests, said that President Johnson had come "to the world of fantasy" only to find "the world of fact."

We had dominated the news, shown the world shocking photos of rats and tenements. White people were on notice: justice or "the fire next time."

The stall-in's publicity also lent support to the civil rights bill that was stalled in the Senate.

Six weeks later Eleanor called, screaming, "It's over! The filibuster's over."

"What?"

"The bastards talked for sixty days. Sixty fucking days! But they couldn't stop history. Dirksen got the votes and it's over. They invoked cloture. The Civil Rights Act is going to pass!"

"Oh my God."

"I can't believe it," Eleanor said, her voice choking. "We're gonna get the fucking law."

And we did. Nine days later, on June 9, the Senate approved the Civil Rights Act, and on July 2, 1964, Martin Luther King Jr. and Rosa Parks stood with President Johnson as he signed the law. The monumental act banned segregation in public places, barred employment discrimination, established an Equal Employment Opportunity Commission (which Eleanor would later chair), secured voting rights, and mandated educational equality. It was the most sweeping civil rights legislation since Reconstruction, and the Great New York Stall-In had played a supporting role in its passage.

What I remember most about the stall-in is my terror, from the moment the two cops raced toward Julie as he held the subway doors, to the riot-cop barrier in Queens, the mass of cops moving in on us at the Unisphere, and glowering cops everywhere, all day. They looked like robots. I had never seen a pure militarized state, seen how a government could mobilize massive resources to create a police state for a day, when it wouldn't put a tenth of those funds into housing and schools. Of course, Black people had been living in a police state since the day they arrived in chains, but in my segregated world that had been invisible.

Yet even without knowing that, I had instinctively understood the day would be significant and I had to be there, helping turn history's wheel—with Julie by my side.

The Prime of Life

1964

On June 22, 1964, the phone rang at 7 a.m. On and on the ringer clanged, mixing with my dream until I realized the sound was real. Rubbing sleep from my eyes, I picked up the heavy receiver and heard my best friend, Nancy, blurt, "Mickey's missing!"

We knew Mickey, the younger brother of her husband, Steve Schwerner. The last time we had seen him was in the Village, when he was up visiting from the CORE work he and Rita, his wife, did in Mississippi. It was hard persuading folks to vote, he told us, because every time a Negro attempted to register, white troopers snapped photos. And shot up the house at night— or killed in broad daylight.

"Missing? What do you mean?" We knew it was dangerous in the Delta but here was someone we knew. Someone white. They didn't kill white people.

"Rita hasn't heard from him since last night," Nancy cried. "He and two . . ." Gradually she got it out. Mickey Schwerner was last seen driving back to Meridian with two other CORE staffers after they had investigated a fire, one of twenty church burnings that summer.

Nancy and Steve were our best friends. Julie and I often played bridge with them, laughing deep into the night, talking politics. Nancy had been an Antioch roommate and Steve, a jazz aficionado, once took us to Birdland, where John Coltrane blew his saxophone straight into our hearts.

Only weeks before Mickey's disappearance, on the eve of Freedom Summer, when civil rights workers would flood Mississippi, Julie and I had marched in Washington with Nancy and Steve.

Julius and Joan in Washington for civil rights demonstration, June 1964. (author's archive)

At a party after the march, wearing the same blue sundress I'd worn to call Simon and Schuster, with my hair pulled up in a Simone de Beauvoir bun, I had nodded knowingly to Steve. "It'll take some white kid to get killed for anybody to notice."

Now I wanted to bite those words back into my mouth.

All day Nancy and I waited for news. I could hear her pacing, moaning. "Where could they be?" She kept repeating it as if her question would conjure up their vigorous selves.

I tried talking about other things, wanting to shut out images of Mississippi bodies like Lamar Smith's, shot at close range on the lawn of the Lincoln County courthouse when he helped others fill out absentee ballots. Or George Lee. Gus Courts. Herbert Lee. Louis Allen. All murdered for trying to vote or organizing others.

Mickey and Andy Goodman, also missing—on his first day in Mississippi—were New York Jews, and James Chaney, the third man, was a young local Negro. Their presence together in a car was enough of a crime in Mississippi, never mind that they were the most hated of creatures: civil rights workers. Two outside agitators—*Jews*, hardly white themselves—

come to destroy the southern way of life, riding with a hometown "boy" who should know better.

By night we had no information. The next morning I called at dawn, knowing they wouldn't be asleep. "Any news?"

"No." Steve, usually so warm and easygoing, sounded bleak. "It's all over national TV. White people never go missing there. Even Unitarian Jews." He tried to chuckle at his own feeble joke. He had told me for years, without really meaning it, that he wasn't Jewish but like so many other secular Jews, a Unitarian. "They haven't found anything."

"I'm sorry. I'm so sorry." Missing in Mississippi could only mean death.

Another day of keeping vigil, jumping with every ring of the phone. Mickey's blue station wagon was well known to the Neshoba County sheriff, we learned. As CORE staff, Mickey and Rita had started a boycott with the slogan "Don't shop where you can't work," until one Mississippi store hired its first Negro clerk. Highly visible, they had organized voter rallies and already been followed at night by the KKK. Carloads of white men would jam their bumper, careen around them, and screech away.

Forty-eight terrible hours later, police dug up the burned Ford station wagon in a Neshoba County swamp. (A car that CORE had bought with money Lorraine Hansberry sent from a Croton, New York, rally she organized, raising five thousand dollars for the movement.)

Now we had to anticipate their mutilated bodies.

For forty-four days that awful summer, we waited, with long hours spent poring through mail at Mickey's parents' home in Pelham. It overflowed a large straw basket: hate messages mixed with overwhelming support. I had never seen letters like the ugly ones, scrawled words wishing "Your son rot in hell." And worse.

Other letters offered encouragement to the grieving family. They had given their son, their brother, to a noble cause. "Thank you," these writers said. "How can we help?"

Julie spoke at packed rallies or sang Freedom Songs alongside Mickey's father, Nat. Julie had been singing at coffee houses in the Village and had even held a concert, so it was natural now to sing in public. And everywhere he went that summer, I went, too.

We wept and shouted, marking off the days. Still, my heart beat with a shred of hope. Could the three be alive, even if barely, hidden away in some cracker jail? Bruised and battered maybe, but breathing?

MISSING CALL FBI

THE FBI IS SEEKING INFORMATION CONCERNING THE DISAPPEARANCE AT PHILADELPHIA, MISSISSIPPI OF THESE THREE INDIVIDUALS ON JUNE 21. AN EXTENSIVE INVESTIGATION IS BEING CONDUCTED TO LOCATE GOODMAN, CHANEY, AND SCHWERNER, WHO ARE DESCRIBED AS FOLLOWS:

ANDREW GOODMAN · **JAMES EARL CHANEY** · **MICHAEL HENRY SCHWERNER**

RACE	White	Negro		White
SEX	Male	Male		Male
DOB	November 23, 1943	May 30, 1943		November 6, 1939
POB	New York City	Meridian, Mississippi		New York City
AGE	20 years	21 years		24 years
HEIGHT	5'10"	5'7"		5'9" to 5'10"
WEIGHT	150 pounds	135 to 140 pounds		170 to 180 pounds
HAIR	Dark brown; wavy	Black		Brown
EYES	Brown	Brown		Light blue
TEETH		Good; none missing		
SCARS AND MARKS		1 inch cut scar 2 inches above left ear		Pock mark center of forehead, slight scar on bridge of nose, appendectomy scar, broken leg scar

SHOULD YOU HAVE OR IN THE FUTURE RECEIVE ANY INFORMATION CONCERNING THE WHEREABOUTS OF THESE INDIVIDUALS, YOU ARE REQUESTED TO NOTIFY ME OR THE NEAREST OFFICE OF THE FBI. TELEPHONE NUMBER IS LISTED BELOW.

DIRECTOR
FEDERAL BUREAU OF INVESTIGATION
UNITED STATES DEPARTMENT OF JUSTICE
WASHINGTON D C 20535
TELEPHONE, NATIONAL 8-7117

June 29, 1964

FBI poster of the three missing civil rights workers, Mississippi, 1964. (Federal Bureau of Investigation, "The FBI Wants Information about Three Missing Civil Rights Workers," *SHEC: Resources for Teachers*, accessed May 1, 2020, herb.ashp .cuny.edu/items/show/1173)

The FBI created a missing-persons poster and organized massive searches while the country waited for news.

Local whites openly jeered FBI agents who searched, dredging rivers. "Hey, why don't you hold a welfare check out over the water," one white man yelled at a boatful of agents. "That'll get that nigger to the surface."

Eight black corpses were found as investigators combed the woods, rivers, and swamps of Mississippi. Among them were the bodies of Henry Hezekiah Dee and Charles Eddie Moore, two nineteen-year-olds recently kidnapped and tortured by the KKK, then dropped into the Mississippi River. Another mangled corpse wore a CORE T-shirt. All those bodies, but not Mickey, Andy, or James.

SNCC workers like our friend Ralph Featherstone, later killed by a car bomb, searched ravines. They shone flashlights into wells. Searched empty houses. Tension rose. Day after day the country waited to hear, while Julie and I spent the entire summer with Nancy and Steve.

But the three men had vanished.

"The South don't mess around," Julie kept telling me. "Those crackers know they're stone losers. Their time is up. I hope they don't kill us all before they go!"

On August 4, news at last: a mystery informer pointed to an earthen dam near Philadelphia, Mississippi. The FBI dug and found a sickening grave with three tortured bodies. Mickey, mutilated, unrecognizable, was identified by the draft card in his pocket.

The FBI arrested eighteen men, but the state refused to prosecute. "No evidence," they claimed. It would take years for the federal government to take the case, charging "conspiracy to deprive the murdered men of their civil rights," and forty years until *one* accused murderer was convicted.

We learned later that after the three young men left the smoldering church, Deputy Sheriff Cecil Price in Neshoba County arrested them on a bogus traffic charge and held them incommunicado until he released them at 10 p.m. Soon patrol lights flashed them over. Price pushed the three men into his patrol car and sped off, followed by two carloads of KKK members. He dumped Mickey, James, and Andy out on a remote road, where a group of raging white men chain-whipped and butchered them. (In 2014 Barack Obama awarded them the Presidential Medal of Freedom. Mickey's was accepted by Nancy, Steve, and Mickey's widow, Rita.)

My response to grief was direct, put-my-body-on-the-line activism. Unfathomable as it may be now in an era when even first graders write "personal narratives," the idea of writing about my secondhand encounter with Mississippi brutality didn't occur to me. I hadn't yet discovered the personal essay as a literary form. Soon the women's movement would embrace such essays as a means of giving voice to our stories, declaring, "The personal is political." But in 1964 few wrote them and those few were male.

Instead, barely three weeks after the bodies were dug up, I was part of a rag-tag group sleeping on pews in an Atlantic City church. "We shall overcome, someday." My blue sleeping bag, borrowed from Ann Mari, was sticky with sweat. Enfolded in the soft case, I tossed in the muggy church, eager for morning. Eager for justice. I heard several people softly singing, "Ain't gonna let no beatings turn us around, marching up to Freedom land" and fell asleep to the song.

We were in Atlantic City to pressure the national Democratic Party. For years the Mississippi Democratic Party had excluded Negroes by saying, "They aren't voters," while keeping them from registering. The governor, head of the state party, mocked the NAACP as "Niggers, alligators, apes, coons, and possums."

In response, sharecropper-turned-activist Fannie Lou Hamer, SNCC's Bob Moses, and others formed the Mississippi Freedom Democratic Party (MFDP), a parallel party open to all. They registered 50,000 voters at Freedom Registration polls and elected sixty-eight delegates, Negro and white, to the Democratic National Convention in Atlantic City. *This* delegation was legitimate, they argued, and should be seated instead of the all-white "regular" Mississippi Democrats.

In the morning I crawled from my sleeping bag to wait for the MFDP to chug into town. Wiping our brows in the ninety-degree heat, we paraded on the boardwalk with our signs: "Break Segregation" and "We Are the Freedom Democrats!" I had driven from New York with Mickey's parents, plus Nancy and Steve, to ensure that the credentials committee seated the Freedom Party. Julie was skipping the demonstration to write but had sent me off with a hug, promising to follow the news.

"Keep your eyes on the prize, hold on!" we sang while we marched in a circle, our feet tramping the beat on the wooden boardwalk. All morning we stamped on the boards. "Paul and Silas bound in jail / Had no money for to go their bail / Keep your eyes on the prize, hold on." We marched in the fierce sun as we sang, holding signs or handing them off to others so we could clap to the beat. "The only thing we did was wrong / Was staying in the wilderness a day too long."

My old friend Eleanor was there, too. As a new Yale Law School graduate and veteran of the previous summer's Mississippi Freedom Schools, she had helped write the MFDP brief. It opened with a challenge, asking "whether the National Democratic Party takes its place with the oppressed Negroes of Mississippi or their white oppressors?"

The Freedom Democrats arrived at the boardwalk towing a flatbed truck holding Mickey's charred station wagon, a stark emblem of the horror Mississippians faced when they tried to vote. Chest heaving, I joined others shouting greetings to tired MFDP delegates, most of them farmers in overalls, pouring from the caravan.

I had no doubt that exposing the regular Democrats' reign of terror would guarantee Freedom Party certification. The evidence was right there in that car they mounted on the boardwalk, its skeleton breathing fire. A vivid, grisly illustration of the apartheid that existed a thousand miles south of Atlantic City. All day we marched, until evening when we huddled on the boardwalk, still calling out our Freedom slogans.

That first night we returned bone-tired to the church, where our ragged group of demonstrators found Ms. Hamer waiting for us. I had heard of this legendary sharecropper from Sunflower County, thrown off land she and her husband lived on for eighteen years the day she tried to vote. She had answered the eviction by blooming into a voting rights organizer. One of the best.

I watched this large, dignified woman laboriously climb stairs to a stage and launch into the story of her recent Winona, Mississippi, arrest. "I guess if I had any sense," she told us, standing at the edge of the stage, "I'd have been scared—but what was the point of being scared? The only thing they could do was kill me, and it seemed they'd been trying to do that a little at a time since I could remember."

I sat cross-legged on my sleeping bag while Ms. Hamer, a beautiful woman with a broad face, stood above us and lifted her skirt. Her legs were thick, covered with dark bruises, the inside of her massive thighs one continuous blotch. "This is what those Mississippi sheriffs did to me," she said in her deep voice, tears rolling down her cheeks. "What they forced those Negro prisoners to do to me in Winona. Said, 'I want you to make that bitch wish she was dead.'" She stopped, choked up, and began to moan softly, "This little light of mine, I'm gonna let it shine . . ." She swayed, clapping, until she could talk again. "When one beat me with a blackjack until he was exhausted, they made the other one start in." Still crying, she bellowed out her song, "This little light of mine, I'm gonna let it shine." We joined in as she added a new verse. "All over Atlantic City, I'm gonna let it shine. All over the Democrats, I'm gonna let in shine!"

I watched, transfixed. Her courage was like a tent flapping around her, one that extended to embrace us all. That night when I lay on the hard pew, I vowed I would do whatever it took to end segregation. "This little light of mine," I hummed, tears trickling into my ears.

The next day we held vigil again on the boardwalk. Suddenly Dr. King and Mrs. King swept by. Compared to our grimy selves, they looked majestic: heads high, faces lit. They glided next to me, perfume lingering, their feet barely seeming to touch the dusty planks. Looking back, I imagine them swathed in furs, though in that steaming heat they couldn't have been. Yet that was the grand image they exuded as they flowed by with their entourage.

Dr. King addressed our rally on the boardwalk while we held posters of the murdered three overhead, wanting everyone to see the brothers we had lost. His thunderous voice rolled over us like clear water, soothing our pain.

When Ms. Hamer was going to testify to the credentials committee on national TV, Steve slipped me a Convention floor pass. I pushed deep inside. Ms. Hamer recounted her savage beating in the Winona jail. Tears flowing, she asked, "Is this America, the land of the free and the home of the brave, where we have to sleep with our telephones off the hooks because our lives be threatened daily because we want to live as decent human beings—in America?"

Credentials committee members were visibly upset. Of course the Freedom Democrats would be seated. We had no doubt.

But the same President Johnson who had twisted Senators' arms to pass the Civil Rights Act the month before now twisted them back in an effort not to seat the Freedom Democrats. Afraid to alienate powerful Southern Democrats and "lose the South" (the white South), he dangled judgeships and imposed threats on committee members. His tactics flipped the committee. Even those moved to tears by Ms. Hamer ultimately voted against seating the Freedom Party.

We couldn't believe it. The proof was so clear: the burned-out car, the beaten bodies, the legal brief recounting unconstitutional exclusions, and Fannie Lou Hamer's personal testimony!

Instead, the White House offered a compromise: two at-large seats (to be filled with one white and one Negro delegate), while the regular all-white Mississippians remained seated. The MFDP, shaken but defiant, refused. "We didn't come all this way for no two seats since all of us is tired," said Ms. Hamer.

Crushed, I crawled into the sodden sleeping bag back at the church.

In the morning, no one sang. Everyone reeked of three days' sweat, our smell as sour as our faces. The drive back to New York with the heartbroken Schwerners was painful, all of us stunned and angry. We had gotten a Civil Rights Act, but we mourned: If the Democrats were abandoning us, where could we turn?

At home I eased my pain, as I often did, with a book, volume two of Simone de Beauvoir's memoirs, *The Prime of Life*. Like me, she was a young adult during the period this book covered, the prewar Paris years. I resonated with her sense of invulnerability when I copied her sentence: "The world existed, in the manner of an object with innumerable folds whose discovery would always be an adventure, but not as a force field capable of threatening me." She retained this youthful imperviousness until World War II showed her that catastrophes can happen to anyone. All human life is uncertain.

I had not understood that either, until the summer Mickey and the others suffered a horrible death and the MFDP wasn't seated. Life, I discovered, didn't guarantee that right action would always be rewarded. Such a belief, which I had held fast until my midtwenties, had been fostered by white skin and the privilege of attending college, even if my parents had to scrape together loans to send me. I hadn't realized what a bubble I inhabited until de Beauvoir's words made it clear.

But now my bubble wobbled. Daily life with Julie amid the barrage of Theresa's insults—"Nigger, nigger, filthy nigger, get out!"—proved continuously challenging.

"Hey," Rap Brown exploded one afternoon at our kitchen table. He often visited since Julius—who now claimed his "grown-up name"—had met him in Mississippi. This day he sipped a mug of Bustelo coffee I had poured through a cloth bag and then blended with scalded milk as Ann Mari taught me. "Look what happened when they burned down Harlem! Bed-Stuy. Chicago. *Now* Johnson calls for 'massive spending in the ghettoes.' So that's what it takes. 'Burn, baby, burn.'" He laughed bitterly, his soft gray eyes hardening with pain.

"We could start with a clean slate," I agreed, as if the racist conscious-ness we wanted to change were a place. Burning it or blowing it up would transform everything. "Start over." The fire next time. The MFDP defeat had shifted everything. White people were hopeless. If only we could blow up the Pentagon and Congress and the White House, destroy all existing institutions with their racist structures, we would be done with it. Free to create a fairer world. Like young people everywhere, I was sure we could do a better job.

The next day I muttered to Ann Mari in her East Harlem kitchen, "All the bad people should be taken out and shot."

Ann Mari was now thirty-four to my twenty-four, with a single impres-sive braid that hung to her waist. She put down the bright-blue yarn in her lap, rested her knitting needles, and, lifting her eyes, cast me an odd look. "Who are the bad people? The ones with the Bs on their foreheads?" Those two shocking sentences silenced me. Burned into my mind, they became indelible guides.

Julius, equally angry, composed bitter songs about lynching. He began traveling occasionally to Mississippi to lead singing at mass meetings, where he saw the terror firsthand. When he hung a gruesome, life-size poster of a lynching on the wall by his typewriter, the brutality of life in America crept further into our home.

Confused about where to turn, I fled to our saggy bed and listened to the rat-a-tat-tat of my husband, who pounded furiously on his noisy old typewriter revising a novel, composing essays on folk music, and, increas-ingly, writing militant political commentary.

I felt honored to be his first and usually only reader, commenting, cross-ing out sentences, asking, "Why does this follow that? Wouldn't it be better to put this line at the end?" I loved his eager receptiveness to my suggestions. Loved and admired him. When the *National Guardian* asked him to write a regular column, a platform that brought his first fame, I got to edit them all.

Little did I understand how I lived a 1950s life, radical version: man as actor, woman as helpmate. It would take three years for that realization to arrive and erupt, with fireworks that challenged us to adopt a new paradigm—or split.

Dr. Spock's Baby
and Child Care

1965

"First comes love, then comes marriage, here comes Joanie with a baby carriage." When I had skipped rope gleefully as a girl, enjoying the thrill of Double Dutch with two ropes thwacking the pavement—splat! splat! splat! splat!—I had no inkling of the ditty's power, the way it encoded a cultural imperative. The chant had so engraved itself into my cells that pregnancy seemed inevitable, like the rain or the wind. Or marriage.

When I had gotten pregnant in New Haven at twenty-one, my psychiatrist lover had arranged an abortion with a doctor friend, a true back-alley, late-night appointment. Six weeks later a painful pelvic infection landed me in a hospital where a grim doctor, white coat flapping in mourning strips, towered over me shouting like a vengeful apparition, "This is God's punishment for your sin. You will never have children!"

I believed him.

Now, when Planned Parenthood phoned the lab results, I held the receiver out and shrieked, "Pregnant!"

Julius and I hugged.

"Yes!" we shouted.

No abortion this time. We would expand our little family. What a joyful new focus. I would not have to face the burden of actually committing again to my vague writer dream. Never suffer again the shame I had felt after my Simon and Schuster call, nor stretch to see what I had to say beyond academia. Brave the blowback to my words. Leave all that to him. I could aspire but not have to produce. The baby gave me the perfect out.

As for the child-to-be, I was wildly unrealistic, planning to merely add him or her as an adorable carry-along toted to concerts, avant-garde films, and demonstrations. A small bundle to cart along with Julius's guitar and books. I would take the baby to class, no problem. I never anticipated how a new person would transform my life.

The City University doctoral program in American history had lavished me with fellowships, grooming me for success as a historian, but I waved it all off, erasing my achievements with the disclaimer, "Well, I'm the only student who does the assignments on time." It was if a patriarchal spirit laid a chloroform cloth over my face, intoning a spell of forgetfulness about my true nature. "Breathe deeply, my child, Breathe in the vapors of amnesia. You're a wife and soon-to-be mother."

Though I remained in school throughout the pregnancy, propping books on my swollen belly, at last I warned the department chair, "I'm going to take a year off."

"Why?" He looked stricken.

"I'm going to have a baby!" I said triumphantly, pointing to the bulge under my tent dress.

"That's alright, we'd give you time off. You're doing so well—we wanted you to teach an introductory course next semester. But we could postpone it a year."

"All right, I'll try to keep up once the baby is born," I said, dubiously.

But from the moment I saw Rosa, nurturing her became my one desire. I marveled at her perfection, admired every finger twitch, and soon all I wanted to do was gaze at her rosebud lips and luminous dark eyes. I pored through Dr. Spock's *Baby and Child Care* ten times a day. My paperback copy, stained with spit-up and tears, became my Bible.

Yet despite my fog of infatuation, for six months I kept up with graduate school. Julius took care of Rosa while I was in class, and we seemed to be managing until the evening he told me, "I've decided to move South." He gazed at me from the stove where he stirred cloth diapers with a long wooden spoon. Every day we had to dump and swish the soiled diapers in the toilet, then boil batch after batch to sterilize them.

"What?" I stubbed my cigarette in a blue ceramic ashtray Ann Mari had made. Rosa slept in her carriage by my side.

"I want to be a cultural worker for SNCC in Mississippi." He paced our dark narrow kitchen. "It's an opportunity. I need to go."

"We said we'd never be apart." I looked at him in disbelief while I rocked the carriage. "We promised." It seemed especially unfair that he would be the one to engage full time in movement work when, of the two of us, I was by far the more radical, the more political. "We have a baby! She needs you. I need you. I can't do this by myself."

"It took this long for the movement to recognize cultural workers. Up till now there hasn't been a space for me. The time has come. I've got to go." He faced me, pleading, "I'm being called."

"Take me with you. Take us. I'll drop out of school. We'll all move."

"I can't take a white wife. It's too dangerous. We could be arrested! Or killed." His ever-somber face looked even more wretched.

"I'm willing to risk it."

"I grew up in the South. It's home. I don't want to take you as a tourist. I'm called to go. By myself."

"We're a family. We're married." I looked at the arm I had caressed so often, the large, perceptive hands that had traveled my body. And I stared directly into his eyes, which he averted. "No. You can't go."

"My father traveled constantly for his job as a minister on a national board. My mother coped. That's how it is sometimes. Lots of families live apart." He strode down the hall.

I trailed him, pushing the carriage. "This is where you belong!" I rocked furiously. "What am I supposed to do about school?"

"I've been thinking about this for a long time. I couldn't tell you until I was sure it was the right thing to do. I have to hear the words of my people. I've been away too long." He looked desperately homesick.

"You can't go," I said, steel in my voice. "You're the father of a six-month-old!"

"It's my revolutionary duty," he said, impatient now, before he lifted his old brown suitcase onto our bed in the living room. "I probably shouldn't have had children. At this moment in history, I'm being called."

"But—"

"I thought you would be glad I was joining the revolution!" He whirled. "This is what you wanted, isn't it? 'Property is theft.' You're the one who taught me that. Well, I'm going to do something about it and see that those goddam Mississippi crackers don't keep robbing my people blind!"

"Shit, that isn't what I meant. You can't just go!" I sobbed, leaning against the doorjamb. "What will happen to our marriage?"

"A physical separation might be an inconvenience, but it can't affect our marriage," he said brusquely.

Two days later he picked up his suitcase, hugged me, cried, and walked out the door. Stunned, I wondered, how can men make such unilateral decisions without concern for how others are affected?

For days I steamed, complaining to anyone who would listen to my tale of woe, and eventually tried to consider this trip from his point of view. From the needs of the revolution we were trying to make. And his own need for self-realization.

A week after he left, I announced to my department chair, "I'm going to do something more useful than study. I'm going to compile a book of letters home from soldiers stationed in Vietnam, to show how horrible the war is."

"You'll be welcome back whenever you're ready," the kind man said.

"Thanks," I said breezily, never giving it another thought.

Despite my fury, which alternated with forgiveness, Julius and I talked often. He visited every few months, and I kept editing his writing—abandoning my soldiers' letters project. Instead my life centered on Rosa and my new colleagues at City University, where Ann Mari got me a job researching urban policy. Three dollars an hour, pretty good pay, and I needed every penny of it, since I had given up my graduate fellowship and Julius no longer brought in money from teaching guitar.

In the South he grew closer to SNCC comrades, to the Black southern culture he had left behind, and to his ambition as a writer. Soon I hardly knew who my husband was anymore when he returned for visits, though we groped each others' bodies and talked for hours, trying to connect. Julius and I had started as two young intellectuals in love. Now our worlds couldn't have been more different. He spoke with world leaders like Ho Chi Minh and Fidel Castro—who I, the Marxist, had mentally introduced him to, I fumed—and I was a housewife talking to a toddler. While his sphere had grown to the world, mine had shrunk to the block. "I traded in Frantz Fanon for Dr. Spock," I complained bitterly to the notepad I still didn't call a journal.

Not yet knowing who I was, I let myself be flung whichever way the winds blew, searching for creative outlets to stay afloat. At Christmas I painted designs for holiday cards, signing "Yours in struggle." I brushed newspaper with red and green watercolors for wrapping paper as Pete Seeger advised, "instead of buying it, stuffing the pockets of capitalists." I molded masks out of clay. Baked stuffed pork chops and fruitcakes wrapped in rum-soaked cheesecloth. Attended endless meetings.

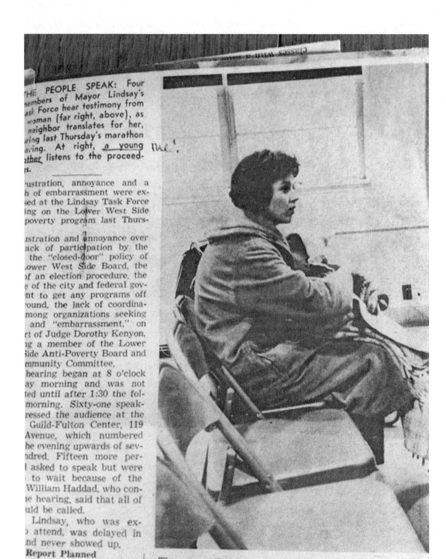

THE PEOPLE SPEAK: Four
members of Mayor Lindsay's
Task Force hear testimony from
woman (far right, above), as
neighbor translates for her,
during last Thursday's marathon
hearing. At right, a young
mother listens to the proceed-
ings.

...ustration, annoyance and a
...h of embarrassment were ex-
...sed at the Lindsay Task Force
...ing on the Lower West Side
poverty program last Thurs-

...istration and annoyance over
...ack of participation by the
...the "closed-door" policy of
...ower West Side Board, the
...of an election procedure, the
...e of the city and federal gov-
...nt to get any programs off
...ound, the lack of coordina-
...mong organizations seeking
...and "embarrassment," on
...rt of Judge Dorothy Kenyon,
...ng a member of the Lower
...Side Anti-Poverty Board and
...mmunity Committee.
...hearing began at 8 o'clock
...ay morning and was not
...ted until after 1:30 the fol-
...morning. Sixty-one speak-
...ressed the audience at the
...Guild-Fulton Center, 119
...Avenue, which numbered
...he evening upwards of sev-
...dred. Fifteen more per-
...l asked to speak but were
...to wait because of the
...William Haddad, who con-
...e hearing, said that all of
...uld be called.
...Lindsay, who was ex-
...attend, was delayed in
...nd never showed up.
Report Planned
...rpose of the hearing —
...l be 16 throughout the
...to come up with a report

The report is due to be completed in about a month.

grow. The program
men who attempt to

Newspaper photo of Joan at a public hearing for Mayor Lindsay's task force,
with Rosa in her arms, Lower West Side, where she was testifying on the need
for a War on Poverty. (*Chelsea Clinton News*, February 17, 1966, author's archive)

Alone, I agitated more fiercely than ever. One afternoon, when Steve Schwerner told me he and Nancy bought their groceries in the Pelham suburb where his parents lived "because food's a lot cheaper there," I thought of my neighborhood A&P. The same chain where Steve and Nancy shopped. "That's amazing! It's so much higher here," I said as we compared prices on toilet paper, sliced cheese, and milk. "Man, that's almost a 10 percent difference!" I calculated. "Okay, 7 or 8 percent more here."

"And the produce is better there," Steve added. "Fresher. Plus the meat, a whole different quality!"

"For a cheaper price." What kind of gouging was this? I didn't know then that A&P was notorious for dumping spoiled food on poor neighborhoods of color. But I could see with my own eyes the high prices and poor quality compared to what Steve described in Pelham.

The next day I talked to Rosie, my best friend on the block, the cheerful young woman I had met on her stoop when I'd come years before to look at the apartment. Now we met almost daily in her apartment to drink coffee and chat, bouncing babies on our laps. She was the one who had instructed me, right after Rosa was born, to tape a penny over my baby's belly button so she would have an innie instead of an outie. It worked. And I'd had Rosa's ears pierced like all the Puerto Rican girls on the block, including Rosie's toddlers. "Look how they're cheating us, Rosie! Most of us don't even have a car. We can't get to the suburbs."

"As if we knew the way!" She giggled. Two of her girls, both under three, dodged between our legs under her kitchen table. When one tagged the other, they squealed. "Shh," Rosie hushed them. "So injusto."

"Let's boycott A&P." It was just two blocks away. "They should match the Pelham prices."

"Sí." Her wide face lit up, full of outrage, for she harbored an activist soul like my own. "And we should demand better food, too. No rotten stuff."

We started talking to neighborhood women, gathered a group in Rosie's apartment, and wrote a flyer to hand out on a picket line. "DON'T BUY HERE! They're stealing money from us! Prices are much cheaper for the same items at their suburban stores. And better quality! Boycott until they give us Same Food for Same Price!" The Woolworth's demonstrations six years before had taught me the power of boycotts, and Rosie's husband, Armando, an experienced union organizer, helped us think about what to write. Then he translated our flyer into Spanish so we had a bilingual leaflet. Now all we had to do was set up a schedule.

"¿Puede usted piquetear mañana? Can you picket tomorrow?" Rosie asked each of the Spanish-speaking neighborhood women. "Or the day after?" Going door-to-door on the nearby blocks, I rounded up eight English speakers. "Thank you." I told them, "Here's a schedule. Please sign up for a slot. We're paying way too much for groceries."

Every morning we had at least two women on the line, one English speaker and one Spanish speaker when possible. Sometimes more. "Don't buy here until they lower prices like in the suburbs," we called out. "And give us better food! No spoiled meat."

"No compre aquí hasta que ellos tengan precios bajos como los que tienen en el suburbio," another woman said, handing out our leaflet while she admired a baby. "¡Qué hermoso bebé!"

And exactly as we did in the Woolworth's boycott I had been part of in New Haven, we turned a surprising number of shoppers away. Day after day we trudged out there, rain or shine, convinced the store was losing money.

But after two weeks our picketers slacked off. We could barely keep one woman on the line. "If you can hold out a little longer, they're sure to fold," Armando told Rosie and me. "Don't give up now!" He had started going to work late at his job in a Long Island paint factory, even though it cost him pay, so Rosie and I could picket. A sweet man, he took care of one-year-old Rosa along with his own small girls.

Some days I didn't believe we could keep going. I thought of how the civil rights movement had kept people's spirits up throughout the long Montgomery bus boycott, and later during Mississippi registration drives, by holding mass meetings at night. Preachers, with all their rhetorical skill, urged people to stay strong, invoking biblical parallels to their struggle. In Mississippi, Julie was one of the singers at those meetings, with Guy Carawan and the Freedom Singers, who had all sung around our kitchen table. But Rosie and I couldn't call mass meetings. The women in our boycott, all poor mothers, were too busy in the evenings with children. We had no shared community, no space for large meetings, and no singers. What could we do to rally our people?

We hit on a plan: give them pastries and coffee back at Rosie's cozy, sunny apartment after the morning shifts. We bought cheap boxes of donuts, and Rosie brewed up her strong coffee laced with sweet condensed milk. Every day a few women sat for an hour or so, babies crawling everywhere, and we talked. About all the ways we were getting screwed, not only by the grocery store but also by the landlords, our husbands, and our pay, which was mostly under the table. Women began to linger. More and more showed up on the morning line and then sped over to Rosie's crowded kitchen table. We were almost shutting the store down in the mornings. Our afternoon shifts remained sparse, but we couldn't keep gathering women during the busy dinner hour. Still, we knew we were cutting sharply into profits.

After four or five weeks, the manager called me, since my number was listed on the leaflet. Rosie and I hurried to his cramped office in the back of the store, which stank of rotting fruit and vegetables. Crates of old produce were stacked all over the room.

"Buenos días," Rosie greeted him.

"What do you ladies want?" He glowered, ignored Rosie, and motioned for me to sit. I glanced over at her and didn't respond, forcing him to deal with her.

"It's here," she said, pointing to the leaflet. "Aquí. We want the same prices you charge in Pelham. And better food. Don't dump your old frutas on us!"

"We have different costs here." He spoke to her as if she were a stupid child.

We raised our eyebrows.

"Different security costs," he tried.

Silence.

"Trucking."

"Don't you truck to Pelham?" Rosie asked.

"Right," I chimed in.

"It's different here," he repeated. "It's a different neighborhood."

"So?" I said. "What does that mean? That we deserve lousy food?"

"The food doesn't move as quickly."

"Maybe because the prices are too high!" Rosie said.

"You girls don't understand. It's business."

Rosie jumped up. I stood, too, infuriated at his patronizing tone. "Vámonos," she said.

"Okay." We started toward the door. "*You* don't understand," I threw over my shoulder, unable to resist.

"Wait. We can shave three percent off most of the prices." He smiled broadly, as if he had given a great gift.

"We want the same as Pelham." Rosie was adamant. "Lower prices, better food."

"Four percent," he said sourly.

"No." We stood by the door with folded arms. The stench of rancid meat was overpowering and I couldn't wait to leave. But the manager kept upping his offer.

Rosie and I negotiated a 7 percent price cut that day on every single item, matching the Pelham prices. "And fresher produce and meat," he said reluctantly, without even the grace to be embarrassed about all the spoiled food he had put out.

"We'll be watching," I promised. "And if you don't keep your commitments, we'll be back."

Outside Rosie grabbed my arm and said, "Let's have a party!" Giddy with victory, we strode back to our block. That evening we celebrated with some of the picketing women at her apartment, singing, shouting, hooting with laughter. When Armando got home from his long commute, he beamed at Rosie before he gently tucked their four girls into one double bed.

That night I felt a huge sense of pride. We had done it. Rosie and I had organized our little corner of the world for justice, and won. I was so satisfied, I didn't even think of writing about my political work.

But someone else did.

Things Fall Apart

1966

On a sticky August afternoon, the doorbell rang.

"Who is it?" I asked through the closed door.

"FBI," came a deep voice.

"What?"

"FBI. Open up."

I hesitated. Did I legally have to open? My heart pounded so hard I was sure they could hear it through the door. "What do you want?"

"We'd like a little of your time," a man said.

"Why?" I stalled.

"Background, nothing serious." This sounded like a second man.

"Background on what?"

"General background."

I was quiet.

"This is an official visit," the first voice said.

Not wanting to get Julius in trouble, I decided to let them in. Slowly I removed the pole-in-the-floor door lock and slid open the dead bolts, trying to figure out what I should say.

Two white men, looking like generic movie extras, stood in the doorway flashing badges.

I wanted to slam the door but instead tried to show my dislike by not inviting them in.

"Mrs. Lester?" the tall one asked blandly, sounding as though he were taking a survey. He didn't sound threatening.

"Yes."

"Where is your husband?"

"In the South," I said, deliberately vague. I wasn't going to tell them he was in Mississippi with SNCC, inspiring potential Negro voters with his music. That this was revolution. A revolution we both wanted. But I worried aloud, "Has anything happened to him?"

"You tell me," the shorter agent snickered, lifting his arms in a "Who knows?" gesture. The taller, nicer one said, "We don't have any information to that effect."

Okay, I would try to talk mostly to him.

The three of us stood uneasily. I shifted from one leg to another, determined not to give any specifics about Julius.

"What were you doing in New Haven?" the short one suddenly demanded.

I wondered how they knew I had lived there and why they even cared. But this was a good diversion. "I was working at Yale Medical School."

Rosa, attuned to the fear bubbling from me, toddled over from her mat in the corner and hung onto my leg. I touched her head, trying to soothe her. Soothe myself.

"Didn't you participate in a march for Communist Cuba?" the short one barked.

Surprised he knew so much about me, I corrected him. "Independent Cuba."

"Did you march or not?"

"Yes." I remembered the 1961 march in Washington vividly. I had been entranced by a phalanx of Cuban men with black berets, who explained, "We're members of the 26th of July movement. Movimiento 26 de Julio. It commemorates Castro's 1953 attack on the Moncada Barracks, which launched the revolution." We walked all day, raising our fists, chanting, "¡Viva Cuba! Hands Off Cuba! Fair Play for Cuba!" That night I slept with an artist I met at the march, spending the night in his New York tenement. In the morning I lay in bed watching light slant in the window, highlighting laundry hung on lines over a back courtyard. Oil paintings in bright colors scattered the floor in the one-room apartment; his easel was propped against a wall. The man brought me steaming coffee in a handmade mug and I felt like a true bohemian.

"Why did you participate in a Communist march?" The FBI agent yanked me back to the present.

My hands trembled, but these men were pissing me off. "To normalize relations between two neighboring countries."

"A Communist country!"

"Listen, I was protesting US attacks on a sovereign country!" My voice rose. "James Baldwin supported the group I marched with, Fair Play for Cuba. Is he a Communist? Is Allen Ginsberg? Is Norman Mailer? Truman Capote. They all supported Fair Play for Cuba."

"You wrote a letter to the Department of Justice about opening diplomatic relations with Communist Cuba."

"Stop calling it that! It's Cuba. Period. That's the name of their country."

"Yes?" the shorter one prodded. "Did you write it or not? A propaganda letter to the DOJ."

"DOJ?"

"Department of Justice."

"I wrote a letter. My own, not propaganda."

"And you circulated a petition." He glared.

"Why are you asking?"

"Background," the tall one said softly. He jotted a note in a pad.

We remained standing uneasily at the door. Still believing I was protecting Julius, I answered everything. "Yes, I wrote to Congress about dismantling the House Un-American Activities Committee." "Yes, I sent in that petition." "Yes, I was on that march for civil rights in New Haven." "Yes, yes," I dutifully replied to it all, correcting them occasionally although I was tiring and so was Rosa, who began to cry. Who did they think they were, barging in like this?

"It's okay, sweetie," I tried to comfort Rosa, wondering how long this would go on. But I couldn't risk refusing to answer. I had heard the FBI kept civil rights workers under surveillance and had a long history of making trouble for organizers. I had to be careful or Julius might get in trouble.

The men bent their heads to write everything I said and searched through a notebook, evidently finding questions to ask. Their tone grew more aggressive. They moved closer. Every time I stepped back, they moved toward me.

Leaning down, I picked up Rosa, balancing her on one hip while I carefully answered. "Yes, I was in Atlantic City in '64."

"Why were you there with a Communist organization?"

"What Communist organization?"

"The so-called Mississippi Freedom Democrats," the shorter man sneered.

"They aren't Communists! They were the only legal delegates to the Democratic National Convention. They were nonsegregated. They should have been seated." How long could I keep this up? Did I dare throw them out?

"And these book reviews?" The same agent held up Xeroxed copies of two *National Guardian* reviews. "By you. This one, about 'the end of capitalist,'" he said, not even getting the word right. He frowned, rippling his forehead. "Are you anti-capitalist?"

"Yes," I said proudly. When were they going to get to their real subject: Julius? This was a lot of background.

"Are you a Communist?"

"Not officially."

"What does that mean?"

Fatigued as I was, I had to keep them interested in me. Had to keep stalling. "I'm not a member of the party."

Rosa began to scream and claw at my leg.

The tall one asked pleasantly, "Where can we sit?"

"In the kitchen," I snapped. The only place with chairs other than Julius's desk chair, which he didn't like anyone to touch. I carried Rosa, squirming in my arms, back to the kitchen and quickly scattered bright red, blue, and green wooden blocks on the floor. For a moment I crooned a lullaby. Keeping one eye on her as she played with the blocks, I kept answering questions.

The men stayed another half hour, asking about things I had done, all of which I felt were innocuous—and legal—enough to confirm. How did they know so much? They must have been watching Julius. Probably tapped the phone. We had long suspected a tap, with all the mysterious clicks and whirring noises we heard, and sometimes we yelled into the receiver, "Did you get that?" Or when we were really pissed off, "Pigs!" But Julius had been cautious on the phone. When he talked with SNCC's chair Stokely Carmichael, he spoke in code. They had secret names for each other. And if Stokely was at our apartment, they whispered.

When the two FBI agents finally said, "That's it for today," I felt dizzy with relief. Rosa climbed into my lap and I held her tight against me, rocking her until we both giggled. There, I thought proudly, I had done it. Shielded my husband.

All night I wondered what the agents wanted. What were they hoping to learn that they didn't already know? Had they imagined they could flip me to be an informer, but given up when they heard how adamant I was?

When Julius called the next day, I said, "The FBI came to the apartment, but I didn't tell them shit!"

"They came to the door? What did they say?"

"Oh, getting 'background information.' I don't know exactly what they wanted, they were sneaky, but I made sure I didn't say a word about you."

"Thank you."

"It was awful, Rosa was crying, and they stayed forever."

"You let them in?"

"Yeah, I thought I had to. But I was really careful."

"They've been going around to lots of folks."

"It was scary. They're so creepy, and they knew a lot about me. But they hardly mentioned you. Maybe they wanted me to let down my guard and let something slip, something they wanted to know. But I was super careful."

"Good job, Joan. You're a true revolutionary."

I confided an account of the visit to my counselor friend from Camp Gulliver, Claire, who had recruited me for the job at Church of All Nations. We often saw each other for coffee or a walk. Maybe she would have some insights.

But instead she astonished me by standing up from my kitchen table after I told her the story. "I can't be friends with you anymore. I'm sorry. It's too risky. I don't want to subject myself to that. It's too dangerous." She physically backed away and fled out the front door.

Shocked and hurt, I didn't argue. Maybe association with Julius and me had grown dangerous. Claire had been one of my best friends in New York, but I never saw her again.

My questions about that FBI visit lay in my mind for ten years, until Ann Mari wrote a book instructing folks how to request their FBI files and helped me get mine.

Once the thick bundle of pages arrived, I had a strange sensation, reading about that FBI visit in my heavily redacted file. The agents' asking about Julius was "a pretext," I learned. It was me they wanted to interrogate. Me they considered dangerous.

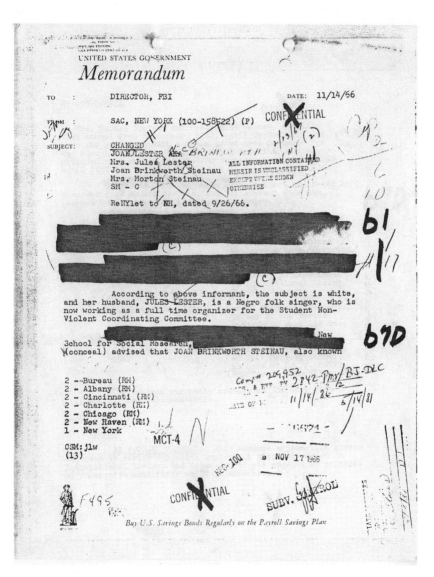

UNITED STATES GOVERNMENT

Memorandum

TO : DIRECTOR, FBI DATE: 11/14/66

FROM : SAC, NEW YORK (100-158522) (P) CONFIDENTIAL

SUBJECT: CHANGED
JOAN LESTER aka
Mrs. Jules Lester
Joan Brinkworth Steinau
Mrs. Morton Steinau
SM - C

ALL INFORMATION CONTAINED
HEREIN IS UNCLASSIFIED
EXCEPT WHERE SHOWN
OTHERWISE

ReNYlet to NH, dated 9/26/66.

b1

b7D

        According to above informant, the subject is white,
and her husband, JULES LESTER, is a Negro folk singer, who is
now working as a full time organizer for the Student Non-
Violent Coordinating Committee.

                                                New
School for Social Research,
(conceal) advised that JOAN BRINKWORTH STEINAU, also known

b7D

2 --Bureau (RM)
2 - Albany (RM)
2 - Cincinnati (RM)
2 - Charlotte (RM)
2 - Chicago (RM)
2 - New Haven (RM)
1 - New York
CSM:jlw
(13)

MCT-4

Buy U.S. Savings Bonds Regularly on the Payroll Savings Plan

CONFIDENTIAL

SUBV. CONTROL

9 NOV 17 1966

AL 100-19682

b7D

[redacted] observed nothing
concerning Mrs. STEINAU that would indicate that she was
engaged in any type of subversive activity while at Putney,
Vermont. [redacted] Mrs. STEINAU, now Mrs. JULES
LESTER, is married to a negro and that she is very much
interested in the civil rights movement and the negro cause.
She said Mrs. LESTER'S husband is employed by the Student
Non-Violent Coordinating Committee and JOAN herself is ,
taking courses at CCNY and is believed to be employed at
City College, N. Y. [redacted] as no
knowledge of the outside activities of JOAN [redacted] husband
other than that set forth above. [redacted]

        Records of the Vermont State Police, Brattleboro,
Vermont, law enforcement agency covering Putney, Vermont,
as searched by [redacted] on
12/7/66, advised that there is no record in the files of
that office identifiable with JOAN B. STEINAU or JOAN
LESTER.

        [redacted] Brattleboro, Vermont, on 12/7/66, advised
that the records of that Bureau failed to reveal any record
identifiable with JOAN B. STEINAU or JOAN LESTER.

-2-

Document from the FBI file for Joan Steinau Lester, December 1966.

NY 100-158522

Records of the Business Office, Yale University
Medical School, mentioned above, reflected that all of the
above employments were under the Antioch College Co-op
Program.

E. Residence

b7D

the subject resides in Apartment 1, 329 West 21st Street,
New York, New York with her husband and infant child.

II. AFFILIATION WITH THE COMMUNIST
MOVEMENT

A. Evidence of
CP Sympathies

b1

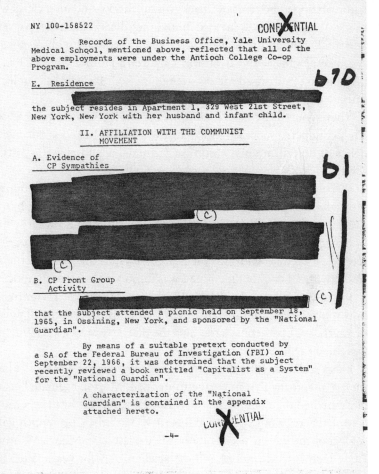

(c)

(c)

B. CP Front Group
Activity

(c)

that the subject attended a picnic held on September 18,
1965, in Ossining, New York, and sponsored by the "National
Guardian".

By means of a suitable pretext conducted by
a SA of the Federal Bureau of Investigation (FBI) on
September 22, 1966, it was determined that the subject
recently reviewed a book entitled "Capitalist as a System"
for the "National Guardian".

A characterization of the "National
Guardian" is contained in the appendix
attached hereto.

CONFIDENTIAL

-4-

Document from the FBI file for Joan Steinau Lester, November 1966.

It turned out that when I had demonstrated with Fair Play for Cuba, I had triggered an FBI investigation into my "subversive activities." They tracked me for seven years, fastening page after page into an impressive file.

FBI letters flew for all those years between Vermont, Ohio, North Carolina (my birthplace), Albany, New York City, Chicago, and New Haven, summarizing police records, background checks, and interviews with former employers. One, unnamed, found me "the intellectual type, very alert and intelligent and was at her best when furnished with responsibility." A spokesperson at the Evanston Children's Home, which I had left so precipitously, surprised me by stating, in the FBI's words, "Subject was a satisfactory employee."

They scoured my past, finding letters and book reviews I had written. They conducted surprisingly exhaustive searches but concluded with "evidence of no Communist action" or "criminal or subversive activity." After seven years of investigation, they closed my file.

What a waste of time and money, I thought, despite feeling vaguely pleased that my small contributions had been significant enough to trigger FBI interest. Later, after I'd had a chance to digest the file—what I could read of it, with extensive blackouts—I remembered my assumption during their interrogation that Julius was their target. Despite all their questions about my activities, I couldn't imagine I was important enough to notice.

My amazement at being the FBI object of interest made me realize how much I had diminished my own accomplishments. For all those years of marriage, I had considered him the Star and myself the Wife. I never imagined I would be deemed dangerous.

I also realized, with shock, how incompetent the FBI was. They gave me an imaginary first marriage to my dad, Morton Steinau, because we had marched together at a Fair Play for Cuba rally in New Haven, and they completely overlooked my real flirtations with the Communist Party, the subject of the whole investigation. They missed Dr. Niebyl, a Communist Party member, who mentored me academically for years, often inviting me to his New Jersey home for tutorials. They missed the weekly Marxist study group he led, where our goal was learning how to overthrow capitalism. They missed my attendance at the national Communist Party USA Convention in New York, where Dr. Niebyl took me one afternoon to meet the scholar Herbert Aptheker, who offered to publish one of my research papers as an American Institute of Marxist Studies monograph.

How much did it cost the FBI to send letters back and forth between seven bureaus for seven years, have an agent monitor our phone, write up their nonsensical reports, and fund a personal interrogation by two agents?

But every shadow has its sliver of light. Right then, reading my file ten years after the visit, I began to take myself more seriously. If I was worthy of all that attention, I must be Somebody after all. The FBI spent a lot of money to give me the gift of self-worth. So "thank you" to the FBI, although I do have to urge a better use of funds: as my friend Rev. Andriette Earl says, "Feed the children!"

Trying to stay afloat in Julius's absence, I played with Rosa, talked to friends on the phone, and wept with loneliness. But I did find a novel to ease my solitude. Each night I feasted on Chinua Achebe's mesmerizing *Things Fall Apart*. Published in the US in 1959, the first widely available book by a Black African author, it told a tragic story: Okonkwo, an Ibo (Igbo) man, is a great warrior "well known throughout the nine villages and even beyond," confronting the nineteenth-century British invasion of Nigeria. Simultaneously he's navigating internal pressures of his traditional culture, where norms of manliness already stress him before the colonizers arrive. Confirming my research about colonialism's impact, this novel shows the human cost when Christian missionaries and imperial governors crush local communities. Like the violent suppression of languages when the US forced Indigenous people into English-only boarding schools, British suppression of culture had equally devastating results.

Though the book's brutality upset me, I was thrilled to discover complex characters in a Nigerian village from a Nigerian perspective. All the "Africa" books I had previously read—staples of the 1950s English lit curriculum—portrayed "ugly" Africans, "rudimentary souls" with disturbingly black bodies, like those in Joseph Conrad's novel *Heart of Darkness*, which I had hated in college. We had also read Rudyard Kipling's poem "White Man's Burden," sympathizing with white men doomed to civilize "your new-caught, sullen peoples / Half-devil and half child." The "lesser breeds."

Unsparing as Achebe's novel was, I found it exhilarating to learn about Nigerian culture, and the clash of cultures, from his insider's view. The writing, clear and direct, was exquisite. Achebe celebrated bonds of kinship and community in prose that felt like folklore, immediately drawing me into the story. Now it is considered a classic and assigned to high school students.

When I read it in the mid-'60s, the humanity and warmth nourished me during the long evenings of Julius's absence.

When would he return? I'd gotten pregnant on one of his visits home and wondered what our relationship would be once he did return, with two children crowding our tiny apartment.

I knew he was taking heat for our marriage. He had told me about the day a SNCC colleague, a man who'd visited our home repeatedly and I thought was my friend, surprised Julius by saying, "I probably shouldn't say this, man, but I don't think you should be married to a white woman." And that man wasn't the only one. Julius was constantly grilled: "How can you consider yourself Black and have a white wife?" On college campuses, where he had begun speaking, that was the most consistent question students—and faculty—asked.

The early '60s movement, which had started as "black and white together" when we had stood, arms linked, singing "We Shall Overcome," had polarized. The Democratic Party's rebuff of the MFDP and the advent of Black Power—plus the spellbinding Black Panthers in their black berets—dramatically changed the mood. After SNCC expelled whites, urging us to take our anti-racist organizing into white communities, more of Julius's friends began to rebuke him for his choice to stay with me. "Man, we gotta wonder where your sympathies lie. Sleeping white, talking Black. Which side are you on?"

The Autobiography of
Malcolm X

1966

The dim light in our basement mirrored my heavy heart in those days, and the constant threat of rats did the rest. Their rank, pungent smell permeated the apartment each time one died inside the walls.

Once when Julius was home, he wrapped a red bandana around his face and hacked into the bathroom wall with an axe to remove a rotting carcass. I stood by, gagging. "There," I said, pointing to the place he should whack. Even after he dug the rat out, destroying the old plaster wall, I could smell that putrid, slightly sweet stink. It lingered in my nostrils for months.

Many nights I sat by Rosa's crib with a baseball bat to protect her. One of Rosie's daughters had been bitten in the face while she slept, the rat drawn by milk drooling from her mouth. I couldn't bear the thought of a big rat sinking its teeth into Rosa. So I guarded her, often falling asleep in our old armchair, and she never got bitten.

Money was a constant problem. Many months SNCC couldn't pay Julius his thirty-dollar wage, which he would send half of to me, so I usually walked the twenty-three blocks to work, saving the fifteen-cent bus fare.

To cut costs on groceries, I applied for government surplus food. Every month, Rosa and I rode the bus to a crowded distribution center, where I picked up a paper bag packed with a huge box of yellow American cheese, a giant number ten can of powdered eggs, an equally large can of peanut butter, and a five-pound sack of flour. Waiting in line with other mothers, babies crying and our backs hurting from standing on our feet with a squirming child on a hip, we joked, "How about those peanut butter cans? I could feed the whole block!"

One morning a woman standing near me holding on to two squab-bling boys turned and said, "I heard that peanut butter is good bait for rats." She wore a pretty flowered dress cinched at the waist with a wide belt, a small white hat, and a scowl. "That's why they give us so much, they know we all have rats." But she laughed, put her hand on her hip, turned her brown eyes on me, and said, "Gracious, child, I don't know how I'll survive these honkies with their slow-ass ways."

I wondered why she said that to me—a honky—but she seemed friendly, so I asked, "Does your flour have bugs in it? What are they?"

"Weevils, child. Flour weevils. Give some chunk to the bread." She laughed. "Substance! Taste like bits of meat."

"You can eat them? I try to pick them out. They're so disgusting. Wig-gling around." I made a face.

"When we don't get meat, we get weevils!" She laughed again, grabbing her boys and holding on tight. "Stay here by me like I told you!"

"How old do you think the cheese is? Sometimes it has a funny smell," I asked this woman who seemed to know so much. Rosa was asleep in the stroller.

"Lord, I don't know. I'm glad for every damn bit of food I can get out of these white folks."

"Hmm." I nodded. "Me, too." And I was. "How do you use the powdered eggs? They taste like metal even when I mix them in pancake batter."

"Put some spice in there. Red pepper. Hot pepper. Chili. Any kind of pepper! That'll cover everything up. Ask me how I know!"

Once we picked up our heavy bags, I heaved mine into the back of Rosa's stroller, headed for the bus, and waved good-bye. "Thanks for all the information."

After that, no matter how I tried to hide the metallic tang with spices, I was still aware of it. But I was grateful, because using the powdered eggs meant I didn't have to spend money on actual eggs.

In the midst of this anxiety about money, a short, grizzled man with a leather briefcase showed up one afternoon at my apartment door.

"I'm Conrad Lynn," he said, extending his hand and bursting into the living room.

I had heard of Conrad, a radical lawyer who defended pacifists, draft resisters, and civil rights activists. And I had listened to him on Pacifica's WBAI radio station, where he commented on civil liberties issues. To this day I don't know what prompted his visit. We had both been in Fair Play for Cuba, but more likely we had met through Julius. Or maybe Rap, since Conrad was his lawyer.

A bearded man with a big grin and glasses, he swiveled his head, looking around my small combination living room and bedroom. "Why are you living down here in the dark?"

"I don't have money for anything else. The rent's only thirty-five dollars a month."

"Doesn't Julius send you any?" He dropped his briefcase.

"Not anymore. SNCC hasn't paid him in months." Seeing the judgment on Conrad's face, I added, "It's not his fault."

"Are you able to work?" He kept peering around. "You don't have any daylight!"

"I know. But it's cheap. I work three days a week up at CUNY doing research. But I pay a dollar an hour for child care, and I make three dollars an hour, so . . ." My words dribbled off. I wanted to hug this respected older man, taking such an interest in me.

"I bet you have rats, too," he mumbled.

"Uh huh."

"Here," he said, reaching into his pants pocket for his wallet. He peeled off four hundred dollars in twenties, counting aloud, and thrust the bundle at me. "Take this and buy groceries, buy meat, buy some clothes for the baby, get a sitter and go out." He shrugged and gestured with both hands. "Go out. Get out of this basement. As much as you can."

I looked at the outstretched hand holding the thick roll of twenties. I had never seen so much cash.

"What?" I gasped. "Are you sure? That's so much money."

"That's okay." He laughed. "I have some clients who can afford to pay me. I've got the money and you need it. What else is there to say?"

"Thank you, thank you. That is so kind." My mind rushed ahead to picture the food I could buy, and I hugged him. "But who can pay you this kind of money? With clients like Rap . . ."

"I know, I know. But there are others who can. So I'm like Robin Hood." He threw back his head and laughed some more.

"Thank you!" I reached for the money and jammed it into my pocket. "Do you want some coffee?"

"Oh, yes." We took the twenty steps to the kitchen so I could boil milk for a cup of Bustelo. I wished I had cookies to offer. Or fresh fruit.

But I did have bread and held a piece on a fork over the gas burner to toast it.

"My wife is white, too," he said, looking at me with genuine affection. "I know what it's like to be a mixed couple. What it was like in 1952 when I married Yolanda." He beamed when he said her name. "Her mother knocked her to the ground and tried to strangle her when she announced she was married to me!" His look was half amused, half pained. "Italian American family, working class, highly prejudiced." He shook his head. "I hope it's better now for you. Though I can't say our life is so great in the suburbs either, in a supposedly liberal cooperative community."

"My parents wouldn't come to my wedding. But they didn't try to strangle me!" I smiled. "I guess I'm lucky." I kept looking at him as if he were an apparition, as if this whole afternoon were a dream. Would I wake up soon and find I had imagined it, with no fat bundle of money stuffed in my pocket?

After Conrad left, I sat feeding Rosa on my lap, thinking how miraculous this gift was. And how strange that an old Negro man would give me, a white girl, money. That wasn't how I thought the world worked.

I don't recall ever seeing him again, but whenever I heard his name or thought of that day, I felt grateful all over again and vowed that if I ever had money, I would share it the way he had, making a significant difference in somebody's life.

—

After Rosa woke from her nap, I rushed to the grocery store with twenty-five dollars in my purse and for the first time in my life bought everything I wanted. Real butter. The juiciest, biggest bright-red apples, with no soft spots. A Sara Lee chocolate cake with thick creamy fudge frosting. The biggest eggs. An imported bottle of Heineken beer. Strawberry jam. Sirloin steak.

The next afternoon when Rosa and I rode up to East Harlem for our weekly overnight at Ann Mari's, where we would luxuriate in her sunlit windows and uplifting company, I didn't lug Rosa's stroller and all her paraphernalia—diapers and lotions and clothes—up and down steps on the subway. We rode in a taxi and I felt like royalty.

Those long evenings and mornings with Ann Mari were my weekly respite, sleeping soundly in her guest room and sitting around her sunny kitchen table in the morning, laughing, eating, talking politics. Feeling the spaciousness of light and heat from her big kitchen window. "Did you see *The Battle of Algiers*?" That would be me, gushing. "It was amazing."

"I know. To see people making a revolution. Hard to watch but inspiring."

"Yeah, I closed my eyes during the torture." We stopped to pour hot milk into our second cup of delicious coffee and chomp a few bites of croissant. "It's interesting to see the conditions that allow people to make revolutions, isn't it?"

"When their bellies start to fill up enough so they can think, they can imagine a better life!"

"Oh." I learned so much from this deeply political older woman. But occasionally I was the leader. "Ann Mari, you have to read *The Autobiography of Malcolm X*. I can't put it down. He had a terrible childhood. White supremacists murdered his father in Michigan. The police didn't do anything, and his mother had a breakdown. Child welfare took him away, and eventually he moved to Boston to live with his sister. He became a hustler and a robber and went to prison, but then he transformed himself completely."

"He was a hustler for the Nation of Islam," Ann Mari said, looking unimpressed.

"But he was really working for Black unity when he was killed. He was so incredible the way he analyzed white supremacy. Brilliant. And he cared so much."

"Hmm . . ."

"Malcolm called his grandfather a 'red-headed devil.' The white man raped his grandmother, his mother's mother. That's why his mother was light-skinned and that's why he had red hair. They called him 'Detroit Red' in New York. Imagine carrying a rapist's blood. And hair!" I shook my head.

"One of the perks of the white patriarchy. Why do you think Black and brown people are so many shades?"

"I know it's common. But to see your father murdered, your mother put in a mental hospital! And he was only thirteen. Then he was murdered himself."

She didn't look as outraged as I wanted her to, though she said, "I heard him speak in Harlem a couple times. He was magnificent."

"I listened to him on the radio a lot."

She smiled and we sat in a companionable silence. The sun on my shoulders was like liquid gold, massaging every tired muscle. And the conversation fed me for days.

All summer Rosa and I took taxis to Ann Mari's, both ways. We ate better, I got a sitter one night to attend a movie with a friend, and I bought books. Records. I rode the bus to work instead of walking, at least on the way home. I eked out the money from Conrad as long as I could, even sending fifty dollars to Julius.

But eventually it ran out and I was back in the same predicament.

At work I began to cheat on my time sheet, penciling in an extra hour when I clocked out by hand. Sitting at a desk in the hall by the sheet, I checked around to make sure I was alone. Sometimes I felt so nervous I would erase the false arrival or departure time I had entered and write in the correct one, only to think, Three dollars an hour! How much food would an extra hour buy? Milk. Bread. Meat. I would calculate and erase it again, feeling worse by the minute and ever more worried about the great smudge I was creating. Wasn't it evident by the gray blotch almost tearing through the paper that erasures had been made? What would my boss think? But no one ever questioned me. Probably that Waspy look, my honesty pass. So historically inaccurate, but effective.

I started shoplifting from Woolworth's, my old antagonist, where I found it easy to slip a pack of baby socks or kitchen sponges into Rosa's carriage. I would drop something in, then stroll nonchalantly out the front door, heart pounding, skin slick with perspiration. But those blue eyes, pale face, and dishwater blonde hair carried me right through the exit, a racial checkpoint. My white skin supplied an invisibility shield that cloaked even my Negro baby in the carriage.

I had stolen a few things in high school. I especially remember a soft, green, long-sleeved cashmere sweater I desperately wanted. It cost twenty or twenty-five dollars, a fortune in the midfifties. I had never owned clothing so beautiful. Tired of hand-me-downs and rummage sale leavings, once I tried it on in a small dress shop, I decided to steal it. Heart pounding with fear, I kept it on under my jacket and fled the store. Once I cleared the door, I began to run.

That sweater was my favorite piece of clothing for the next ten years. I still recall its velvety warmth against my skin, its perfect fit, and how the dark green set off my light-colored hair. When I pulled it on over my head,

I felt like a movie star. In all the years since, I've never had a sweater as fine. I wore that sweater until it shredded.

Now, ten years older, I picked up the habit again. The clerks near the door of Woolworth's never looked at me twice as I sailed out with a smile. Even as I benefited from their blindness, I thought, Racism is bad business. While they're busy following people of color around the store, I'm busy popping things into Rosa's carriage.

Each time I felt mixed about my success: pride and relief that I had gotten away with my thefts, anger that corporations—especially that old segregationist Woolworth's—made so much money when I had so little. And shame. Shame that heated my body and rippled through my veins. But swamped in money worries, I kept it up until the day I confessed to my mother, when she came for a visit.

"If you get caught, it could be serious," she said, looking worried. "What would happen to Rosa?"

I stopped breathing.

"If you promise not to do it anymore, I'll send you twenty-five dollars a month." She gazed solemnly at me and squeezed my hand.

"I promise." It was the first time since I had left Antioch at nineteen that my parents offered money, and my mother continued her monthly gift for the next year. Her generosity put a bounce back in my step. But even though I gave up shoplifting, I never thought to stop lying altogether.

Years later I met Jamie Washington, a born-again gay Christian who became a friend after we started traveling together as training partners, leading diversity trainings. Once on a break we sat holding hands, our fingers laced together. After I questioned something he said, Jamie told me, "I've taken a vow to tell the truth at all times."

"Wow. All the time?"

"Yup," he said with his radiant smile. "No exceptions."

Impressed and quietly embarrassed about my dishonest past, I promised myself, "From this moment on, only the truth." I knew this included no stealing. No exaggerating. No fibbing.

In the forty years since, what a relief it's been to stand on this principle. I never need to wonder whether to tell the truth. I made a vow.

—

Early summer of 1967 brought good news. A legal case, *Loving v. Virginia*, was contesting Virginia's Racial Integrity Act of 1924, which criminalized sex or marriage between white and "colored" people. Mildred Jeter Loving and Richard Loving, a Negro woman and white man who had traveled from their Virginia home to marry in Washington, DC, had been arrested in 1958 by a sheriff shining a flashlight onto their bed as they slept. Their marriage license, obtained just six weeks earlier, was posted on the bedroom wall. "I'm his wife," Mildred Loving protested. But the marriage was invalid in Virginia. Sentenced to a year's prison term, the couple fled the state and filed suit.

They lost the first time in a US District Court that announced, "Almighty God created the races white, black, yellow, malay, and red, and he placed them on separate continents." Thereby demonstrating His segregationist intent. Many Virginians agreed with Him, including some who burned a cross in the yard of Mildred Loving's mother.

After Richard and Mildred Loving lost again, this time in the Virginia Supreme Court, their ACLU lawyers appealed to the US Supreme Court. When his lawyers asked Richard what message he wanted to send the Court, he said, "Tell them I love my wife."

On June 12, 1967, nine years after the Lovings were arrested for their marital crime, the Supreme Court issued a unanimous decision overturning their convictions and striking down anti-miscegenation laws. Mildred and Richard, with their children, could finally return from exile and settle down again in the state they both called home.

When I heard the decision on my kitchen radio, I yelled, "Yes!" startling Rosa, who was asleep in my lap. "Yes, baby!" I kept murmuring, tears trickling. "Maybe now we can go South with Daddy. We just became legal. A legal family, from sea to shining sea."

⁓

Douglass, born a month later in summer heat, a day shy of Rosa's second birthday, was a sweet, contented boy, so unlike his high-strung parents and sister. Julius, briefly home, joked, "Where did this baby come from?" Had we given this easygoing child too heavy a name?

Yet as undemanding as Douglass was, and as helpful as Rosa proved to be, I now had two babies to care for. Alone. Was I crazy to put up with this life, to stay married to Julius when he wouldn't live with us?

Aretha Franklin's *Chain of Fools* seemed written for me that year. After Eleanor brought over the record so I could hear the song, I blasted it whenever I could find it on the radio. "You got me where you want me, I ain't nothin' but your fool."

Here I would shriek, "Ya treated me mean, Oh you treated me cruel."

Dancing around the kitchen in the narrow space between table and wall, I screamed at the climax, "One of these mornings the chain is gonna break . . . Chain chain chain of fools."

Aretha's voice, so wide and deep, lifted me up and gave me strength to hold on. Now, with *Loving* decided, it wouldn't be so dangerous for us all to go South, I thought, waiting for the right chance to bring the idea up with Julius.

On one of his quick trips home, we decided to visit Central Park with Rap Brown, now the SNCC's chair, who had become a close family friend.

"Let's take a picnic," I said, excited by this chance for an outing. "And go swimming!"

"Okay," Julius agreed with a smile, packing up his guitar while Rap offered, "I'll make sandwiches." While he slathered mustard and slapped baloney on bread, I changed into a bathing suit and helped Rosa with hers. We stuffed a sheet and towels into a bag, packed a cantaloupe, pulled clothes over our suits, and, gathering up baby Douglass, set out.

I hadn't been to Central Park since the previous year, when I had carried Rosa on a cold April day for a Vietnam War protest. I had marched to the UN behind a Native American contingent chanting, "Americans, do not do to the Vietnamese what you did to us." Later, when I listened to the news, I was surprised to hear, "President Johnson let it be known that the FBI is closely watching anti-war protests."

But now the five of us enjoyed a rare holiday, boating and laughing. Late in the sunny afternoon, full of food and happily sleepy, Julius strummed his guitar and began singing "Stagolee" in his beautiful, rich voice. "Well, when I was a little boy sittin' on my mama's knee, she said, 'Son, let me tell you 'bout that bad man Stagolee."

The children, Rap, and I sprawled on the grass, entranced by the tale Julius had recorded on his first Vanguard album three years before. Rosa and I, knowing it by heart, sang along, and Rap chuckled, "Tell 'em, brother," at the painfully witty bits, like "Stag's town Hang-a-Nigger, Georgia, where all trials are conducted Southern style, 'Nigger, you guilty.'"

Julius had taken an old Stagolee myth about one man who killed another and had given it a civil rights sizzle. Even heaven, in his version, had gotten rid of Black people because, as a sheepish St. Peter told Stagolee, "You know, they's up here playin' the blues on the harps, you know, and flattin' thirds in the hymns, and flattin' fifths and all that. We couldn't have 'em up here. All we got now is white folks and some middle-class Negroes, you know, some of the bourgeoisie, you know, we had to send all the bad colored folks down to Hell."

Rap, over six feet tall, jumped up with Rosa in his arms. "Now ain't that a blip? Colored folks kicked out of Heaven 'cause we got rhythm and soul!" He stretched back on the grass, holding Rosa, who adored him. The man was gentleness personified, so unlike the media image of a rabid, antiwhite extremist.

After Julius finished "Stagolee," he sang his "Cockroach Blues," which we belted out with him: "Lord, I wouldn't mind roaches if they would help pay my rent. But you know a roach said to me, 'You better move. I want me one of the luxury apartments.'" We laughed along, knowing the truth of the song. "I bought a spray last night and I sprayed all over the house. I got up this morning, roaches thanked me for killing a mouse."

Every time I heard the song, I marveled anew at his ability to take an upsetting situation—our inability to rid our three rooms of roaches— and use humor to turn it around, just as people had so often used the

Boating in Central Park with H. Rap Brown and the children, 1968. (author's archive)

blues. "There were some roaches on the stove, they were standing around in a crowd. I walked over to 'em; roaches turned around and yelled, 'Freedom now!'"

Rap lifted his fist, pumping it while he chanted, "Freedom Now!" Rosa, who followed everything Rap did, raised her own small arm, piping, "Freedom Now."

We lingered in that magical mood, savoring the sun and the breeze coming off the water until sunset, long after Douglass had fallen asleep. But seeing Julius so at ease, watching him hoot with laughter and feeling mellow myself, I was loath to leave. Three blue jays began to squawk near us, running off a flock of chickadees.

Finally Rap said, "They're telling us it's time to go." Slowly we packed up, making our way back to the basement where roaches scattered whenever we turned on a light. But that night I fell asleep with a smile.

Looking at the photo today, it's hard to believe more than fifty years have passed since that idyllic summer afternoon. The children are now in their midfifties, Julius has joined the ancestors, Rap (now Jamil Abdullah Al-Amin) is entombed in solitary confinement, and I'm eighty years old, writing it all down.

Rap has had the hardest slide. Because he publicly demanded that police stop killing Black people, in 1967 J. Edgar Hoover ordered all FBI offices to "expose, disrupt, misdirect, discredit, or otherwise neutralize" Rap, Stokely, and two others. They focused on Rap mercilessly, framing him repeatedly, especially after his book *Die Nigger Die!* came out in '69. Stokely stayed in the public eye because he fled to Guinea and became an international speaker until his death thirty years later. But Rap was intentionally eclipsed. Following one of his many arrests, after the FBI had hounded him and his mother nearly to death, I raised money for his bail. Soliciting funds from my parents, Julius, and old SNCC comrades, I sent a few hundred dollars to his brother, wishing it were more. Wishing that a man so committed to justice could find some for himself. But he was charged with murder—framed, many believe—and it seemed unlikely.

Despite these rare happy moments as a family, Julius's life and mine ran on different tracks. Yet I tried to believe that someday things would get better. Even though Julius insisted he still couldn't take us South—"Are you crazy?"—I thought that someday he would move home and we would be a proper family again.

Look Out, Whitey!

1968

Stunned, I finished the final page of Julius's manuscript. The lyricism of his early stories remained, but he had added a new dimension: a furious passion for Black liberation. As my pencil sliced through repetitive words, I felt tears gather. What a gifted writer I had married, one who cared so much about humanity. How lucky I was to share an intimacy with such an artist, to be part of his creation. And how fortunate for his writing career that we had stayed in New York, the literary hub of the country.

Though I agitated for a move to Madison, Wisconsin, where the university had exactly the radical American economic history doctoral program I craved—I had applied, had even received a fellowship—he refused to leave New York because he was meeting the editors he needed. I wouldn't go without him.

As for my own subterranean trickle of a half-remembered writer dream, there was no way my talent could compare with his. Maybe someday I would get to write political essays again, but until then I would continue trying to change the world, one demonstration at a time. And I would keep editing my husband's brilliant work.

Julius's dapper literary agent, Ron, whom Julius called the HNIC (Head Nigger in Charge), often came by our basement. The two men would lean back around the yellow kitchen table while I served Bustelo or the Cokes Julius loved. "Man, you check out "Sonny's Blues" yet?" Ron asked one evening. "Jimmy Baldwin is one fucking genius. Damn! Roll over, Shakespeare. Jimmy Baldwin's in the house. *Going to Meet the Man.* Yes, sir." Ron shook his head. "The man is baaad."

"The cat is brilliant, but hey, check out *Jubilee*. That Margaret Walker's no joke either. She kills off mammy in one fell swoop, to be forever laid in her grave." Julius mimicked digging with a shovel.

"Farewell, mammy." Ron chuckled. "And none too soon. None too soon . . ."

Ron, who lived nearby at the Chelsea Hotel on Twenty-Third Street and Seventh, devoured Julius's new manuscript in a weekend and sold it within days to Joyce Johnson at Dial Press. As an early manifesto of the new Black Power movement roiling the nation, with the delightfully outrageous title *Look Out, Whitey! Black Power's Gon' Get Your Mama!*, the book was explosive.

Before publication, the prestigious *Kirkus Reviews* wrote, "The book should make 'honky' check out his siege supplies because this black power spokesman means it when he says 'It is clear that America must be destroyed. There is no other way' . . . A deliberately inflammatory tract." The *New York Times* praised it in language as incendiary as the book itself, saying it "arcs over the rotting outposts of the Republic like a mortar shell shedding its sulfurous glare, and lands plump in the heartland to detonate the conclusion that 'it is clear that America as it now exists must be destroyed.'"

The day I saw the book in print, I burst with pride. I had believed in Julius before he published a word. Read and approved every draft, so the world's praise seemed natural. With his deep confidence and talent, it had been only a matter of time. This box of books simply acknowledged what we had both known would come true.

On the first page, Julius profusely acknowledged my editing skills and commitment, validating all my hard work, my sacrifices.

My deepest gratitude must go to my wife, Joan. It seems to be a cliché for authors to thank their wives, but the wives know why, and know that it is no cliché. Wives are the ones who suffer the loneliness and pain while husbands are away, physically or spiritually. They are the ones who must live with a commitment that is so complete that the family is something that gets attention in the husband's spare time, and in a revolution there is no spare time. Yet, they remain wives to the husbands who are more often a source of pain than joy. Wives also deserve the most gratitude because they are good editors. At least, mine is. She deserves a special place in Heaven, right close to God's big, rosy rocking chair and if she doesn't get it, God will have to be on His guard, 'cause Black Power will be there after His mama, too.

This almost made everything okay.

We held no book party—nor did Rap or anyone else I knew—but the provocative title created its own publicity. Reviewing *Look Out, Whitey!*, the *Times Book Review* called it "a magnificent example of the new black revolutionary writing that could generate the tidal force to sweep aside all the tired and dead matter on our literary shores."

Julius rocketed to celebrity status. Suddenly every radical benefit wanted him as a speaker. College campuses begged him to come. Everybody sought his attention.

Reeling from Julius's sudden fame and the incessant demands on his time, my resentment flared. "We need you here," I complained, feeling like the worst shrew in the world. "You have two babies."

Silence was his usual response. And he kept ramping up his public presence. When Phyllis Fogelman, editor in chief of Dial Books for Young Readers, proposed he write a children's book, Julius set to work. Within months, *To Be a Slave* came out, winning a Newbery Honor. His touch was golden.

New York's listener-sponsored radio station WBAI offered Julius a weekly radio show, which he named *The Great Proletarian Revolution*. For his first guest, on December 26, 1968, he invited Les Campbell, a founding member of the African American Teachers Association, to read a student poem. Les arrived after a bitter fight over local control of public schools in Brooklyn's Black Ocean Hill–Brownsville neighborhood. The fight pit Black parents against the United Federation of Teachers, which struck, trying to stop community control after the neighborhood board dismissed the union teachers—mostly white and Jewish.

I had been active in my neighborhood supporting the Ocean Hill–Brownsville folks. At the time, I described it in a letter to Pam Allen.

You know, this school strike is an absolutely incredible thing which has polarized this city (racially *and* along class lines) to an amazing degree. . . . It has radicalized thousands of people (mostly women) who have seen a clear-cut demonstration of the power lines in this city and of the racism. For instance, we have had 50–60 women from our local elementary school (located on our corner and serving mostly the projects where I live and the ILGWU co-ops across the street) sleeping in every night (rotating of course) for 2 weeks after we broke into our school to open it, had meetings almost every night in the school to discuss cirriculum [*sic*] changes, how we can get community control of our school, what we want, the whole rotten educational system and what function it serves in this society, and we've been operating that school during the whole strike. . . . This fantastic thing is happening all over the city, in literally every district (it's hardly reported in the press, of course) . . . while the (mostly) poor women of this city are liberating their schools.

Into this charged atmosphere, Les Campbell brought a group of his students' poems, and Julius chose one for Les to read on air.

"Are you sure? Are you crazy?" Les asked him.

"Yes," Julius answered, insisting, "Read it."

Dedicated to Albert Shanker, the poem began, "Hey, Jew boy, with that yarmulke on your head / You pale-faced Jew boy—I wish you were dead." And continued in that vein. Julius defended the reading to listeners as helpful, "to know the feelings of at least one Black teenage girl."

Huge protests erupted. The Anti-Defamation League demanded: "Fire Julius Lester." The UFT filled suit against WBAI and also tried to fire Les Campbell, making the story front-page news. Julius was quoted in the *New York Times*, "An ugly poem, yes, but not one-hundredth as ugly as what happened in the school strikes, not one-hundredth as ugly as what some of those teachers said to some of those black children."

Now the constantly ringing phone delivered death threats. I never knew whether to answer. Once when Julius did pick up, he looked ashen after he hung up. Sitting by the window, he stared out like a zombie.

"Another death threat?" I asked, cradling Douglass in my arms.

"It was the FBI," he said slowly.

"Why?"

"There's a plot to kidnap me."

"What! By who?"

"They uncovered a plot, that's all they said."

"What are they going to do?"

"Not much." He looked tense.

"Aren't they going to protect you?"

"No, they said all they do is give me the information. And to 'be careful.'"

"What idiots!"

"They probably want me dead anyway . . ." He stared out the window again.

What were we supposed to do with that information? Julius took to looking over his shoulder wherever he went. Each time he left home, I wondered if he would return.

At WBAI a gang of men with clubs, Jewish Defense League members, surrounded the station. "Fire the anti-Semite!" they yelled as they charged police, trying to break through the cordon surrounding the station. Some got to the roof, attempting to get inside—to Julius. He had to be escorted in and out of the building by armed guards, but he continued his show.

"Another article in the paper," he said wearily one morning, pointing to a denunciation calling him the most anti-Semitic man in the nation.

While I wouldn't have gone that far, I agreed with the critics. "Why did you choose that poem?" I asked him one night in bed.

"Les had a right to read it." I could feel his arms fold against his chest. "That's how lots of Black people feel about Jews. They run the schools; they don't give a damn about Black kids. They run the grocery stores. They take money from our community. They cheat people."

I was silent.

"It's true. You don't know."

"But to have such a hateful poem! There could have been other ways to talk about that power dynamic. And the history of alliance, how Jewish lawyers defended the Scottsboro Boys. And think of Mickey, and Andy Goodman. There were so many Jews in the movement. And Nat. It's a long, overlapping history . . ."

"That was then, this is now," he said, rolling away. "And this got peoples' attention."

He was right about that. By the spring of 1969, everybody in New York City, and many nationally, knew his name. His books flew off the shelves. For that I was glad. And as always, proud. But concerned about his eagerness to stoke controversy.

There was one controversy he wasn't willing to court, though, and that was to take his white wife and biracial children to the South. "It's still not safe," he argued. "If the crackers don't kill us, the niggers will. Especially those Black women. They can't stand to see a brother with a white woman. Lord, they'll whip out a knife before you know what hit you." Only years later would I learn that he often slept with those Black women on his trips, even set up housekeeping with one of them. But at the time, the only thing I understood was his resistance to taking us, and considering how many murdered civil rights workers we had known, his caution seemed well founded.

Julius stayed in the South. Each evening while the children slept, I wrote, stuffing pages into a manila folder tucked between two books on the kitchen shelf—de Beauvoir's *Memoirs of a Dutiful Daughter* and Du Bois's *The Souls of Black Folk*. I typed at the kitchen table, banging out my loneliness, my longing for an at-home mate. And when the night grew late, with the world outside finally silent and my brain full of beer, I let the words flow freely, moving beyond day-to-day frustrations.

Once I wrote a two-character play. Julius and I were the dramatis personae. In the opening scene, he explained on the phone why he had had to go South. I answered as I tried to do in real life, understanding that at this historic moment, he was making a significant contribution.

But then another version popped out, almost writing itself. The character Joan answered Julius's attempt at explanation with, "Fine. That will give me more time for my work. I'm writing like mad on a book."

"What kind of book?"

"About a white mother with Black children. Showing daily life. Here are some lines from it: 'Wherever the white mother goes, people ask, "Where did you get that child?" After she answers "From my body, like every other baby is born," they ask, "How did she get that tan?" "She was born that way." "Who's the father?" When she says, 'A Black man,' they freak out.' It's going to be a great book, there's nothing like it. Oh, and the children and I will be moving to California next month.'"

"What?" Julius says in the play. "You're moving to California?"

"Yes, the land of milk and honey. I'll forward the address."

The writing flowed onto page after page as I imagined myself rising up, refusing the role of abandoned wife, and setting out for my dream destination. Satisfied, I finished my script well after midnight, dated the pages, and shoved them into the folder before stumbling off to bed.

Yet in the light of day, my words looked pitiful, a vengeful role reversal, the fevered fantasy of an exhausted mother who rushed four days a week from home to unreliable sitter to job, running the entire way. And ran back in the evening. An author? Hardly likely! Better to focus on the tasks at hand. Laundry. Groceries. Meals. Dishes. Bedtime reading. Doctor visits. Research at work. Run home. On my days off, I pushed the double stroller to the nearby seminary, with its pocket park inside the heavy gates. There

Rosa played, twirling, jumping, running while I kept my eye on Douglass, so he wouldn't swallow the pebbles he liked to stuff in his mouth.

Desperate to stay engaged in a domain beyond my job, where I submitted research to scholars who wrote it up for urban studies articles, I joined the tenants group Metropolitan Council on Housing, which had helped me fight eviction from our basement. Proud to stand up in court for tenants who had withheld rent, I learned how to win concessions from landlords who neglected their buildings.

But try as I might, I could not find a way to win equity in my marriage. It would take an army of women to show me how to escape.

The Second Sex

1968

The army arrived first in the form of a book.

"It's amazing," Eleanor raved uncharacteristically. Tall and thin, dressed for work, she stood erect at our apartment door and thrust a thick paper-back at me. Its pages were frayed, corners turned down. "Read it, Joan. You won't believe it."

"Oh, Simone de Beauvoir," I said when I saw the name on the tattered cover. "I've read her novels. And her autobiography. I love her. *The Second Sex*, what is it?"

"A manifesto that will change the world." She wagged her finger. "If Fannie Lou Hamer's testimony stopped the clock in America, *The Second Sex* will stop it all over the world."

"Really?" Eleanor's self-assurance always made me feel like saying, "Yes, ma'am," and saluting.

"We'll talk about it after you read it." She laughed her deep, infectious chuckle.

That night, once Rosa and Douglass fell asleep, I lay in bed, eyes burning. Eighty pages in, my brain burst with the hurricane force of de Beauvoir's words. Men, she wrote, oppress women by framing us as Other, defined only in opposition to life's central actors. We are always peripheral. Men regard themselves as essential and transcendent, while women are inessential, incomplete. He creates, acts, and invents; she waits for him to save her.

It was the blueprint of my life, laid out in academic formulation. Exactly as I had read about for Black and other colonized people, but this time it was me being subdued. Was this otherness why I felt hollow inside? Why

I felt constant, blistering rage at Julius for not doing child care and rarely sending money, for not giving me time to explore a creative life?

"The book *is* amazing!" I told Eleanor over lunch at a midtown restaurant. I had left the children with Rosie while Eleanor picked me up in her sleek black city car. As New York City Commissioner on Human Rights, she had a driver. "A white man," she loved to point out while we rode in the back.

Eleanor nodded. "De Beauvoir lays it all out. The sister tells it like it is!"

"It's infuriating!" I growled. "It's gone on forever."

"Time for a change!"

"What will we do?"

"Organize!"

"How?" I asked, unsure how to apply my neighborhood organizing skills to such a global, eternal problem.

"The transition to feminism is easy for anyone who's been associated with civil rights or labor rights. The analogies are intellectually compelled."

"I know, it's shocking how similar the lies are. What we've been taught to believe."

"What I don't understand is why the transition doesn't happen to everybody who was in the civil rights movement." Eleanor shook her head in disgust.

"Did you see what Roy Wilkins said? He told the *Times*, 'Biologically, women ought to have children and stay home. I can't help it if God made them that way, and not to run General Motors.'"

"The executive director of the NAACP! That's criminal!" she said. "It's exactly what those white bastards said. 'God made them that way,' so we had to be slaves."

"I can't believe they don't see the similarity."

"Stokely said the same thing." She shook her head. "'The position of women in the movement is prone.'"

"He said he was joking."

"Yeah my ass he was joking. People don't joke about things they don't believe."

I thought about him sitting at my kitchen table, eating my food. Is that really how he saw women?

"We need to kick some ass. Like Shirley," Eleanor said.

"Shirley?"

"Chisholm. She had to fight her way out of a Brooklyn Democratic clubhouse, where the men ridiculed her every damn day, to get into Congress."

Visible Black feminists were few at a time when Black men were calling for unity, but Shirley and Eleanor weren't the only ones. Dorothy Height of the National Council of Negro Women was another, as was Fran Beal, a friend of mine who led SNCC's Black Women's Liberation Committee (later renamed the Third World Women's Alliance).

"I'm gonna work with Black women, you go find the others!" Eleanor said over dessert, shaking her head again at the fact that we had to.

Robin Morgan, whom I had met through Julius, told me about other white women who were equally fed up, women who had given their all for civil rights and were furious at their go-make-the-coffee treatment in the movement. Fifteen or twenty women, she said, met weekly at the Southern Conference Educational Fund (SCEF) office on lower Broadway, talking about *our* oppression.

I made my way down to the high-ceilinged loft, while Julius, home for a month, stayed with the children. "I'm with you, with women's rights," he assured me, making me all the madder.

Robin, Kate Millet, Roz Baxandall, Shuli Firestone, Anne Koedt, Ti-Grace Atkinson, Flo Kennedy, and others who would later publish our thinking crowded the room, sitting cross-legged on the floor. "Why are women on the bottom everywhere?" they asked.

"Yeah, even in sex!" we howled.

"Why don't we know anything about the women's rights movement of the early twentieth century?"

"It's a blank in our history books, just like Black history!"

"We've been obliterated."

"By male supremacy," someone added sharply.

"We never put our own interests first."

Spellbound, I returned every week to this group of voluble, high-powered women. We tore everything apart, exactly as we had done with race, scrutinizing all aspects of life through a gendered lens. Each revelation shocked me with its personal impact.

"Housework?" someone asked. "Why is it our job to start with?"

"Child care, same thing."

So I wasn't alone. Every woman was expected to shoulder these jobs and count herself lucky if her male partner "helped."

"What about when I try to talk about how we don't share household jobs and he says, 'What, I have to listen to some trivial shit about house-work?'" one woman exploded.

It was uncanny how many stories mirrored mine. I had wondered what I was doing wrong, but everybody's husband or boyfriend acted the same, dismissing us with: "Baby, the *real* struggle is ending the war in Vietnam, where people are way more oppressed than you'll ever be." Or "It's *Black* Liberation. Not women's lib. You're jumping on the bandwagon, distract-ing from the real issues."

Even as I laughed when women mimicked the put-downs, every word reverberated. I dove into research on the history of the family, the basic unit of women's oppression, and discovered it derived from the Greek *familia*: a man's property, including his slaves, children, and wife. In ancient Rome, the *pater familias* held the power of life and death over every member of his *familia*.

I read Engels and found that the control had started even earlier, when agriculture yielded a surplus and men wanted to be sure their wives' babies were theirs, to pass on inheritance. I wrote up my research in a five-page paper, unsure what to do with it other than pass out carbon copies to other women in the group.

Once we looked with new eyes, everything was separate and unequal, from Male/Female Help Wanted ads with their differently paid jobs, to the paltry number of female authors and the skewed image painted of us by male writers. Even Allen Ginsberg's *Howl*, I saw when I reread it, portrayed woman as a crusher of the creative male, a "shrew" who "does nothing but sit on her ass / and snip the intellectual golden threads of the craftsman's loom." Domestic life left men "mouth-wracked and battered bleak of brain all drained of brilliance." It sounded like Julius, codified in an iconic poem, though he wouldn't like *Howl*'s image of Black neighbor-hoods as playgrounds for white boys, "dragging themselves through the negro streets at dawn looking for an angry fix."

"Even sex, where the 'missionary position' doesn't stimulate us the way it does men," a woman at one meeting said to hoots of agreement.

"It isn't our individual failings holding us back. It's the uneven play-ing field, which we've accepted as nature's handiwork," another woman threw in.

I reeled with the implications. Why did Julius's powerful confidence run roughly over me as he built his life around what *he* needed—apologizing occasionally but never agreeing to change our household arrangements.

"What can we do?" a woman asked.

"First, tell our stories, understand what we have in common."

"It's what women have always done," another voice chimed in. "Told stories around the kitchen table. That will lead to action."

"Yeah. Like choice around motherhood. That's key."

One afternoon I rode uptown to Ti-Grace Atkinson's apartment, where three of us were to plan a demonstration. Ti-Grace was a tall, willowy, white Columbia doctoral student in philosophy, who wore berets and looked as though she would speak with a French accent, though hers was southern. Flo Kennedy was a formidable fifty-year-old Black lawyer, famous for her stinging, witty jabs. She swaggered in wearing her trademark cowboy hat, laughing that we had to "rattle the cage door, let 'em know we're in here!"

We stood in Ti-Grace's kitchen searching for a slogan that would capture the spirit of our upcoming Legalize Abortion march. We tried out various catchy phrases until Ti-Grace proposed, "Up against the Wall, Motherhood!"

"Yes!" Flo roared. "That's it."

"Um, it might put mothers off," I, the only mother, demurred. "We're not against motherhood itself, just the lack of choice."

Flo took a step back and eyed me silently for a minute before she spoke, hand on hip. "You're so uptight. Afraid to put some spice on it."

"No, I'm not. I simply don't think that would appeal to mothers."

"Or not to *you*," she said darkly. "What are you so afraid of?"

"I want to attract mothers to the demo—"

Ti-Grace jumped in. "Motherhood is bourgeois. We have to get past trying to prove we're 'good women' by becoming mothers. It's a perfect slogan!"

"But it sounds as though we're attacking mothers," I objected.

"Folks can distinguish between mothers and motherhood," Flo sneered.

Facing the united disapproval of these two powerful women, with free lives unencumbered by children, I felt caught in the odd position of appearing to defend the patriarchal family even as I railed against it at home. Used to being the radical in any gathering, in this new women's movement I often ended up, as a mother and married heterosexual, on the traditional side. It was a strange feeling. But our pro-choice work paid off. Two years later, New York State passed the nation's most liberal abortion law, three years before the Supreme Court's *Roe v. Wade* affirmed national abortion rights.

New women arrived at the SCEF office weekly, jamming the space, so we split into autonomous clusters we called "consciousness raising" groups. Forerunners of the women of today's #MeToo and Time's Up movements, we built solidarity—and fomented change—by sharing our stories.

Twelve of us, mostly wives or girlfriends of SNCC staffers, began to meet in my new public housing apartment, painted a sunny yellow. I had called the Housing Authority every week for two years to advance us along the waiting list until we moved, at last, out of the basement, away from the rats and Theresa's ugly shrieks. Four small, clean rooms on the sixteenth floor, looking like heaven.

Ann Mari rode the train from East Harlem, and we all crowded into my living room, sprawling on the floor and a cot that doubled as a couch. Smells of fried fat from the kitchen six feet away permeated the air, but no one minded. We named ourselves New Women and dug deep, wanting desperately to understand why we each felt so alone, so defeated, as we tried to forge satisfying lives. Every Wednesday evening at eight, the stories flew.

"Every man I know has put the moves on me."

"Me too!"

"We're relegated to service: typing, mailing, and food. With sex on the side." Knowing groans.

"At my job, same thing."

"The summer I turned sixteen, I had a job at a roadside stand," I said one night, glancing down at my beautiful son asleep in my arms. "I had to kill lobsters with a knife before we put them on the grill. I felt like a big shot, with a white sailor hat and a paycheck every Friday. I nicknamed myself Smoky and wrote it on my hat." I smiled. "I loved that job until the owner, Whitey, asked me to come in early one Saturday. Said he wanted to cook me a special lobster meal. I was excited. But after I ate, he grabbed me from behind and tried to kiss me." I blushed. "He was really old. When he touched my breast, I had no idea what to do, except wiggle away. I never told anyone.

"That night I slept at my friend Becky's house, like I always did on Saturday nights because it was too far to drive twenty miles home at midnight when we closed. In the morning Becky's whole family went to Catholic Church. Except her father. He walked into my bedroom and tried to get in bed with me. I was shocked to see him in his pajamas. I said 'No!' Even though he begged. Later I told Becky and she laughed it off with, 'Oh, he tries that with me all the time.' I thought I was losing my mind. All in the same weekend. That Monday I quit my job and worked as a soda jerk for the rest of the summer, so I'd never have to see Whitey again and never sleep at Becky's."

Women clucked with sympathy. For the first time, we put these harassments in context. They weren't simply a matter of a creep here or there. It wasn't about how pretty we were. Or careless. Or stupid. Or provocative. It was sexism, a brand-new concept.

That night I lay awake thinking of all the men who had tried to force themselves on me. The English professor at Antioch. An elderly painter in Vermont who invited me to his art studio when I was eighteen and working nearby. Thrilled, I had trotted over to the great man's studio, only to be repelled by his, "Would you lie down on my cot with me?" I remembered a friend's husband coming upstairs one morning while I was going down after my friend left for work. He lunged and kissed me, saying smugly, "I've wanted to do that for a long time."

Each time I had frozen with shock and slunk away, wondering what I'd done to attract such unpleasant attention. Avoidance had been my only strategy, embarrassment my response. I hadn't had the tools to place these actions in a context: of power, entitlement, and male privilege. What a relief to drag these humiliating events up and submit them to the light. Still, it would be ten years until Eleanor, as chair of the federal Equal Employment Opportunity Commission (EEOC), issued the nation's first sexual harassment guidelines, providing a concept—sexual harassment—to women all over the country.

In New Women we dissected everything, from our supposed penis envy (Ha ha!, we laughed, Fat chance) to our lost names. As slave masters imposed their surnames on people they owned, ours came from husbands or fathers. "Anonymous" was usually a woman, and we were all anonymous.

We and others in similar groups gathered radical essays about our lives from a new feminist perspective. We circulated these poorly typed, explosive booklets hand-to-hand and devoured them like food, necessary food.

⁓

The stories that spun around my living room that summer were matches to an oil that lay everywhere, coating the crevices of our minds. It was a flammable time. We watched Newark and Detroit explode. "Desperate

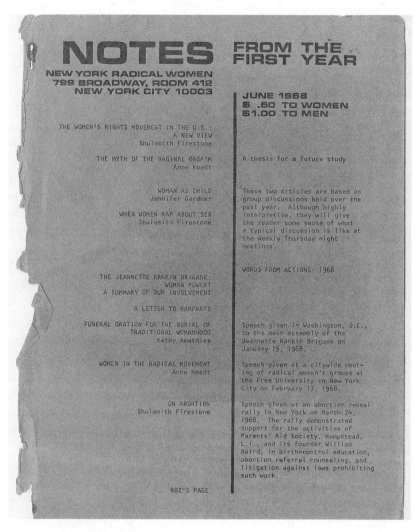

Cover of Women's Liberation booklet, "Notes," New York Radical Women,
June 1968. (author's archive)

people trashing their own neighborhoods in despair that change isn't coming quick enough to pay the rent," Julius said. "Or to protect them from
the pigs, who're using the rebellions as an excuse to shoot any nigger they
see." Even *Bonnie and Clyde*, the hot new movie we loved, showed us that
guns might do the trick if you wanted to help the poor. Maybe that's what
women needed, too.

The SCUM Manifesto

1968

One evening as our meeting broke up, a woman slid a mimeographed booklet into my hand. "A friend gave it to me," she said softly. Looking down, I saw the words *SCUM Manifesto*, Society for Cutting Up Men, and the author's name, Valerie Solanas. "Flo Kennedy is her lawyer," Kathy whispered. "She's going to need one. She shot Andy Warhol last week. She's in a hospital prison ward."

That night I laughed out loud reading the manifesto snug under my covers, a solitary haven with Julius in the South. The booklet was so outrageous it was hilarious, but with a deep seriousness running under the satire, like *Gulliver's Travels*.

SCUM opened ambitiously: "Life in this society being, at best, an utter bore and no aspect of society being at all relevant to women, there remains to civic-minded, responsible, thrill-seeking females only to overthrow the government, eliminate the money system, institute complete automation and destroy the male sex."

For the next forty pages, Solanas laid out flaws of the typical male, who was "obsessed with screwing; he'll swim through a river of snot, wade nostril deep through a mile of vomit, if he thinks there'll be a friendly pussy awaiting him." He constantly has to "prove that he is a Man." His main means of attempting to prove it is screwing. "Big Man with a Big Dick, tearing off a Big Piece."

Solanas details defects, too, of the brainwashed women who service men. "If all women simply left men, refused to have anything to do with any of them—ever—all men, the government, and the national economy would collapse completely. In contrast would be the women of SCUM," who "will become members of the unwork force, the fuck-up force; they will get jobs of various kinds and unwork. For example, SCUM salesgirls will not charge for merchandise. . . . SCUM will unwork at a job until fired, then get a new job to unwork at."

Solanas's audacious writing reminded me of another pamphlet I had read, by "Anonymous." The writer proposed that the same evening all over the country, when our shiftless men arrived home, they would open the front door, and *Bam!* "One shot for every diaper you never changed." We would aim at their feet. *Bam!* "One toe for each infidelity." *Bam!* "For the broom you never picked up." *Bam!*

A generation before *Thelma and Louise* struck the same nerve, I played with the blasphemous image. At odd moments, when I pictured Julius roaming the Georgia and Mississippi countryside "making revolution" (and maybe babies, too), while I raced to the babysitter before my 9 a.m. job, I flirted with the reckless scenario. *Bam!*

Yet despite its allure, eventually I let the daydream go and released it to my graveyard of fantasies, next to the one where, like Joan of Arc, I waved a banner at the head of my troops. Or the one where I frequented cafés, like Simone de Beauvoir, and wrote stories all day. Instead I contented myself with the power that came from heretically naming ourselves Women instead of girls, which provoked a predictable response: "So you're a women's libber?" asked with a sneer. Some of the braver women even took to calling men boys, as in, with highway construction, "Boys at play."

One topic we never discussed in our women's group was how it felt to be white women with Black men. We were an all-white group except Ann Mari, who was Puerto Rican, and several Jewish women, who, as targets of racist violence themselves, hadn't fully crossed the imaginary line to be "white." Over half of us were partners of Black SNCC men. Here we were, baring our souls about everything else, but our racially complex lives never came up.

I had shied away when white SNCC wives or girlfriends tried to be friends. When I saw them with their Black mates, the mirror was too intense. It was easy to avoid the reality that this was how Julius and I looked, because I never saw myself with him. Our only mirror was a small bathroom one, and photographs of us were rare, showing reassuringly familiar us. These other couples appeared so unusual looking in the '60s.

What if we had discussed our troubles: the stares, the shouted curses, the fears for our family's safety? Our coupling was still so verboten, I didn't want to acknowledge the complexity, the layers of meaning in our choices. Or the danger we faced in this roiling civil rights moment.

When Dinky Romilly, Jessica Mitford's daughter and the wife of James Forman, visited me and asked, "How is it for you as Julius's wife?" I looked away. Dinky sat in my kitchen playing with her baby, little James, and I saw a white mother with a brown child. I had never seen a picture like that before.

"It's fine," I answered her. "What do you mean?"

She gave me a quizzical smile. "You know, white and Black. What's it like for you?"

I couldn't answer, except to mumble some platitude and turn away.

Similarly, when Pam Allen, Robert Allen's white wife, had tried to be friends, "because we have so much in common, married to Black men," I'd recoiled. Later I wrote her, "I'm glad I feel so close to you now—and I half-hated you when you were in NYC (did you know?) because I saw you as very threatening to the false consciousness I had devised for myself as a means of surviving in my situation. So just wanted to let you know that I'm glad I'm free to like you now, and I do—and glad you were around before to make me uncomfortable!"

Julius and I were just *us*, I wanted to keep believing, despite my desire to explore the social context of every other issue. We were so much more than Black and white, I thought. The stereotype about our coupling was that it was mainly erotic. I wanted to rebut that, show a fuller picture.

Looking back, I wonder: Did everything with Julius simply feel too fragile, so I didn't dare examine the politics of race, gender, and sexuality as it pertained to us? How much of our attraction had indeed been the thrill of an outlaw romance, as well as our compatible devotion to literature? The fascination of exploring the unknown, the forbidden. And our commitment to desegregation, which we embodied. Marrying had felt bold and brave and interesting. As well as a delicious chance to extend a giant middle finger to the culture, which in my early twenties was not to be sniffed at.

Given that I was trying to prove something, though I didn't realize it, I couldn't reveal how troubled my marriage was. Trying to keep my marriage intact and raise these children, I simply didn't have the emotional capacity to delve into an issue that felt so fraught. I had to show the world—even other biracial couples—that we could make it, that we were normal, and not focus on our so-called racial differences.

Not only were we normal, but in our love we embodied the healing of a great wound, a great wrong. Our marriage, if happy, could show the folly of separating people by color. To prove the point, for several years I wrote on the back of every envelope I mailed: HELP STAMP OUT NEGROES! MARRY ONE. Today I cringe remembering that. It looks horrible—embarrassing, tone deaf, offensive. But in the early '60s I felt clever, flipping the common, infuriating white question, "Would you want your daughter to marry one?"

After a summer spent bitching—a word we reclaimed from men who charged, "You're diverting the real struggle, bitches"—I set out in November 1968, with Marilyn Lowen, another white partner of a Black SNCC man, to represent New Women at the first national Women's Liberation Conference.

Julius, after much negotiation, had agreed to stay home with the children. Once more I borrowed Ann Mari's blue sleeping bag, and I boarded the train to Chicago, feeling a different person than ten years earlier when I had ridden the same route to the Evanston Children's Home.

Eighty women met far out in the woods, shivering at a rustic YWCA camp. I curled in the frigid sleeping bag the first night, missing my children, wondering, Why am I here? I was twenty-eight. Most of the other women were younger, childless, and white. Would they have anything relevant to say to me?

But when we hung off bunk beds for workshops, listening to words we had never heard before, a redhead from Florida asked me in front of everyone, "Don't you vet everything your husband writes before he publishes? I read his acknowledgments. He says you do."

"Yes," I nodded proudly. "I read every draft."

"I've heard about you. Your name should be on his books."

"That's intellectual theft!" someone else called out.

Women clapped.

"Wow." After all the kudos the world was throwing Julius's way, I basked.

But women were angry. "Why is he getting all the credit when the ideas are yours, too?"

"You should be coauthor!" a few screamed. That seemed a stretch, yet the unaccustomed support cheered me. Maybe my ideas were worthwhile, editing not only "something I do after dinner."

Later that day I heard a woman proclaim, "The sexual caste system pervades *everything*, starting right in the delivery room."

Yes, I had seen it with my own children. Strangers always cooed, "What a beautiful girl," to Rosa. But they slapped scrawny little Douglass, deepened their voices, and predicted, "You're going to be a fine ball player, aren't you, son?" They didn't compliment *his* looks, adorable as he was. Nor mention a career for her. Make sure Rosa knows she's smart, I added to my mental mothering list. Help Douglass be sensitive.

"Who ever talks about jerking off?" another woman asked, to applause. "We should." The room exploded with shouts and cheers.

"I do it with a pillow."

"On my stomach," someone else said.

"There's only one area for sexual climax," declared Anne Koedt, a tall blonde I had met at the SCEF loft. "The clitoris. And men don't even know where it is! They've perpetrated the myth of the vaginal orgasm. But the clitoris is where all the fun is."

I sat listening, silent and flushed. I had never heard such talk. I, who enjoyed sex so much, had never masturbated. Never even thought of it. I couldn't wait to get home and try.

After three days soaking up radical ideas, I told Julius, "I want to extend the trip one more day." Huddled at an open pay phone outside the dining room, I cradled myself against a chilly wind that cut through my thin jacket. Wet leaves stuck to my shoes, exuding a damp, homey smell of fall woods. "It's so incredible here."

"No, I'm sorry," he said, sounding truly regretful. "You had your three days, as we agreed."

"I haven't been away from child care for three years." My voice rose. "I just want one more day. I'm learning so much. Women are making all kinds of plans, about actions and writing and—"

"Joan, I'm here with a sitter but I can't get any work done. You know that. I need complete silence."

"And you have a sitter," I said bitterly. We never had money for me to have one. "I want to come back one day later, that's all. One day."

"Look, we had a deal. Three days." He sounded exasperated.

"Please," I begged, near tears. "One extra day. Everyone else is staying. The conference is amazing. All kinds of ideas . . ."

"No, I need you to come back." His voice was firm.

"I really want to stay one more night. I might," I said defiantly.

"Listen, if you don't come back, I'll put them in a shelter."

"What?" I screamed. "You wouldn't do that." An automated voice warned, "You have twenty seconds left" and I was out of change for the phone.

"Temporarily. I'm sorry, but after tomorrow they're not my responsibility."

"You can't do that. How can you even say that?"

"You said you'd be gone three days. That's what we agreed on. You better come back."

The phone went dead.

Furious, I returned home, pouring hot anger into what I now called my journal. Sitting up late at my tiny desk stuffed into a corner of the kitchen, I wrote. "Unthinkable thoughts about Julius's 'exploitation' of me. How could it be since he is so good, so understanding? But I edit him, I free him from child-raising to create. And I was so damn grateful for those three days. What can I do, go on strike?"

I began to scrutinize every word he said, analyzing it for sexist content. "Your revolutionary duty is to stay with the children, so I can fulfill my God-given potential" gave me text for weeks.

"What about *my* potential?"

"What is it?" he asked. "Go fulfill it."

"I'm like a slave," I muttered, doubly furious because I had no idea how to fulfill my potential. But I did know one thing was unfair: Why should he be able to choose his revolutionary duty, while mine was assigned by gender?

Afraid to break up this family I found so unjust yet essential—for how could I raise my children alone, where would we go?—I scrawled secret lines, living out fantasies of leaving.

Silly Womanly Thoughts

The model wife sits
in her rocker-recliner,
thinking of going out for the evening paper . . .
and never returning.

Smiling, chatting with her husband as
she imagines it . . .
sudden disappearance.

No, but the children!
How could she think of it?
So she walks to the newsstand,
And returns, of course,
Kissing her husband as she
  comes in.

Silly womanly thoughts.

Variations of this daydream played out in script after script. Tucking
these furies deep in my desk, I wrote about all the women in history—
herstory!—who stole moments while laundry dried on the line and babies
napped, women hiding manuscripts in shoeboxes. I felt part of a long subversive trail, leaving crumbs for other women to find.

The writer Robin Morgan, a warm and witty woman who had become a friend from the SCEF meetings, began to visit and hash over ideas
for anthologies about our new movement. We would each edit one, we
decided. Eager to create an outline, I spent evenings making grand plans,
focusing on economic aspects of women's oppression.

"Great," Robin encouraged one afternoon when sunshine lit my small
kitchen. Rosa played on the floor with crayons while Douglass napped.
"Fifty essays, that's about right." We brainstormed names of women who
might write them.

Her outline took a broader form, covering history and every possible manifestation of the Women's Liberation Movement. We pored over
sheaves of paper at the kitchen table. Our camaraderie was warm and
easy, in no way competitive. After all, we were sisters in collaboration.

But Robin, with a background as a professional writer and no children,
surged ahead, contacting women we knew, including my friend Eleanor.
Soon she had a Random House contract for her anthology. Not confident
enough to believe I could publish my book, I stayed stuck in the mire of
children's strewn toys, endless readings of *Little Bear's Visit*, and the constant stream of phone calls for Julius.

Women sought the solace of his deep, understanding voice when they were looking for a "sensitive man" to hear their troubles; men asked him to write an article, serve on a board, give a speech. After a woman asked him to appear on a panel about feminism, I swore, "I'll picket the talk and tell people how unfeminist you are at home if you have the nerve to participate!"

"You're out of your mind," he fired back.

"Yes, I am. Completely out of my fucking mind. That's what happens to women who do too much child care!"

He didn't answer, but he didn't join the panel.

Now Julius, often home, retreated to his desk for days at a time, carving out an invisible study in our new public housing project living room.

Once I said, "You haven't talked to me for three days! Damn it, I need you." I thought longingly of days past, when his poetic sensitivity was turned toward me, not to others or the crush of deadlines. "I miss you."

His response was silence. And the metallic click of typewriter keys furiously hitting their mark. How did he find the fortitude, the selfishness, to carve out time for his writing, I wondered, no matter the needs of the family.

One evening as I cooked, I fantasized throwing my heavy cast-iron skillet at Julius's head, watching his brains splatter on the wall. I could imagine no other escape as I bounced between need ("We're a family!"), flashes of love for my soulmate, and a bottomless pit of fury. Even Dr. Spock, my friendly parenting god, infuriated me when he wrote in his new book, *Decent and Indecent*, "Women on the average have more passivity in the inborn core of their personality. . . . I think that when women are encouraged to be competitive too many of them become disagreeable." Statements like this made me feel quite disagreeable.

Writing my cross-country friend Pam Allen, I told her I might leave Julius.

On your question about self-respect and how much to sacrifice when the man *is* producing important stuff, the thing I've kept working toward, and which since Douglass was born especially has not worked, is to get myself to a point (in attitude and in activity) where I give myself a sense of self, i.e. where we really are equal in many ways, and then the things I have to do around the house, or the psychological demands which are made on me don't seem like a sacrifice. We did have this kind of a relationship for 3 years before the children were born—with kids it seems to me just about impossible and I'm frankly very discouraged and often feel little hope that it's possible for us to have a good relationship while the kids are little. They simply demand so fucking much and drain so much energy that there's not much time for any kind of development of one's self, and if the husband is involved totally, well, there you are. I had pretty much resigned myself when Douglass was born to 'accepting my role' until he was three and could go to nursery school—but when I read the article you sent the dam burst and I realized I couldn't repress myself for two more years, and that a fantastic amount of resentment and other ugly feelings have built up toward Julie. I do think that however rationally the case for the man's more important work may be made, that essentially that case is unacceptable emotionally— that kind of judgment about human beings is really impossible—and you must keep struggling for one's own survival, development and contribution, and that maybe it's just easier to do it alone without having that other presence around reminding you of what they aren't doing.

At least, that's the way it appears to me now. And I have the feeling that living separately, Julie is going to do a lot more child-care than he did before. It's just a constant struggle however you do it, being a wife to that kind of man and a person with a sense of self at the same time, but at least if one has engaged in the struggle and realizes that that's what it is, that's something positive. . . .

I do think you have to primarily do whatever it is you have to do, and then you'll be able to give the love and whatever else it is and the shit-work that the husband needs; if the latter is seen as the primary role in your life, then you can't really give what needs giving ungrudgingly if you've got any self-confidence and self-respect at all, and it ends up that you really aren't capable of doing anything.

But I didn't leave. Where would I go with the children?

Instead, Julius announced gravely one morning, toying with a pen on his gray metal desk, "I'm going South again next week."

I was so shocked it took me a minute to answer. "What? For how long?" The children played on the floor. Their teddy bears, dressed in tiny hats I had knit, ate lunch from pink plastic plates.

"I don't know," Julius said, looking as if he were pleased but trying to contain it. "I got a call from headquarters in Atlanta. They want me to come back and lead a cultural workers' project."

The teddy bear drank from a tiny pink cup I held to his lips.

"Can we come?"

"You know I can't take a white wife. And children." He stared me down, holding the black telephone receiver in his hand, waiting to dial. "It's too dangerous," he said, muttering, "Not only from the crackers."

"You can't leave us here again!" I cried. "Indefinitely. I'm sick of this shit."

"We've been through this over and over, Joan! No, you can't come."

He turned silently away, disappearing into a Black Revolution where I could not follow, while I fled into an imaginary Woman's Room where I would shut him out and write, if only I had such a room.

Revolutionary Notes

1969

Finally, after two years of working with SNCC in the South, Julius returned to stay. With his author money from *Look Out, Whitey!*, which students tucked under their arms on every college campus, we escaped New York for a marvel: Martha's Vineyard, where we rented a beach house in Gay Head. Suddenly not poor, how strange it felt to leave our public housing—"the projects"—for this elite enclave. After the dirt of New York, the rats and roaches, I felt plucked up by a great benevolent hand and set down in a peaceful, meandering paradise. Years of movement stress leached from my pores. "Shall we wage armed revolution?" gave way to "Where shall we fly kites today?"

Four-year-old Rosa and I walked all over our end of the island, enchanted by the hills and waving grasses. At our beach house I felt a familiar churn of emotions—pride, longing, and anger—while Julius wrote or flew alone to New York for his weekly radio show. Still, the nurturing I felt when embraced by sky and sun lifted me up.

When fall days arrived, we chose to stay on the island and move inland, away from the harsh winter winds roaring off the ocean. Then, living my dream of creating unfettered New Children, who would grow up to be the New Man and New Woman that Baldwin and Fanon showed was necessary, I followed my mother's footsteps and opened a school. It would be a Free School—free of tuition and mentally free. Thinking back to the time we'd liberated public schools during the Ocean Hill–Brownsville rebellion, I imagined truly radical education. I had read A. S. Neill's *Summerhill* about his British school where children were empowered, as we wanted everyone to be. These schools treated the learner as a co-creator of knowledge rather than an empty vessel to be filled. Having watched how Rosa discovered things for herself, figuring out how to create a book or open a complicated window or climb a tree, I wanted all children to enjoy that freedom. The Gay Head Town Hall donated space; parents contributed books and snacks. The eleven children that first year, including Rosa, were all Black or members of the Wampanoag nation.

At the Island Children's School, as I named it, we offered choices to three-, four-, and five-year-olds, trusting that successful choosing now would carry over into later life. They mixed their own bright blue-and-red finger paint and cooked fresh bluefish, which we ate with gusto. They created lists of their favorite words for reading lessons, and they built a wooden shack outside and painted it with vivid colors.

As the school expanded, I wrote essays for the local paper about our child-centered philosophy. "Education at Its Best Is Ecstatic," I titled one article. Still, I didn't think of these pieces as writing but as advocacy, seeking to convert adults to child-empowerment philosophy. Since we had assigned the category of Writer to Julius, who was so different from me—and so like the male authors of my college education—even when I published, even when I thrilled to the effort and pleasure I expended on these short essays, I never considered them serious writing.

On fire with my child-empowerment cause, my enthusiasm was contagious. Parents flocked from all over the island. Off-island educators visited, gushing, "This is a model of the new Open Education. Everyone looks so happy!" James Taylor, whose nephew little James was a student, generously gave us fundraising concerts. Occasionally we would see his lanky body coming through the door with little James. Once he brought Joni Mitchell, who strode in, tall and thin, a sheet of white-blonde hair hanging over her eyes.

"It's grand," she told me, with a strong Canadian accent and a huge toothy smile. Too busy with the children to be more than momentarily starstruck, I said, "Thank you," before I ran to help a boy mix water with sand for some glorious mud.

At school and with the parents at community meetings I organized, I was a leader, able to think clearly and inspire others. But try as I might with conversations deep into the night, I couldn't convince Julius to commit himself to our family.

"I'm thinking about living in a monastery," he told me one evening, after rereading Thomas Merton. "That may be my true calling." His furrowed brow rippled even more tightly.

"But you can't!" I grabbed his hands and held them. "You're a father."

As Julius ran farther afield and I tried to rein him in, we recycled our old conversations about his "calling" and my need for a co-parent, a mate. Attempting to shackle this unhappy writer felt as awful as my inability to do so.

"Let me go," he cried, thrusting his thin shoulders back.

Yet he stayed. And loved me, as best he could. Once he came home from New York with a new wedding ring, "a symbol of our renewed marriage," he told me, slipping it on my finger.

When his book *Revolutionary Notes* came out in 1969, only a year after *Look Out, Whitey!* and *To Be a Slave*, he wrote in the dedication:

> To Joan, whom I often confuse with myself, because the longer we live with each other, the more difficult it is for me to know where I leave off and she begins. That is as it should be.

> To Joan
> who is so much a part
> of my Being that to call her
> wife is to dehumanize her
> and vulgarize our relationship.

> So I will call her Joan
> because the sound of that name
> reverberates from every word
> I have written and every breath
> of my being which is also
> Joan

We were so entwined, I believed that someday, somehow, our marriage would improve. He would stay home, and I wouldn't be angry all the time. We would be free to express the love that still gurgled under our separate lives like a subterranean stream.

As I built a school community on my own, I felt a lightness in my step and noticed myself whistling when Julius wasn't around. He hated whistling; it hurt his ears. I remembered this was the way I used to feel, years ago. Powerful. Engaged. Smart.

Friends visited from New York and admired our country life on the Vineyard. "You have it all," envied one long-legged blonde, Prudy, the young white girlfriend of Julius's cut buddy Charles—who, I would later discover, had a Black wife back home. Charles, a round-faced man with glasses, had been beaten by a deputy sheriff in the Selma county jail, like many others. He was staunch, a full-time organizer for SNCC.

"Your school, your children, your marriage . . ." Prudy trailed off, looking around at the green lawn sparkling in late-summer twilight. "You know, you're a model for me," she gushed. "You're such a strong woman. I think about how you do the school, you have these beautiful children and a great marriage . . ."

"Julius and I are talking about separating," I cut her off, only half believing it myself.

"Why? I thought you two were the ideal couple."

"I hardly know any more. He doesn't want to live with children. Or me, really." I felt my face heat.

"Why?" She looked bewildered.

"Julius dreamt I smothered him with a pillow," I said, embarrassed. I, who so fervently believed in the evolution of all human potential, whether in New Children or Deep South sharecroppers, was chaining an extraordinary Black man, he had implied, by tying him down to family.

Rosa wandered over and rested her head in my lap. I stroked her forehead, brushing tendrils of curly hair from her face while Douglass nestled against my leg. A cool island breeze whispered against our bodies.

"I don't know what I want anymore. I'd like to keep trying to work it out." I lit a cigarette. "But he's gone so much . . ."

"I thought you liked his trips to New York. It gives you time to yourself."

"No, I don't, I hate it. It's too much, alone with the children for days. I feel crazy up here in the woods. At night I can't even see any house lights. We're so isolated. The nearest occupied house is a fifteen-minute walk away. And that's the only one for miles."

Her eyes widened, astonishing me, showing me how I came across to others. My capable appearance—and actions—covered such a tangle of difficult emotions: jealousy of Julius in the city, where he spent time with hordes of admiring women; anger at his free and easy ways, while I was left to cope with two messy young children; and self-hatred at my inability to rise above these nasty bourgeois feelings. Or to find my way into the writing career I craved. Would I forever be tossing off small pieces for newspapers or spending my nights on furious poetry and essays no one would read? At the core of my anger was resentment that Julius did so little child care, not allowing me time on my own, and my distress that as much as I cared about the school, I had not found a way to "be a writer." How I envied Julius his three books, his radio show, and a voice that everyone wanted to hear.

Trailed by children, Prudy and I strolled into the house. I peeled onions for a rice-zucchini-cheese dinner and rubbed a clove of garlic into my wooden salad bowl, inhaling its pungent aroma.

Soon Julius and Charles emerged from the corner of the vast living room where Julius's desk anchored his space. Serving the hot casserole and salad, I poured wine, with juice for the children. We four adults sat at our round oak table for hours, as Prudy and I listened to the men tell tall tales of the South.

"Man, them whiteys were so white I thought they had sheets on their faces."

"I know what you mean. . . . I damn near wet my pants. But I held my head up, I was a *man*."

"Man, you could put some shade on that shit." Julius and Charles howled and slapped hands.

"White folks so scared of us, I heard they takin' classes," Julius said, "learning to sleep with one eye open!"

"Shut up, fool."

While we laughed, my children trailed Charles's chunky six-year-old, Alicia. The three children capped their heads with red plastic bowls and marched naked through the living room, tooting imaginary horns and holding stuffed animals high until I scooped vanilla ice cream and called them back to their card table.

"Can we bring our bears to eat?"

"Yes," I said. "They can sit on your laps. Or we can make a special teddy-bear chair. Let's do that, so you don't drip ice cream on them. They're hard to wash." We settled all the bears into an extra chair I pulled up to the table.

Julius picked up his guitar. "When I get to heaven I got a question for the Lord," he sang in his deep bass voice. "How come you make a poor nigger's life so hard?"

Early in the morning after our peaceful evening, Julius and I quarreled.

"Do you have to leave again tomorrow?" I asked while we dressed. "Can't Charles go on without you this time?"

"You know I have to go. Why are you bringing this up again?"

"Black men," I threw out, "leaving their children. You're following in a long tradition."

"What?" he spun around, looking flabbergasted. "How dare you?"

"Charles," I backtracked. "He once suggested it, last year . . ." I trailed off miserably, shaking my head.

"I don't want to hear that garbage again. That's beneath you. This is not about race!"

"I know," I mumbled. "I'm sorry."

Later that day we argued again about something else. It could've been his upcoming departure or what I called his selfishness—the usual topics. Underneath these tired words of mine lay something deeper: jealousy. He was living his life to the full, wandering hither and yon at his pleasure, sharing beds with many women, I believed, though he denied it. And while I felt proud of the school I had founded, loved the students, honored their hardworking parents, and cherished time with my own children, I suspected there was something more for me that I didn't know how to actualize. So I blamed him.

Or politics could have been the subject of our dispute that day. More and more, politics were a charged topic for us. "Movements, ideologies, and causes destroy identity," he insisted these days. Despite being hailed as a radical hero after *Look Out, Whitey!* thrust him into a national spotlight, he had grown disenchanted with the movement. And it with him. "My Self can't survive a revolutionary movement. I'm an individual first," he maintained.

"Sometimes the need of the group is greater than that of individuals," I argued. "We're called on at this time to subsume our individual needs." (Strange that I took this position, since I had been infuriated when Julius made the same case for "your revolutionary duty is child care," so he could go South. And since he often used the line for his need to go South.)

"Individuals have as a first duty a commitment to unfolding our souls. Our destinies," he said.

I, with no idea yet of either a soul or a destiny, shot back, "After all the killings we've been through, you can't commit to the revolution?"

"I'm a poet. A writer. Artists have a higher calling. I have to be responsible to my gift."

This drove me crazy. "You can't commit to me or the children or the revolution, or even Black people, and you cloak that in this bullshit about God and the soul and being a mystic and a poet! Meanwhile people are dying. You know, Black people like in the Black Panther Party are trying to help, people who submit to revolutionary discipline."

"It's dangerous for writers to believe they should submit. Look at Baldwin. He's a spokesman now and what happened to his art? *Fire* was his last decent work. He's given up his calling as an artist: to be true to his own soul, not Black people's needs."

"Or their family's," I muttered.

Ignoring me, he said, "Baldwin no longer gives us a vision of who we can be."

I looked at him quizzically.

"All anybody can see now is Blacks as victim." He sounded bitter. "My only duty is to my soul, not any group of people. Like the ones who tell me I shouldn't be married to you." He paused for emphasis, letting that sink in. "And," he added for good measure, "the Black Panther Party is a gang of street thugs!"

"They're defending themselves against the cops! Who are murdering people every single day. They're inspiring Black people everywhere. Get some respect."

"Whatever happened to the beloved community? Now you're holding up men with guns who terrify people. Lining up in rows saluting. Groupthink."

"They're more than that. They feed children! They take people to the doctor. And the only people they're terrifying are white men in power. Maybe that's a good thing."

"They're a street gang who found themselves a good hustle."

We were talking from two different planets. But our bond was so deep it took years to fray, even as our battles wore us down.

"Let's go to therapy," I proposed. "We need help."

"Black people don't go to therapy," Julius said, dismissing me.

And so it went. That year, 1969, in an article for *Evergreen Review* called "White Woman—Black Man," Julius wrote, "Being black means you carry the world on your back twenty-four hours a day. Being black and married to a white woman means you carry it forty-eight hours a day. . . . Like the ol' folks used to say, 'Sometimes my cotton sack gets so heavy.' Every time we leave the house together, which is at least once a day, I can feel the people looking at us. . . . I'd just like to walk in [to a restaurant] and not be noticed by anyone except the waiter. . . . The fact that [my wife] is white is not uppermost in my mind. That's important in everybody else's mind. I'm not even sure I know what white means in relation to her. She doesn't communicate whiteness. She communicates [herself]."

"Did you mean that?" I asked him after I read the article.

"Yes. We have the right to be married! Black people have never accepted interracial relationships. Never. And now they're saying it loud and clear. If you're Black in America, it means you're not an individual," he sputtered. "You have to conform to a cultural idea of Blackness." In 1969 that meant hanging with other Black people. The proscription enraged him. "When I was a child, Black people demanded a certain kind of behavior from me because of white folks. What they'd think. Now Black people are demanding a certain kind of behavior from me because of other Black folks. I had one cat tell me the reason LeRoi Jones is a revolutionary is because he left his white wife."

Yet much as he might reject it, the Black Power imperative ate away at him. When he simply had to be around Black people, he split for the South.

But he always came home to me. And so we struggled on.

Until Tanya.

Over the fall of 1970, letters from Tanya, a woman Julius had met in Santa Fe, arrived with outrageous regularity. Soon, when I flipped open the metal box at the foot of our hill, I recognized her blue envelopes and round script.

Walking the mile to pick up the afternoon mail hadn't been a chore before. I cherished time alone on the path, soaking up the radiance of my beloved woods. Sunlight streamed through fir and birch groves, ferns spun endless pools, deer and cottontail rabbits darted ahead of me. Picking my barefoot way down the hill until late fall, when I pulled on boots, I had smiled all the way. But now making the trip back I struggled, wanting to tear up what I was sure were love letters. Dutifully I carried the stinging bundles home to Julius, who waited at his big gray desk. "What are they?" I would ask, storm in my voice.

"Nothing much." He waved his hand to suggest little of consequence, while he ripped them open.

"Who are they from?"

"You're so suspicious, Joan. Leave me alone. Let me have a life."

⁓

Julius and I hovered on the edge for months, with endless midnight talks. "I don't think we can make this work," he would say, while I argued for us. Weeks later he would buy me a gift for our "new start."

But ten months into the '70s, eight years after we had pledged to never spend a night apart, Julius, rolling out of bed, whispered, "I'm moving today." He hung his head and slid his eyes away, while I lay frozen.

"Moving? Where?" My body understood before my mind comprehended.

"I'm going to live with Tanya. In Boston." I had seen her at the conference where they met. He had taken the children and me along, and I had glimpsed them holding hands. He denied it, but I had seen their knotted fingers with my own stricken eyes.

Panicked at the abyss before me, I repeated my mantra. "You can't go, you can't leave the children and me here alone." I felt my eyes swell.

"We've talked about this for years," he said, sounding weary. "You and I can't live together."

The specter of loneliness cut through me like the chill island wind. I pulled covers up over my ears while he continued to talk, detailing my flaws—my poor housekeeping, my mercurial moods—and the virtues of his new lover: especially her adoration. Plus she was a woman of color, thereby letting him off the hook, at last, for "talking Black and sleeping white." Protecting him from the charge that he either hated himself or hated women of color.

"Tanya," he said with pride, "is reclaiming her Native American roots. She walks barefoot all the time, even through the winter in Boston." As my tears trickled over the quilt, he added, in a voice filled with awe, "She doesn't own any shoes."

Stunned by grief, I was nonetheless impressed, trying to imagine the toughness of the woman's feet, the resolve in her heart. I thought about the coldness of snow. Ice. Slush. All barefoot. I wiggled my toes at the foot of the bed.

So this was the end.

But it wasn't. Two weeks later he returned, saying, amid tears, "I missed you too much." And I let him stay. I cried so hard at any hour of day or night—or, alternately, raged at full volume—that he soon left again. Back to Tanya, who called every day, supplying her own fulsome tears.

And so it went for a couple of months. He bounced back and forth while we unwound ourselves from each other. As he had said in his dedication to *Revolutionary Notes*, he didn't know where he left off and I began. The same was true for me. We had grown up with each other, fused together in the heat of the '60s.

And now, as we closed the first year of a new decade, it was over. He wrote me, "I know that probably one of the things that has gone through your mind is the 'unfairness' of my leaving, that I leave to lead the life I want to, unencumbered by children. . . . From the inside, though, it looks different. . . . In a way, I think we, as individuals, face the same basic problem: Building lives without the other. And if the prospect is alternately exciting and depressing for you, it is the same for me. There was a certain security in our being together, a security because we were dealing with what was known, what was familiar. Now, perhaps more even for me than for you, there is nothing but the unknown. And, sometimes, it scares me. I want to come back, because no matter how bad it got, at least being with you was familiar. Being married was familiar. There were few dangers. Now there are many." He was even afraid to try writing, he said, because I had read every word he had written. Could he do it alone?

Months later he wrote me, "I approached the typewriter like an athlete recovering from an injury, afraid that the former suppleness of his muscles will not return." Yet he did it, wrote a book review for the *New York Times*, and knew then he would be able to go on alone.

Reading his letter, I felt a familiar churn: pain that he had moved on without me, excitement about my own possibilities, and the old rage at his assumption that I would raise our two young children alone. Much as I adored them, I couldn't imagine how I could handle my own life and theirs, without a mate.

Sisterhood Is Powerful

1970

At first Rosa, Douglass, and I played hearts and gin rummy until all hours, gorging on strawberry Pop-Tarts. When their eyes drooped, I bundled them into their beds, which I had moved to my room.

Now that the children and I could do whatever we wanted, what I wanted was to run my hand across paper with a pen or pound on the typewriter. Once the Writer disappeared, my need shot up like a geyser, and soon I reverted to normal bedtimes for the children. Evenings, after I cleared the dining table, read stories, and tucked them into bed, I poured questions onto paper, composing poems deep into the night. Julius's desk sat empty in a corner of the living room, but the dining table had been my spot for so long that I stuck to it. Bent over my old Underwood, fingers nestled into its round white keys, I sipped red wine and played Carole King's *Tapestry* album, warmed by her promise, "You've Got a Friend." The carriage slammed back and forth as I hammered out poems.

"Housewife, I didn't plan to marry a house," I wrote bitterly, starting "Thought Interruptus."

We begin, beginnings to end
Abrupt
Thought interruptus
Yes you told us
Women's work is never done. We are always on call
Midwives to other lives.
Where are your scientists?
You ask us

Proving proof.
Painters poets presidents
(Aching breaking bones flung from careless cars)
Were you ever burned
Nine million female heresies?
Were you ever denied a job
Because your uterus held
Unfertilized potential?
Or because there was no separate toilet
Fitted for your sex? State law.
And how can I tell you
My head holds grocery lists real good
But I'm suffering from a kind of brain damage.
A certain tightening of the muscles is my symptom
When I hear you say
And what did you do
Today?

The act of writing, selecting the perfect word, holding it in my hands to assess its weight, the feel of its sound against its neighbor, gave me strength.

Dream-ravaged eyes turn inward
Soon I will scream if I cannot write
It out, release the pain
That is torturing me insane.
I lay thinking of calling you to say
You must take the children for more than a day
And raging already at your kind
Patronizing
Insulting
Refusal.

Reams of poetry piled up. But I never considered publishing. Believing the world's dismissal of words about women or children as craft, not Art, I viewed my nighttime writing as something to soak in while I healed. The way a gardener inhales the nourishing aroma of moist earth, I inhaled and exhaled words.

The mere movement of my pen across a lined yellow pad, or the feel of the smooth indented typewriter keys against my finger pads, soothed me as I tried to ease the stab in my chest. I wrote instinctively, like an animal craving water, typing up multiple versions of poems until every word fell into its proper place and my soul was at peace.

A thirty-year-old woman living deep in the woods, I tried to let the winds of life blow through me as the children squealed, slid down stairs on an old mattress, or climbed out our mullioned windows onto a wide ledge spanning the back wall.

"I have to pee," Rosa would announce, grabbing her crotch.

"All right, climb out." The only bathroom was downstairs in our upside-down house. Upstairs, the children loved cranking open our high narrow windows, stepping onto the wooden birdfeeder, squatting, and peeing onto the ground below. The house was built into the side of a hill; the drop-off was six feet, with grass below. I trusted my sure-footed climbers to stay up, and they did. And in the free years of the early '70s, climbing out a window to squirt pee seemed exactly the right sort of daring adventure to allow the New Child.

"Ma." Rosa, my shadow, was ever at my side. "Why isn't Daddy living with us?"

"It's hard to explain." My stomach boiled. "He needs to live somewhere else. He'll always love you, though. And he'll always be your daddy." I knew the right words yet hardly believed them myself.

"My rage is as strong as the force that is my life / And that is very strong," I read to my best island friend, Amy, announcing, "This poem's to Julius." I took a drag from a cigarette and set it back in the blue astray. "Every time I hear a midnight child's door open / I silently scream. Our two worlds meet at knife-point."

Amy looked stricken. "How sad," she said. Not "How profound," as I had hoped.

Julius and I tussled still. He visited occasionally to see the children; each time I harassed him, citing "your abandonment, your lack of child care. Your *promises* to me." Tugging on the robe of betrayed wife, I rarely let up on him, though I did puzzle privately over what I had done wrong to suffer like this. Julius and I talked frequently on the phone, trying to bandage our hurt, but these conversations often ended in tears—usually mine and sometimes his. Soon he visited less and less.

Drowning in loneliness, choked by pain and resentment, I wondered how I could survive.

While the children played around my ankles, my brain went clickety click. Scribbling poetry that seeped from the nights into the day, I cared for them with my mind half present. Loss—and working out lines in my poems—gripped me until I struggled for breath. Douglass and Rosa scampered like wood urchins onto paths near our house, shrieking with joy. But my center, for the first time since they had been born, was elsewhere.

"I've covered all the pain with paper-mache," I wrote about my teenage past, not understanding why I had felt so despairing I had tried to kill myself. Instinctively, using Scottish psychiatrist R. D. Laing's book *Knots*, where he recommended "falling apart" as the necessary prelude to "falling together," I allowed myself to shatter. Letting go of any pretense, I functioned at a minimal level: meals for the children and meetings with staff for the school I directed. The rest of the time I drifted.

Doris Lessing's novel *The Golden Notebook* gave added permission to my disintegration. For months I read and reread it, puzzling out a story spread over a series of colored notebooks, with "Free Woman" sections scattered throughout. In the center lies Anna Wulf, an accomplished author. Frantically coming apart, depressed, she tries to integrate her splintered parts: mother, author, lover, citizen. I admired Anna, identified with her struggle for wholeness. A woman's mental breakdown can be a means to healing, Lessing showed, when she lets go of her illusions about life.

I had believed in two illusions, I saw. Contradictory ones at that: Julius and I were two free intellectuals, à la de Beauvoir and Sartre writing side by side in cafés, unencumbered. And there was truth in this. Julius did see my mind as kin to his, even if it was handmaiden to his talents. That was a gift in a world where the intelligence inside my blonde, blue-eyed head was often overlooked. But once we had children and their care fell to me, the café fantasy was hard to sustain. Even before children, I had to admit, I wasn't writing "creative literature." Only papers for school or radical book reviews.

Simultaneously I carried an image of the nuclear family based on a child's-eye view of my parents' devotion, my affectionate father reliably returning home every day at six. That was never going to work with Julius at this stage of his life, yet I held on to the dream, tried to force it, way beyond any reasonable expectation.

Stripped of my two models for women in love, all I could do was stay true to my rage, "a motor strapped to my back that keeps me afloat," I wrote, and see where it led. As I spiraled downward and grew unable to read or concentrate even on a newspaper, I wandered the woods and wrote, spewing pain, turning bits into poetry and letting the rest hang loose like entrails from a dying horse. Where could I go, stuck like this on an island with two small children, my emotions unraveling?

One day when I could hardly care for the children, I left them with my visiting sister while I drove off to spend the night at Amy's house. Rosa chased my car, screaming, "We hate you!" Understandably, since my gaze, so long directed at her, had become unfocused.

If I couldn't even cope with my own children, how would I manage for the rest of my life? How would I earn a living for us to supplement what Julius sent, and how long would his checks continue? What would our lives become?

In the depth of winter, when our mile-long dirt road—where ours was the only inhabited house—turned to mud and the tires spun uselessly every time I tried to go out, I hit bottom. Standing in mud up to my calves, trying to dig out the car once again, I began to bawl. "I'm losing my mind. I can't go on in this isolated house. Stuck."

As my tears grew more intense, with chest heaving I dropped the shovel and threw myself into the cold mud. If I couldn't even dig the car out, how would I dig myself and the children out of the mess we were in, living without a mate deep in the woods?

Nauseous, I finally dragged myself up, covered in mud, and staggered into the house to vomit. But what I threw up in the toilet were tiny figures who tumbled out of my mouth into the bowl. I saw them clearly. Small rounded beings, fully dressed.

Panicked, I called the only psychiatrist on the island, whom I had met when he donated to the Island Children's School.

Soon I sat in his office crying.

"How can I help you?" he asked kindly.

"I threw up little bodies into my toilet bowl. I saw them spinning through the air waving their little arms and legs before they fell into the toilet."

He looked at me with concern.

"Am I psychotic?"

"It sounds to me like a drug reaction," he said quietly. "Have you taken LSD?"

"No. I've never tried anything like that. I'm afraid I'd never come back from the trip."

"Any other drugs?"

"No. Wine."

"Perhaps someone put it into a drink you had?"

I shook my head. "No. Except a little pot every once in a while."

He persisted, "Maybe somebody slipped LSD to you without you being aware of it."

"No." I was crying heavily. "Where can I go? I live at the end of a dirt road with no occupied houses for a mile. I can't even see a light through the trees. It's just me and the kids in a big lonely house in the middle of nowhere. I'm falling apart."

"I have something I think will help." He scribbled a prescription. "Try this," he said as he ushered me out of his office.

The following day I swallowed one of the pills. Thorazine. But it made me feel so woozy, like a zombie, that I flung the bottle in the garbage. "I can't believe he gave me this," I fumed to Amy. "If I was barely functioning before, this would be the knock-out! I can't believe people actually take this stuff."

I never returned to the psychiatrist.

As January ebbed into February, I kept furiously writing, following R. D. Laing's advice to heal myself by exposing all my pain. The small figures I had seen, I decided, were people from my past that I was releasing. Purging. Trusting Laing, I stopped worrying about losing my mind and put all my energy into restoring myself through writing and exploring the woods. I soaked up tree medicine, inhaling the rustic smells, touching solid bark. I lay on the earth, its rich loamy aroma grounding me. I wept at the beauty of sky medicine, its brilliant blue pulsing into my chest. Cloud medicine. I drank every drop in the bottle.

I never did figure out where all the pain came from. Was it simply being a smart female in a man's world, suffering daily harassments? Or was it finding myself alone, responsible for two other beings, without my soul mate?

Whatever the source of my collapse, nature's medicine worked. By March I had passed through the worst and birthed a small, authentic self, feeling as tender as a newborn turtle without a shell. When spring buds burst, I wrote to Ann Mari,

> I've felt so strange, in a dream-world of my head, and I yank myself out just enough to respond to the children's most insistent needs, and my god how I don't know how, I kept the school together and did snap myself into that kind of reality for meetings and again, the minimum necessary to do the

job . . . but all the time underneath my head was swirling confusion. And all that writing . . . drawers full of my tattered self. But I came through, and here I am. Pretending I'm still the me that everybody knew but I'm not. Somebody else is growing inside me, pushing, who needs room. I like her/me.

I enjoy the children so much again. I enjoy feeling the breeze on my body. I had forgotten how much joy I used to get out of life. Come soon, we'll play in the meadow.

⁓

Ann Mari, a breath of solid sanity, did visit for a week. Life was returning. Then Robin Morgan arrived, toting her baby boy and a copy of her new anthology, the wildly successful *Sisterhood Is Powerful*. She had done an epic job, including essays by every influential feminist. Eleanor was there, Flo Kennedy and others, plus fifteen poets raging free of "proper" diction. Robin credited me in her acknowledgments, as Julius had. Again I was pleased to be thanked, though painfully aware I had let the opportunity for my own anthology slip away.

But poring through the book, six hundred pages, linked me to the world again. My suffering wasn't simply my individual failing. Women were all failing in patriarchy, trying to accommodate ourselves, find wiggle room, rebel. "There is no adequate personal solution."

"Every woman who heals herself heals all women," Robin reminded me while we lounged, looking out to the pine forest surrounding my house. For the first time in months, I could hear robins calling to each other, see the slant light falling tenderly on their orange and red breasts, watch sunlight dapple trees.

"We took over *Rat*," Robin exulted. "WITCH sat in and took it over completely. We put out a Women's Liberation issue. The male left is on notice: no more sexism. We mean it!" (WITCH, the Women's International Terrorist Conspiracy from Hell, had seized control of the famous New York underground paper *Rat*.)

After nights of inspired conversation, I felt filled and nourished. How much I had missed my connection with activist women. Robin left me with Toni Cade's new anthology, *The Black Woman: An Anthology*. Alice Walker, Paule Marshall, Abbey Lincoln, Grace Lee Boggs. The assembled voices lifted my spirits. What was I doing out here in the woods?

The three of us stuck out in our mid-island town.

"The Fresh Air Fund?" one puzzled white woman hazarded a guess at the grocery store when I pushed the children, for a lark, in a metal cart. Rosa was five, Douglass three.

"What?" Her comment momentarily confused me. "No, they're mine." I steeled myself for the grilling, decided against it, and rolled away, leaving the woman to puzzle out our family on her own.

"What's the Fresh Fund?" Douglass asked, turning his sweet face up to me.

"Oh, I don't know. It's about city children. She doesn't understand we're a family. She's a silly lady."

If the probing looks made me clasp them more tightly—"These are my children!"—they also fanned my longing to flee these woods filled with white dropouts. I didn't know if I could survive another island winter, with the whistling winds and rains, the deep muddy ruts and barren gray trees. The isolation.

Maybe it was time to venture out of the cocoon. Though I had no idea where to go, the idea of leaping into a new life grew more appealing every day. And I was free to jump. The Island Children's School had stabilized enough that it would survive without me. (And it did. Fifty years later, it endures with the same child- and community-centered philosophy.) I could move on. In New York City one weekend, when I was visiting Nancy and Steve Schwerner, I put my dollar in a photo booth slot and snapped a roll of pictures. Yes, they showed me, it was true: I had birthed a new self and there she was, eyes sparkling.

Later that weekend I met a man in a bar, a warm and wise ex-prisoner. Prentice Williams had done sixteen years in a Greenhaven cell for teenage drug sales—set up by police, he said—and robbery. He had been so lonesome in prison, he told me, "I'd have loved a garbage can if it loved me back." In an era when Eldridge Cleaver's prison memoir *Soul on Ice* was a best seller and *Soledad Brother: The Prison Letters of George Jackson* was every radical's Bible, I saw Prentice as a former political prisoner whose real crime had been growing up Black and poor.

He visited our island home, playing his trumpet into the evening air while I lay on a giant rock in front of the house, hearing jazz tones sail through the open windows. The children, their exuberant bodies always in motion, climbed this big, strong man the way they climbed trees in our yard. And after Julius, the cool intellectual, maybe this unlettered man who was all heart was precisely what the three of us needed. He would be the perfect,

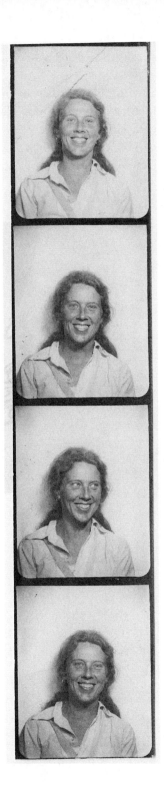

Photos of Joan from a New York City photo
booth, circa 1971. (author's archive)

attentive Black father for my biracial children. After so many years with Julius, a comfort around Black culture and people gave me an immediate ease with Prentice.

After three months I hugged him and said, "Yes, we'll move back to New York with you. We'll come in the fall."

How little I understood the man he really was. Or the woman I had become.

They Shall Not Pass

1971

One object stood in the Brooklyn apartment: a giant oak rolltop desk. I lunged, pulled on carved handles to reveal deep drawers, and opened tiny doors shielding small cubbies. This substantial desk dominated an entire side of the dining room, where built-in cabinets covered one wall and a fireplace centered another. A splendid, formidable desk, left by the landlord when he moved south. I claimed it even before unpacking.

That first night I pawed through boxes until I found sheets for my platform bed. But Prentice angrily pulled the sheets from my hand.

"I won't lie on a bed you've slept in with another man!"

"That's ridiculous." I tugged on the sheets. "What difference could it make that a year ago Julius slept on it?"

Prentice wrapped his muscular arms around me. "But you're my woman now."

"I'm not 'your woman.' I'm my own woman." I tried to yank away. "I suppose we can't use these sheets either? He slept on them!"

"You're mine," he repeated, squeezing me tightly.

"I belong to myself!"

I squirmed away, while he drove off. Hours later my new partner returned with a rusty brass headboard, a mattress smelling of piss, and a smattering of scratched, mismatched furniture. *My bed was disgusting—and this one isn't?*

"Feeling submerged already," I scrawled that night. "I hate my plastic modern no-character living room and the bedroom too." But I had made this enormous move and needed to affirm it, no matter how much I was rattled by the noise of the city, the crowds.

Our first Saturday, Prentice, the children, and I drove to the Chelsea Hotel, where Julius lived. At first my ex seemed tense. "Hey, brother." He slapped hands with Prentice.

"Nice pad you got here." My new man, wearing a green, gold, and black dashiki, rocked back and forth on his heels while Rosa and Douglass climbed on him. "I'm their jungle-gym," Prentice joked. Proud.

I hung back, wanting these two men in my life to get along.

"So brother, what work do you do?" Julius asked, though I was sure I had told him.

"I direct an ex-prisoner job program." Prentice lifted the children, one hanging from each bicep. "These are my climbers." He smiled, swinging them back and forth. I melted, watching this handsome man pay rapt attention to my heaven, the two stars upon whom my days rose and nights fell.

Julius gravely blessed his in-home replacement. "I think you'll be a good father," he pronounced. "Catch you later, brother."

As a father, Prentice at first proved to be everything Julius wasn't. He drove carpool, asked the children about their days, and helped with school projects. Quick to spin words and passionate about his ex-prisoner cause, he seemed to float easily from the rubble of his impoverished childhood into middle-class life. He held me all night, wrapped in embrace. I felt safe, cherished. Home. Until the afternoon he said, "My parole officer warned I'm in big trouble, living with you. It's a parole violation."

I stared blankly.

"We have to get married."

"I don't want to get married," I said, standing by my desk. "It contradicts all my beliefs."

"You want me back in prison?" He paced, which he often did. Like a caged animal. Or a caged man.

"No. Of course not." I touched my desk for strength.

"It's only paper. What difference does it make? I have to have it for us to live together." Prentice stood in front of me, a hulk of massed energy.

"I stopped using 'Mrs.' years before Julius and I split. I don't want marriage to ruin us. The institution. The structure."

"It won't," he swore.

"I want us to just be two people."

"We are." He smiled his radiant smile. "Marriage is only a piece of paper. Like this one." He snatched a blank paper from the top of my desk and dramatically tore it in half. "See. Paper. That's not us." He pointed to me and then himself.

"Marriage does something to people, Prentice. Chains them."

"Not us. Don't you think we're smarter than that?"

"I don't know." I shook my head.

"Baby, I have to have it! There's no option."

I didn't answer for a long while. "If it's merely a piece of paper . . ." I faltered. "So okay, if it's only paper and you need it. But don't ever call me Mrs."

Once again I fought back tears on a wedding day, pledging "I Do" before fifty friends jammed into our dining room. A raucous party followed our vows before a prison chaplain, our stereo blasting, "I heard it through the grapevine, and I'm just about to lose my mind." I wasn't sure if I was losing mine, with these Black ex-prisoners and reformed prostitutes in tiny skirts who didn't look all that reformed, mingling with the Schwerners and Ann Mari, plus Maxine Wolfe, a white professor living upstairs who wore a brown-and-white-checked pantsuit. *What's going on?*

While Prentice poured his extravagant energy into his job with the Fortune Society, helping men emerging from prison, I spent my days teaching at a nearby Community School. "I can't believe I get paid to do this," I marveled. Three nights a week, I ran to catch the train to Manhattan for Bank Street graduate classes, adding an underpinning of theory to my ad hoc educational methods. Every class fascinated me.

Yet being a wife automatically threw me into battle. My own contradictory beliefs—men are patriarchal pigs / we need a man in this family / nuclear families oppress women—kept me reeling.

After we married, Prentice said, "I'd like you to change your name."

"If I'd thought about it the first time, even known it was an option, I wouldn't have done it," I refused, feet planted wide apart, hand on hip in the kitchen. I turned to hand him the old-fashioned I had blended from a powdered mix.

"You've got another man's name!" He smashed down his drink.

"It's my name now." I sprinkled garlic powder in a pan. "I've had it for ten years. I'm used to it." I added a pinch of oregano. "And the children would feel strange having a different last name."

"How do you think I feel with the three of you having Julius's name?" Prentice leaned against the wall of the kitchen wedged in the middle of our apartment.

I took a sip of his drink, feeling bourbon heat my chest. "Oh, every woman has some man's name. What's the difference, my father's or his name or yours?" I stirred the spaghetti and muttered, "Slave names."

"If it doesn't make any difference, then take mine!"

"Which some ancestor of yours got from a slave owner."

"So did Julius's!"

"No, I'm not going to have a different name from the children! And I'm not going to be Mrs. You."

He glowered but couldn't move me on that one.

The more I sat at my massive oak desk, writing on its grainy surface, filling its drawers with my journals, the more I felt my 115 pounds swell into importance. I stuffed its cubbies with memorabilia: a red Lenin pin, smooth stones from Ann Mari, a piece of turquoise my sister sent. This desk was my land, my nation. Huge and imposing, it formed a carapace over my tender new psyche. After I closed the wooden roll, no one else slid it open. Even Prentice understood this zone of personal space.

Yet I despaired, writing, "I'm sinking down into housewifery and all those feelings that go with it: jealousy, envy, feeling incompetent, demoralized, unsure of everything, don't know how to cope. Kids gnawing at me, want to scream. I've lost myself already, and thinking what I've left, sky, woods, and a beautiful school, for this."

Whenever I lay in bed reading, Prentice complained, caressing my shoulder, "You've always got your face in a book. That's not real life. It's only stories."

"I have to read," I would say, turning the page. How had other women found their way? I devoured *They Shall Not Pass: The Autobiography of La Pasionaria* by the Spanish Civil War icon Dolores Ibárruri. Three hundred fifty pages of inspiration. How did she, a mother who had once been a maid, bloom into an organizer, an orator, a writer? She survived lethal poverty by pure grit and spirit, educated herself, and blossomed into a leader.

I gulped down every book I could find about women's lives. Doris Lessing's Martha Quest novels, featuring a rebellious young woman stifled in marriage, resonated strongly. How can I have love and be my own person, Martha Quest agonized. How, indeed? What a terrible choice: loneliness or swamped by male entitlement.

Marge Piercy's novels *Going Down Fast* and *Small Changes*, burning with anger, reminded me that other women had exactly the same questions.

How could I maintain autonomy in marriage? Hadn't Prentice promised me this would be "just a piece of paper"? Now that seemingly innocuous paper was deploying bombs into every area of my life.

Like driving. Marge Piercy's stories about women showed I wasn't crazy to insist on a driver's license in my own name, instead of the one New York state automatically issued after this marriage. I wasn't Joan Williams and never would be, but that was the name on this important document. My bank account, credit card, and everything else used Joan Lester.

Cashing checks became an ordeal. "Photo ID please," a clerk would ask pleasantly.

"The state made me get this in my married name," I would start to explain to the clerk. "I don't ever use that name."

The clerk would look at me with a puzzled frown. We would argue, and eventually I usually got what I needed. But it was a huge hassle. I began to dread any official dealings, trying to prove that Joan Lester and Joan Williams were the same person.

So I petitioned the Department of Motor Vehicles to get my name back.

But I lost. My legal name, they ruled, was Joan Williams. I had to use the driver's license in that name. Mandatory. No exceptions. "You could go to court to try to legally change your name," one DMV manager told me. "But I don't know if they will. Since you're married." He gave me a significant look, as if I were demented, perhaps not even capable of realizing I *was* Mrs. Joan Williams.

Prentice and I fought constantly. "You're my wife," he would say, trying to clinch arguments. Meaning: I should submit. "I thought it was just a piece of paper!" I would shout and run from the room.

Marge Piercy showed me I wasn't insane to insist that Prentice not grab tape from my hand, if it took me a second to rip a piece off the roll. "Let me do it!" I heard myself say over and over, like a child. "I may not be as strong as you, but I can manage tape!"

A man herded from cell to cell, shackled for sixteen years, now determined exactly what he would do and when, and no one better give him any lip. Everything infuriated him. Slow waiters in restaurants ("It's because I'm Black!") caused him to drag us all out, loudly swearing, "This fucking white racist dump."

Humiliated, I began to resist family outings.

"Now you're too good to go out with me? Little Miss Sunshine, living in a dream world where you think everybody's nice, like in your books. They're not!"

"That's not it, goddam it!" I shook my head in frustration.

Ignorant of the habits required for the middle-class life he had entered—like noting the amount of a check on a stub, putting oil in the car when the gauge read empty, or obeying alternate-side-of-the-street parking—Prentice frequently stumbled. Each fall triggered fireworks.

I was equally unfamiliar with the customs of longtime marginalized folks. "Why are you going to take the electric payment all the way there in person?" I would grumble when he planned to set off on the subway. "That's such a waste of time. Mail a check!"

Or the telephone bill: "Why pay cash when we can write a check?" His habits made no sense to me. "Don't cash your paycheck at the loan shark! And have to pay a fee. Deposit it at the bank! And enter it in the check-book." Which he rarely did, so for the only time in my life, I bounced checks.

After two years of fighting, one grim morning when Prentice had stayed out all night—again—and slunk in at six with long red hair all over his jacket, I said, exhausted, "You have to move."

"No."

"Yes, I can't take this pain anymore."

"I'm sorry," he whispered. "I love you too much. I had to do something on my own that doesn't involve you. To get myself back."

"Like making out with a red-haired woman? You had to do that?"

He stared at me. "But I love you both. I want both of you."

"You can't have me then. No way!" I was shouting.

"Couldn't we all three live together?"

"Are you fucking crazy? No way! You have to leave, Prentice. Go with her. I'm tired of the pain. This marriage isn't working," I heard myself say. Exactly what Julius had said to me before he left: "I'm tired of the pain."

"I don't want to hurt you. I always end up hurting people," Prentice whimpered. "I'm bad." He put his head in my lap.

Startled, I let him lie there. "You're not bad," I said wearily.

"But bad people go to prison. I must be bad." He began to sob.

"Poor people go to prison," I said through my own tears. "Look at all the good work you've done." He cared deeply about the men in his ex-prisoner program. But he had no idea how to live on the outside.

"I'm sorry. I haven't been easy, either." Riddled with my own contradictions, plus fierce in my insistence that I knew what was best for *my* children, I had hardly been a trouble-free wife. "But you have to pack," I insisted, despite the strong erotic attraction that remained. I was adamant that he leave, so after we made love, weeping, I repeated, "Take everything. Take it all."

He left on Christmas Day. While he tromped through the living room dragging load after load in black garbage bags, I rocked in a chair near the decorated tree. Pine fragrance suffused the room. The children slowly opened presents, trying to distract their disconsolate mother.

"Look, Ma." Rosa showed me a homemade wooden jigsaw puzzle from my parents. She sat near my chair spilling brightly colored pieces on the floor, gazing anxiously up at a face that must have looked wretched. "Don't be sad. We're here."

Douglass zoomed by with his new battery-operated car. "Shh," Rosa said. "Ma needs quiet."

He softly patted my leg and nestled his head against me.

Soon clothes and toys, torn wrapping paper, and pieces of ribbon littered the room. As twilight fell, I sat in the gloom, looking out at silhouettes of bare trees until I rose, shuffled to the kitchen in my ragged white terrycloth robe, and rummaged in cupboards. I opened a can of chipped beef, melted butter in a pan, stirred in a heaping tablespoon of flour with a sprinkle of salt and pepper, added a cup of milk for the white sauce, and popped three pieces of bread in the toaster for one of our favorite meals: chipped beef on toast.

The next day I raced to Macy's, an unheard-of occasion since I relied on free boxes or friends' castoffs. Only for the children's back-to-school clothes did I brave department stores. But I splurged on a comforter: white with lilies of the valley, long slender stems with green leaf sprays scattered over the lovely field. And matching sheets. Just looking at the flowers calmed me, reminding me of the Vineyard's beauty.

When Julius and I talked that evening, he said, sounding truly grieved, "I'm sorry. I thought Prentice was a good man, a good father."

"He was. We were too different, though. He wanted a compliant wife," like you did, I thought. "And I was anything but."

Julius was silent, until he surprised me by saying, "You're a good woman and you deserve a good man. One who will appreciate you. I'm sorry I couldn't give you what you wanted. Or needed."

"Thank you," I said, comforted by my old companion's words. After all we had been through, he knew me better than anybody, and when we talked at length, as we often did, it felt like old times. Held by this warm, familiar voice, my grief subsided.

That night I snuggled alone under the new comforter and let the peace of the household wash over me. Again the children and I would be left to our own ways. Once more I was free. A new year, 1973, was about to begin. How would I meet it?

Power

1973

Late evenings I sat at my rolltop desk and wrote, filling page after page while Marvin Gaye wailed, my fingers thumping on the typewriter keys, keeping time with the trumpets, drums, sax, and guitars. I latched onto the desk as if it were a raft carrying me across a boiling sea, calming my soul.

When I tired of writing, I would call Julius, a night owl who was always ready to chat in the wee hours. One night he told me, "We were mere children when we married, afraid of the wolves which materialized at the edge of the forest at dusk."

I marveled, just as I used to, at his eloquence.

"We were magnets of need," he said. "Using each other as shelter from the terror of trying to be a person."

"Although actually," I said, "you clung to me when you moved in after I'd found my own apartment. Remember? How you showed up at the door? I really wanted it, wanted to be alone. Why did you come?"

"I was afraid. Afraid of losing you. Afraid I might not survive alone any longer."

"Really?"

"I was afraid I might commit suicide."

I was silent, shocked.

"I'm sorry," he said. "If I'd given you that time to define yourself, we might have had a better marriage."

"Yes, we might have." I paused. "I'm sorry too, that I was so angry all the time. I just couldn't accept you being gone most of the time. And I was riveted to 'fairness.' If I had accepted the way things were . . ."

"We were young, and you were finding your way."

Self-portrait, pencil drawing, circa 1975. (author's archive)

"I still am."

Once more I scribbled poems deep into the night, drank red wine, nodded to Coltrane's *A Love Supreme* or to Otis Redding wailing on *Dock of the Bay* and filled legal pads with pain and fury, unaware that I was practicing my art. The act of writing again became medicine, soothing me until Les McCann's scratchy voice on "Compared to What" sent my questions into overdrive. I shouted along each time the line came up: "Trying to make it real—compared to what?"

I took to sketching my face as I stared into the ornate mirror over the fireplace, trying to capture my essence in pencil strokes. If I could only see myself clearly, maybe I would know how to move forward, fulfill whatever promise was in me and avoid another heartbreak.

And I wrote.

Jazz Riffs of the Fifties

Miles magic, swirl nostalgia. Jazz refractions shatter light-time. Spacious nights of jazz.

15 years ago I wandered barefoot in Chicago into a club where I heard a confusion of notes, the real Dizzy. Unknowing what the notes meant or who he was . . . the sounds penetrated deep.

Bird was a poem on the wall.

Chuck Berry made the fifties bearable.

Lady Day. Only now I get angry, as at Janis Joplin, for singing the mas-o-chi-sm woman blues, 'Leave me baby so I can hear the crying sound.'

Mingus, that big fat thumb dominated and dwarfed the giant bass. Last week I heard him, thumb diminished, said to have been analyzed. Sure refined his tone.

Birdland Coltrane, sounds I didn't know existed reverberated through the night. Sax notes poke lovely anguished holes in my soul . . . when he plays, I'm whole.

Still I followed the tradition of women spiriting pages into private drawers, stowaways sheltered from critical eyes. As Honor Moore wrote, much of our literary history lies "buried as ladies' poems have been / in bureau drawers for years." I saw myself as a woman who wrote. Constantly. But not a Writer.

Other women were braver. I discovered Audre Lorde's poem "Power" in the *Village Voice*. It narrated the trial for the killing of ten-year-old Clifford

Glover, who had been walking with his stepfather in Queens when they ran into two white undercover cops looking for Black robbery suspects. One officer ordered, "Stop!"

Believing Shea and his plainclothes partner were robbers, Clifford and his father ran. Officer Shea shot Clifford twice. When put on trial for murder—the first NYC on-duty officer ever tried—he said, "I didn't notice the size nor nothing else, only the color." His acquittal triggered days of "riots," meaning cops beating Negro protesters who were marching in the street.

That could have been eight-year-old Douglass, I thought, when he walked with Prentice, whose slow, deliberate rock was a jailhouse roll. A pig would not have thought twice about executing them, not noticing "size nor nothing else, only the color." Or Douglass could have been walking with Julius. Being an intellectual didn't necessarily protect a man, I had learned. Sometimes it only made the cops madder.

Lorde's poem described the jury in Officer Shea's trial: "eleven white men who said they were satisfied justice had been done" and the heartbreak of "one Black woman who said, 'They convinced me,'" meaning that after four hundred years of terror they had made this small woman so eager for white male approval she relinquished her first real power and "lined her womb with cement."

How had Audre Lorde found the clarity of these words and the courage to publish them? How did she dare? I taped the poem in my top desk drawer, where my eyes lingered on it daily.

Women's poetry began to appear all around me as more women found their voices. Adrienne Rich's "Diving into the Wreck" reminded me I wasn't the only one questioning my female/mother/wife role. Or my sanity. Her forceful, personal lines resonated; I read them over and over, along with Marge Piercy's book of free verse, *To Be of Use*. Their anger and confusion matched mine, as Piercy wrote, "like a woman whose mouth hardens / to hold locked in her own / harsh and beautiful song."

I discovered May Sarton's *Journal of a Solitude* after she wrote an op-ed for the *New York Times* affirming the pleasures of single life. The silence, the space to contemplate. Digging deep inside, I wrote:

I do like myself tonight, even if my typewriter is clanking horribly and I'm cold and my throat hurts and my neck hurts. I feel thin and tough and the sharp edge of self, and I am going to struggle on. This is a very big changing time/point in my life and I'm not going to mess it up.

Writing, writing, it's becoming an obsessive knife in me, hurting and cutting. Writing has become some sort of end-idea in itself, regardless of content, but the act of it, the producing of it. I must get it from my father, and Julius, and now I do really have to work on that as a reality, if I'm to have any peace at all.

⁓

My poems came spilling out:

how to be a poet

so what was it I thought this afternoon about a vision
about seeing from an angled perspective
that was so important?
but it was.
i lay, taut and almost coming,
and a poem came, and went.
and I came.
that was more important than getting up
to write the poem i liked.
i let it go, so
I could feel my body throttle, charge,
be involuntary for a few moments, ecstasy and
exhaustion.
i lay, i let the poem go,
and now i miss it.
i don't regret the spasms that threw me
across the bed.
but how to be a poet?

Slowly I understood how hyperaware I was of others' gazes, especially the omnipotent male one affirming, "You are worthy." Bit by bit I worked to strip that gaze from my mind and body:

Clean clear tunnel in my chest
free-fire zones liberated daily
reclaimed one by one,
each victory a sharded rest
until I am shot down again
and again.

The smile on a man's face
to which I, not I,
respond.
Seeking the look in the eye
which will tell me I,
not I,
am beautiful.

As I continued to reclaim my psyche, the state even returned my name with the divorce papers. "ORDERED, ADJUDGED and DECREED, that the plaintiff is authorized to resume her prior surname." Although I had never used my "Mrs. Williams" married name except for the state-mandated driver's license, once more my license matched all my other identification. I was one whole person.

I got a jolt, however, when Julius's memoir *All Is Well* appeared, just five years after our divorce. Much of it was about our marriage. I came off horribly: a wife incapable of true love, hampering a serious artist. Reading it, all the pain I had felt with him, the rejection, bubbled up. Shattered by the revelation of his seven affairs during our years together, I called the ACLU, eager to sue. "And I once apologized to Julius for being so angry all the time," I told friends. "He ain't seen nothing yet." But since Julius had changed my name in the book, the ACLU lawyer told me, "You're not identifiable. You have no case." For weeks I stewed, denouncing Julius to anyone who would listen.

My only satisfaction came when the *New York Times* review called *All Is Well* a mass of "jejune reflections," writing, "Lester speaks at length of his pain and suffering in dealing with what seem to have been the minimal demands of Arlene (his former wife of eight years, the white mother of his children) from whom he was absent much of the time while tending to his success as a writer and lecturer, tending to the revolution, tending to other women."

My gratification was bittersweet though. I still wanted to be proud of him and enjoy the close friendship I thought we had built. The book snuffed that desire for several years, until he called one afternoon to apologize. "I treated you terribly in that book. It was a bad time for me. I wish I could retract it. It's embarrassing now. I'm sorry."

"Thank you. It was hard to read."

"That isn't who I am now and it's not how I feel. I have more perspective now."

"Thank you. I appreciate it." By then the sting had softened.

"You deserved better. Please forgive me," he said in that sonorous voice, and I did. His apology almost sealed the wound, although I still noticed heart-sparks from time to time, especially when he got some rapturous write-up in the newspaper.

But what about love? Looking for inspiration, I tried Jean Rhys's novels featuring single women. Yet in each one the woman ends up destitute, waiting for a man. These tales of desolation reminded me of the Italian New Wave films I had seen in the late '50s, where women without men spiraled into suicidal depression. Even Anaïs Nin's famous journals, supposedly so feminist, showed me a woman who tied her fate to men. Was this to be my destiny? Or could I savor solitude, as May Sarton and Sidonie-Gabrielle Colette described it? Was there another option?

One of the mothers at the Children's School I opened in my apartment dated a woman, I heard. Early one morning I saw them: two sparkles bouncing along the street holding hands. They glowed. The mother of my student, dark hair falling around her face, leaned over to stroke her lover's cheek. Her lover, shorter, younger, and blonde, laughed. What was the relationship like? I had no image, no idea.

Late one afternoon Rebecca, my carrot-topped co-teacher, confided, "I'm thinking of getting involved with a woman." She grinned a lopsided smile. "But I'm not sure. I want to try it." We spent that evening in my living room sipping red wine, discussing the possibility. As the night grew late, I realized how drawn to her I was.

The next evening I invited Rebecca over again. We drank one bottle of red wine, opened another, and, like the preschool teachers we were, lounged on the floor while we talked and flirted. Soon she grabbed my hand to pull me down and we playfully wrestled, the way I did with Douglass and Rosa. We rolled back and forth until, panting, I pinned her and stayed lying on top of her.

Tentatively, we kissed. And kissed again. Passionately.

She slid one hand under my shirt up to my breast and caressed it, which sent jolts of heat through me.

Within minutes we were rocking on the floor, hands inside each other's pants. She felt moist and "just like me," I thought with shock. The erotic attraction, laced with a smidgen of distaste, intensified.

Finally we pulled back, finished the second bottle of wine, and Rebecca tottered off into the night. In the morning, a Saturday, she called. "I'd like to start dating," she declared softly. "I think I'm in love."

"No!" I blurted, the attraction mysteriously vaporized, replaced by revulsion. "I don't want to." Shamefully, like many a straight woman before me, I let fear overcome all feelings of warmth, of friendship, and hung up.

On Monday morning I kept my distance, as did she, and over the coming weeks I watched as Rebecca became lovers with another woman, eventually moving in with her. We never again regained the intimacy we had shared before that night, as I strove to put the incident out of my mind. We continued to operate the school, but for the rest of the year we kept all conversation on a careful, professional level.

Today, decades later, it's hard to acknowledge how callously I acted. Normally I think of myself as a kind person, but at that moment homophobia overruled all instincts of care for another. I wonder, is that what happens when people act in racist ways, fear blotting out their natural inclination of concern for others? It's helpful to have had an experience of being on the other side to give me compassion and remind me of the power of fear, giving a glimpse into otherwise incomprehensible behavior.

One morning I sat in Ann Mari's kitchen drinking coffee, soaking up the sun heating my back. "I need to make more money. I have to find a way to get a better-paying job."

"Why don't you go back to graduate school?" She had recently earned a doctorate in political science. "You could do it. You could make five times as much once you became a professor. You'd love it, doing research, teaching. Writing!"

"How would I support us while I was in school?" Much as I admired her, we seemed fundamentally different. Ann Mari had a longtime male partner, a full-time research job, and no children.

"You could get a fellowship. Be a TA."

"What's that?" I gulped my coffee.

"A teaching assistant. They pay graduate students to do it."

Maxine, the college professor upstairs from my apartment who smoked weed with me, seconded the idea. "I'll help you figure it out," she said, holding her breath to keep the smoke in. "You could earn a decent living."

Could I really lead an expansive, professional life of the mind? Leave the nursery school grind behind? Life with three-, four-, and five-year-olds, once so delightful, was wearing me down. I longed for intellectual conversations with adults.

The clincher was Douglass. Believing that a prepubescent boy needed a father, I had sent my eight-year-old up to Amherst to live with Julius, who, now a UMass professor of Afro-American Studies and more settled than he'd ever been, eagerly accepted the idea.

Rosa cried for days after he left, and I missed Douglass more than my heart could bear. During vacations when he visited for weeks at a time, he and I slid easily into each other's rhythms, sharing sweet, quiet moments. As we walked to Prospect Park or shopped for groceries side by side, we shared a companionable silence. It was like a gentle rain falling on dry ground, nurturing my mother spirit. Each time we parted at Penn Station, I couldn't hold back tears. "I love you," I would choke out, squeezing him good-bye.

"Please don't cry, Ma," he said as his own tears dripped.

Once he mailed me a dollar, his allowance, the most valuable gift he had to send, with his block-printed words of love.

I applied to a doctoral program at UMass Amherst with a letter of reference from Maxine, who concluded, "Lest you think that Joan is the perfect human being, I have tried to think of a 'weakness' to describe. The only thing I can say in that vein is that I'm not sure she's aware of the extent of her competence and she tends to underrate her abilities."

On a deliriously happy day, I opened the university's acceptance letter. "We've awarded you full tuition with a $6,500 assistantship." Rosa and I hugged, twirled, and danced. We would be near Douglass and Julius. Once more we would leave behind the noise and dirt of the city, the mounds of garbage, and my dead-end life.

This time I would make something of myself. All alone. Instead of using up energy railing at a man, I would expend it on myself. The day before we left, I wrote in my journal, "I wake before dawn, wanting to take the day by its ankles, so tomorrow will come sooner."

Diving into the Wreck

1977

On June 21, 1977, I pulled up to the two-story Victorian where I had rented an apartment. Douglass and Julius stood on the front porch waiting. The welcome sight let me know I had come home. Julius looked different: heavier, wearing a wide-brim cowboy hat. Even his face, with a broad smile, appeared like that of a happier man than I had known. Evidently the country life of a professor, plus his new girlfriend, whom I had met many times, suited him. And my ten-year-old son looked like a piece of heaven.

All day Douglass glued himself to my side, following me from room to room, reminding me of his toddler days. When I walked outside, he was my shadow. In the kitchen I stumbled over him.

Once more Julius, my old confidante, was nearby. We talked on the phone for hours, mostly discussing the children but also his writing or my studies. "Can you believe I'm going to get a doctorate?" I marveled.

"Uh huh. Why not? You're smart enough."

His words were balm on the wounds he had left.

Despite our painful past and increasingly divergent politics, we maintained a compatible familiarity. As Julius grew more conservative in the world's eyes but more true to his soul, he became calmer, more peaceful.

Soon I would see the familiar sight around town of this man I knew so well yet barely recognized in his recent incarnation, rocking his new style: the large cowboy hat that became his trademark. We rarely talked in person now beyond a brief hello; the telephone was our medium. Plus the occasional warm letter he wrote with the monthly child support check. With our divorce, we had never negotiated a support agreement or other settlement, deciding we could work it out amicably ourselves. "The adversarial nature of the court system is horrible," I had proclaimed. "We don't need the bourgeois court to tell us what to do! We'll figure it out."

Flush with book advances and royalties, Julius was appreciative. "I'll give you $15,000 in one lump sum," he promised at the time. "Very soon. Since you helped earn this money with your editing and raising the children, it's half yours. And I'll send child support each month until they're eighteen."

A year later, when he hadn't sent the $15,000, he brought it up on a call while I still lived in New York. "I'm sorry," he said. "Truly sorry. I had to use the money on taxes. I don't have it."

"Not at all?"

"No, I had to use all it on taxes. I don't have any left."

"That's okay," I said casually.

"I thought you'd be mad."

"No, I'm fine."

"Really?"

"Really." And I was.

Later, though, once Rosa and I got to Amherst and had to live on my graduate student stipend, I kicked myself for this nonchalant reaction. And for not getting a court-ordered settlement. Julius did send child support checks every month, though, right on time, and for that I was grateful. Plus he sometimes sent notes about my good mothering with the checks. His failure to give me the promised $15,000 was one grievance I didn't hold on to. It was over.

Back in the country, I could breathe fresh air again, let sunshine bathe my skin, and best of all, love my son close-up. I dug up my rented lawn to plant a garden and watch life grow. With Douglass often by my side, I relaxed into small-town life, savoring the beauty of green leaves on oak trees and soft grass caressing my bare feet.

This time I moved not to follow a man but to reunite the family and establish a career. Eventually I would be Dr. Joan Lester, a title that would cause others to take me seriously—and maybe help me do the same. As for my writing dreams, perhaps at thirty-seven even those would be fulfilled.

Can a poet set the washer to rinse / hold?
Can a teacher be oh so sexy?
Can a mother fix a faucet, dry and fold?
How can I be all of me?

With my rolltop desk dominating my new living room, occupying the same space Julius's had taken in every home we had shared, I was finally ready to be the intellectual I had dreamed of becoming.

Yet "Amherst is so fucking WHITE," I wrote in my journal. "So coupled off. I want revolutionary america. Black america. Woman america. Or slummy america. Something I'm used to."

I made a beeline to the UMass Everywoman's Center, with its simpatico comrades—women of color, political women, lesbians—amid inspiring murals and political posters tacked on the walls. There I met Aquila Ayana, a quiet, elegant artist with the Third World Women's Task Force and mother of a son. With her hair in braids tied up in great swirls, and dressed in perfectly coordinated Afrocentric materials, we may have looked mismatched (me in ragged pink overalls and old T-shirt). Yet over tea at her peaceful apartment filled with art and light, we confided our dreams: she of painting full time, me of writing. And we laughed, oh did we laugh, about the indignities of race. She was a great mimic. "Can I touch your hair?" she would say in a mincing voice, describing the latest affront by a simpering white woman.

With her I felt at home.

My crammed schedule soon had me running—supervising student teachers, attending classes, writing papers—but a series of assaults on women jolted me into a women's self-defense class. Night after night at the UMass gym, I kicked, thrust my fists, and tried to trip a padded "attacker" lunging from behind, before I returned to my amazing children, textbooks, and the rich, disquieting voice of Nina Simone: "It Be's That Way Sometime." Being with ten-year-old Douglass again made every difficulty of the move, every adjustment to a white suburb full of green lawns, totally worthwhile.

～

Every Wednesday I got a hit of Brooklyn when I rode the Peter Pan bus to sign for my unemployment check, visit friends, and eat good Chinese food before returning to Amherst the next morning.

One November night I emerged, shivering, from the Grand Army Plaza subway. I started out for Maxine's apartment when a white couple caught my eye. The young woman looked as if she might be struggling against a tall, thin man. His arm circled her. "Is everything all right?" I asked, flush with confidence from my self-defense class. Although I had been unafraid before and had once charged a group of teens in the subway, shouting "Stop it!" when they sprayed mace on a sleeping man, I felt even stronger now.

"This is my woman," the man answered angrily, while she remained silent.

The couple hurried on.

His response, and her lack of one, made me uneasy. And of course his claiming her as "my woman" galled me. They were heading in the opposite direction, so I turned and followed. What was going on? Was that his girlfriend or his wife, and was this a case of domestic violence?

The man kept peering back, scowling.

After a third of a block, their awkward gait made me call to the young woman, "Are you okay?"

She turned slightly, her wavy brown hair snagging on his jacket button. I saw huge brown eyes, shocked wide open. She shook her head slightly, her back pressed against his chest. Now I saw that one of his arms held her firmly around the waist. The other gripped her throat while he pushed her ahead.

He looked back and called, waving a glint of steel, "If you say anything, I'll kill you."

The woman's head spun to me again. "Help," she mouthed. "Help me."

My heart pounded wildly. How could I save her? He had a knife. If I tried to attack him, he would probably slit her throat. Or mine. He was tall, too. Probably close to six feet. It would be hard to take him down.

I glanced around. Half a city block off, three men strode away from us. I yelled with all my power, "This woman needs help. Help this woman!" and kept screaming while I clenched my fists and raised my arms, crouching in a self-defense stance.

As I write this forty-two years later, using my contemporaneous account for details, I look ridiculous to myself: a thirty-seven-year-old woman barely over five feet tall, weighing 115 pounds, with eight weeks of self-defense training under my belt, confronting a tall armed man who had already threatened to kill me. Yet at the time my actions seemed entirely reasonable. I never thought of abandoning the woman, and I did feel physically competent. Adrenaline-fueled, I kept screaming, "Help this woman" while I prepared to fight the man.

Startled, he momentarily loosened his grip on the woman. She bolted in my direction and fell against me. I reached out my arms to embrace her, feeling her body tremble against me.

All three of the other men down the block raced toward us. One held his umbrella straight out as he ran. Another shouted, "I'm a policeman." The third, I could see as they came closer, whipped out a walkie-talkie.

The cop and the walkie-talkie man lunged for the attacker, slammed him against the low stone wall bordering the park, yanked his arms behind his back, and cuffed his wrists. This all happened in seconds.

A police car screeched to the curb. The two cops forced the man's head down and thrust him into the back seat of the car.

The woman shook in my arms, weeping. "Thank you, thank you."

"You're my sister," I said, holding her shuddering body.

The two plainclothes officers came over, ignored me, and brusquely asked for her name, which promptly slipped my mind, her age (twenty-seven), and her address (somewhere in the Village). She said between sobs, as I continued to hold her close, "When I came off the train, he grabbed me from behind."

He had cut her ear, which dripped blood onto my tan jacket.

"He made me go with him." She cried so hard she could barely speak.

Where was he taking her? Prospect Park's nighttime emptiness beckoned from across the street. It was vast and dark.

"We're pretty sure this is the guy who did one hundred rapes in Brooklyn," one cop said flatly.

"Please show us your badges," I asked them when they instructed the woman to get into the squad car. "Don't get in until we see their badges," I told her.

The two flipped out IDs, and suddenly, without warning, it was over. She jumped into the front seat—with the attacker in the back!—and they zoomed off while I stood alone on the street, heart pounding. I stood, still in shock, for a few minutes until, sobbing, I walked slowly toward Maxine's apartment in my old building.

That night, agitated, I called the Park Slope police station. "Can you tell me the woman's name?" I asked the person who answered.

"No."

"Or how to contact her?"

"No."

"I'm sure I'm in the police report. I was the one who spotted her and yelled to the police to save her."

"No, we can't give out any information."

"Can you please give her my name and number? I think she'd want to contact me."

"No." Flat voice, no affect.

"Could I speak to a supervisor?"

"No."

That night I shook in bed, replaying the scene over and over.

Since I couldn't reach the woman and I needed to cleanse that terrifying incident from my body, once back in Amherst and safe at my desk, I did what writers do. Then for once I mailed the essay to a national paper, *In These Times.* On December 14, 1977, my article appeared, headlined "Personal Intervention Can Make a Difference."

To my amazement, women's centers and women's papers all over the country reprinted it for months. Several years later, Melanie Kaye/Kantrowitz published the essay in her book *The Issue Is Power.*

Looking back, I wonder why I submitted *this* essay, when for so long I had published so little and submitted nothing to national media. Newly fired up by friendships at the Everywoman's Center, and furious at intensifying assaults—a backlash to women's gains—I considered it activism more than literature. As I explained in the essay,

I am writing this for several reasons. First, people should know about a case where intervention did work. The woman was probably saved from rape, other physical injury, or murder. I was not hurt and the attacker was captured.

Although it was incredible luck that two plainclothesmen were half a block away at the instant I yelled, I think the attacker was preparing to run anyway, as soon as I shouted. He released the woman as I screamed for help, and he did not move toward me. The third man, who was not a cop, told me that as soon as he heard me yelling he prepared to act by pointing his umbrella so the metal tip was directly out.

The attacker might not have been caught if the police weren't there, but probably the woman would have been released and I would not have been hurt. I would act the same way again in a similar situation, although I have had moments of terror thinking about the experience in the days since it happened.

Second, the woman involved helped to save herself by struggling continuously against her attacker. Her struggling gave me the clue as to what was going on. Resistance was effective.

I hope that I can trace the woman. We shared a profound moment. Her face, with her mouth stretched wide, exposing her teeth, her eyes enormous with fright, and her courage in continuing to struggle and to act on her own behalf by shaking her head when I asked her if she was alright, although he must have had the knife against her—all these images of her keep going through my mind, and it would be good if we could connect again, and perhaps put closure on the event. . . .

Acting together again, we might be able to turn that terribly frightening experience into a source of strength for ourselves and other women.

I had found a style that fit me perfectly—the personal essay, a structure Julius used extensively. My form wouldn't be feminist poetry or academic discourse but accessible essays serving equality. All those years I hadn't known what to write about, except, as a married woman, endless iterations of "Silly Womanly Thoughts": my musings about leaving Julius. On the Vineyard I had published articles on child-centered education, but now I had unashamedly used the "I" viewpoint to tell a personal and political story.

Using writing as a tool of activism came naturally, meshing my two great passions. The era encouraged the form. In the '70s, with the explosion of women's magazines and papers, our stories began to see widespread print; this, after all, was the device we had used in consciousness-raising groups. I had needed those years on my own, with nightly writing sharpening my skill, to claim the form.

But above all were writers like Adrienne Rich and Ntozake Shange, whose choreopoem *For Colored Girls Who Have Considered Suicide / When the Rainbow Is Enuf* had electrified Broadway. They, along with James Baldwin, Audre Lorde, Muriel Rukeyser, Grace Paley, Vivian Gornick, and others I absorbed like water, had abandoned the supposed objectivity of the white male author's omniscient viewpoint. When these older white men wrote of pain, it had come detached from social life: a lost love (Auden) or a fleeting moment of beauty (Shelley and Keats). Now all these new writers, mostly women, focused on a first-person voice embedded in their times, "gaining access to their emotional as well as political lives on the page," as the poet Claudia Rankine would later introduce Adrienne Rich's *Collected Poems 1950–2012*. The disembodied voices of earlier generations of essayists and poets gave way to a storm of outrage: children napalmed, Black bodies brutalized, women denied agency in every area of our lives. The writer engaged herself. Nothing happened "out there."

By the late '70s, these women had created a new literary landscape, one that invited me to participate. Rich wrote in "Diving into the Wreck": "The words are purposes. / The words are maps." This was an urgent art. "Art means nothing if it simply decorates the dinner table of power which holds it hostage." Rich, with the others, dared us to take ourselves seriously, create new language that could forge a path out of our wilderness.

They created an opening I ran through. Living in the heart of a vibrant Amherst/Northampton women's community, I was ready to write my way into my own voice, which was emerging in tandem with its subject: women on the rise.

Soon I sent an essay to the *Amherst Bulletin* decrying the term *broken families*, with its intimations of pathology. My family wasn't broken, I insisted, simply different. We weren't diseased or shattered, but normal: a psychologically healthy mother and children, getting along just fine, thank you. The nuclear family, with its patriarch, stay-at-home mom, and 2.5 children, was dying, and none too soon.

For weeks women stopped me on campus. "Are you the woman who wrote about 'broken families'? I've worried about my kids ever since the divorce. You made me feel so much better."

I had found my voice.

The Women's Room

1978

At night when I felt especially lonely, or hot, I sang along to Nina Simone's "I Want a Little Sugar in My Bowl" and reminded myself to "be my own love." I'd spin Archie Shepp's *Four for Trane* or Keith Jarrett's *The Köln Concert*, replayed until his piano runs were part of my bloodstream, and write. And read.

I feasted on a new novel every white feminist was reading, *The Women's Room* by Marilyn French. Depicting trapped housewives, women who had expected egalitarian marriages but ended up at home scrubbing floors, the book described my life as no other fiction had. When the protagonist, Mira, newly divorced, goes to Harvard for a PhD in English literature, I thought, *This is my story*. It reminded me once more that I wasn't alone, and it inspired me to hold steady. I pledged in my journal, "When will my one outline impressed into the air of this earth be enough? When will I feel the gentle air love me, let the sky be my lover and the wind caress my cheeks? When will the flowers be the faces of my lovers, when will I control my life? NOW."

Still, despite my feminist commitment, after several mostly-for-sex encounters with men that busy year, I called Prentice in New York.

Oh no, a wiser part of me interjects. After that disastrous marriage. How could you? What can I say? He was warm, handsome. Massed energy, like a spring coiled, ready to explode. My fantasy Great Love. And amnesia struck again, as it had when I had first gotten pregnant. I forgot who I was. But you'll see. I did act differently this time. In the end.

"You look wonderful." I gazed at Prentice on the Brooklyn corner where we met one sweltering May afternoon. Flatbush Avenue traffic roared by.

"You're dressed completely in white." I looked down at my own all-white outfit.

"No coincidences." He smiled broadly as he planted an arm on my shoulder, letting his hand dangle over my breast. Thus entwined, we strolled to Junior's Restaurant for my favorite meal: bagels, lox, and their world-famous creamy strawberry cheesecake. Once inside, Prentice chose a red leather seat facing the door. "You don't know who might jump you. I never want my back to a door."

Shocked at this reminder of how threatened he felt, I tried to make allowances for his volatility. He hadn't had an easy life. Yet he had retained a big heart. There was an openness about his wide smile that I found as engaging as ever.

Thus we began Phase Two.

Prentice first visited Amherst on a Saturday afternoon. After he opened the door to the living room and sauntered in, Douglass flew into those great waiting arms while I looked on, elated. Douglass wouldn't let go and remained pasted against Prentice's midsection. Finally, when he could peel the boy off, Prentice bumped fists. "Hey, little man!" The two wore broad smiles the rest of the evening.

Rosa was more restrained. "Hi," she said politely, reaching out for a token hug. Oh well, I thought. She's used to having me all to herself. No man is going to please her.

That weekend the energy between us sizzled. I felt the old magnetism. He was irresistible. It was delightful to feel those strong arms around me again.

For months we shuttled by bus between New York and Amherst. Life felt perfectly balanced. Both children were fine; I had exciting work and occasional weekends with my exhilarating lover. I wrote an article for the *Daily Collegian* describing Simone de Beauvoir's influence in creating my ideal life, closing with this:

> I read and reread the tale of Simone's love affair with Nelson Algren, in her writings and his, and I absorbed intensely the story of her independent yet intimate, lifelong association with Sartre, always wanting to have that kind of relationship, but not knowing how to impress my changeable, excitable image upon the haughty, self-contained model who gazed at me from the jacket of her many books. And she grew ever more haughty with the years.

Ah . . . yet, at thirty-eight, I see that it has happened. I am living a life much like Simone de Beauvoir's, albeit with children. I do lead an intellectual life, productive, with a feminist awareness at its core, and I have developed a lifetime, supporting, non-live-in relationship, after many years of struggle; a relationship which nurtures me, spiritually, intellectually, and sexually. Yet I live alone, proud and independent.

I have become, finally, the woman I always wanted to be.

But Prentice began to want more.

"I thought we could see each other sometimes, give each other sustenance, and be lifetime friend-lovers," I wrote him. "It's not unreasonable."

"You're still living in a dream world," he replied by return mail. "Make up your mind. Am I your man or not?"

He began to spend more time in Amherst. Early one thundering evening, when storm clouds loomed but no rain fell, Prentice and I sat on the splintery front steps of my apartment, seeking privacy from the children. "I don't like it when you say I'm 'your woman.'" I twirled my hair. "I'm my own woman, that's all, nobody else's, and I won't ever be."

"You are my woman," he teased, his face with its wide cheekbones crinkling, until he got serious. "You're crazy." He glanced around at the broad green lawns, the large maple trees and white clapboard Victorians, all back-lit by the storm, like a stage set. "Living up here in Sunnybrook Farm, you think life is perfect. Wake up, it ain't."

"I'm not crazy, I'm terrifically sane," I protested. "I've found there's so much more to life than being loved. I want you, and myself too."

"It sounds to me," he said, "like you're trying to keep this nappy-headed nigger at a distance. Living up here in this white town." He shook his head. And then the rain came. A great sheet drove us off the steps. We moved to the porch floor, sitting cross-legged with our backs against the house. Savoring the smell of fresh dirt that summer rain brought, I pleaded, "It's not about race. It's about being my own person. Please try to understand me."

Later that night he wrote a note in his lovely round script. I found the message, written in purple ink, on my pillow. "You are you. Therefore acceptable."

"And you are you." I smiled. "Therefore I love you."

Still, the next morning he pressed to move into my small apartment. The thought of his volatile energy smoldering in our home terrified me, just when I had gotten myself, finally, on a clear path: a doctorate, challenging work, the respect of my colleagues and a small writing public. Eventually there would be money.

But after all those years, he and I did have an ease with each other. I appreciated his tenderness with the children and admired his strength. He had survived a rough world. "You're anti-white, I'm anti-male," I wrote him after he left. "Now you want to settle down, while I want to smash dragons. What do you know of my work, of how I love my desk, and the joy I feel hearing music when I'm alone?"

Torn by conflict, for the month of October we kept breaking up. "That's it," I would swear, guiltily. "You're too demanding. It's never going to work. I want peace and calm." But after two weeks of missing his ardor, I would call.

Viewpoints

What is this energy, which fills my body and turns
Toward you?
The poets call it passion
Psychologists: pathological obsession.
Feminists name it dependence
You say it's love
And I call it struggle.
I WANT TO WORK

This back-and-forth persisted until Prentice's fortieth birthday, on November 20. We all four sat around my oak table celebrating. The children had made place cards and party hats. "Here's my special roast chicken," I announced with a flourish as I set it ceremoniously in front of Prentice.

While eating he gulped down glass after glass of red wine until, with a great splash, he opened a bottle of champagne. Bubbles fizzed all over the tablecloth. Douglass and Rosa teased, "Look at the mess you made," and we all laughed, though I grew concerned about the amount of alcohol Prentice was consuming. Rain from a storm lashed the house.

After the meal, I carried a cake from the kitchen, four tiny striped candles flickering in the darkened room. Rosa, Douglass, and I had made the chocolate cake, his favorite, with coconut frosting. Prentice's jaw looked tense, his eyes glassy. I glanced at the empty wine bottle and saw the champagne was nearly gone.

"Happy birthday to you," we sang, clapping. High wind rattled the windowpanes.

"Will this be my last birthday here with you?" Prentice asked vacantly.

"Blow out the candles!" I urged.

"Goddamn it, I've got no place in this family," he railed. "I want this chair to be *my* permanent chair." The tension rose. "And no one else to sit in it."

This sounded like Julius with his living room desk chair no one else could touch, but an unhinged Julius, a man with a demented undercurrent in his voice. Ignoring him, I plunged on, leaning over the table with the cake and melting candles. "Blow out the candles."

"Fuck!" He pushed back his chair, slamming it against the wall.

"Damn it, blow out the candles!" Rosa said quietly, staring at him.

"I deserve a chair!" he shouted.

She jutted out her chin and whispered, "Shut up, you bastard."

He jumped up and in a flash was inches from her face. "If you *ever* call me a bastard, I'll kill you! And don't tell me to shut up, you little bitch!"

Equally astonished by my thirteen-year-old daughter's outburst and his fury, I leapt to my feet and, peering up at this muscular man, said, "If you kill her, I'll kill you." Douglass, four-and-a-half feet tall, ran to stand by my side. We all began to cry. Prentice swore, "That little bitch called me a bastard" as tears streaked his dark face.

"Stop calling her that," I said. The children clutched my sides.

"That little bitch . . ."

"Stop saying that!"

Shaking, I pulled the children into the kitchen and shut the door. I could hear Prentice muttering, "She called me a bastard!" and whimpering, "This is *my* chair." Grabbing both children's hands, I led them down the narrow back stairs to our landlady's kitchen.

"Prentice has gone crazy upstairs." I took a huge breath after she opened the door. "Can the children stay here until I get him calmed down?"

"Sure," said Susan, a junior psychology professor. She looked unfazed.

"He threatened to kill Rosa." I tried to show the significance of the crisis.

"Oh, I imagine he didn't mean it." She turned her neat blonde head toward the children. "Do you want to watch television? And have a snack?" I wasn't sure Susan understood, really, what had happened only minutes ago, but her calm reassured me that a quiet, normal world did exist just below the madness above.

"Yes" to television, "No, thank you" to snack. The children were subdued, robotic.

"I'll bring you some birthday cake," I said, feeling wretched leaving them. "And I'll come get you really soon." I squeezed by and made for the door. "Everything's going to be all right."

Hurrying back, I found Prentice sitting, staring blankly at the cake, candles melted down to small pink pools. I cut three large slices, threw them on plates, and carried them down for the children and Susan. Then I quietly returned.

"You have to leave," I said.

"You know I didn't mean anything." He stared at me with bloodshot eyes. "I'd never touch a hair on the head of any of you. I'd kill anyone who tried to harm you."

"But you have to leave." I stuck to my point. "I can't have this nightmare going on when I'm trying to study, the children have to study and go to bed. We can't live this way. You have to go."

"There's no bus until morning."

"I know." I couldn't send him out into the Amherst streets. Rumor among people of color in town had it that the police owned a thick book full of their photos. Every dark-skinned resident of Amherst was supposedly in it. With a police department like that and Prentice's prison record, he couldn't afford to spend the cold, windy night on the town common, bordering the police station. Aside from the possibility of getting roughed up, one arrest might send him back for a long stretch. I looked over at him. Sitting quietly, all the fight drained out of him, he looked harmless enough.

"All right, you can stay until morning, but you have to be out of here for the first bus." I pushed up my rolltop and rifled through a cubbyhole until I found the blue-and-white schedule. "It's at five thirty. You have to leave here by five." It was a ten-minute walk to the center of town.

"I'll be on the first bus out of this fucking town," Prentice snapped, the creases on his face ravines. He looked dazed and beaten.

I realized it was nearly nine, minutes before Julius would pick up Douglass. Racing into my bedroom alone, I dialed, reaching Julius before he set out.

"He threatened to kill Rosa tonight," I burst out, hardly believing the wreckage of the evening. "It was horrible. He's calmed down now, but it's been awful. A nightmare. I've kicked him out. He'll be gone in the morning for good."

"I've always said that's what's wrong with prisons. It turns out this kind of violence." Julius sounded sad.

"I know," I agreed, appreciating his understanding.

"I'll be over in ten minutes."

The warmth in his voice comforted the shakiness welling up from deep inside. Now that the storm had passed, my legs felt as if they might sink into the floor. I sat on my bed, not sure I would be able to rise.

"I'll pick him up on the porch. I'm truly sorry this happened, and that it's ended this way."

I willed my teeth to stop clattering. "Thank you." He sounded so sane.

I did manage to stand and rush downstairs to bring up the children. Minutes later I heard Julius's car horn. Leaning over, I hugged my son and plodded by his side down to the front door.

"I'm sorry," I said, feeling terrible he had witnessed such a brutal scene. "I'm so sorry, Douglass. It won't happen again. He'll be gone in the morning."

I returned to find Prentice and Rosa scowling at opposite sides of the living room. We just have to get through this night, I thought. Then the world will be back to normal.

Numbly, I pointed to our wooden rocking chair and told Prentice, "Stay right here until I come back." Taking Rosa's hand, I led her into her room and closed the door. "Go to bed, sweetie," I said, wrapping my arms around her.

"Ma, I'm scared." My thirteen-year-old looked five.

"It's all right. He's not going to do anything." Now that my adrenaline had simmered down, I could hardly talk. Every word felt forced, almost slurred. "Go to bed, sweetie. I won't let him out of my sight. And you know he didn't really mean he was going to kill you. People say things like that . . ."

"But he looked like he meant it."

"I know." I had little energy to reassure her further. And what feeling I did have in my body let me know my heart was cracking. "He'll be gone before you get up, I promise."

Her face ashen, my daughter pulled on her pink flannel pajamas and crawled under her comforter. I bent to kiss her and instead lay down, willing the warmth left in my flesh to nurture her until morning. Tomorrow, I thought, I'll have strength to tend her. Now, please stay in your room. Once she slept, I gently opened her door and tiptoed out.

There he sat, stone, in the chair, not rocking, simply staring straight ahead.

"Come into my room with me," I told him, feeling like a jailer. "I'm going to watch you all night." Seven hours until I could eject the tempestuous ex-husband I had loved so dearly. He followed me, hardly talking.

This man, used to waiting in lines, stood motionless by the window while I forced myself, lying dressed on top of the covers, to stay awake. Both of us shivered in the cold room although I huddled inside the thick Guatemalan sweater he had given me. He, ready to go, wore his brown leather jacket.

Once, he started toward my bedroom door.

"Where are you going?"

"I have to piss, woman."

I trailed him, waiting outside the bathroom door.

Finally, at 3 a.m., feeling pity, I invited Prentice to lie down with me on the bedspread. We lay facing on opposite sides of the bed. A small reading light illuminated his exhausted face, his shiny jacket and large, cracked hands. The night was silent.

"You're living in a dream world." He spoke in a hushed tone. "You think by banishing me, everything will be nice and clean. Life isn't like that."

Was he right? I wondered if my desire for quiet, for calm, was simply a white girl's fantasy. Now that I lived in this upper-class white college town, was I absorbing its mores, leaving behind my poor Black lover? But just because his life was chaotic didn't mean mine had to be. There must be another kind of solidarity.

"Life can be," I maintained. "That what I want, anyway. Maybe it's me, maybe I am crazy, but I can't take this intense love we have, like a volcano. I never know when you're going to explode."

"You want to smooth everything over," he whispered. My heart caught at the tenderness in his voice. *I will not be tempted*, I repeated to myself. *Don't touch him. That was too scary tonight. This has gone way beyond what I can handle.*

"I'm sorry I've been so indecisive," I murmured. "I should have let you get on with your life and never called you last spring, starting this drama all over again."

"I'm glad you called," he said. "It's our destiny."

No, I thought. *Not mine. I'm going to get my doctorate and be sane, raise these children, and become a writer. No more ordeals like this night.*

We lay untouching, talking quietly, lapsing into long silences. Those dim hours felt like a wake, and we the hushed mourners. When the clock read 4:30, I rose, made him a cup of strong coffee, and waited to push this lover-mate out the door for the last time. Stopping before he stepped through it, Prentice looked at me and said, "All the hard time in Greenhaven, nobody ever got to me like this. Sixteen years in prison couldn't do it. But tonight a little girl broke my heart." He dramatically wiped a tear from the inside corner of his eye and shook the drop from his hand.

I stared as the streetlight shining through a window behind him framed his head. Grief-stricken and worn down as I was, my mind said, *Go, go, go.*

"Good-bye."

He reached for the knob, strode out holding his head high, and never turned to look back.

Relief, exhaustion, and despondency flooded me. The children and I would have our own lives back. I'll have to be vigilant, I thought, not to let any sentimentality lead me into ever seeing him again. I stared down at the white-and-burgundy Guatemalan sweater, ripped it off, and thrust it to the back of my closet. I began to quietly wail. But even as I cried, I knew I had done right. Painful as it was, this final ejection marked a turning point. I was walking a road I needed to stay on, one it had taken twenty years to find, and I would never again allow myself to be sidetracked by a man's needs at the expense of my own.

Two weeks after he left, I wrote in my journal:

Finally, I want integrity, authenticity, more than I want happiness. But strangely of course, integrity brings beautiful happiness. A happiness of the soul. A delicious completeness, supreme satisfaction with the atoms of the universe.

I need integrity, I need myself if I am to keep moving. Growing. To survive the way I see fit. Wholeness. These words keep recurring in my thoughts. I guess I've achieved that. Now I can begin living.

At thirty-eight years old, I was my own woman at last.

In the years that followed, Maxine occasionally glimpsed Prentice on the subway. Each time she reported, sadly, "He looked more strung out than ever." Ten years on, his prison buddy Tom, the white "ex-cop gone bad" who had attended our wedding, wrote me in pencil from prison to say, "Prentice died. Heart attack." Even as I blessed his soul, hopefully now at peace, layers of clenched muscles in my chest unfolded. He would never arrive on our doorstep again, leaking that volatile energy into our home.

Silences

1979

The Common Woman Club in Northampton held four simple rooms carved from the parlors of a classic Victorian, opening sacred space. Whenever I entered, pulling aside sheer white drapes, I left the hurly-burly world with its assumptions about who I was, what I wanted, and what I could do. Crossing the threshold, I felt the tingle of transgressing into safe, protected, women-only territory. Curling up on a wicker couch to write in my journal, I relaxed; other nights I sat alone at a corner table reveling in the soft light. No man intruded while I ate, luxuriously, enjoying fish and vegetables I had not cooked. No one asked smoothly, after he had slid into a chair, "What's a beautiful woman like you doing, sitting alone?" An hour stolen from motherly duties felt like heaven, a jolt of rejuvenation until I could once more walk the streets with equanimity.

Emboldened, I signed up for my first writing course. Twice a week I pedaled my bike four miles through the warm country air, winding up Route 116 to the sign for Hampshire College. I turned in and glided past a white farmhouse until I arrived, sweating and panting, at class. I sat nervously among the college students, aware that my teenage daughter was only a few years younger than they. But as I dove into exercises ("Complete this sentence, write for ten minutes . . .') and read aloud, my courage grew.

Soon the *Valley Women's Voice* published "Sisterhood," an essay I wrote for class. "To have been beaten, the way a rug is beaten. Assaulted, the way a problem is assaulted. Attacked, the way weeds are attacked. But I'm not a rug and I'm not a problem and I'm not a weed. I'm a woman." One man, I wrote, had grabbed my breasts as he dashed off the F train. Another rubbed my ass as he passed by on Eighth Street. Yet another stroked my butt in a crowded subway car. My psychiatrist lover in New Haven had whopped my head with his fist until my ear bled.

Maybe if enough of us spoke up, I reasoned, and saw that our shame was shared, we could stop the assaults. Helped by an emerging late '70s consciousness about violence against women, I wanted to contribute by sharing my story. Sexual coercion, battery, and street harassment, we called the indignities; the new term *sexual harassment* hadn't yet surfaced in public conversation. "Words like drops of blood on the page," I wrote in my essay. After it was published, women on campus smiled and said, touching my hand, "Thank you for being so brave. That's happened to me, too." Stories tumbled out. "He beat me when he was drunk. . ." "He grabbed me and tore my blouse off . . ." "When I went into his office, he closed the door and locked it. And then . . ."

Women began speaking out about these humiliating, frightening episodes. It was a heady time, shining lights all over our shame. I plunged forward, publishing at least once a month.

In "Letter to My Younger Sisters," published in the *Valley Women's Voice*, I wrote,

> We revolutionary women of the late '50s and early '60s lived our daily lives much as other women did around us. In nuclear families. Dutifully. Dependently. Midwives to other lives. We may have read Marx and Brecht at the playground, but still . . . there we were at the playground, and the personal and the political hadn't a hope of glimpsing each other, it seemed.
>
> How that decade of the '60s ripped open our hearts, and in the upheaval of our anger we were transformed. . . . Sometimes still, it seems I've lived too long in the old regime. Unexpected old emotions ripple this much-rippled heart and the arena in which I move seems suddenly, eternally the same—the struggle for ever-deepening independence and the self. . . . But that, after all, is part of participating on the cutting edge of history. . . . Using oneself as a razor, cutting out new arcs of space in which we can move, may not be easy, but there is a reason we open our mouths to the future. . . . The fruits of reconstruction, however dearly paid for, are sweet.

I had puzzled my way forward, stumbling and screaming as I fought my way out of mythical womanhood, birthing a new feminist creature in full possession of myself, without, in the end, any models at all. Even Simone de Beauvoir, who I learned was not happy with Sartre's philandering, no longer served. No children, what a different life she had. Or Angela Davis, also childless. Or Agnes Smedley, the author of *Daughter of Earth*, who had foundered on her own love affairs with men and never had children. Or Marge Piercy, whose utopian/dystopian novel *Woman on the Edge of Time* I had loved—another female author without children.

I had had to forge a customized life as an intellectual with children. And now I was sailing, publishing, gaining local recognition as a feminist writer. I refused to end up like the women Virginia Woolf described in *A Room of One's Own*, those who never got their words on paper, "possessed" women who dashed their brains out on the moor, crazed with the lack of space or time to write.

Tillie Olsen's book *Silences* became my manifesto, offering compassion for my late writing start. Most of what we considered the great works of humanity, she said, came from lives able to be wholly surrendered and dedicated. As Joseph Conrad explained the environment necessary for his art, "the even flow of daily life, made easy and noiseless for me by a silent, watchful, tireless affection." Even Rilke, whose poetry I had loved, wrote— reminding me of Julius—that his only responsibility was to writing. That was why he could not take a job to support his wife and baby or even live with them.

Tillie Olsen also talked about her own hard time getting to paper and pen, often delayed by child raising, housework, and secretarial jobs. But she had done it finally, cleaving to her own spirit so tightly, she said, that she nearly died.

I learned it wasn't only the mundane life tasks, of which women had an abundance, that kept so many of us from writing. It was the self-confidence, as Virginia Woolf wrote, "to find the form for one's own life comprehensions." The will and drive. Difficult for anyone, but almost im-possible for women bred to fulfill others' desires. As de Beauvoir demon-strated in *The Second Sex*, we learn early to contort ourselves into shapes fitting male expectations.

No wonder I had been silent so long. Daily life pressed on. "Children to dentists, car to garage, laundry to the line, head to my studies, heart to the children. Little red spider crawling up my pad, and the breeze blows the curtain in and out."

By May I wrote:

This Astonishing Spring

Has spring ever burst forth like this before?
Did beauty always double every time I looked?
Were leaves ever so large at this time of year?
Were their undersides just that shade of pink?

Did spring ever amaze me like this?
Was I ever so affirmed and this planet so adorned?
My various planet. One day soft, pink and green.
Another, blazing white lace.
Today, kiss me gray and even sky.

Was it always like this? Sudden, unexpected grace.
Was Winter's reprieve ever so total?

Other springs, my toes have sifted the dry dirt.
I have exulted and drunk pools of fern growing in the woods
Where nothing grew before.
I marveled at their undulating movement.

But this year I stand awe-struck before God.
So this is what those skeletons were meant to bear!
Was it ever thus? And how could I forget?
Was winter's snow so deep, or was it that I never knew?

Has my planet always been so green
Or is it just
This one astonishing spring?

But I couldn't only write feminist essays and poetry; I had a doctorate to complete. Trembling, I began my dissertation. This would be a research study about how young children understood race and gender. Did I have the scholarly chops to do it? So many before me had faltered at the feet of "the Big D." Amherst was full of ABDs: old graduate students who had completed All But the Dissertation. They imagined for years they would someday write it, but never did complete the work.

What would become of me if I couldn't finish? "Maybe I'll be lucky and die so I don't have to do it," I wrote. "Rock myself, love myself, hold me sun, hold me leaves, hold me planet. Hold me and rock me so I can write what I have to write. Hold me birds and my beautiful porch. Hold me blue vase that Ann Mari made, hold me flowers Douglass gave me. Hold me Israeli cup from Maxine. Hold me friends and planet and trees and sky, and I can write, nestled safely in all those many loving arms."

My days grew impossibly full: teaching five classes, interviewing for jobs, with the dissertation crammed into every spare minute. My nights jammed with sound. "Lord," I wrote to myself one night, "Nina Simone is belting it out. Tell us about it. Thank God I have music, and the children. How I love to look at their beautiful faces."

Curled over my ancient black Underwood, tears of relief flowed as my fingers beat out the final words of "Democratic Education as the Basis for Multicultural Acceptance: A Case Study of Five-Year Olds." I concluded by citing a well-meaning white teacher reading a book about a Chinese girl to a class of white children: "The lack of Third World personnel in the school is revealed as a critical one. When multicultural social relations are absent, any piece of literature about difference cannot be fitted into a daily reality, examined, assessed and then used appropriately as part of the child's broad knowledge about another culture. Thus, the book remains exotica, a discrete bit of information unrelated to the rest of life."

I dedicated the dissertation to my ultrapatient children. When I had typed the last page, I rested my head on the typewriter and sobbed. I had finished!

But worry nibbled at the heels of relief. In spite of Section 8 housing assistance—"the GI bill for women," my friendly caseworker called it, winking—and a fuel subsidy, I barely paid our bills. What was next, and would I still be able to write?

The week my dissertation, bound and delivered, sailed from home, my fingers itched for the worn metal keys where they felt at home, skipped and sang. I typed a journal page: "Words I love you, the ring of you, the precision of you, your variety, the way the right one of you pops up for each occasion. Words burn your way up and down my page merely for my pleasure. Be my playthings, let me love you, watch you dance and leap."

But life clamored. Though I had cleared away the distraction of men, the puzzle of money pressed. My Holyoke Community College teaching job, where I had replaced a professor on leave for one enjoyable year, would end in a month. I had interviewed elsewhere but foundered on my refusal to leave Amherst, with the children so ensconced. "I'll commute," I promised the UConn president when he grilled me as a finalist for a tenure-track job. "I'll stay in Storrs three nights a week." Or Cambridge, I told potential Boston employers. But everybody wanted employees who lived in town.

Ultimately I realized I would have to find a local position, not so easy in a place where new doctorates and ABDs littered the landscape. I considered directing the Che-Lumumba School. Or a bilingual/bicultural public school program. Other possibilities emerged—a migrant worker education program, an independent school directorship—yet nothing seemed right. I worried in my journal, "The real question is: social justice, money, and can writing be involved? How to balance them? That is the task now."

Writing personal essays seemed a luxury. I had tasted the joys of a writer's life with the dissertation: fingers tapping smooth metal keys, brain turning over a phrase, bending it this way and that like an ocean polishing stones in its tumbling waves. I had basked in writing the way I savored a swim, naked, in warm summer rain. "Words dancing green like fern, blue as the sky, weaving me into a sturdy basket." But the moment had passed. It was time to settle into a career, defer the literary impulse. My writing zeal, driven underground, would be left to smolder until, one day, it would finally ignite and force itself to the surface.

This Bridge Called My Back

1980

The children's brown glow stood out in a sea of Amherst white. "How can you cast the only dark-skinned student in the one Gypsy role?" I fumed to the school drama coach backstage. Rosa had told me, shivering with pleasure, "I can't wait for opening night," wanting to surprise me with the play. But when I sat front and center, I had been incredulous. Rosa, head-wrapped, sat silently off to the side during the entire show.

"I don't want her typecast as the exotic stranger!" Like Lena Horne. How could this still be happening?

"But she fit the role," the drama coach stuttered.

"How?"

"She fits the part perfectly." He turned to help a white boy tug off his non-Gypsy costume.

"By her skin color! It's a stereotyped role in the first place, the 'mysterious' Gypsy. And to put your one Black student into it! She has other talents," I stormed. "She's brilliant. She didn't even have a speaking line, just sat in the corner looking dark!" I stomped off, tears sprouting, as much from confusion as fury. What would a Black mother do? Those I knew gave me conflicting advice, from "Let no slight go unchallenged" to "Let her handle it."

Checking with Julius, I heard a little of both, outrage and resignation. "I had to meet with the principal at Douglass's school when kids nicknamed him Chocolate," he said wearily. "Virtually all the administrators are white and they don't get it."

"I know. When I have talked to the school, nothing really changes. I read that piece you wrote for the *Times* about Douglass being called Chocolate. I was shocked."

"Hmm. What does Rosa want?" he asked. He never used to ask for their opinions.

"To leave it alone." She had begged me, "Please don't complain to the teachers anymore, Ma. They make it worse on me afterward."

At the time when my children were growing up and roaming more widely, an Amherst liquor store owner hurled a Black Amherst College student to the floor. "She *threw* her money on the counter," he claimed. "Disrespect-fully." Police, despite the student's vehement protests, "subdued" and cuffed her. The newspaper report terrified me. If upper-class college status hadn't protected her, what would shield my teens? I couldn't let Douglass and Rosa venture out into such a dangerous world. As the lawyer and activist Pauli Murray had told friends forty years before, "I'm really a submerged writer, but the exigencies of the period have driven me into social action."

James Baldwin had taught me that if white people would lay down the mantle of supremacy, everyone would benefit, including themselves. After all, having a delusional sense of superiority couldn't be good for us, because we weren't viewing reality as it was but in a distorted version. Could I reach whites with this message? Working in white communities is what SNCC leaders had asked white activists to do fifteen years before and it still made sense, since white people were the source of the problem.

I would try by expanding the few anti-racism workshops I had conducted at UMass. Ricky Sherover-Marcuse, an anti-racism educator in Oakland, California, generously shared her curriculum with me and, buttressed by my newly minted doctoral degree, Dr. Joan Lester's Unlearning Racism business was born. My artist friend Jan Winston designed a brochure, my Women's studies faculty friend Arlene Avakian took a photo, and I launched myself at the beast.

After all, my generation had dismantled eighty years of legal segrega-tion, expanded voting rights even in kill-on-sight Mississippi, and created affirmative action to grow a new African American middle class. Plus I had the shiny new *Dr.* in front of my name. "It's like having a penis," I joked to friends. "It's my honorary male status."

"You're going to make a living this way?" they asked skeptically.

"Yes," I assured them, though I wrote to myself, "I am wondering whether I can make it doing workshops. Then I think: I have to! Nothing else I want to do right now. I have to protect Rosa and Douglass. But what will I do when winter comes on? I'm SCARED about using up all my money to pay for heat. What if the rent supplement gets cut off? Took Douglass out to dinner tonight. $22.75. For two people. That's too much! From now on I'll cook up special treats."

Organizations under attack were willing to pay what looked like good money after years of graduate school wages: hundreds of dollars per workshop. Often they signed on for a series. Plus I offered Unlearning Racism classes in my living room for white people, who registered month after month. I wanted to unravel the myths we had been fed, our shame and guilt for accepting the lies, and ask participants to commit to radical change. What would they do to interrupt the institutional racism in their workplaces and the prejudices in their families or out on the streets?

There was nothing else like it offered to the public then. Radio stations aired interviews with me, and the *Daily Hampshire Gazette* wrote features. Requests poured in from all over New England for my programs. Though I had little experience conducting workshops, I gave myself to each one heart and soul, until participants enthused, "I don't feel hopeless anymore. Thank you."

My venture was working, though I wrote to myself, "Sometimes I want to step back, be more contemplative, look at the sky, and WRITE!" But fear for the children's lives drove me on.

I found a new book to use for my classes: Cherríe Moraga and Gloria Anzaldúa's *This Bridge Called My Back*, an electrifying anthology of essays by women of color telling deeply personal stories. They wrote about a new concept: overlapping identities. Aurora Levins Morales described the race, class, and gender issues that shape Puerto Rican women. Audre Lorde asked feminists to recognize our different sexualities. Moraga and Anzaldúa challenged white feminists: Could we please do the necessary anti-racism work so the women's movement would be representative and relevant?

This Bridge Called My Back became urgent reading, the text I assigned in all my workshops.

On fire with the need and passionate about the work, I still wondered where I fit.

Between worlds. Why is it ever thus for me? Black/white, whose world am I in? Straight/gay, whose world? Families/single people. Unemployed/ employed. I feel everywhere in between. Writer/activist. Who am I?

Who is my community? I bring together people from different worlds— because they are all my friends!

Worlds colliding in me or coexisting? This morning I feel splintered, ALONE, nowhere. Unlike everybody else.

Yet the sky has small blue patches behind the clouds, what a pretty blue and white sky. It looks like an oil painting with the painter having just put splotches of blue and white on the canvas, the white fades into the blue.

The writing calmed me, even if I didn't have answers.

Compulsory Heterosexuality
and Lesbian Existence

1981

"I've tried men from A to Z," I told Maxine. We sat on my screened-in porch watching fireflies, their lights flashing like tiny falling stars. Max lit the joint in her hand, sucked in a deep draft, and handed it over. "The sensitive ones, the political ones, the quiet ones." I enumerated my list of Amherst lovers: the solar engineer, the truck driver. "And Ari." I smiled, remembering winter afternoons in his sunny room. "A beautiful young Ethiopian Jew, a Marxist. He was a graduate student. But a pure intellectual, totally uninterested in children."

She nodded.

"Finally there was Pumpkin Man. A white farmer. He courted me by saying, 'My contribution to the future of the planet is vegetables. We'll need to grow our own when the Reagan economy tanks.' He would feed us all after the economy collapsed. He was out doing something useful. For the people!" I pumped my fist, laughing. "But he treated the children like five-year-olds. Oh God, Max, it was horrible. I wish you hadn't been on that damn Fulbright." How I had missed her, rereading each airmail letter, microscopic script on thin blue paper, my spidery lifeline. "I let him move in when he had nowhere to go. The day I kicked him out I hung new curtains in the kitchen to celebrate."

Max laughed. "Those little dotted-Swiss ones over the sink?"

"Yeah, from the thrift shop. He laid out pumpkins and squash all over my apartment, trying to dry them. He never picked up anything from the floor, but he covered it with pumpkins!" We howled. "He was always leaving his clothes lying there, too. Last week I read about a woman who *nailed* her husband's clothes to the floor. I wish I'd thought of that."

The rest of the evening, we lamented all our failed relationships with men, laughing at their foibles—and our own.

A month later Max called to say, "I've started dating a woman, Sandy. She's political, working class. It's so different without sexism in the relationship. It's a hundred percent better than being with a man."

I listened. Max, like me, had been straight so long, married twice. How did she make this leap?

"My whole body's an erogenous zone with Sandy," Max said, uncharacteristically giggling on our next call. "She kisses me anywhere on my body, on my neck, my shoulder, anywhere. And I have this giant orgasm!"

I listened, enthralled.

My sister visited from Minnesota with her longtime lover, a woman. During the entire week I never heard a raised voice or unkind word, and no one seemed in charge. They walked the street holding hands, spoke thoughtfully to each other, and took turns cooking breakfast.

This is what I wanted, an egalitarian partnership at last. Something like the one Julius and I had started out with, before children—except, I remembered with chagrin, his expectation that I nurture and edit his writing, with no reciprocity. Maybe I could have a truly equal relationship with a woman. Terrifying as the thought was.

Three days after my sister and her lover left, I circled Womanfyre, the Northampton bookstore. Twice. I crept in, scurried to the corner marked Lesbian, slipped two books and a journal off the shelf, and slapped them face down at the cash register. That night, lying on my stomach across the bed, I pored over the *Signs* issue featuring Adrienne Rich's essay "Compulsory Heterosexuality and Lesbian Existence."

Sexuality exists on a continuum, and most of us are inherently bisexual, she wrote, as Kinsey's research had showed twenty-five years before. Yes, I thought, I certainly am, although I hadn't dared admit it. Looking with desire at the naked breasts of a roommate in my late teens, I had forced myself to turn away and ignore the feelings. Likewise with my best friend Amy on Martha's Vineyard, whom I knew I was in love with. And so did her husband, who was furiously jealous—like the husband of a college friend years earlier, who once threw an encyclopedia at me. These husbands saw what I had been unwilling to recognize.

Rich wrote, "What deserves further exploration is the doublethink many women engage in and from which no woman is permanently and utterly free. However woman-to-woman relationships, female support networks, a female and feminist value system are relied on and cherished, indoctrination in male credibility and status can still create synapses in thought, denials of feeling, wishful thinking, a profound sexual and intellectual confusion." Yes, the synapse. A gap in my thinking. Confusion. I wasn't the only one plagued by this contradiction.

Like an armchair Red, I became an armchair lesbian. Maybe escaping heterosexual doublethink—I need a man / men are hopeless—would be my reward.

"I'm thinking of being a lesbian," I confided to Ann Mari, who slouched at the opposite end of my couch on a visit from New York. My left-wing friend, fifty now, was the same blunt woman I had admired for twenty years. Her hair, suddenly gray, had surprised me when she arrived, but now I was accustomed to her weathered look: the craggy, square face, the short silver hair. Here she was, taking precious time from her work at the Center for Constitutional Rights to visit me, and I was grateful.

"Why not?" She threw her hands in the air. "I know lots of women who've chosen women later in life, and they're happy. I'd try it myself, but I'm terminally heterosexual."

"Oh, you must be one of the five percent."

"What's that? I've never been part of any elite."

"Kinsey said five percent of people tend to be exclusively heterosexual, five percent homosexual, and the rest somewhere between. I think I'm smack in the middle."

"I'm on the end, definitely on the end. Worse luck for me," she chuckled.

That night I wrote, with some bravado. "At last, my own blue eye reflects me back so well. No male eyes have to be looking. I am the strong, independent woman I decided ten years ago I needed to be in order to survive."

Soon I told a few surprised friends, "I'm becoming a lesbian."

"You haven't even kissed a woman," Jan objected. We sat hunched on her back step. "So you can't know."

"I did once in New York," I said, recalling that drunken late-night grope with my red-haired co-teacher. I had never thought this one unconsummated night counted. Now I elevated it to Lesbian Initiation.

"But how can you *decide* you're a lesbian? Don't you have to fall in love?"

"Why should I let my hormones lead me into calamity again? Maybe it's time to live more rationally. I gave up cigarettes and meat at thirty-five, sugar and caffeine at thirty-seven, alcohol at thirty-nine. Why not give up men at forty?"

Jan's eyes darted around her yard.

"They're toxic for me. Why not explore something else? Or leave relationships alone altogether. I can't put myself, and the children, through any more dramas."

"You'll be lonely when you're old," she said quietly, giving me a searching look. "How will you live without somebody then?"

"I'll manage. Lots of friends, my work."

"It's risky."

"As if men aren't!"

"You can't *choose* to be lesbian. People are born gay!"

"I can so choose. Why not? People get to choose their religions. Why can't I choose my partner? Most of us are bisexual. We simply grew up accepting heterosexuality as normal. Like people used to believe they had to stay in their own race or religion for marriage, we thought we had to choose opposite-sex partners."

"That's true. But . . ." Her face puckered. "I thought you liked sex with men."

"I did. It wasn't the sex I didn't like. It was the se*xism*."

"Who does? But most of us don't become lesbians. I don't know if you can choose, Joan. It's a matter of desire."

"The desire's already there. It's simply a matter of allowing it to surface. I've been attracted to women for years; I never thought it would be okay to pursue it. Coming up in the '50s, I never even knew of such a thing as lesbians."

Later, when I told Aquila, staring at her beautiful oval face to gauge her response, she surprised me. "I'm bisexual," she said with her wicked laugh, like a mountain stream rushing over rocks.

I looked hard at her.

"No. No disrespect, Miss Ann . . ."

We cracked up.

"But no."

Oh well, that really wasn't what I had in mind, even though I adored her.

My astonished parents had endured so much with me, my thrice-married brother, and my sister, who had come out at twenty. "Yes, dear," was their loving response. "Whatever makes you happy." And they meant it. Since my marriage to Julius, they had become practically full-time anti-racists; now, with two lesbian daughters, they would soon begin attending Pride marches with me, my dad trembling with fear in those early days, when some marchers—especially teachers—wore paper bags over their heads.

Joan with her mother, Barbara Steinau, circa 1980. (author's archive)

Daily life—absent any actual practicing lesbians in my apartment—rolled on. The children were only mildly alarmed when they heard me tell friends of my new lesbian status. Without the shadow of a father figure hovering over our fun, the three of us frolicked, enjoying each other's company more than ever. "The children are growing so well. I'm not their mountain anymore. They're becoming their own."

Yet despite my public pronouncements, I found the habit of men as hard to break as smoking, which took years of swearing off, then tumbling back over and over to the seduction of "just one." Caffeine had been tough too, forgoing the sweetness of evaporated milk in a bitter mugful of coffee, the pleasing jolt along my nerves. "It's the same," I reassured myself. "I feel like Odysseus lashed to the mast." I could resist. "I have scraped my fingernails into the dirt, my fingers have held me to this planet, my arms reached out across the sky. My feet are rooted to my own planet."

And they held.

Hearing there might be lesbians in the softball league, I practiced all spring before nervously joining a team, the Yellow Jackets, not sure what to look for. Each night of a game, I watched the women, wondering who was a lesbian. Hmm . . . maybe the pitcher. Or the catcher.

It took me the entire summer to figure out that I was the only straight woman in the entire league. The only one who carried a dainty pink pocketbook rather than a slim wallet jammed into a back pocket. No wonder nobody made a move toward dating me; many had experienced the same suffering I inflicted on my co-teacher thirteen years before, when I "experimented" with her and then ran away.

One night after a game near the end of summer, I joined a few teams celebrating at Checkers, an Amherst watering hole. No longer a drinker and shy among these younger lesbian athletes, some of them serious softball players and none with children, I stood alone on a staircase dressed in my red game shorts, pink purse dangling.

A woman loped over to a spot below me, placing one black-cleated shoe on my step. "Are you Joan Lester?"

"Yes." I looked down at her, relieved that someone was talking to me.

"I'm Carole Johnson. I've heard about you. You do anti-racism training."

"Yes." I smiled. "It's my passion."

The intense, athletic-looking woman had dark hair waving around her face and olive skin. "I do anti-racism work too. Let's sit down."

We found stools at the bar, where I unzipped my purse to pull out one of my brochures.

"We should talk. I do desegregation training for teachers all over New England." She attended law school at night, she said, intending to practice civil rights law, which impressed me. "I'll give you names from my Rolodex."

A week later we sat across a table at Silverscape, a small Amherst restaurant we each claimed as a favorite. As Carole and I dug into quiche, dark bread, and fresh salad, I listened to hear if she ever said "we." When she buttered a thick slice of bread, I wanted to ask. By the time we arrived at cheesecake, I had to know.

"Are you in a relationship?" I tried to catch my breath.

"No."

Lingering over second cups of peppermint tea, we covered our compatible politics. Plus she had had women lovers, as well as men.

"I can't believe you were Julius's wife. I carried his book with me everywhere in college. *Look Out, Whitey!*"

Though that last comment didn't usually win points, her political savvy impressed me. Plus my body kept up an insistent chatter: I like her, I like her.

"I've wanted to date a woman with children," Carole said, surprising me. I had thought that might put her off.

"Have you read *Woman on the Edge of Time?*" I asked.

"It's my favorite book," she answered, practically sealing the deal.

"Every child in the good future has three co-mothers, men or women. It makes so much sense."

"And nothing's thrown *away*. I love that. Because . . ."

". . . there is no *away*." I completed the thought. "What a concept. No place to throw trash that's truly away. Marge Piercy's brilliant."

She shuddered. "The bad future! Where people are 'walking organ banks' for the 'richies.'"

"I know, and that fem Gildina, who lives in one room with a holographic set like a big TV, and the multies keep her for sex. She's like a cartoon woman."

"We have to make sure the bad future never comes," she said, her green-gray eyes both resolute and kind. Like she really cared. "With Reagan elected, we have our work cut out. He's scary."

"The way he's trying to break the air traffic controllers' strike, did you see that? That's horrible for unions. Everybody's thinking, 'Oh, the air controllers make so much money.' But if he breaks them, it's all over for unions."

"The future is in our present, Marge Piercy says. Our actions choose."

I nodded. *I like her, I like her.*

Two days later I nervously handed Carole a handful of my published essays. They were so personal—what would she think? Was it too soon to reveal so much? For a week I wondered, distracted while I prepared workshops or met with groups. She would know everything about me now. Would this end our budding relationship?

"I love your articles!" Carole said on our next Silverscape date. "You're a beautiful writer. I can't believe you wrote them. They're so vulnerable. Thank you for sharing them with me." Her eyes shone.

The thought flashed: This is how I acted with Julius when he first showed me his work. Now someone's looking at me the same way.

"I'd love to read anything else you've written," she said, carefully. "That you'd want to show me. Your writing's amazing."

As September faded into October, she kept encouraging me whenever I gave her more essays. "I love your writing," she said every time. "You have a gift."

One afternoon I read her a journal excerpt aloud while we sat on my couch at dusk, watching the silhouettes of trees form against the darkening sky. Was this too intimate? But again she responded, taking my hand, "Your writing is incredible."

I couldn't believe I was getting this kind of encouragement. Some readers had complimented my articles, but I had never had anyone read so much of my work and be so enthusiastic.

At last, on Halloween, after two months of walks, dinners, and one quick kiss, I asked, "Do you want to come to Sunday brunch tomorrow?" I had waited long enough.

Promptly at 10 a.m. she arrived. I opened the door with a smile and pounding heart. "I'm not hungry, are you?" I said.

Carole looked startled. "Wasn't this for brunch?"

"Let's lie on the couch and make out instead."

"Where are the kids?"

"They're at Julius's."

"All right," she gulped, looking shocked. But pleased.

I led her to my old floral couch. Awkwardly, we lay down. Softly at first, our tongues sought each other's warm mouths. Her fingertips stroked my flaming face, my arms, while I pulled her closer. Pressed against Carole's soft body, I sputtered, "This is what men have been getting all these years! This soft body . . . these breasts . . . and what did we get? Hard bodies like boards." I couldn't believe the inequity. "With that thing poking us!" She laughed in disbelief, but I meant it. "That was so unfair!"

That afternoon, lying wrapped on the couch for three rapturous hours of kisses and caresses, we pledged, "I won't go out with anyone else, and we'll never discuss our relationship after 11 p.m."

"This time," I swore in my journal, "I choose to love with all my intelligence."

Yet lying with a woman triggered reactions I hadn't expected. The first time we tumbled into bed at the house she shared with three other lesbians, I insisted on wearing my panties, plus a T-shirt.

"Do you want to take off the rest of your clothes?" Carole asked while we lay, passionately kissing.

"God will strike me dead if I take everything off," I said.

"God?" She knew about my atheist upbringing and beliefs.

I nodded, amazed that the religious prohibition had penetrated even my bohemian bubble. It was the first time I truly understood the power of mass consciousness to affect everyone, even nonbelievers.

She was patient, and one afternoon soon thereafter I removed my T-shirt. Felt our naked breasts touch. I waited. God didn't seem to mind. She didn't even throw a warning lightning bolt outside the window.

Finally I slid my underpants down to my ankles, wiggled my toes free, and threw the pants on the floor. God didn't smite me. Carole's bare skin felt sumptuous and I couldn't get enough of her body pressed against me. I had usually found sex with men satisfying—often the best part of a relationship—but Carole took me to new crests of joy.

One winter weekend Carole and I strolled the cold, deserted dunes on Cape Cod's Ballston Beach. A briny smell of seaweed and salt swept me back to the Vineyard, to the years Rosa and Douglass were small, following me everywhere, holding onto my legs while I cooked. A gull flapped by, wheeling with a scream. "I miss the children," I sighed, a tide of longing pulsing through my body. "Even with Douglass not living with me, I think about him all the time. Every afternoon he runs in from the Junior High and I light up. Rosa . . ." I hesitated, without words for the intensity of my love. "I hate to be away from them. But it's been so hard, raising these children alone."

"You're not alone now." Carole reached for my hand.

"Yes, I am!" I exploded, shaking her off. I wasn't going to trust anyone else with them, not after all they had been through.

"I'm right by your side," she said softly.

All winter Carole showed her steadiness, making friends with the children, listening, cooking up batches of popcorn. She shook and rattled a saucepan on the stove while kernels exploded. By spring sixteen-year-old Rosa asked her, "If my mom dies, can I live with you instead of my dad?"

"Yes," Carole assured her. "But your mom isn't going to die."

This relationship wasn't in any text I had seen. Not in Doris Lessing or Simone de Beauvoir novels, not in Marge Piercy or Alice Walker books, not even in *This Bridge Called My Back*. I was writing my own script.

Yet while the lack of a map was confusing, it liberated me. I didn't have to fight sexism, or accommodate, or fight for my space and respect as a woman. We started fresh. Two women. Both activists. One about to become a lawyer, the other a new "Dr." and aspiring writer. How would we organize our lives? I wrote, "It's only my will that keeps me alive, Jimmy Cliff sings. Yes, true. So now, I'm not used to floating on a never-ending river of happiness. What's interesting about that? Can I detail the many twigs of bliss in the river? What's to talk about, what's to think about, as I leave my bone of pain behind? Why am I so afraid to say to myself how excited I am about being with Carole? I don't realize how alone I am used to being: in my work, in my bed, in my house, as I cook. As I parent. I'm missing it a bit. Though it's also nice to be so cared about."

Carole supported me as a mother and writer with a passion no one else had ever shown. But how would the world receive us?

One afternoon at Douglass's hockey game, we climbed high in the bleachers where Julius, his face shaded from view under a black cowboy hat, sat alone on an aisle. I pulled Carole over and introduced her. "She's my sweetie," I told him, beaming.

"I don't know what that means," he answered in a monotone.

Dumbfounded, I mumbled, "My sweetie," again.

He extended his hand to Carole, said hello, and stared straight ahead.

"How could he be such a jerk?" I fumed to her when we fled to our seats. Should I have explained our relationship differently? Would "partner" have conveyed it? That sounded so businesslike.

"You surprised him, that's all. The way you surprise me all the time." She laughed, gripping my hand. "It was a weird response. But that's who he is."

"I don't know. Willfully obtuse?" I never knew these days what to expect from him: warm on the phone; freezing cold in person. Or indifferent. I had been excited to introduce her to the father of my children, as I had once introduced Prentice. His chilly response struck me to the core. How could he be so unfriendly?

"You didn't do anything wrong. He's just odd," Carole reassured me. "He loved you, and he didn't expect this. He couldn't connect the dots quickly enough, that's all. He'll figure it out. Don't worry about it. He's eccentric." She laughed again. "And so are you."

"He definitely is eccentric. Jan Winston told me he's converted to Judaism!" I looked to see how this bombshell would land. "You know about the Les Campbell mess, when Julius had a teacher read an anti-Semitic poem on his radio show on WBAI?"

She looked blank.

"Back in the '60s Julius was a famous anti-Semite! And now he's a Jew." I shook my head. "He always has to be odd man out. That's his specialty. Like the cowboy hat. Now he's going to wear a yarmulke? He even has a Hebrew name, Jan said. Yaakov Daniel-something. Which is interesting, because his father's name was Daniel."

"He's a seeker, Joan. Just like you. You two are so much alike. But you're cuter." She squeezed my hand.

"I'm like Julius?"

"Are you kidding? Creative, eccentric, brilliant. Go your own way. You're a lot like him. Except happier. And like I said, cuter." She smiled and pressed my hand again, showing me she would like to kiss but didn't dare, out in public. "Let's watch the game. I think Douglass just scored a goal."

Harlem

1982

"I want to use my law degree to combat racism and gender discrimination outside the legal system," Carole told me one night after dinner on my screened-in porch. "Let me join your consulting business. We can form a nonprofit."

"Really?"

"I know a lot about nonprofits. Like how to get legal status. And fundraising. I'd love to work with you."

"Yes!" I quickly agreed. I loved her sensible, grounded mind, which complemented my visionary one.

For weeks we met, writing our plans in magic marker on newsprint taped around my living room. We would do everything we could to make Marge Piercy's good future in *Woman on the Edge of Time* come to pass. Gathering a few friends as advisors, we named ourselves the Equity Institute. I coined a slogan, "Turning Isms to Wasms," and we established an office on my tiny screened-in porch.

To apply for tax-exempt status, we needed a board of directors, so I called Eleanor. She had recently resigned as chair of the Equal Employment Opportunity Commission, an agency she had whipped into shape over three and a half years. Now a senior fellow at the Urban Institute, Eleanor was traveling the country, spreading a message of resilience in the face of President Reagan's retrenchment on equality efforts. As an advocate for our demoralized movements, she fit perfectly with Equity Institute's mission.

"Hey, I've got myself together and I'm doing something really good. I want to ask you to help us with it," I told her.

She surprised me by saying, "I always thought you *were* together, what are you talking about?"

"I'm creating a nonprofit to do anti-racism work with organizations. We need a board. Would you be on it?"

"Sure. As long as I don't have to go to any meetings! I have zero time. But you can send me stuff and I'll sign on."

Once we added other friends to the board—Aquila Ayana, Jyl Felman, Muriel Wiggins, and local professors Sonia Nieto, Martha Ackelsberg, Barbara Love, and soon Beverly Daniel Tatum—we were set.

Our first high-profile job was sensitivity training with the Amherst Police: all thirty-three were white, thirty-one of them men. They had read about me in a local newspaper profile. Since Carole was in law school and had to study every minute she wasn't at her UMass day job, I conducted the series of full-day trainings alone.

"You're in for a tough time," Julius warned me one night on the phone. "They don't play. More power to you."

First I got to know the police officers, conducting private interviews with each one, listening to their concerns. Most were furious about the mandatory training, feeling they had been unfairly branded as racists after the Amherst liquor store incident. "We're just doing our jobs," they complained. "Nobody understands how we're caught in the middle. Nobody knows what it's like to be us."

I listened and nodded, projecting calm confidence. But soon I wrote, "Sept 29, 1982. The first day of an eight-week workshop and I'm terrified. Ah! Why did I choose this business, or, why did it choose me, which is the way it feels. I feel I had no other choice. This is what I could do here, what needed to be done. It is clearly the right work at the right time, but oh, how scary!'

A few of the younger cops privately admitted their horror at "sadistic beatings of colored people." One confessed, "I vomited later," in a note he wrote for me to read anonymously to the group. They faced a tough internal culture, I learned, with a job as frontline enforcers for the status quo. Each one was afraid of peer retaliation, perhaps violent, if they didn't follow the unspoken rules for the cruel "justice" they were expected to dispense. Additionally they felt besieged by a critical public, their superiors, and the lawbreakers they confronted.

Each day I, who had so recently called cops pigs, looked at a Jan Winston painting on my living room wall titled "Every seed is awakened with love," and I tried to love each one as well as I could, open them to the devastating impacts of their behavior. By the end of the series, I had gotten through to a few and given them strategies for change.

Though I was beginning to be publicly regarded as a leader on anti-racist efforts, friends and coworkers of color sometimes lambasted me for my clueless "white demeanor." Once, Maria Alvarez, a stately Puerto Rican woman who had been a graduate student with me, as well as a friend, complained over our regular dinner at Amherst Chinese Restaurant, "You're always so upbeat! So positive. So optimistic. So white! People of color can't afford to be so happy all the time." Her face was smiling, as usual, so her words startled me. "It's irritating. As if you don't get it. You don't care how serious racism is, how it's killing people. You're so *white*." She flung the word at me like a curse. "Your attitude, it's offensive."

Stunned, I dropped my forkful of chicken with cashews and forced the swiftly gathering tears back. No "white girl tears" for me, as I had counseled in anti-racism seminars for whites. "Don't take the attention off what the person of color is telling you," I advised. "Listen! It's a compliment that you're so safe. Someone can finally vent directly to you. They're hurting, that's what they're saying. This is not the moment to defend yourself. Just listen and learn. You can cry later. Don't expect them to comfort your hurt feelings."

Taking my own advice, I sat and listened, though pain shot through my chest.

"People of color are dying in this country! Dying. And you go skipping around like everything's fine."

"Tell me more," I managed to choke out.

"That happy-go-lucky attitude is like *Leave It to Beaver*. People of color can't afford to go around smiling all the time."

I thought of my African American training colleague Barbara Love, a UMass professor who got the same rap. I had heard people of color, including my own daughter, complain that Barbara was too constantly sunny. "Too white," despite her dark skin.

"Who does it help if I'm miserable all the time?" I asked.

"At least it would show you're serious. That you get it. You understand the seriousness of the situation. You're not just some white girl prattling on."

I wanted to say, "I do get it!" but kept my mouth shut.

"Do you have any idea about how Puerto Ricans are treated? Do you know about Lolita Lebrón, about the independence movement?"

I had heard of this legendary Puerto Rican nationalist, imprisoned for twenty-five years after joining an armed attack on the US House of Representatives. And Maria herself would take me, several months later, to meet Lolita Lebrón at an Amherst party celebrating her release from prison.

"Puerto Ricans are treated like shit. The worst jobs, the worst slum housing." Maria, usually so composed, was animated. "And you smile on. Do you know how many times white people have said to me, after they realize I'm Puerto Rican, 'You speak English so well!' I was born in Brooklyn, you know. Brooklyn! But I'm regarded as an outsider. An *exceptional* outsider. Not like 'the others.' Who are all thieves and stupid or cleaning ladies, not academics like me."

I nodded again, trying to express everything I felt with a tiny warm smile: "I hear you, I'm sorry it's been so hard, my life has not been a bowl of cherries either but of course I've not faced racism directly, only through my children, and I'm working as hard as I can to change things. I'm sorry for all the kinds of racism Puerto Ricans face and every brown or Black person faces and for my role perpetuating it. I'm trying to learn as fast as I can. I maintain an optimistic view because I think we have to have hope in order to go on." But I didn't say any of it, simply tried with my eyes and warmth to send her the message that I cared. About her. About racism. Understood something if not the half of it.

After several more minutes telling me how obliviously, annoyingly white my attitude was, Maria, who had always been kind, reached across the table to squeeze my hand. And changed the subject. Evidently she had said all she had to say. We ate our dinner and, as usual, hugged good-bye at the restaurant's front door, then set off in different directions.

I walked the long way home to my apartment, trying to absorb everything she said. Racism distorted everything, I knew, but this lodged the knowledge deeper into my bones.

⁓

I plunged ever harder into our work at Equity Institute, trying to win over the white men who held so much power. Could I convince them that inclusive workplaces were good business? I traveled the country speaking to leaders of universities, public agencies, corporations, nonprofits. Detroit. Minneapolis. San Francisco. Miami. Dallas. Des Moines. Charlotte. Santa

Barbara. New Orleans. New Haven. New York. New Bedford. Athens, Ohio. Boston.

Usually I traveled with one of my training partners—Jamie Washington, Barbara Love, or Beverly Daniel Tatum—modeling our egalitarian biracial relationships. Spending days with each of them was a joy, a privilege. But the work felt like rowing upriver, even when participants wrote at the end of our three-day or week-long programs, "I learned so much." "My eyes are opened." "Thank you!" "I will take this to my department."

While I focused on extending my energies outward, Equity's bureaucracy became a riptide pulling me under. As executive director, my writing was reduced to performance reviews, presentations to the board, and contracts. Each time Equity Institute expanded, hiring more staff and developing new programs, my administrative work grew. But I kept up my private journal. "Thinking how I used to write about curtains blowing in the evening breeze, yellow curtains rippling. That was so much my treat and my salvation. . . . I need to get back to the habit of writing. Carving out beauty, creating. I live so differently now. Business luncheons. Conferences. Vacations at the Cape, massages, and saunas."

Carole, Equity's development director, bought me work clothes, gorgeous suits in bright colors. Red. Blue. Purple. Jones New York, Ann Taylor. I had never known brands existed. Peasant blouses on secondhand racks didn't carry labels. I had grown up with rummage sale clothes and plaid dresses from a Sears catalog. Now, clad in wool skirts with matching jacket and heels, swinging a brown leather briefcase and sporting my first professional haircut, I half gloated, half mourned, "I'm a career woman."

We rented the Equity Institute a nine-room suite with a classroom. I hauled myself to a used office supply store, where, poking among stacked furniture, I spied a cherry desk with a matching table and chairs. Its graceful detailing caught my eye: curved drawer fronts, mahogany panels, leaves twining up each side, an expansive desktop. This gorgeous piece of furniture, an elegant version of my rolltop desk at home, was the feminine analog to a presidential desk. I could peer across it with authority when I met clients or interviewed employees. Or fired them.

I trained constantly. Yet no matter how hard or how long we worked, dawn to dusk and into the night, more was needed. We were bailing out a sinking ship with a spoon. But when Douglass visited one day from college, I was reminded why I couldn't stop.

"Tell me everything," I implored at our restaurant lunch. I wanted details.

"Ma," he pleaded. "I can't. I don't know what to tell."

I had learned that if I were quiet, no questions, he would talk nonstop. Finally he opened up. "I'm writing for the school newspaper. Here, I brought you these." He dragged three crumpled articles from his backpack.

I smiled at my radiant son. "How wonderful, let me see them!" He had conducted interviews with famous people like Elie Wiesel. "You're such a good writer. Like your dad."

"Can we stop at the bookstore?" he asked after the meal. Meandering into a small shop, we scanned the new books display table.

"There's that new Langston Hughes biography." I pointed.

"By Rampersad," he said. "It's gotten good reviews."

He wanted a Kerouac book. His ferocious interest intrigued me. Was this the bohemian side of my buttoned-down son? Some wanderlust dream passed down in his genes? I paid and we strolled from the dusty store into the sunlight. As we walked back to my car, he thought of a game we had played when he was young.

"Race you to the car, Ma!"

"All right," I happily agreed, tossing him my large handbag, trying to equalize the race with this college athlete. We ran the few blocks, grinning. As we neared the car, two young white men yelled. I couldn't make out the words and paid little attention. When we arrived at my old turquoise Toyota station wagon and leaned against the hood panting and laughing, the men walked by, staring.

"Sorry," they mumbled as they passed, heads down.

In a flash I understood. My body turned to stone. They hadn't seen a family. They had seen a thief, a young African American man running off with a pocketbook, chased by a middle-aged white woman. What could have happened if they had carried guns?

Soon I wrote about the encounter and used it in my programs as an example of the daily danger dark-skinned people faced. In Boston I mentioned it at a seminar for senior bank managers, all white. That night a workshop participant asked his son, a police officer, "What would you have done if you'd observed the scene?" Next day he reported his son's chilling response: "I'd have shot out his knee-caps."

I shook again and received terrible confirmation: I wasn't insane to continually notice race, to try to ameliorate its distortions. I had to. From then on, whenever Douglass and I were in public, I never handed him my pocketbook, no matter how heavily laden or tired I was. My slip could've been deadly. Being part of a biracial family wasn't an inoculation against ignorance.

The terror drove me to keep on with the work. We were changing the culture, one institution at a time. But how long could I hold on? The writing hunger kept pressing, insistent, a stone lodged against my heart. Would I never get the chance? Weeknights all I could manage were late dinners with Carole, a quick snuggle, and instant sleep. I had never worked this hard, never been a breath away from burnout, year after year.

I jotted down private schemes for leaving Equity: I would write, make pottery to sell, counsel a few clients on their "ism" issues, which I already did for Equity, and revert to a marginal existence. Calculating budgets, I figured I could live on $15,000 a year. In a tent if I had to.

It sounded like bliss. I would never again have to present a budget to the board, explaining why we came up short. Never have to fire anyone—and each time agonize over my own white-boss role in their failure. Never again speak to an auditorium packed with tight-lipped, arms-folded white businessmen (rarely women). Never have to dress up in an uncomfortable suit, stockings, and heels. Year after year, I scribbled desperate plans.

"Not yet," Carole said gently each time I confessed them. "Someday you'll write, I know you will, but we have to build this first."

At those moments, I hated her. Didn't she understand? Sometimes my anger led to a fight, usually over the children. "You need to run anything you want to say to them by me first," I would demand. "They've been hurt by my partners before. It's not going to happen again!"

"That's unreasonable. I have my own relationship with them. Don't you trust me?"

"No!"

In a minute we would be screaming, slamming doors. Finally we went to a marvelous therapist who opened our sessions each week by asking, "What do you love about each other?"

"Nothing!"

But miraculously, within the hour we would work our way to appreciation and sort through the tangles that had us tied in such knots. For several years we saw her, until the space between visits lengthened, and gradually we learned to handle those furious, frightened feelings ourselves.

Acquaintances often told me, "You were so brave to start a business doing what you love. I wish I had the courage to do that." Their faces beamed admiration as they shared their own pent-up dreams.

"This isn't what I want to be doing!" I felt like shouting. "I'm petrified every time I travel to a new city and have to spend days with arrogant white men who don't want to be in my seminars and try to argue their way out of taking responsibility. Out of acknowledging the evidence right in front of them. I hate traveling. I'm scared about making airline connections, the pickup at the airport, the lonely hotels. The speeches where I wonder if I can pull it off again. Do you know how tiring this work is? How tough?"

But I didn't say it. Instead I encouraged people to live their dreams. And it was true: I was living *one* of mine, the one where I helped end racism. But it was taking so damn long.

How much more could I wait to write before I exploded? I reread Langston Hughes's poem "Harlem," with its famous lines about a dream deferred. But I couldn't figure out how to turn writing into my work, how to make money with it, how to end racism with it.

So I kept trudging to workshop after workshop, wondering what would happen to me if I continued postponing life as a wordsmith. Would I really explode? Or simply wither like a raisin in the sun?

The Color Purple

1987

Desperate for time to write, I invited my father, a poet who rarely composed poetry as often as he would like, to a self-styled writer's retreat. We would camp for four days, just the two of us, in a remote wilderness campground.

"Yes," he answered immediately.

A month later, in October, he and I drove winding mountain roads to Mount Greylock State Reservation, deserted that late in the year. We hiked a quarter mile to the campground. Deep layers of blazing red and orange maple leaves on the ground gave off the ripe, delicious smell of autumn. I inhaled deeply, feeding my country girl soul. We unrolled sleeping bags on metal bedsprings in a lean-to, foraged for kindling, and huddled contentedly around a fire my dad built. Smoke blew first one way and then another, shifting with the winds. After a scrambled egg supper, we watched flames tear at the dark.

"Tell me about Black Mountain," I urged him, ever eager to learn more about the idyllic college where I had been born, which figured mythically in my childhood. He told me again about the time he had nearly drowned when the river flooded and he had tried to save a fellow student, who did drown. Mort survived the rushing waters only by holding on to a tree branch for hours, until rescue came. Each time I heard that story, I shivered. Then his face lit up when he remembered the students and faculty organizing poetry readings, plays, and dances. "It was a magical place. And time," he said.

"Tell me about your childhood," I begged. We hunched on adjacent logs long into the night while Mort poked at embers, sending sparks flying. He

Joan with her father, Morton Steinau, fixing cars at Black Mountain, circa 1942. (author's archive)

vividly recalled the ease of his early childhood in the 1920s, then bitter years after his family lost both their business and home when he was eight or nine, and the rented single rooms where he lived with his parents from then on.

"My dad was a bookie in those years," he reminded me as I listened to familiar tales: How Mort had to leave their shabby single room and wait outside when "business" called. Or when cops showed up for their take. His father, Jacob, sixty-five at Mort's birth, was an old man by then. "My dad was born in 1852, before the Civil War. He hated Black people, couldn't tolerate being in the room with them." My father gritted his teeth, paused, and said, "I brought an essay to read to you. About Dad."

"You wrote about your father?" Having died before my birth, he was a remote figure.

"Yeah, twenty-five years ago." He pulled two yellowing pages from his knapsack and began reading, choking up.

Frances had cleaned and cooked for us as far back as I can remember. She belonged in and to our house as much as did my big brother or Mom or Dad or the huge faded oil painting, over the fireplace, of a squatting loin-clothed Indian from India blowing a thin horn and making a snake rise from a jug in front of him.

Frances had brown-black skin. She was so fat that when she sat on a wooden kitchen chair it looked like she was sitting in the air if I stood right in front of her because I couldn't see any part of the chair.

When I was little she would give me my bath and dry me and help me get my clothes on. Usually she left in the late afternoon and Mom fixed supper which we ate in the big dining room that we had to go through the pantry to get to, at a big round table that could be pulled open and made as big as you wanted when more people were there at Thanksgiving and Christmas or when I had a birthday, and those times Frances stayed and fixed the food and served it to us in the dining room.

"I never knew you had a maid."

"Those were the early years in Louisville, before Dad's eyesight got so bad he lost his jewelry store. But listen."

Sometimes, if Mom and Dad went out for supper Frances would fix it just for my big brother and me, and she would put me to bed. She never read stories like Mom did but would make them up out of her head. When she sat on the bed to tell me a story the bed tipped way down on that side and I would roll downhill to the low side of the bed and lay next to her warm body, listening to her stories of jungles and animals talking to each other the way people do. If I asked, "What was the name of the lion or the fox or the snake?" she always knew, and would say, Gloriana, or Belinda, or Jehoshaphat, or whatever its name was.

Before I was big enough to go to school and ate lunch at home, Frances fixed the noon meal for Mom and Dad and me and we ate it in the kitchen and not in the big dining room. Frances ate when we did, but at a small table in the pantry, sitting on a stool that was kept there to stand on for reaching the high pantry shelves over the wide two-door icebox. The icebox was built right into the wall and had another door on the outside of the house the iceman could open and put ice in without ever coming into the house. Sometimes, if I heard him, I'd open the inside door and talk to him while he chipped and fitted the ice, because it seemed so different than just plain talking to someone, like through a tunnel, and he would usually hand through to me a piece of the ice he'd chipped off.

My father walked home for lunch from his jewelry store, which was a block down our street to Main Street and then half a block up Main Street without ever having to cross the street. He always got home just after a loud whistle blew that meant it was noon. He would always call out, "I'm home!" as he walked through the back door into the kitchen, even though Mom and Frances and I were usually right in the kitchen and could see that he was home because Mom would always say a few minutes before the noon whistle blew, "It's time to get ready for lunch. Your father will be here in a few minutes." Dad would go to the kitchen sink and wash and dry his hands and then sit at the table and he and Mom and I would start eating, as if someone had blown a second whistle.

If we needed something at our table as we ate lunch my mother would tell Frances, who ate at her small table nearby. She would stop eating and bring it to us. If my father wanted something, such as another cup of coffee, he'd say, "Mother, will you ask Frances to bring me another cup of coffee, please," and she would tell Frances. If I wanted something more I'd usually call to Frances, but then my father would always say, "If you want anything, ask your mother to ask Frances." So I'd tell Mom again what I wanted and she'd tell Frances and Frances would get up and bring it to the table.

One day, after I was old enough to be going to school, I had to stay home because I had a fever. Frances was cleaning the upstairs where the bedrooms were, and she looked quietly into my room and seeing that I was awake, she said, "It's a long time to lunch and you haven't had no breakfast. I'll fix us some nice hot tea with milk and sugar. You come on down to the kitchen where it's warm. And besides, you'll spill tea over the covers if you try to drink it in bed."

I don't think Mom had ever given me tea, and it made me feel almost grownup. The sweet hot tea tasted good, and so did the toast sprinkled with sugar and cinnamon. Frances and I were sitting at the table where Mom and Dad and I ate lunch, and she had put a fresh tablecloth on, saying, "This here's a tea *party*, not just havin' tea."

My father walked through the kitchen door, started across the room to upstairs, and stopped, his mouth opening, looking first at Frances and then at me. His face became red, and he walked slowly to the table, slowly wound the hanging edges of the tablecloth around his hands. He leaned over to the table, his red and quivering face almost touching mine, and shouted in a hoarse voice, "Don't let me *never* catch you eating at the table with a nigger again!"

He jerked the tablecloth across the table and into the air and tea and cups and plates and milk and sugar and spoons and toast crashed to the floor and ran in streams under the chairs and crashed against the wall and trickled down behind the stove. He wadded the tablecloth into a ball and threw it on the floor, turned, and walked across the kitchen out the kitchen door. As he walked across the kitchen floor, the grating of the sugar under his shoes was the loudest sound I've ever heard, and has never quieted down.

We sat silently. I had never heard of Frances before. He had told me before that his father once yanked the tablecloth off, but I had thought Mort was a teenager offering some benign dinnertime comment about how it would be okay to eat with a Negro. "I never knew there was an actual Black person at the table when this happened," I said slowly, imagining how horrible it must have been for Frances, as well as my six-year-old father. "What did she do?"

"She cleaned it up," he said.

I flashed on an image of a middle-aged woman (Was she? Or younger, with her own children at home?), a heavy woman, bending to sweep up the broken glass, grabbing a mop, swirling that old rag mop with fury across the floor, back and forth. Wishing she dared quit. Wishing my grandfather dead.

And I could see my bookish dad as a little boy, staring with big eyes, wishing he dared cry. Or shout. He too, for an instant, wishing his father dead.

"Your father must be turning over in his grave," I said. "With African American great-grandchildren."

"He was a difficult man," my father said after a pause.

We sat listening to a high-pitched owl call, and the crackle of leaves as raccoons and possums and maybe bears scurried outside the glow of our fire. I tried to breathe deeply, absorbing this aspect of my family history: a Black maid, my grandfather's violence, my dad's sense of justice kindled by this brutal act, only later understanding the everyday oppression.

My heritage.

Was this part of what drove him to stand, with my mom and a few others, protesting a Ku Klux Klan meeting in backwoods Connecticut? They had waited all evening on a small dirt road, holding up signs for civil rights. I had been frightened for my parents, and immensely relieved to hear later that night that they'd safely escaped.

"The sound of the sugar grating under his shoes. It's haunting," I said.

"It's haunted me all my life."

"Me too," I said. "Without even knowing about it. That violence in our history. That hatred. Are we still atoning?"

"Probably." Mort's hands shook as he put away his papers. "We should be."

In the morning, after a smoky breakfast, I hauled out the small portable typewriter I had bought for the retreat, a secondhand gem from Green's Typewriter Shop—Amherst's rare Black-owned business. For hours I crouched on a log, jacket collar turned up against a chilly wind, and let my fingers pound out words. They surged as if stored in my brain ready for the page. How much I had missed this kind of floating-mind time away from the pressures of Equity Institute. How easily my thoughts relaxed out here in the woods. Ideas and sentences magically appeared. My own form of atoning, I supposed, my writing a gesture of social repair.

Mort, sitting on a log nearby, jotted a few lines in his notebook, scavenged for kindling, and, restless, whittled sticks for toasting marshmallows. His presence cheered me while I pounded out sentences and struck words, revising as I wrote.

By lunchtime I was eager to hike; then write until supper, while the father I adored more each year heated a bean stew he had cooked at home and frozen. Again we sat up late in the empty campground. We chatted briefly about our writing of the day, but mostly our talk consisted of me asking for more stories about his 1920s Louisville childhood.

"I was a studious lad," he began, a twinkle in his blue eyes—a glint I could hear more than see. "But we had no money for books, nor did I have time to read, since I caddied at the golf course after school for money to pay our rent in the single room where we lived. I rode my bike there, ten miles. And back again. By the time I got home, it was dark. I was hungry and ready for bed."

My heart filled with Mort's stories, the woods, the pungent smells, his loving presence. That night I slept soundly, relishing the cold lean-to, my father's gentle snore, and the scent of moist, decaying leaves.

Each day we repeated the pattern. Mort puttered gathering wood, penned a few poems, and was my companion while I huddled on a log dressed in long johns, flannel-lined jeans, and a winter jacket, contentedly striking the small typewriter with fingers flying. The writing fire in my soul flamed up, ever ready, it seemed, if allowed space to burn.

When the enchanted days came to an end too soon, my dad and I plodded out to his car with our memories, sleeping bags, trash—and our writing. "Give my love to Carole," he said when he dropped me off in Amherst. "Tell her I'm sorry I missed her."

I arrived home buoyant, with an eight-page article, "What Happens to the Mythmakers When the Myths Turn Out to Be Untrue?"

Carole read it that night. "It's terrific. I can't believe this is a first draft." She proved to be a natural editor, with a good ear and a fine-tuned sensibility, supportive but also pointing out subtle flaws in my reasoning or word choice.

The myth was white supremacy. Both the blatant kind my grandfather represented, and the more subtle kind the rest of us inherited. I suggested we whites had to shed that false premise, about ourselves and others, so our beliefs could match reality. Then we could join the majority of the world's population as equals and learn how to take our true power. Steeped in James Baldwin's lacerating words, I encouraged white readers to draw on our rich history of being allies, like nineteenth-century abolitionists or gentile supporters of Jews during World War II. "What can we do out in the world?" I asked white readers, reminding them to use our relative privilege for change.

My tone was encouraging rather than admonishing. Reading in Alice Walker's novel *The Color Purple*, how the heroine Celie reconciled with her brutal ex-husband Mister, had softened my outrage, shifted my racial writing to a healing voice. "Mythmakers" was the written analog to my compassionate workshop style.

I mailed the essay to a Boston Unitarian church where I had trained staff—and to my shock they published it in their newsletter, exactly as written. "Look!" I screamed to Carole when they sent a copy. Then the Peace and Freedom Party newsletter published an excerpt; other Unitarian churches and underground papers printed it whole. The Equity Institute issued it as a pamphlet.

Those four days in the woods with my dad proved so powerful I was determined to repeat our retreat, but months slipped by, and then years. We never returned. But the stories remained.

I did carve out another brief space—a single weekday at home—and wrote "The Multicultural Organizational Change Process: Seven Essential Components." Again the words rose up, fully formed, after years of talks. Closing with Henry Adams's prophetic 1906 words, I paraphrased, "Whereas society had been (philosophically) unitary for a thousand years, multiplicity was increasing at such a rate that within one generation we would need a new 'social mind.'" The honoring of diverse viewpoints I had seen in *The Alexandria Quartet* and *Rashomon* twenty years before had flowered by the '80s, gaining credibility in a broad social dialogue. Again Carole edited the essay, suggesting a few key changes before I sent it off to *Black Issues in Higher Education*. Would they publish me, a white woman?

The editor called a week later, booming in a deep voice, "We'll print your essay in our next issue—February 15, 1989—and feature it on the back page."

"Thank you!"

The moment he hung up, I leaped from my desk and jumped in the air, screaming, "Yes!" I ran through Equity's rooms pumping my fist. "Yes, yes, yes! *Black Issues* is going to publish my article!"

When it came out, Carole celebrated by taking me to dinner at Silverscape, our old romantic spot. She laid a copy of the journal on the table back page up, where my article and photo beamed all through the meal as a candle flickered between us.

These two articles, "Mythmakers" and "Seven Components," were the slender threads that stitched up my fraying writer's soul during the entire 1980s, keeping me barely alive. Along with occasional activist events—like

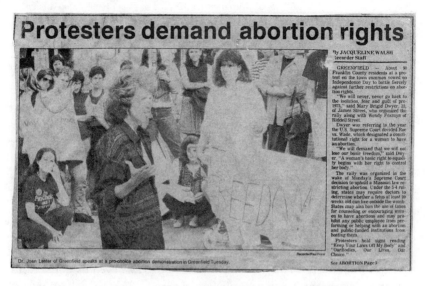

Protesters demand abortion rights

By JACQUELINE WALSH
Recorder Staff

GREENFIELD — About 90 Franklin County residents at a protest on the town common vowed on Independence Day to battle fiercely against further restrictions on abortion rights.

"We will never, never go back to the isolation, fear and guilt of pre-1973," said Mary Brigid Dwyer, 32, of James Street, who organized the rally along with Wendy Foxmyn of Riddell Street.

Dwyer was referring to the year the U.S. Supreme Court decided Roe vs. Wade, which designated a constitutional right for a woman to have an abortion.

"We will demand that we will not lose our basic freedom," said Dwyer. "A woman's basic right to equality begins with her right to control her body.

The rally was organized in the wake of Monday's Supreme Court decision to uphold a Missouri law restricting abortion. Under the 5-4 ruling, states may require doctors to determine whether a fetus at least 20 weeks old can live outside the womb. States may also ban the use of taxes for counseling or encouraging women to have abortions and may prohibit any public employee from performing or helping with an abortion and public-funded institutions from hosting them.

Protesters held signs reading "Keep Your Laws Off My Body" and "Our Bodies, Our Lives, Our Choice."

See ABORTION Page 5

Dr. Joan Lester of Greenfield speaks at a pro-choice abortion demonstration in Greenfield Tuesday.

Newspaper photo of Joan speaking at an abortion rights rally she organized, July 4, 1989. (*Greenfield Recorder*, author's archive)

a rally I organized for abortion rights one July 4, thinking to commemorate freedom that way—I managed to make it through the decade.

California still beckoned. Home of the free speech movement, the underground paper the *Berkeley Barb*, the Black Panthers. Land of sunshine, gay people, and a diverse population. I had dreamed of California since childhood, when my mother, face shining, told me stories about her Laguna Beach adolescence and showed me pictures of herself on the beach with her friends. It looked like heaven.

California, where I had gotten a scholarship to Oakland's Mills College before I met Julie—and had given it up to stay with him in New York.

California was my other dream deferred.

She's Got Her Ticket

1990

I often flew to San Francisco for donor meetings and to Santa Barbara, where an Equity Institute board member hired me for faculty seminars on diversity. "Please," I begged Carole. "Let's move to the Bay Area."

"Equity Institute's not ready. Not yet."

For three years I kept up my pleas, growing ever more urgent until, on April 1, 1990, sitting across a table at Napi's, a noisy restaurant in Provincetown, Carole shocked me. "Let's move to California," she said, reaching for my hand.

"Really? Do you mean it?"

"Yes, I can see you need to go. But it will take a year to transition the organization."

"This is the biggest gift of my life," I choked out. "Maybe six months?"

"No. It will take a year to get everything set with the board and new clients, closing out in Amherst, finding an office." She squeezed my hand and beamed broadly, her wide cheeks turning pink with pleasure. "And a house."

"One year from today?" I repeated, wanting to hear it again.

"Yes."

With every nerve on fire, my enthusiasm never flagged during the year we made our preparations for moving Equity and ourselves.

April 1, 1991, would be our moving day.

The afternoon before we planned to leave, Rosa visited from graduate school for a final farewell. We sat on high stools at our butcher-block kitchen island, chatting about her classes and my upcoming move while

I glanced, satisfied, around the room stacked high with boxes. Every dish was packed, every kitchen utensil. We had switched to paper plates.

"Ma," she said, "I'm going to miss you so much."

"We'll visit and you'll come to us." I reached out to comfort my sensitive first-born, now a full-grown woman. "I'll send you tickets whenever you want. We're flying back for your graduation next month, and you're coming out soon. It won't be that different, you'll see."

She cried then, astonishing me with her vehement love. So many years of confidences, nestled on the old flowered couch doing foot rubs, reading P. G. Wodehouse aloud, roaring with laughter. So many years since she had left home, when we had spoken every few days while she established her own life. I had no doubt she would be fine. Much as I adored her, I couldn't wait to go.

Fifty years old and once more I would make a new start. I imagined myself immersed in a literary culture, Asian American, Latino/a, and African American cultures, gay and lesbian life. Cutting-edge thinking. Feminists everywhere. Political demonstrations. Intellectual stimulation. Spiritual nourishment. Sparkling weather year-round.

Carole and I bought a tiny Berkeley bungalow with skylights, a smooth wooden deck, and a wall of brilliant red bougainvillea in the rear garden. The house was so small we left most possessions behind, abandoning them to a bulk purchaser. But I had to bring my rolltop desk, even though it took up a preposterous portion of our new pale-yellow living room. I needed its heft and the history embedded in its brown oak. I had penned my feminist articles on its vast surface, grappled with my dissertation while staring blankly at its grain, and written thousands of journal pages at this desk.

A garden shed behind our new home would be my writing studio. Before we moved, the old owners renovated it for us with a French door, skylight, and a bright-blue door calling me inside. Somehow I would find time to use it. If, in this great whirling universe full of light and fire, I could not find a path like a shooting star, blazing my words across the heavens, I could not go on, did not want to go on.

Before we left, I called Julius. We enjoyed a unique friendship, extracting the best qualities from our early years. I had forgiven the rest by now, and so, evidently, had he. His warm deep voice on the phone comforted and stimulated me when we spoke of the children, or our latest observations about the world. Though our viewpoints had diverged—his more conservative, mine the same as always—he was such a creative thinker that talking to him invariably stretched me. And our old bond, despite its tatters, remained. On our last evening in Massachusetts, I dialed his number. "Hey, wanted to say good-bye."

"I can't believe you're finally doing it. You've wanted to live in California so long." He sounded almost wistful. Definitely fond, like someone who had known me nearly thirty years. Someone who cared.

"Yeah, my whole life, basically, ever since Barb [my mother] showed me those teenage pictures of herself on the beach. Now I know how cutting-edge the thinking is, since I've been traveling there a lot. I can't wait."

"You've done a great job raising Rosa," he said. "And Douglass too. They're both remarkable adults and you're a big part of that. They're socially aware, responsible citizens. Chips off your block, not mine." He chuckled. "I have to congratulate you, Joan. You've been a wonderful mother."

"Thank you." To say I was stunned would be an understatement. Julius rarely lavished praise, instead excelling at critical thinking and confrontation.

"Now it's your time, Joan. May California be everything you're looking for."

This was the Julius I had loved so fiercely, the generous, sensitive man who could penetrate to the heart of a situation, or a woman, in a minute. "Thank you. Good-bye." It felt strange saying farewell, not knowing when, or if, I would see him again.

In fact, a few years later he would surprise me by showing up at a reading I gave at a Northampton bookstore. I next saw him at Douglass's Minneapolis wedding. That was a time replete with emotion as we prepared, with my parents and other family members, to watch our son get married. At the rehearsal dinner, we each toasted Douglass and his bride; mine was unremarkable, but Julius gave a moving toast, saying essentially, "It was Joan, Douglass's mother, who came up with his powerful name, she who was the devoted political parent, the one who cared deeply about justice and passed that commitment on to our children. She's been passionate about social justice since before we met and kept at it ever since. A toast to Joan, too, for Douglass has inherited her compassion." Open-mouthed, I stood stunned. Carole's squeeze of my hand and pleased smile let me know that I had heard correctly.

The following day, Julius and I walked down the aisle together while Carole sat, front row, awaiting me. In that moment, and after the previous evening's tribute, I felt healed.

The last time I saw Julius was a decade later, at my father's memorial service. He had remained close to my parents for the thirty-five years since our divorce, calling, visiting annually, and sending them a copy of each book he published. I knew they cherished the contact. Sometimes their pleasure with him annoyed me—did I really need to hear about his latest call or visit?—but on this day at my parents' Cape Cod Unitarian church, I treasured their long friendship and was grateful that Julius, who rarely traveled anymore, made the trip for this painful occasion just three days after my dad's passing.

During the service, Julius brought us all to tears when he threw back his head and sang, in his beautiful cantorial voice, "You Gotta Sing When the Spirit Says Sing," inserting a verse with my father's name. "You gotta Mort when the Spirit says Mort." My brother, sister, and I clung in a huddle while Carole and my aunt orchestrated the event. I stood on stage weeping with Julius and the rest of the family, including my brother's ex-wife. As she later quipped to the crowd, "You can never really leave this family. We're all here forever."

Once we shared grandchildren, Julius and I often exchanged emails with the latest news. After the third child he wrote:

Thanks for the email. I was pleased when Douglass told me the new child's name [with Julius's father's as a middle name]. And I'm sure my father would be very pleased. I have no doubt that your thoughts and energies in that direction reached Douglass in that mysterious way communications happen.

Thanks also for the email about the various ways Mort's life is being commemorated. We're hoping to get down to the Cape some time in April and will see Barb and I'll give her something on the stone [a memorial we placed in their yard] which sounds beautiful. Four hundred pounds! It reminded me of John Brown. He and some of the men who died with him at Harper's Ferry are buried under this huge boulder that sits in front of what was his home in upstate New York. It is quite wonderful and the stone you all bought for Mort made me think of it.

Thanks for being in touch and take care of yourself.

He sent long emails updating me on retirement ("wonderful"), his joy with photography, relatives who had passed as white, congratulations on my various publications, details of his declining health ("mitigated with my meditation practice"), and an occasional apology: "Thinking about your parents last night and thinking about how many years I've known them and they me, put me in mind of something that happened for which I owe you an apology. When my parents came to Amherst in 1980 you wanted to come over and visit with them. I felt fine about that but [his second wife] got angry about it. I recall telling you that my parents didn't think it was a good idea to see you, or something to that effect. So, I apologize to them and to you for not standing up to her . . ."

Years later he wrote, after my mother's death: "One of the rituals I love in Judaism is lighting a yahrzeit candle on the anniversary of someone's death. I light one for Barb each year and did so from sundown Monday to sundown Tuesday. It's a little ritual that I love, especially to have the glow of the candle through the night. It is as if the person's spirit has returned to be with me. With affection to you and my best to Carole, Julie."

And another time, another apology: "I spent much of my seventieth year reviewing the previous sixty-nine. . . . This kind of introspection has been quite good as well as painful. You have been on my mind a lot, and I was going to write you to apologize for the ways I knowingly and unknowingly hurt you over the years we've known each other. To make excuses or to try and explain this, that, or the other would not diminish the hurt. I am sorry for having hurt you, knowingly and unknowingly."

His emails were so lovely that every now and then I wondered, Who is this warm, chatty man? In person I would have felt awkward with him. But, as I joked to friends, "Email's the perfect medium for ex-spouses." Julius was finally happy, with a committed partner, his third wife well suited for his chosen life of solitude, twelve acres of land, and no pressures to lecture or travel, which he had completely given up. Always he was laudatory about my writing, saying repeatedly, "Take care of yourself, and again, you write well. There's nothing harder than writing fiction, as far as I'm concerned, and you handled many voices and many characters with admirable skill. Congratulations!"

Sometimes we would get surprises in the mail from him: beautifully printed photos of baby Rosa and me, or an annual calendar he created with his photographs, marked with quirky dates like National Handshake Day. But when I said good-bye on the eve of Carole's and my California move, I had no idea how our lives would continue to intertwine.

On April 1, 1991, Carole and I set out, driving to the Boston airport in a cold, icy sleet. "Good-bye, East Coast" we exulted. "No more freezing rain, no more sliding around on ice. No more driving snow. California, here we come!" All morning we shouted our good-byes, interpreting the terrible weather as a sign. "We were right to leave!"

When I heard Tracy Chapman on the car radio, I joined in, lungs bursting. "She's got her ticket, I think she's gonna use it, I think she's going to fly away. No one should try and stop her, persuade her with their power. She says that her mind is made up." Yes, my mind was made up.

As the plane lifted off, I murmured "Good-bye, Julius," surprised to leave him back in the Old World while Carole and I set out for the New. This time I was the one sailing off for the grand adventure, while he stayed behind.

Their Eyes Were
Watching God

1991

In the fall, I tore myself from the Promised Land and flew to Bozeman, Montana. Two visionaries, Albie and Susan Wells, had created a retreat, Windcall, for burned-out social justice leaders. Four at a time we flocked to the idyllic setting, eager to rest and heal. When my application was accepted on my second try, I knew I would use the time to write.

A spacious sky and October-brown hills surrounded our residence, where we each enjoyed a quiet luxury—our own bedroom and bath—plus an individual studio. There we could write, putter, or make art with the many available supplies.

In those days before laptops, I had arranged for a rental computer. A slight young woman looking barely over twenty knocked on the front door of the main house. "I'm here to install this," she said, hoisting a giant computer.

Oh no, I thought. How will she figure out how to hook it up, with the printer too? Aware of my sexist and ageist beliefs, but in the stress of the moment unable to block them, I fretted, *I really need this computer to work.* "I'll show you where it goes," I said, and uneasily led her to my studio. "It's the last on the left. The corner."

Twenty minutes later, everything worked. Printer and all.

"Ah," I sighed happily, looking out my windows to the forest of pines beyond a meadow. "This is perfect."

I tapped on the computer keys. An essay quickly took form, based on lines I had used in workshops describing "affirmative action 'family style.'" Even low-income white parents like mine, I told students, had amassed more wealth than their African American peers, due to favored work and mortgage treatment. No closed doors in their faces when they applied for jobs; no neighborhood redlining for them.

All day I wrote and rewrote. My inclination to write about the world in the first person, telling stories that made me vulnerable, came naturally now after fifteen years of flourishing women's publications and the new call for multicultural articles. By midafternoon I had printed out a six-hundred-word op-ed. The voice I had used for women's essays in my early Amherst days was back, spiced now with humor.

Every day I hiked and wrote, putting on paper set pieces I had honed over years of talks and seminars. The lie of race—an arbitrary category designed to raise newly minted "whites" over others—had become viscerally clear to me the day Rosa was born. "Who is Black, Who is White?" I wrote. And about the "rioters" who "looted" stores in moments of civil unrest, I wrote another piece: "Who's Looting Whom?" After all, who had violently looted people, land, and a vast trove of resources from an entire continent—not merely diapers or boom boxes from a corner store? Who had plundered wealth from forced free labor for hundreds of years?

Every night I pulled *Their Eyes Were Watching God* from my bedside table and groggily read myself to sleep, with Zora Neale Hurston's inventive images leaping through my dreams. It was the first book I ever read like a writer. Until then the books I had feasted on had been devoured with the eyes of a woman hungry for life guidance. I had never heard the admonition "Show, don't tell," and for all my education I didn't know there were books on the art of writing. But this time I noticed the artistry; I peered behind the curtain to study the arc of Hurston's dramatic scenes, took note of how she built tension and character. With *Their Eyes Were Watching God*, I found a mentor. A brilliant one. I examined the structure of her novel. And her metaphors—creative word paintings—which inspired me to let my mind fly free and grab at wisps of words floating by, tethered by unlikely conjunctions.

After seventeen days soaking up every Windcall moment, I emerged with twelve op-eds. Bundling the essays into my suitcase, I reluctantly moved out to the porch steps for a group good-bye. Posing for a final photo and embracing a last fellow resident, I wanted to hang onto the overhead beams and yell, "No, I won't leave!" These weeks of pampered solitude, with long endless days of writing, were the most luxurious I had ever known.

Back at Equity, the crush of backlogged calls, meetings, and client programs overwhelmed me. The first night home, I wrote, "How often have
pen and paper sustained me? Somehow I learned long ago to release myself
in it and through it." But feeling I had had my fun and needed to buckle
down, I stuffed the twelve articles into a folder. Though Carole urged me to
pull them out and as usual was a careful and supportive editor, piles of work
at the office came first. I didn't have time to research publication outlets.

Several months later, I took a few minutes to query Sandy Close at
the Pacific News Service and send four essays. She didn't accept any but
kindly invited me to tea, where she advised, "Submit to the *Contra Costa
Times*, a small local paper, as a way to get started."

When I consulted Julius, he agreed. "Start small. Remember when I
was publishing in *Sing Out* and the column in *The Guardian*? That helped
build my audience, until places like the *New York Times* wanted me."

I sent one to *Contra Costa*. Then—what made me do it?—I faxed six
articles to *USA Today*. I believed the essays were good and Carole agreed,
but Sandy Close's turndown made me wonder. Still, I took a leap.

Within an hour, *Contra Costa* called with a yes. I hadn't been completely
off in my assessment. I would work my way up to bigger papers.

But moments later my assistant buzzed. "A man from *USA Today* is on
the line."

Oh my God. Why is he calling? Is he going to tell me to leave them alone,
they don't want to see this junk? My brain a jumble, I said, "Hello."

"Joan?" he asked in a husky voice.

"Yes."

"Sid Hurlburt, the op-ed editor at *USA Today*."

"Hello," I said again, heart in my throat.

"We want to take three op-eds."

"What?" Would the mirage vanish, the phone disappear in a puff of
smoke, and would I be yanked back to the paper blizzard on my desk,
my fate as an administrative drudge sealed forever?

"You have a great voice. Light-hearted about serious issues."

"Thank you," I managed to mumble.

"Send a head shot with your social security number and we'll get started."

"Thank you, thank you, thank you," I nearly shrieked but bit my tongue.

"Have you got others?"

"Yes," I murmured, thankful again for those expansive Windcall days
when my soul had sung its way onto paper.

Parity for women in government

53% of the population should have 53% political representation.

"No taxation without representation" was a rallying cry I learned in elementary school. It was a cherished part of U.S. folk history, that canon of stories we tell and retell, establishing who we are and what we believe.

"No taxation without representation" was the clarion call to dump British tea in Boston Harbor. That act initiated the process culminating in the representational democracy we have today.

By Joan Steinau Lester, executive director of Equity Institute, Emeryville, Calif.

Today, when an amazing 53%, of the U.S. population does not have political representation. We have never had one of our own group as a president. We have 2% representation in the Senate and 6% in the House. Our particular visions, styles and agendas are not represented in our governing bodies. Yet we are taxed.

"One man, one vote" was a significant slogan of the 1960s. It's past time for an update. For the '90s: 53% population, 53% representation.

Our cherished history has indeed been *his* story. It's time we added *her* story and made *our*story.

Until that is fully realized and we are indeed coequal governors of our affairs, perhaps we should pay taxes proportionate to our representation in national bodies. Or perhaps we should not pay taxes at all until we have representational parity in this political democracy.

Then again, maybe it's tea-dumping time.

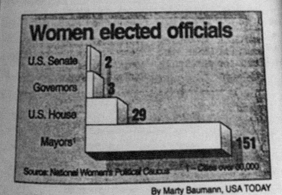

Women elected officials

U.S. Senate	2
Governors	3
U.S. House	29
Mayors¹	151

Source: National Women's Political Caucus   ¹ – Cities over 00,000

By Marty Baumann, USA TODAY

Joan's first *USA Today* article, March 24, 1992.

"Send them along. I'd like to take a look."

Hanging up, I screamed at the top of my lungs, "Yes!"

The largest newspaper in the United States, circulation six million, was about to publish my articles. Not one. Not two. But three. And they wanted more.

On March 24, 1992, my guest editorial debuted. At Carole's urging, I used my maiden name, Steinau, as part of my nom de plume: Joan Steinau Lester. "Start that now," she suggested. "You'll get known that way. Give your parents some credit. Don't only have Julius in there."

The article opened, "'No taxation without representation' was a rallying cry I learned in elementary school. It was a cherished part of U.S. folk history, that canon of stories we tell and retell, establishing who we are and what we believe."

Amazingly, 53 percent of the US population was hardly present in our government: women had 2 percent representation in the Senate and 6 percent in the House. "Our particular visions, styles and agendas are not represented in our governing bodies. Yet we are taxed." Tongue in cheek, I suggested that perhaps we should pay taxes proportionate to our representation. Or not at all. Or maybe, I closed, "It's tea-dumping time."

That night Carole's brother Paul bellowed from Oklahoma, "I saw Joan's picture in *USA Today!*"

Massachusetts friends called. Aquila, who had recently visited, laughed that deep throaty chuckle I loved. "You did it, girl."

"Yeah, now you have to get on with your painting," I reminded her. A talented artist caught in the UMass administrative grind, she had long shared with me the I'm-stuck-in-this-job-how-can-I-do-my-art blues. "Your turn." (She did start holding one-woman shows a few years later.)

My mother called, pride in her voice. "We heard from a Black Mountain friend we'd lost track of for thirty years. He figured by the name we must be related and somehow he found us." She and my dad drove fifteen miles to Orleans on Cape Cod for four copies of the paper. Carole and I snatched up three.

Days later a second *USA Today* column appeared.

More congratulatory calls. I pinched myself every time I saw the photo and byline.

In politics, diversity promotes excellence

The candidates' white-male model has gone stale.

None-of-the-above looks to be gaining ground this presidential campaign season. Voters are sending the message; commentators decry the pallid choices and wonder where the A-team is.

Among other aspects, all of the nationally recognized candidates appear to share several startling similarities: their race, their gender and sexual orientation.

The heterosexual-white-male model may be a good idea, but it's gone stale as the only game in town.

When a sports team uses the same play repeatedly during the game, its effectiveness declines. Likewise with this rerun.

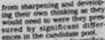

By Joan Steinau Lester, executive director of Equity Institute, Emeryville, Calif.

The candidates this season have been limited as a group, in that they represent such a narrow range of possible life experiences and perspectives.

It's as if only one food choice were available to us as consumers. Our bodies could not sustain themselves on the homogenous diet. Likewise with the body politic. We need variety to survive.

Their striking similarities also prevent these candidates from sharpening and developing their own thinking as they would need to were they pressured by significant differences in the candidate pool.

This view — that diversification of candidate pools benefits everyone, including the candidates themselves — challenges some traditional notions of how best to accomplish the search for excellence.

Discussions of diversity in academia, in corporations and on the shop floor often include fears of "lowering standards" and vague talk of "qualifications."

Recently, these concerns were expressed at Yale University via a flier plastering the campus. It said only: "War is peace, freedom is slavery, diversity is excellence."

Yet common sense indicates that the larger and more diverse the pool, the larger the chance of finding great talent, fresh perspectives and creative solutions.

Nature flourishes on diversity.

In genetics, without a diverse pool, the species degenerates.

In a presidential race, without a diverse pool of candidates, the level of discourse degenerates.

Variety may be not only the spice of life, but the meat as well.

Or the tofu, depending on your preference.

Joan's second *USA Today* article, March 30, 1992.

Another week, another op-ed. When a $150 check arrived for the first column, I taped the stub inside my top desk drawer, next to Audre Lorde's poem "Power."

People all over the country reached for *USA Today* in glass-fronted boxes or bent to pick up a copy at hotel doors. Seeds could be planted in millions of minds. Thus was born the Equity Institute's Media Project, adding writing to my job description.

I was now officially a paid Writer.

Two hours per day of work time to do my writing. Words dripping upon the page. I will have, I have made, the time and space to paint my words across a large canvas. Writer—about social issues—is indeed my life's work. I feel about it the way I did about teaching preschool in the early years. I haven't had that with Equity. Yet these ten years have given me the base to write, write, write, as Carole promised. I am excited! Grateful for the experiences I've gotten to write about. And access to two national media so far: *USA Today* and *New Directions for Women*. A year ago I told Aquila my goal was to write 6 pieces in the next year. I wrote 15 and published 12. I don't know why writing gives me so much pleasure, but it does. Writing, like teaching young kids, makes my heart sing.

Lynn Ludlow, the *San Francisco Examiner* opinion editor, invited me for coffee after I sent him a piece. We sat in a grubby café near his office, with me stunned into silence by the reality that an editor wanted to meet me. "You're a talented writer," he said gruffly. Kindly. "Send me everything you've got."

I couldn't believe I was hearing this.

True to his word, he began printing every op-ed I sent. An excellent editor, he slashed through my articles before they went to press and became my first real writing teacher. Grateful for professional edits, I steadily improved. When the *Chronicle* and *Examiner* merged for a Sunday edition, my editorials regularly graced the Sunday page.

Papers all over the country that were part of the Hearst syndicate were free to reprint the columns; ten or fifteen usually picked mine up. I engaged a clipping service to track them and learned about papers like the *Honolulu Star-Bulletin*, the second-largest daily in Hawaii, which appeared to be a regular fan. The *Miami Herald* frequently printed my articles, too, which delighted me since it was Dave Barry's home paper. Laughing aloud at his columns, which Douglass mailed me each week, I had studied his skill, analyzing how he covered topics like men's stunted emotional intelligence with such good humor.

—

Op-eds kept pouring out. I wrote about everything, and everything got published. *New Directions for Women*, our first national feminist newspaper, which I had subscribed to for years, delighted me by printing every article I sent. Again I was lucky to find a great editor in Lynn Wenzel.

Essays flooded out of me like an ice melt. I had an inexhaustible supply of topics: from the harassments Carole and I experienced as women and as a couple, to the daily news, to my biracial children's lives. I steadily churned out commentaries, recording many for NPR's *Marketplace* and San Francisco's *Perspectives* on KQED. Clerks in stores began to recognize my name when I handed them my credit card. They would say with a smile, "I heard you on the radio."

—

As I stared out my cottage window one afternoon, brain churning with ideas for an article, I acknowledged my amazing life: twelve years into my relationship with Carole, she had turned into the life partner, writing supporter, and editor of my dreams. I remembered the Rolling Stones lyric: "You can't always get what you want, but if you try sometimes, you just might find you get what you need."

I had gotten what I wanted, what I needed, and healed myself in unexpected ways. In sunny California, once I began to publish and enjoy wide recognition, I even found myself telling a new story about Julius. I had blamed him so long for my lack of artistic development, but it had been my own responsibility. Two lonely souls hardly out of adolescence, we had clung to each other for strength. He had burst forth from our nest, streaking like lightning into the publishing world. I hadn't. That wasn't his fault.

In California, far from the Amherst/East Coast orbit of Julius, out here where most people had never heard of him, I was free to start fresh. In California, all things were possible.

Half of a Yellow Sun

1993

"Have you thought about gathering your pieces into a book? I've seen a few. They're original." This was a New York literary agent who had called me at home.

A book? I hadn't thought of that.

"I could help you write a proposal," she offered.

"Really? I don't know anything about that."

"I'd love to represent you."

"Thank you. Let me think about it."

Excited, shaking, I ran to the library to research her agency. It was huge, prestigious. Maybe the leading agency in New York. "Yes," I said when I called back.

Under her tutelage, I struggled through proposal drafts, not entirely sure what she wanted. I created one after another, trying to organize my op-eds into some order and present them in an original way, since that was what she kept saying she liked about my work.

I called every two days, leaving messages with her indifferent assistant. "Did you get my last fax? I haven't heard back from X, the agent. Just wanted to make sure."

Draft after draft failed her approval.

I sped up, faxing new outlines every six hours. What did she want?

Now she became the impatient one, furiously demanding, "I need a better version!" until the day she stopped returning my calls.

I redoubled my efforts, desperate to send her the perfect proposal. But it was hard to know what that was since now I was getting no feedback.

Finally, one bitter afternoon the agent dropped me, snapping, "This isn't working," before she hung up.

Stunned, I sat alone in my writing cottage and sobbed. Why had I pestered her? Was my career as an author over? I had blown my chance at the big time. What a fool I had been not to handle this better.

I had gotten too big for my britches, my mother would have said. Who did I think I was anyway? I was an op-ed writer, that was all. Better stick to that and give up the idea of a book.

Humiliated and embarrassed, for weeks I could hardly write anything. The voice for my columns had come so naturally, but I'd lost confidence. I had wrecked my chances by acting like an unsophisticated, greedy idiot. I kept lacerating myself until an Equity Institute board member, John Eastman, counseled, "Oh no, you've got some great stuff." He gave me a short list of agents and I wrote down the names but stuffed them into a drawer. One evening when I spoke with Julius, starting off about our grown children, I told him what had happened with the agent.

"Publishing is tough these days," he said. "It's getting harder to sell something."

"Well, you seem to put out a book a year."

"But you'd be surprised how many even I can't sell, after all these books. Don't give up," he urged. "You have to find the right agent, and that one publisher who loves your stuff. That's all it takes. One."

"Do you think so?"

"I know so. If all these newspaper editors are so interested in publishing you, why wouldn't an editor at some house? You should send the proposal to other agents." He even gave me a name.

But still I didn't do anything.

"Have you sent off a proposal yet?" John, the Equity Board member, asked me each time we spoke.

"No," I answered vaguely, not wanting to tell him how horribly I had acted, how ashamed I felt.

"Do it," he said a few times. "The names I gave you are good agents. They'll be aligned with the way you're thinking." One of them, Faith Childs, was an African American woman Julius had mentioned.

Partly to get John off my back, I finally sent my book proposal to two agents and a small press.

I waited.

Days passed, weeks.

Nothing.

After a month Faith Childs replied with a long, generous letter, telling me she admired my writing samples, but sadly, "Collections of essays don't do well."

Defeated, I wondered if I should simply stick to columns, which *were* doing well. I decided not to send the proposal anywhere else.

The next day I was caught off guard when Mary Jane Ryan, the publisher of Berkeley's flourishing Conari Press, called to say, "We're totally interested!"

Really?

"We love your stuff!" she said. "Let's meet to discuss it."

Did that mean my proposal was okay?

Over dinner at Bucci's restaurant, Mary Jane and her husband, Will, assured Carole and me, "We'd know how to market this book. It's like Molly Ivins's collection." Ivins, who cracked lines like, "Our attorney general is under indictment. He ran as 'the people's lawyer'; now we call him 'the people's felon.'"

"We'd like to offer a book contract," Mary Jane said. "We'll do a good job for you, and your backlist will always be available."

"After the birth of my children," I gushed to Carole after we left the restaurant, "and meeting you, this is the happiest day of my life!"

The next morning I raced to a Shattuck Avenue photo booth, inserted a dollar, and snapped a roll of grins, two thumbs up, to record my joy.

⁓

Yet I worried in my journal, "Is this book just a myth? All I really have are some chapter headings. But I think I'm on to something." I plunged ahead, organizing the text one way and another, plugging gaps with new essays.

By March of '93 I wrote:

The book. It will be (is) FUN. That's the perspective to keep—not the $, the fame, the hassles, the pressure, the book tour, the contract, the critics, the reviews. I realize all those questions and concerns started to take over, instead of the joy of the writing.

What has been so precious about the columns is that they are FUN. It's felt like a hobby, one I've gotten good at and get intense pleasure from. The book (THE BOOK) already feels like Business. This is an important crossroads. It's entering the professionalization of my writing. I don't want this to become my bread and butter. I want to keep it as the strawberry jam, my treat.

Self-portrait as a writer with children, 1993.

On May 28 I rejoiced:

The world couldn't be giving me a better fifty-third birthday present than my two articles coming out on Sunday. One in the *LA Times*, one in the *Chicago Tribune*. My creativity is being given full scope. Here I stand. One tough bird. Celebrating Chapter 3: Girlhood, Motherhood, Cronehood (mehood). In the first two phases I tried so hard not to be selfish, putting others first. Especially motherhood. But I'd been told that was how a good girl lived. Now at last I dare to put myself first. It still feels bold and almost risky, after playing midwife to other lives. But I cherish this space. The crone rides . . .

By fall the manuscript had been written, edited, revised, and reedited. Anne Lamott's *Bird by Bird* explained the process I had been through. "Very few writers really know what they are doing until they've done it," Lamott assured me in her chapter about the "shitty first draft," that initial writing where we pour thoughts and feelings onto the page. The shape of my book didn't become clear until I had drafted it all.

For months I gathered endorsements for *The Future of White Men and Other Diversity Dilemmas*, the title a humorous portrait of the angst white men were expressing. The cover of *Newsweek* had screamed "White Male Paranoia" after the Senate Judiciary Committee's dismissal of Anita Hill during the Clarence Thomas hearings ushered in the Year of the Woman: twenty-four new women elected to the House and five to the Senate, the greatest increase ever. *Business Week* followed up with its own cover, headlined "White, Male, & Worried."

After months of brainstorming, my publisher came up with my effective title, designed to provoke. Only later did I realize its uncanny echo of Julius's first book, *Look Out, Whitey! Black Power's Gon' Get Your Mama!* Two long tongue-in-cheek titles, both referencing white men's fears of a cultural transformation, in which they would have to cede some power. How does the universe make this happen, when every person involved in my book's naming was unaware of the similarity? The content was alike, too: each a manifesto on current events, motivated to engender change. I was following in Julius's giant footsteps without even noticing they were there.

One of my salty heroines, Texas governor Ann Richards, blurbed *The Future of White Men*: "Terrific writer!" And Urvashi Vaid, the former executive director of the National Gay and Lesbian Task Force, wrote, "Lester's generous voice sheds keen insight, humor and practical advice." Conari designers came up with a neon pink cover, highlighted by green cutout letters. A cheerful photo graced the jacket flap.

I waited anxiously for reviews, which Mary Jane told me would come a few weeks before publication. One afternoon she called, sounding worried. "We got the *Publishers Weekly* review." *PW*, the industry Bible. "It's not good." I felt a hot flush of shame. "But they're tough. The others will be better."

"Okay," I gulped.

Photo of Joan by Irene Young, 1994.

When she faxed the review, I read that they found my short essays "superficial." I was devastated. Why had I thought I could be a real writer? I should have stuck to my bite-size pieces; I didn't know how to write with the depth worthy of a book. Was *The Future of White Men* going to be dead before it even came out? Criticism was sure to come from all corners. I waited anxiously for other reviews, wanting to crawl into bed.

But the American Library Association's prestigious *Booklist* came next, and to my relief the reviewer recommended the book "for all libraries." The *San Francisco Chronicle* reviewer Pat Holt wrote, "In its chatty, no-nonsense way, puts all the taboos on the table. . . . It's tricky territory, but in Lester's hands, the paths are clear and easily followed." *Ms.* magazine followed up with an enthusiastic endorsement, saying, "You can learn from this book." Even the conservative *Orange County Register* liked it.

Conari Press was going all out. They planned a national tour for our fall '94 release, booking me on scores of TV shows and morning-drive radio. Every white male hosting his own radio or TV talk show wanted to battle me. The provocative title had done its work. Now I had to carry the flag for inclusion.

I crisscrossed the country. United Airlines was lavish with upgrades in those days, if one was a frequent flyer. So I always flew first class, reclining in leather seats and eating shrimp cocktail.

Media escorts drove authors everywhere; they became confidants while I tried to tamp down my terror. In Boston, a retired teacher hired for my three days in the city plucked me from the Four Seasons Hotel every few hours to zoom me to an interview or two, and return me to the hotel, where I rested before another round.

"What *is* the future of white men?" my interlocutors invariably began, hostility coating their voices, as if my title alone proposed sending them into permanent exile. But generally my response—"White men simply have to learn to *share* power, not *abdicate* it"—and friendly tone won them over, and we parted on good terms.

But national TV was different. How did I look, would my unruly hair stay in place, my scarf? The interviewers were often sharper, asking more pointed questions, which I, in my anxiety, had more trouble answering, though Carole swore I sounded fine.

In New York the *Donahue* show put me up at a disconcertingly strange midtown hotel. It featured an entirely black interior, mirroring my mood. All night before the show, I quaked alone in a tiny room, my dark cell. By morning, when an escort from the show arrived, I was a bundle of nerves. At the NBC Rockefeller Plaza studio, an assistant producer ran into the green room holding a clipboard. "Jump right in on the panel," she instructed after I signed the release. "Don't hold back. Even if you're not called on. Phil wants you to mix it up." She shepherded me down a maze of hallways into an auditorium, repeating, "Speak up. Don't hold back." I sat on stage with the other panelists, one my Equity Institute colleague Jamie Washington, whom I had insisted we include. I was the only woman, he the only African American. The others were white men set up to be our antagonists.

Phil Donahue appeared below us, pacing. "What's the future for white men?" he asked, turning first to me and halfway into my answer interrupting to ask the same question of a white man. "Women and minorities are taking all the jobs," that man said to audience applause.

"*All* the jobs?" I asked. "Last I checked, white men still ran over ninety percent of American companies, governorships, police departments . . ."

"White men can't find work," he interrupted. More clapping.

"I know it's a change. Other people are just starting to crack open a few high-level jobs. That can feel unfair when white men are used to having them all." I heard a burst of audience support.

"It's affirmative action. That's what's unfair. What about affirmative action for me? My grandparents were from Poland. Do you know how many Polish jokes I hear, how we're stupid?"

"I'm sorry. But still—"

"Political correctness, that's all it is. Hire the best person for the job."

Jamie jumped in, saying, "Political correctness is a phrase used to demonize any policy some people don't like. It's a—" People applauded until Donahue cut him off, turning to one of the white men.

And we were off, until the interminable show ended at last and I could breathe again.

In Washington, DC, I spent an hour sparring in a radio studio with G. Gordon Liddy, the infamous Nixon operative convicted in the Watergate crime. Now he hosted a national show and was eager to wrangle. Sitting on adjacent high stools with headphones on, we went at it. But I discovered I liked him, and he appeared to reciprocate. He was so up front about his opinions ("prejudices," I called them) that they were easy to parry, laughing as I did so. And somehow we respected each other. We parted with a warm handshake.

Boston again, Los Angeles . . . I grew used to wearing the large radio-station headphones, which I much preferred to the glare of television cameras. For television I had to dress up in one of my two bright TV suits and worry about makeup as well as words. For radio I simply had to keep my wits about me.

Back in Berkeley, Conari Press signed me up for a series of seventy-five radio interviews to do by phone from home. The East Coast morning-drive programs came on at 4 or 5 a.m. Pacific Time. I grew used to rising a few minutes before the show and answering my phone in a nightgown to parry questions from the white male host. When the live shows occurred later in the day, I did them from Equity. I never paid attention to host names since I had never heard of any of them, but I was generally able to bond with them quickly and put them at ease. No, I wasn't out to kill or castrate them, I reassured them, simply urging, "It's time for equality everywhere." A few honestly wanted to understand my thinking. Most thought they had found a juicy subject with a woman whose ideas they could ridicule, although they learned I could counter their thrusts and even, to their surprise, get them laughing at our joint human foibles.

One noon I was scheduled for twenty-five minutes on WABC radio. When the producer called, I awaited the plug-in to go live, listening to the usual booming music and ads preceding the conversation. A strident male voice suddenly boomed into my ear, "Here she is! Joan Steinau Lester, the woman who advocates putting white men out to pasture! We're done for, *Dr.* Lester says." He exaggerated "Dr." in an unpleasant way. Like a talking horse, his tone suggested, a brainy woman with a doctorate was ludicrous.

Well, I thought, that's aggressive. He's not wasting any time on the pretense of a cordial introduction. But oh well. I adopted my most reasonable-sounding voice, attempting to make a joke. "Oh, I think we can find better uses for white men than putting them out to pasture," and I expected a friendly reply. Or at least a chuckle.

But the man attacked ferociously, asking questions like "Are you ugly?" and interrupting before I could finish replying, "Why do you ask?" Soon he was actually screaming, impugning feminism, peace activists, and "minorities" in the vilest terms. I began to shake. Who is this guy? I looked at my media sheet. Rush Limbaugh. Never heard of him.

Using my well-practiced reasonable-woman voice, I started describing how the expectations that men lead and know everything aren't good even for *them*—thus the greater incidence of heart attacks—when I heard him shout, "Feminazi! You're a feminazi!" and dead air filled my ear. He had hung up. In the middle of my sentence.

"Who was *that*?" I wondered. But soon I forgot the unpleasant incident, chalking it up to a crazy man's antics, until months later I heard Rush Limbaugh's name again and thought, *Oh.* I had tangled with a bear for fifteen minutes and given his listeners a taste of another view.

My provocative title, *The Future of White Men and Other Diversity Dilemmas,* which I had thought an amusing way of showing that white men were simply one more demographic—albeit a powerful one—was doing its work.

The Future of White Men

1994

As the date for my book party approached, my heart beat with excitement—and anxiety. I had only been to two book parties, and they both intimidated me.

The feminist writer Susan Griffin had invited me to her book launch for *A Chorus of Stones* two years before. Thrilled and honored, I'd wondered what to expect. The reality awed me: a jammed living room on a Marin hillside, with huge glass windows, wooden beams, art everywhere, women (and a few sensitive-looking men) clad in black. Turtleneck black. Wrapped-in-shawls black. Even the raw-wood bathroom, with its stained glass tchotchkes artfully arranged, was bohemian heaven.

People crowded book-filled hallways, sipping drinks as they chatted. I overheard Judith Butler passionately arguing postmodernism, essentialism, and contingency with another woman. I understood nothing. Urgent conversations swirled around me. Had everyone written books? Feeling privileged to be among them, I was acutely aware that this rarified literary environment—a white upper-middle-class setting—wasn't my natural habitat.

Unsure, I headed to the large wooden dining table laden with food and filled a plate with hors d'oeuvres. Mostly brown. Mushroom pâté? Small wrapped items in crusts, a profusion in three different shapes. Various cheeses and small seedy bread slices. Two kinds of crunchy crackers. Brilliant clusters of red grapes heaped in great bunches. The hosts, Naomi Newman of the Traveling Jewish Theater and her partner, the drummer Barbara Borden, had provided the spread. Their lives looked perfect in this setting, with their art, that impressive bathroom, and their intellectual friends.

Finally we all piled onto couches and floor pillows to hear Susan read. Naomi introduced her, people applauded her reading and asked a few intelligent questions, and she signed books. Would I ever reach such an exalted state?

Susan also took me to Jessica Mitford's book party for *The American Way of Birth*, held at a stately San Francisco home. I recall high ceilings with tall windows and lace curtains, many steps up into the house, and a doorway cloaked in ivy.

"I was friends with your daughter Dinky in New York, back in the '60s," I told Mitford when she signed my book.

She clasped my hand and said warmly, "Here's my number. You must visit me sometime." But, bashful in the face of her fame and age, I never did.

Those were my only book party experiences. Now my turn was coming; what would it look like? I had given keynotes and speeches, but this was different. I had never *read* anything to a group. How would I keep their attention? I confessed my fear to Ronnie Gilbert, of Weavers fame, whom we had met with her partner Donna Korones on one of Ronnie's East Coast tours. They had welcomed us to California before we even moved, hosting us in their home while we looked for our own. Now Ronnie, an experienced actor, offered, "Let me coach you."

The following day I hurried gratefully to the North Berkeley studio behind her house and launched into a section of *White Men*. My armpits sweaty, I read as fast as I could but with conviction.

"Take it easy," Ronnie said. "Slow down."

I tried again.

"Breathe! Smile!"

Every week for the next month, I found my way through her side gate and past the garden to her backyard studio. Each time, I practiced the same excerpt, which she helped me edit, omitting nonessential words and sentences.

"Slower!" Ronnie kept coaching. "And pause. Stop. Let people absorb what you're saying."

Once I slowed my pace to the leisurely one she counseled, and didn't allow myself to race through the reading simply to be done, she began working on intonation.

"Remember, this is a story you're telling. Vary your voice."

"How?"

"There's a lot of humor in what you're saying. Let the humor come through in your voice. It's serious stuff, but you've made it light. *Show* that."

I repeated the read.

"Vary the volume," she said. "Start quietly so people have to pay attention to hear you. Then build, louder, to a crescendo. And then soften."

I read it once more.

"Think about the narrative drive," she counseled. "Whisper in the middle to keep the suspense."

Each time, I left her studio exhausted, until four days before the book launch, she pronounced me "Ready!"

Once I had the reading down, with a promise to practice twice a day until the party, I wondered what was a suitable Author outfit. The morning before the party, Carole took me shopping. We chose flowing, black silky pants and a matching vest with Japanese painting inscribed front and back, over a bright white blouse. Suitably sophisticated and simultaneously casual, I thought. Once I added the dangling earrings she gave me, I felt ready.

But a new fear seized me. Would anyone come? We had only been in California three years. Unlike Susan, who had lived here for decades, or Jessica Mitford, I didn't have a network of old colleagues and connections. I wasn't famous, though my name was becoming known through my *San Francisco Chronicle* op-eds and radio essays.

What if, after all this work, hardly anybody showed up?

That Sunday afternoon, people squeezed into the Equity Institute space until there were over a hundred guests. Our suite in the converted warehouse boasted thirty-foot ceilings with exposed beams and heating ducts, the look of the high-tech early '90s. Bouquets of huge balloons floated to the ceiling, flashing colors as they drifted.

Café de La Paz, our caterer, heaped platters of Central American food on a bright-red cloth, a festive table under our industrial windows. Guests swarmed the long table, filling plates with fragrant fried plantains, mango salsa, guacamole, *pico de gallo*, cornbread, and fish studded with pumpkin seeds. Enticing, tangy smells wafted by our noses. The buzz of the crowd swelled, rippling through the air to fill even our high space.

The pianist and composer Mary Watkins opened the program. Her fingers moved fluidly over the keyboard, playing a soaring, jazzy tune with

Ronnie Gilbert singing, with Joan in the background, at book party, 1994. (photo
© by Jean Weisinger)

hints of Negro spirituals. Then Ronnie stood on the stairs above the atrium. Leaning over the wall, she belted out "Agitator," a song she had written for her play about the labor organizer Mother Jones:

> You know the washing machine where you wash your shirt
> Well it's the stick in the middle that does the work
> It tugs and it twists and it may be mean
> But it loosens the dirt, gets the shirt darn clean
> And they call it an AGITATOR.

Seated behind her on the stairs, I applauded with the delighted crowd. More people spilled into the room, filling the doorway as I stepped up to the mike. Looking out at the multiracial crowd, the community we had dreamt of, I was overwhelmed. Honored. After three and a half California years, Carole and I had truly found our home.

Ronnie had coached me, "Make it dramatic! Underline the phrases you're emphasizing."

"With all the talk about the diversity table, what is the place for *heterosexual white men*?" I began, leaning heavily on the underlined words. "Are they going to be the *'has beens'* of our multicultural future?" I stopped to breathe and smile.

"Look like you're having the best time ever," Ronnie had instructed. "They'll join you in that feeling."

"Are white men becoming diversity dinosaurs?" I read and heard people laugh.

A good sign. I paused for a beat, then continued, "It's a fear many have expressed. . . . Each of us holds a piece of the puzzle, with the different perspectives our varying experiences have given us. That giant puzzle of how to make this planet work needs *all* of the pieces to be complete." I paused again to let that sink in. "Heterosexual white men aren't multicultural *'has beens.'* They're becoming *'also* be's instead of *'only* be's.'"

Lots of chuckles. "That's not so bad really. But it's a change, and a challenge, to share power."

Applause rang out after I finished. I had done it. Now I could enjoy the feast, the festivities, and the crowd. Conari Press had sent a cake decorated with frosting that replicated the book cover, a wonder I had never seen. Our friends Leonie and Kate presented a framed book cover. Supporters packed our rooms. When Linda Tillery walked in, the magic was complete.

She had headlined a concert in Massachusetts, where Carole and I went for our first date. Now here she was, a guest at my book party.

While the crowd mingled and munched, I gazed at piles of shiny pink hardcover books. When Susan Griffin saw the cover, she sniffed, on my behalf, "They could have done more with the cover!" Twenty-five years and many book covers later, I've come to agree, but at the time I thought it the most beautiful book ever. People waited in line while I set myself up at a table to sign. I thought of book-signing lines I had stood in for Alice Walker, Anne Lamott, June Jordan, and others. Now they were lining up for me. It was hard to believe.

People bought copies for family, friends, and "a handbook for my office," several said. One young white woman beamed when she told me, "I gave *The Future of White Men* to my mom and we had the best talk we've ever been able to have about race." She held her signed copy close to her chest.

"Thank you for using it that way," I answered, feeling bubbles of serenity well up inside, filling me so I nearly floated to the ceiling with the balloons.

"Do you mind signing mine, too?" an elderly woman asked, her dark eyes glinting with anticipation. She leaned on a hand-carved cane.

"Of course not!" After all the labor that went into the book—laying down that first draft on blank pages; the terror of wondering whether I could finish it; revising, year after year; proofreading; promotion—after all that, signing books was the most pleasurable task in the world. Connecting with readers, gathering energy from their enthusiasm, was pure joy.

The woman, clearly thrilled, handed me her book, open to the title page.

"What's your name?" I asked.

"Akila."

"What a beautiful name. Would you like me to sign it to you?"

"Yes, thank you. My granddaughter has the same name, so it can be for both of us! She's eighteen. I think she'll like it, too."

Oh good, I thought. Different generations. I wondered what conversations they would have after reading the book.

I signed, she smiled, and so did I. Though in years to come several large houses would publish me—Simon and Schuster, the publisher I had called decades before from that Greenwich Village phone booth, and Harper-Collins—I would never again feel the pure, giddy delight of that first book party. It signified my new, certified status: Author. Like my doctorate, nothing could ever take that status away.

~

After Carole and I finished helping the Equity staff clean up, my body sagged, but my mind was on fire. Back at home, too keyed up to sleep, I stepped barefoot onto our deck. The cool, smooth boards sent shivers through me, and a full moon, hanging low, made me gasp. I sank into a chair, closed my eyes, and tilted my head back, bathing in the soft light. When I looked a few minutes later, there it was: that bright, gleaming moon. As its warm light and the sweet fragrance of our climbing roses began to calm my excitement, my mind emptied. For a moment all thoughts of the book party vanished. I was simply there in the night staring at our scarlet bougainvillea lit by the moon.

"Carole," I called into the house. "You have to come out. The moon is beautiful!"

"Wow, it is," she said, stepping onto the deck. "It's almost orange. And so big. It must be a harvest moon."

When she slipped into the chair next to me and took my hand, a deep peace swept through me. The moon, my partner, my book.

"What a party," she said. "I was so proud of you."

"It was the best party ever."

"You deserve every bit of it. All the years you've put into your writing. And now a book. The first of many!"

"I hope so," I murmured, wondering if I could pull off another one. But I knew I would try. "I'm so lucky I found my voice."

"It wasn't just luck. You've worked hard. You paid attention to the call of your soul."

"I know, but I was lucky to have an apprenticeship with Julius. Such a gifted writer." I shook my head in wonder. "I got to see up close how he did it, listen to his cadences, help him shape his ideas." I paused. "His sentences."

"That set you in a direction. Showed you the life of a writer." She laughed. "And if he did it, you could do it. You even got material for a lifetime, marrying an African American man. Having children with him."

"Uh huh. I never thought I'd be so appreciative. I learned so much. About the way he worked, the rhythm of his sentences, his images . . ."

"He's a beautiful writer."

"And I was lucky to come along when other women were finally getting published. Remember what Muriel Rukeyser said, 'If one woman told the truth about her life, the world would split open.' Women have been doing it. I had a lot of footprints to follow."

"Hmm." She nodded.

I closed my eyes again and was thrust back twenty years, sitting at my rolltop desk reading Audre Lorde's poem "Power." Between the solidity of the desk and the inspiration of the poem, something had unlocked inside me.

Memories flooded in as I remembered how I had feasted on each new feminist book as if it were food, nourishment for my hungry soul. Reading and rereading Adrienne Rich's poems while I listened to Nina Simone sing "Mississippi Goddam," my heart beating fast with the excitement of it all: the fearless poems, the courageous music. I had felt so alive, wanted so badly to participate in this great awakening. How I had looked up to authors like Alice Walker. Show me how to live as a creative spirit, I used to beg the Universe, at the same time I'm a mother, a breadwinner, a lover. A student and teacher.

Every Simone de Beauvoir novel and memoir was an event. I searched her words for answers to my question: How does a free woman live? I scoured the pages, reading in bed late into the night until my arms were sore from holding the book, eyes so swollen I could barely see. The same with Doris Lessing's fiction. When each book came out, I was desperate to see how her heroines, who suffered in their pursuit of independence, survived. Tillie Olsen, Agnes Smedley, Zora Neale Hurston. Nadine Gordimer. Free spirits. How had they done it?

"They were giants to me. As necessary as air. I think about women ten or fifteen years older than me, writers who came of age before all these women were publishing. It was tough for them, so isolating. Some of them committed suicide. Or they stopped writing. Maybe more of them would have made it," I said.

"And now you're going to be one of them."

"Of what?"

"Those authors who inspire other women."

"Oh, I don't know about that."

"I do." Carole squeezed my hand.

"I don't know. I'd like to inspire other women, definitely, but that's not the heart of it. It's about getting to express something inside." I searched for words. "For the chance to do that, I have nothing but gratitude. To life. To you."

"And to yourself," she said.

Hand in hand, we walked into the house and closed the door on that glorious night.

Epilogue

2020

When George Floyd's public torment—and death— exploded into a great racial reckoning, I wondered how I could contribute. I realized that after all these years of talking to white people about race, I could help develop allies, so I wrote blogs and offered my mostly white neighbors copies of that twenty-six-year-old "isms" primer, *The Future of White Men and Other Diversity Dilemmas*. Thirty people took one and several asked for follow-up conversations. One woman emailed me about pain from her past unaware interactions with people of color. I suggested she forgive herself and said, "Let's chat."

To create a community gathering space for that kind of dialogue, I made a Black Lives Matter banner from a sheet and hung it by our driveway, placed two green plastic chairs six feet apart, and waited, shivering in summer fog, for neighbors to stroll by.

Soon a curious white man scanned the plaza and paused. I recognized this guy; we'd talked a few years ago. He's short and friendly, older, with sparkling eyes.

"It's Black Lives Matter Plaza, aka my driveway," I called out with a smile.

He peered at colorful chalk pictures—hearts, a unicorn—and read aloud the words that friends had written: REPARATIONS (in blue). LOVE LOVE LOVE (aqua, bordered in pink). IMAGINE (multiple colors). SAY THEIR NAMES (green).

"Feel free to add something, a word or a drawing." I pointed to a bag of chalk. "Anything. Except profanity. Or the name of you-know-who."

"I don't draw."

"Then write a word or a phrase."

On Black Lives Matter Plaza, aka Joan's driveway, June 2020. (photo by Tim Wagstaffe)

He hesitated before inching up to the chalk.

"You live in the neighborhood, right?" I asked.

"Over there." He waved over the hill, then bent to write. Large blue capital letters appeared, one word over the other, spanning half the plaza.

SUPPORT

JUSTICE

"Thank you," I said.

He gazed at the other writing on the pavement. "But I don't know about reparations."

"Why?"

"It's impractical. How would they select people?"

"Nikole Hannah-Jones wrote a great article in the *New York Times Magazine*. She told how Indigenous tribes qualify membership. They have criteria. For reparations, people could trace ancestry back to enslavement."

"How would they give out all that money, even if they could figure out who to give it to?"

"Look at what the government did with stimulus checks for COVID. They managed that."

We chatted for ten minutes before he slumped off. "Come and talk any time," I called after him.

He turned to wave. And smile. "Thanks."

Another day, Alan, an earnest young white man who'd read *The Future of White Men*, arrived, eager to talk. "I only became aware of inequality when I went to Zambia," he said. "I knew about colonialism, but to see it firsthand, what happened . . ." His sentence dribbled off. "And to think about my whiteness. My wife and I are committed to raising anti-racist children, having conversations in a way we never did with our parents. We've joined an anti-racist parent group." He stared and shrugged. "But I have no idea what to do."

"You'll find opportunities," I reassured him, "if you're looking at what's happening around you. It's like anything else: when you get a new awareness, you'll see where you can act. For instance, with African Americans or other people of color—"

He interrupted, "I don't know any."

"Okay, it's time to enlarge your social circle."

"How?"

"At work, or in any kind of activity you're involved in, be bold. Go over and talk to people of color. If there's chemistry, try to make a new friend. Follow up, just like you would with anybody you're interested in getting to know. It'll take time."

"I don't want to make a mistake."

"We all do." I laughed. "I'm still learning after all these years. But most people will appreciate you trying to be an ally, a friend. Believe me, they've heard worse. But that's a first step. As you interact with more people, you'll be more observant. You'll notice times where you can step in to interrupt some discrimination. Or the kind of unconscious bias we all have. That will diminish over time if you make an effort to notice."

We kept talking that day and on following days, building a warm friendship. Conversations like this are taking place all over the world as a new awareness percolates and people grapple with how to make changes increasingly recognized as necessary.

On Saturday, November 7, 2020, when news media declared Joe Biden and Kamala Harris our new president- and vice president-elect, Alan rushed over to Black Lives Matter Plaza. He drew a huge pink heart with Stacey

Abrams's name inside, commemorating her work registering 800,000 new Georgia voters. Another neighbor wrote

CELEBRATE DEMOCRACY

and I chalked in

VP KAMALA HARRIS

The charge I felt that night when she stepped to the podium to accept the win was electric. After a lifetime of advocacy, I watched a glass ceiling shatter—and reveled in the sound. Equally sweet was the connection I felt with a woman of color who grew up in Berkeley, the town I've come to call home.

I wasn't the only one rejoicing. We cheered wildly when our hometown woman, our first Black and Indian American female vice president, stepped onto the biggest national stage. Dancing exploded all over East Bay streets.

Her presence in the White House, along with continued public pressure, strengthens the possibility of ushering in a New Reconstruction, reviving our brief nineteenth-century one. The country is so devastated by misrule and pandemics that a great rebuilding—with equality at its center—may find the white political will that faded all too soon the last time. Meanwhile, girls of every color will see where they truly belong: in the White House.

The breadth of the Movement for Black Lives coalition has given this old heart a mighty dose of what Senator Cory Booker calls "calloused hope." It's a battle-scarred hope, trusting that this moment has the potential to propel changes we can hardly imagine. Julius closed *Look Out, Whitey!* predicting, "The new order is coming, child. The old is passing away." Today, fifty-two years later, I feel more optimistic than ever. A world that works for everyone is indeed emerging, our way forward led by brilliant women of color.

Acknowledgments

A writer's greatest gift is feedback from perceptive readers. I have been graced with many over the five years I worked on this memoir. A huge thank you to many loyal friends, family members, and writing partners who read sections or the whole manuscript (some multiple times) and provided encouraging feedback. I am especially indebted to readers Donna Korones, Nenelle Bunin, Jonathan Poullard, the late Barbara Hazard, Suzette Celeste Johnson, Penny Hunt, Sonia Cairns, Lucy Jane Bledsoe, and Page Lester. I owe an enormous debt of gratitude to you all, as well as Betsy Blakeslee, Mardi Steinau, Zee Lewis, and Carole Johnson, who all listened patiently during the long years when all I wanted to talk about was book titles.

I have special appreciation for my ex-husband Julius Lester, who in the final months of his life read a late draft and sent a long, generous email: "Thank you for allowing me to read the mss. I really appreciate it. . . . It's a good book, and a difficult story to tell with so many parts and emotions to sort through. I thought the parts dealing with our marriage were fair and balanced. I was (and am) difficult to live with, and you were able to communicate that and yet remain fair and as objective as one can be when writing about one's life with someone else. . . . I think it's a fine book. . . . I have no problems with what you wrote." And then he was gone, leaving a greater absence than I could have imagined.

I am indebted to several scholars whose work proved helpful as I read about events I was involved in fifty-some years ago. Erin Pineda of Smith College wrote an excellent essay about the Great New York Stall-In: "Present Tense, Future Perfect: Protest and Progress at the 1964 World's Fair,

The Appendix 2, no. 3 (2014). Charles S. Isaacs gives a passionate account of the conflict that erupted over community control in *Inside Ocean Hill–Brownsville: A Teacher's Education, 1968–69* (Excelsior, 2014). And thanks to Joy Press, who, after interviewing me for her own research on the Women's Liberation Movement, took time to send me copies of my letters archived in the Pam Allen papers at the University of Wisconsin.

My agent, Liza Fleissig, was an early supporter of the project, supplying talented editors who read multiple drafts, helping hone the manuscript. Despite an overfull plate, Liza always returned emails within moments. A true miracle worker.

I am grateful to have such an enthusiastic publishing team at the University of Wisconsin Press, especially with editor in chief Nathan MacBrien. He leads an extraordinary team: Jacqulyn Teoh, Adam Mehring, Jennifer Conn, Sheila McMahon, Casey LaVela, and Kaitlin Svabek, each of whom, radiating clarity and kindness, has been a pleasure to work with. The second-greatest gift for a writer, after insightful readers, is to have a marvelous publisher, one who gets your book and is as excited as you are to bring it out into the world.

Finally, I must thank my extraordinary wife. Not only has she encouraged my writing for our entire forty years together, but she's also a superb editor. She reads every draft—or listens to me read the whole book aloud over a period of days—and has the final word on everything I write, tempering my excesses when necessary, applauding me as only a beloved could. With her, I finally understand the role I played in Julius's early writing career, and I am grateful for being able to play both sides now. Thank you, Carole. The book is dedicated to you with good reason; you deserve that and more.